WITH SIBERIA

COMES A CHILL

ALSO BY KIRK MITCHELL:

Black Dragon (SMP, 1988)

He felt that love had saved him from despair, and that this love of his had grown still more powerful and pure under the threat of despair.

—Tolstoy, *Anna Karenina*

1

STREET-HUGGING FOG.

"Guaranteed to bitch up swing shift," the patrolman said, alone in the black-and-white Chevy cruiser. Keeping his eyes on the street, he slipped the microphone out of its dashboard clip. "Central One, Potrero Three. . . ." The wipers were squeaking over the windshield, leaving damp arcs on the glass and making it even harder for him to inch his way toward Hunter's Point.

"Come in, for Chrissake," he said with his thumb off the mike button.

"Potrero Three, go ahead with your traffic," the female dispatcher finally answered.

"You got a backup rolling my way?"

"Not yet. Stand by. . . ." She then tried to raise another radio car. She tried twice, but the cop was away from it. *Fucking the dog.*

"Central One," the patrolman said, "never mind if everybody's tied up. The wife say anything about weapons in the house?"

"Negative."

"Did you ask?"

"*Affirmative.*"

She had said this with enough spin on her voice for him to add with a soft chuckle, "Just asking, sugar."

The fog-blurred lights on the Islais Creek Bridge had little tin skirts over their bulbs. This was supposed to keep Mitsubishi bombardiers from figuring out the lay of San Francisco Bay, although a battle-damaged destroyer anchored out in the channel was ablaze with cutting torches. Only a couple of canvas shields had been thrown up on its bayward side in case a Jap sub sneaked through the nets just inside the Golden Gate Bridge. Fat chance, these days. All the war left was thousands of miles away.

He started to light a smoke but figured he was too close to the house. Besides, there was a cigarette shortage in town, thanks to all the foreign diplomats pouring in for some kind of United Nations shindig. Even his usually reliable black market sources in Chinatown had dried up.

Suddenly, a hatless sailor staggered out in front of him, wagging his arms like a chimp.

The patrolman laid on his horn and brakes at the same time, and the young seaman stumbled backward on his heels, gaping at the headlamps.

He cranked down his side window, the fog cold on his face, and growled, "Get back to your ship. I'm coming back this way in ten minutes, and if I see you again, you're mine!" He accelerated again, then rounded the next left onto Jerrold Avenue. It would take him out to the tip of Hunter's Point. He kept the window down. Despite the raft of Mickey Mouse calls since briefing, he was drowsy and wanted a clear head for what was coming next.

Dead ahead, the fog was lit up like incandescent gas over the Navy drydocks—from the welding torches, the floodlights slanting down through the rigging. The glow also wavered against the dingy fronts of the boomtown apartments he was creeping past, shoulder-to-shoulder clapboard housing for the war workers.

He turned the corner onto Carbon Street and parked. He was there. "Central One, Potrero Three is ten ninety-seven."

"I copy your arrival, Three. I'll continue to roll the first available backup."

"Yeah, yeah," he said to himself, having hung up the mike. In a ritual of nine years, he patted the notebook and fountain pen he kept in his right breast pocket, skimmed his elbow over the grips of his .38 special to assure himself that the revolver was snugly holstered, and finally donned his cap with one hand and sprung the door latch with the other. The sidewalk was beginning to show dark mottles of moisture. From the fog.

The apartment's blackout curtains were drawn. He didn't like that: restrictions had been lifted in fall of 1943—eighteen months ago now.

He hesitated on the cement stoop, listening. No hollering inside, so he rapped firmly on the door. The trick to handling a domestic dispute was to take control right away.

The door opened a crack. One side of a middle-aged woman's face showed. No blood. No black-and-blue marks. So far so good. "Did you call on your old man?"

She said nothing for a couple seconds, then: "I did."

A real mouse, but he figured she'd once been pretty in a Jewish sort of way. "Well, can I come in?"

"Please, Officer." Her flabby arms were bare. He scanned them for bruises, even old yellow ones. If he had a habitual wife-beater on his hands, he'd step on hubby's toes, goad him into taking a swing. That would earn the guy a goose egg on his noggin and ninety days in jail denim. Of course, a sap tap and a misdemeanor conviction wouldn't stop the wife-beatings, but it would put an end to the nuisance calls. The woman wouldn't phone if it cost her his paycheck. Soon, the patrolman would be rotating to night watch and he wanted no summonses to 233 Carbon to disturb his on-duty sleep among the plasma refrigeration boxes along China Basin.

But the woman didn't have a mark on her.

The husband was sitting at the far end of the sofa. He glanced up at the intrusion, but then tilted his bald head back toward the table radio beside him.

Beyond the man's slippered feet the patrolman could see broken crockery strewn across the kitchen linoleum. A nearly empty bottle of bourbon was standing on the sink counter.

The Station KYA announcer was rattling on about how the week-long invasion of Okinawa, after an unopposed landing on April Fools' Day, was finally heating up with banzai charges and kamikaze attacks. Maybe that was the problem at 233 Carbon. Hell, a nigger woman had taken after him with a hot steam iron when he'd tagged along with the Army brass to follow up on her son's KIA telegram. "You folks got a boy out in the Pacific?"

Again, the man glanced up. "No, we don't." A soft, almost cultured voice. A strange duck, the patrolman instantly summed him up. He was thickset and a little windburned as if he worked on the docks, a notion that was bolstered by his black Frisco jeans and hickory-colored shirt. But he also had gold-rimmed glasses and dreamy eyes. One wall was nothing but shelves of books. Long-hair books, if the patrolman could judge by their unfamiliar titles.

"Can we have a word, ma'am?" Without giving her a chance to answer, he ushered her into the kitchen, their shoes crunching over the shards. Through the open door he kept one eye on hubby, who didn't really seem to be listening to the war news. "What happened, lady?"

"I don't know." She was twining her skinny fingers together.

"What d'you mean? You weren't here?"

"No . . . I was here."

"Then what gives?"

Her eyes darted from his face to his chest as if to check out his badge number. Was she thinking of filing a complaint against him already? What had he said or done that was out of line? Christ, how he hated these calls. "He just exploded," she said at last.

"And emptied the kitchen shelves?"

She nodded.

"He drink most that bottle by himself?"

"Yes. I don't drink."

"What's his beef?"

"I don't know." She had begun shivering, which seemed queer to him as he looked beyond her at the quiet man on the sofa. "I was hoping you might be able to find out."

4

She'd probably been living with the son of a bitch most of her adult life, but after two minutes he, a complete stranger, was supposed to put his finger on what had miffed the guy.

Strolling back into the living room, he ordered, "Stand up."

The husband came to his feet, uncertainly.

The patrolman patted his working clothes down. He ordinarily did this only on the streets, but something made him frisk the man, who was silent but for the whistling of his breath in his nose. "You got a job?"

"Longshoreman."

"Go ahead and sit again." The patrolman eased down into the rocking chair across from him. "What's your name?"

"Laska."

He reached into his breast pocket for his notebook and pen. "That your last or first name?"

The husband didn't answer. His eyes were riveted on the notebook.

"This is just for my own information," the patrolman explained. "You behave from now on and it don't go any farther than my shirt pocket. Okay?"

"Laska's my surname."

The patrolman was unsure if that meant first or last, so he asked, "What's your other name?"

"William."

"Middle initial?"

The man shook his head, but his gaze was still on the notebook.

"No middle initial." The patrolman snapped shut the pad and pocketed it. "Okay, Will—what's the problem here?"

"*William*. Only my friends call me Will."

The patrolman shrugged it off. "Whatever."

The woman crept back into the room and sat beside her husband. That took the patrolman aback. Most women fresh from a spat with hubby wouldn't get within ten feet of him.

Both of them were staring at him like owls.

Then a creak of floorboards came from what was most likely the bedroom.

5

The patrolman rose. "What's going on here?"

"Grandmother," she quickly said. "Grandma's ill."

She had grasped her husband's forearm, and now he gently shook off her hand. With no one to hold, she hugged herself.

The patrolman sighed. They were just oddballs, embarrassed by the ruckus they'd made now that a cop had shown up. "I'm going. And I don't want either of you phoning again with this kind of crap. Seems to me you folks can iron out your own problems."

"Not quite, Officer," the husband said. One hand was tucked under his leg.

"How's that?"

The man lofted a small pistol from between the sofa cushions and fired once.

The patrolman recoiled, slamming against the beaverboard wall, thinking that he'd been hit. But the first bullet had not been meant for him.

The woman jerked upright, then twisted her upper body to face her husband.

"Jesus!" the patrolman cried.

"Forgive me, Emma," the man whispered.

She had been struck in the back of the head, and blood was flowing down her neck. Yet she confronted her husband with an amazed look. She had expected something awful, the patrolman realized through the buzz of his own shock, but this hadn't been it.

She collapsed off the couch to sprawl across a braided oval rug.

Meanwhile, the patrolman had been fumbling under his coat for his holster flap, close to whimpering from the nightmarish slowness of his own reaction, as the husband turned the muzzle of the pistol on him. The patrolman was on the verge of firing when the bedroom door banged open and a broad, ugly face glowered at him from the shadows. With a foreign accent, the man ordered William Laska to get on with it, and by the time the patrolman had spun around again Laska had yanked the trigger twice.

6

One bullet missed the patrolman, imbedded itself in the wall. But the other caught him in the throat.

He let go of his revolver to claw at the gurgling wound with both hands. He felt as if the wind had been knocked out of him, although it was a thousand times worse because of the drowning sensation.

"Is he gone?" Laska asked.

When the patrolman became aware of anything other than his own agony, he realized that he was on the floor, his chin resting against the woman's foreleg. He thought to retrieve his handgun and went so far as to roll on his side before a sleepy indifference took hold of him. His vision was beginning to fade around the edges, but he could see the man in the bedroom door raise a pistol, one like Laska's, to eye level. Strangely, the ugly man directed it not on the patrolman, who expected a finishing shot to the head—but on Laska. "You do it, or I will," he said. "Damn the ballistics test, I will do it. And if I pull the trigger, *he* will know that you have no guts!"

Laska hesitated, shuddered, but then touched the muzzle of his own weapon to his temple.

It was the last thing the patrolman saw.

2

THE GRAY 1939 DODGE SEDAN John Kost now drove at ten miles an hour toward Hunter's Point was his private concession to the war. His rank entitled him to a 1941 model, the last before civilian production had been curtailed, but he gamely let his sergeant have the newest car allocated to the Homicide Bureau. American-born, Vincent Ragnetti had a passion for automobiles, whereas John Kost had none. After twelve years of driving, as long as he'd been on the department, he could not yet shift gears without making the car crow-hop. But beyond this general uninterest in automobiles, the worn Dodge was his penance to the young Americans who were suffering and dying all over the world.

On the Monday morning following the attack on Pearl Harbor, everybody in the Homicide bull pen—then up to a full strength of seven plainclothesmen—had trooped out of the Hall of Justice and down to the recruiting center—everybody except Ivan Mikhailovich Kostoff, or John Kost as he was known at work. All six detectives were glumly back at their desks within an hour, having been summarily rejected for infirmities due to age, gluttony, or alcoholism. Only Ragnetti found the nerve to ask their newly promoted inspector why he hadn't gone with them. "You got something against mixing it up with the Japs, John?"

"No," he answered from the windows, "and I'd go if it fell upon me to."

"Then why d'you look like you're down in the dumps?"

"To understand, Vincent, you'd have to grow up in the midst of a war."

"And you're saying you did?"

John Kost only nodded. And later that Monday, when one of the dicks made a crack about what pushovers the bucktoothed Nips would be, John Kost turned on him: "The Japanese are both intelligent and brave. Make no mistake about that, my friend. Nikolas Romanov did—and it cost Russia dearly."

"Nick who?"

He then ignored the loudmouth, who eventually joined the Marines and was killed in a training accident.

On that day after Pearl Harbor, he had wondered why he'd ever joined San Francisco PD. Had it been for something as silly as that the patrolman's coat resembled the blue *chekmen* of the Imperial Cossacks? And that he wanted to prove to his father that he, too, had a heart to serve, that he had taken more than six feet and seven inches of height from his half portion of Don Cossack blood? Regardless, Mikhail Kostoff had proved indifferent to his son's choice of occupation, even though it became the sole means by which bread came into his mouth. "Why didn't you join the Mounted Patrol?" had been his only comment.

Of course, during the same months he'd thought about becoming a cop, he had also considered going to seminary. Entering the white, or secular, clergy of the Orthodox Church, who are permitted to marry before ordination, had not seemed severe enough to suit his new ambition, so he fixed on his sights on the black, or monastic, clergy. But what bright and sensitive young man in the heady process of demolishing his innocence— and demolish it he had with the help of the prettiest whores of the Tenderloin District—has not found himself suddenly yearning for the cleanest possible life? He had even gone so far as to talk over his perplexity with Father Aleksei, who heard him out, only to sigh and comb his fingers down the length of his then completely black beard. "Oh, my dear Ivan Mikhailovich, listen up now . . ."—he'd learned the expression from cowboy movies—"a fellow thinks about becoming a priest for one of two reasons. Any idea what they might be?"

"No, Father."

"He's fascinated either by good or by evil. I ask you to decide which reason brings you to me. See me again tomorrow after vespers."

Following a sleepless night, listening to his father mutter orders to a long-liquidated White Army from the adjoining cast-iron cot, John Kost returned and gave his answer.

"Very well," the priest said, "become a policeman then."

"Father?"

"A policeman sees nothing *but* evil. And perhaps by that unlikely life you can close the distance between God and yourself."

"But I don't understand—"

"Is God knowable?"

John Kost hesitated only an instant. "No, except as He personally reveals Himself in His acts, His energies."

"Nicely memorized. But always remember this—we can say what God is not, but we can't say what He is. As a policeman, you'll know, and absolutely too, what God is not. Every day you'll see things and be able to say, 'This is not the Lord.' Ambiguity grinds away at faith. But you, Ivan Mikhailovich, will not be an ambiguous man. Now go before I change my mind. You're likable, and it'd be nice to be assisted by such a fellow in my dotage. . . ."

John Kost now pulled into the space between two Potrero Station cruisers parked before 233 Carbon Street, part of a one-story triplex. "Yes," he whispered to himself, struck by the forlorn look of the place with its blackout curtains drawn and a patrolman posted on the stoop, "it was *here* tonight." For a few brutal minutes it reigned inside this shanty—the complete separation of man from divinity. The most engrossing and terrifying thing in the world.

He stepped out of the Dodge into an ensemble of foghorns: the Hunter's Point baritones nearby, bleating in full notes; the bass diaphone on Yerba Buena Island grunting in counterpoint; and a distant soprano siren, perhaps as far away as Oakland. And backdropping all this was the clatter of the work being done on the Navy ships. On an afterthought, he took off his white scarf and cutaway coat and tossed them onto the front seat so they wouldn't be bloodied. His Smith & Wesson .38 special revolver was in a shoulder holster strapped over his starched white shirt.

A few neighbors were rubbernecking from across the street, waiting no doubt for the bodies to come out.

"Evening, John." Nathan Aranov came slowly down the steps. He was a short, lithe man with an ascetic face, iconographically so. John Kost thought him to be the brightest assistant inspector in the department, although Aranov tended to doubt himself. A good man's failing in a world that had spawned Hitler and Stalin. They met on the sidewalk, and Aranov asked with a wan smile, "You dressed for *Boris Godunov?*"

John Kost nodded.

"Sylvia and I made the mistake of going last night. Did Xenia improve any with a day's rest?"

"It isn't a question of improvement, Nathan. The poor girl's miscast. I think she'd do much better in the title role."

Aranov tried to chuckle, but the crime scene was still too fresh upon him. Instead, he coughed into his small white fist. "Damn," he said after a moment, "this is a rotten one."

John Kost lowered his voice as if he didn't want the patrolman on the stoop to hear. "Who was he?"

"Wallace Elliot."

"I didn't know him," John Kost said gratefully.

"Nine years—all of it in Patrol. He's had the waterfront beat from here all the way up to China Basin for two years."

"Family?"

"Divorced, no children," Aranov said.

John Kost started for the front door. "How about the neighbors, Nathan?"

"Defense workers, bachelors. Both on the job tonight."

11

"But you canvassed the block?"

"Right. Nobody even heard the shots. I'll check with the Coast Guard when the foghorns kicked in, but the racket from the shipyards was probably enough to cover the reports."

"Restful neighborhood, what?" In passing, John Kost squeezed the patrolman's arm at the elbow. "Bad business."

"Yeah, Inspector, bad fucking business."

Three strides later John Kost was standing in the middle of the cramped living room appraising the two corpses—somehow, a man and a woman lying dead together suggested sexual intimacy, even though he already knew this not to be the case. It occurred to him for the hundredth time how much Aranov's fluid chalk lines were like Cyrillic calligraphy. That the bodies had already been chalked in meant the Identification Bureau's work was wrapped up; the technician was in the kitchen, repacking his equipment. Shattered crockery on the linoleum in there was the only evidence of an altercation prior to the killings.

He frowned at Patrolman Elliot's revolver—it had failed the man. "Well, Nathan, care to walk me through it?"

"Beginning with the call?"

"Please. I came straight here without being briefed."

"It was phoned in as a family disturbance, wife the reporting party."

"What time was this?"

"Uh, twenty-fifteen hours."

Eight-fifteen. Just as the curtain was going up on *Boris Godunov*, John Kost mused, realizing that during those klieg-bright moments at the War Memorial Opera House, Patrolman Wallace Elliot had yet been a living spirit, still capable of choice and redemption.

"According to the radio log," Aranov went on, "the wife here"—he glanced at the body—"said her husband was 'going to harm' her. Those words exactly."

"Any mention of weapons?"

"That's what hits me funny." Aranov nudged his fedora off his forehead, revealing his sparse brown hair. "The dispatch sergeant took the call himself. He says she insisted there were no weapons involved, that there weren't any in the house."

"Perhaps she didn't know about this." John Kost knelt beside the sofa and inspected the palm-sized, nocturnal-blue pistol. "Dusted for latents yet?"

"An hour ago. Be my guest, John. Spent casings and the cartridges left in the magazine have been bagged and tagged. I put the piece back where I found it—next to the suspect's right hand."

John Kost slid open the action. "Mauser?"

"Yeah, probably a war souvenir. Four rounds were expended. The first went in the back of his wife's head. Apparently didn't come out again—we looked everywhere. And she must've been sitting right beside the suspect, with him here on the end next to the radio." Aranov pointed to the comet-shaped blood spatters arcing across the wall behind the sofa, their tapered ends pointing away from where he then said the woman had been seated. "I'm sure she then fell sideways—see the curve of the spill on the cushion here?—and tumbled onto the rug."

"Poor sister," John Kost muttered.

Aranov looked curiously at him, but then continued, "Next, the suspect took on Elliot. He was standing—oh—about where I am."

"He obviously drew his revolver, but did he have time to return fire?"

"No, all six primers are as mint as the day they left the factory. The suspect let go with two rounds at him. I'd guess rapid-fire—boom boom—because the spent casings came to rest within inches of each other—"

"Where, Nathan?" John Kost interrupted.

Aranov stubbed a chalk circle on the floor with the toe of his wing tip. "Here. One round went though this wall into the john and pancaked against the tile of the shower enclosure. The other wound up in Wallace Elliot's throat. Clipped the left carotid artery but didn't exit as far as I can tell. Maybe after the postmortem we'll have a projectile in decent enough shape for comparison."

"Let's hope. I doubt the bullet inside this poor woman's cranium is in much better shape than the one that hit the tiles."

One side of the patrolman's face was flattened against the woman's calf, corroborating what Aranov had claimed: she had died before Patrolman Elliot.

"You ready for the grand finale?" Aranov asked.

John Kost was staring at the woman's slack expression. "Go ahead."

"With two bodies at his feet, the suspect turned his pistol on himself. But he must've flinched at showtime because the bullet penetrated his skull at an oblique angle—upward from the temple. Into the frontal hemisphere, I'd say." With his index finger, Aranov illustrated the path of the bullet on himself. "And there's every indication it came from less than twenty inches away."

That was the accepted maximum distance a suicide could fire a shot against himself. "Such as?"

"The entrance wound was bigger than the diameter of a Mauser bullet. Singed skin and smokeless-powder residue were evident around the hole. . . ." Aranov paused as if to consider if he'd forgotten anything. "When Elliot's backup finally showed, he was sure the suspect was as dead as the others. But then he found a pulse on the guy."

"Will he live?"

"Probably. The sons of bitches always pull through, don't they, John?"

"Who're we to wish otherwise?"

Aranov's eyes began watering, and John Kost wanted to kick himself for having sounded sanctimonious. He had meant nothing by it, really, but the young plainclothesman took everything so hard. "Anyways, I phoned the hospital right before you got here. They were prepping him for surgery."

John Kost stood again. "Tell me about this man."

"According to the Longshoremen's-local card in his wallet, his name is William Laska. He also had a Port of Embarkation clearance to load for the military. And I found a pay stub issued by the Pier Forty-six office."

"China Basin?"

"Yeah."

John Kost stepped over Elliot's corpse to the wall of bookshelves and began running his fingers along the spines. "Any priors for anything under that name?"

"A return from Sacramento won't come until morning. But nothing in our files. And our ID Bureau wouldn't have rolled the fingerprint card he needed for his POE clearance. Speaking of—I'll go to the hospital as soon as I can break away and print him."

"I'll do it, Nathan. You have enough on your hands here. And who knows? I might get a dying declaration out of Laska."

"Do we really need it?" Aranov asked.

"Yes. We have all the answers except the big one." John Kost turned back to the books. "You know, this fellow was a socialist."

"I had an idea. Some library for a stevedore, huh?" Aranov paused. "There's one more thing we should talk over."

"Shoot," John Kost said, scanning a personalized inscription to "Will" by Harry Bridges in one of the labor leader's paperbound dialectics.

"Delbert came up with this—the inside knobs to both the bedroom and front door have been wiped clean."

John Kost snapped shut the booklet and strode into the kitchen, his shoes crunching over the broken crockery. The round-faced, bespectacled ID technician peered up at him. "Inspector?"

"You sure those knobs were wiped, Delbert?"

"Positive."

"Any fabric-pattern impression left on the metal?"

"Some."

"Any chance of a later match?"

"None."

Aranov had come to the door, and John Kost asked him, "Was Laska or his wife wearing gloves?"

"Nope. And neither was Elliot tonight. I went through all his uniform pockets."

"How about Elliot's backup?"

"Bare-handed, John."

"Besides," Delbert said, "these were definite erasures, not just glove swipes." He paused. "How's that for a dandy little monkey wrench?"

3

JOHN KOST NOSED his Dodge through the fog into General Hospital's parking lot, set the brake, and got out. He opened the trunk and began rummaging around in the largely useless collection of investigative accessories a Homicide inspector was required to carry in his car, looking for the portable fingerprinting kit. He hoped William Laska hadn't died in the last hour: he was in no mood to print a corpse, even if rigor mortis hadn't set in.

The fog had thinned enough for a few stars to show through. He watched the milkiness sift across these pinpricks for a moment, then put his coat on over his shoulder holster. He didn't like to flaunt his .38 special, as the rookie plainclothesmen did, and there had been times when he'd even left the damned thing in his desk's pencil drawer.

Suddenly, he looked up from the trunk.

He was being watched. He just knew it.

Scanning the lot, he noticed a Hudson over the roofs of the prewar Plymouths, Fords, and Chevies.

The Hudson's engine spewed exhaust, and the driver—defined by nothing more than the silhouette of his hat, possibly a boater—drove out onto Potrero Avenue and continued north toward downtown at moderate speed. The license-plate bulb was unlit, which was reason enough for John Kost to think of having the beat cruiser stop the Hudson so the driver could be identified. But then he decided that detaining him would be unwarranted: he was probably a medico on his way home after a long day of surgeries. Had those two doorknobs in the Carbon Street triplex not been wiped he wouldn't have given the Hudson a second thought. But if he had to put money on it, he'd bet that the patrolman supposedly protecting the crime scene, the photographer, or even ID technician had inadvertently destroyed the latent prints on the knobs. It had happened before.

At last he found the fingerprinting kit.

Inside the hospital, he was surprised to learn from the front desk that the surgeon had already finished with William Laska. He caught up with him at a watercooler and flashed his five-pointed gold star: "Inspector John Kost, Doctor—San Francisco PD."

The surgeon eyed his tuxedo. "Yes, what is it?"

"Has anyone from the PD been by to collect the bullet you extracted?"

"No, because I didn't extract it."

"How's that?"

"It's lodged in the patient's frontal hemisphere. In the neighborhood of Broca's area. That makes it inoperable as far as I'm concerned."

"Why?"

The surgeon took a heavy-lidded pull off his cigarette, then chased it with a sip of water. "If I cut, he could lose any number of functions. Like speech."

"Is he still cerebrated?" John Kost asked.

"You probably mean—how cerebrated is he? I don't know. We'll find out if and when he comes around."

The patrolman guarding the prisoner in the fifth-floor room looked so bored and drowsy John Kost allowed him to return to the Hall of Justice, promising that he'd take over until the relief arrived at six in the morning.

"Thanks, Inspector."

"Think nothing of it, old fellow." It was no great sacrifice: he knew he'd be unable to sleep tonight.

Laska's head was thickly bandaged. He was staring blankly at the globular ceiling light.

"This rotten fuck won't answer to nothing," the blue-suiter said, then took his leave with a yawn: "Good-night, sir."

"Same to you now." As soon as the man was gone, he phoned Lydia Thripp, apologizing for his sudden absence from the Opera House—he'd been paged in the lobby during intermission.

"Did it have to do with your poor man who was killed tonight?" she asked, sleepy-voiced. "I heard about it on the radio on the taxi ride home."

"Yes, my dear. I'll be tied up for a few days, but I'll see you on Sunday for sure."

"Not before that?"

"I'm afraid not."

"I love you, Vanya."

He paused. His growing dissatisfaction with this gracious and wealthy woman saddened him, for he knew what must follow—and soon. Yet, without giving her false hope, he would continue to drop by her Sunday brunches after mass at St. Basil's. After all, lovers can metamorphose into friends if the disengagement is handled as tenderly as the entanglement. "How nice of you to say. Sleep well now."

A table Philco on the nightstand caught his eye, and he switched it on.

There was no more news of the homicides, but the announcer said that the San Francisco String Quartet had closed its eleventh season at the St. Francis Hotel tonight and the station would now broadcast the performance, originally scheduled live but pre-empted by the communiques out of Okinawa—a "frightful" kamikaze attack on our Navy, he explained. With tens of millions slaughtered, what did a word like that mean anymore?

Smiling as the first strains of Schubert's C Major Quintet came over the airwaves, John Kost boosted the volume. A quintet performed by a quartet: the pervasive wartime labor shortage.

Laska seemed unaffected by sound—but it was good to imagine

19

that the music might be a solace to him as he lay there, sightless, on the brink of death and eternal hopelessness.

John Kost hung his jacket on the door hook, then carefully folded up his French cuffs to his elbows.

He opened the kit atop the nightstand. Taking hold of Laska's cool and pliant right hand, he inked the fingertips and rolled their identifying friction ridges onto three cards: one for the department, one for the State Division of Criminal Identification and Investigation in Sacramento, and one for the FBI.

He repeated the process with the left hand, then cleaned up the suspect as best he could with a moistened paper towel. "That wasn't so bad now, was it, old fellow?"

Nodding his head in tempo with Schubert, he washed his own inky hands at the sink, wetted a towel, and rubbed the stiff feel of dried sweat off his face.

Finally, he switched off the overhead fixture and made do with the light from the hall leaking in under the door. He took the hardback chair beside the bed. His eyes slowly grew opaque. Silently, he prayed for the redemption of William Laska's soul. For Patrolman Wallace Elliot and Laska's wife there was nothing he could do. They had been cheated of the chance for redemption, and in that lay the true horror of the crime.

The C Major Quintet came to a close, and without announcement Schubert was supplanted by Brahms, the First Quartet.

A nurse came and went, her visit so brief her flicking on the ceiling fixture had seemed like lightning. The darkness returned. Her stout heels clipped away in echo down the corridor. A baby shrieked in a distant ward. And John Kost sat alone with the cop-killer and remembered the child whose only name had been Vanechka.

After that long, dimly recalled retreat of the White Army across Siberia, his soldier-father brought him to Irkutsk, near Lake Baikal. Mikhail Kostoff's manservant—who'd rescued the abandoned Vanechka from the Moscow flat his mother had left one morning for bread and never returned to—had died of pneumonia along the way, so the boy's care was entrusted to a young sailor who'd recently shown up in Irkutsk. No more than twenty years old, but of sinewy build and dauntless green eyes, he claimed to have spent two arduous years making his way home to Baikal, and his threadbare uniform tended to support his story. His name, sadly enough, had been forgotten in the years since. But he said he had first come out to the taiga with his father, an exiled musician, and like Vanechka had lost his mother early. When his father died, he'd been taken in by a family of fur hunters and had eventually come to love Siberia. So Vanechka remembered him simply as the Siberian.

They were billeted together away from Irkutsk, which was swarming with fleeing tsarist gentility, in a village of timber huts out among the birches—Vanechka's first inkling that he was not precisely Colonel Kostoff's son.

Somewhere, the Siberian had found an old gramophone and a half dozen records. Tchaikovsky and Mussorgsky, mostly. It became Vanechka's happy chore to wind up the machine, before running back to the Siberian's lap. The scratchy music would get the young sailor weeping, yet he'd always smile as he wept. "Why do you cry so?" Vanechka once asked.

"Ekh, Vanka," he said, having settled on this more manly diminutive for Ivan, "someday you'll understand how all the bad things are melted away by music. You'll want to surround yourself with music from dawn to dusk."

But one evening in the windless lull after a storm, the Siberian suddenly lifted the needle off the wax record. Quickly, he dressed Vanechka and led him outside, down a lane of packed snow that squeaked under the soles of their boots, then out into the birches when the lane ended, and each time Vanechka tried to speak the Siberian shushed him by clasping a brittle glove over his mouth and motioned for him to keep wading through the snow in his furrow until finally they were what seemed to be a great distance out into the taiga. Here at last they halted. For a long while they stood side by side and said nothing. They gazed up into indigo depths so clear there appeared to be no sky between their dryly burning eyes and the frozen white fire of the stars. But then the Siberian gestured for Vanechka to go ahead and talk.

"What should I say?" he asked, then giggled in wonderment. The voice that had visibly wafted out of his mouth had crackled like the red and blue cellophane in which American oranges came wrapped at Christmastime. "What is it!"

"Star-whispers, old fellow!" The Siberian laughed in his baritone version of the eerie, crinkly voice.

"What?"

"The sound that comes from truly deep cold. On mornings when our voices did this we knew it was no good to take our horses out into the taiga. On those days the sable could keep their skins, what?"

"Will you take me sable hunting?"

"Someday, my dear Vanka—when this war's finished." The Siberian straightened, somberly clutched the boy's gloved hand, and they started back toward the village.

They were almost to their billet, rounding the corner of a darkened hut, when a figure stepped out of the shadows. At first Vanechka thought him to be a Bolshevik, for even his father had admitted that the Red Army was very near now. But he proved only to be one of the violently hungry men Vanechka had seen everywhere in Siberia for the last year. He had Tatar eyes, and they narrowed even more as he growled something in a strange tongue to the Siberian, who pushed Vanechka back out of the way and answered the man in the same language. Whatever the sailor had said, it made the stranger bare his teeth and dig a big skinning knife out of his overcoat pocket.

The Siberian danced away from the gleam of the first thrust, even laughed a little in his star-whispers voice, which sent the man into a fury. His knife whooshing through the cold air, he drove the Siberian up against a woodpile. Rearing back for an overhand stab, the stranger was suddenly aghast to see a hatchet in the Siberian's grasp. Vanechka was surprised too. He hadn't seen a hatchet near the pile.

The Siberian's first blow spun the knife out of the stranger's hand. The second strike was glancing, but still caught him alongside his head. And the final two were to his face as he lay motionless in the drifted lane.

22

The Siberian cleaned the hatchet blade with a few handfuls of snow, then slipped it inside his coat. Finally, he seized Vanechka by the arm and began pulling him toward their hut. His eyes were bright, but his voice oddly mild as he said, "Say nothing of this to your father. He has enough worries as is. Will you promise me, old fellow?"

Unable to speak, he could only nod.

"Good, now you stay inside and crank up the gramophone while I go out again. I shan't be long."

Soon after that night the war was over, but no sable hunt followed. Only years later would Vanechka appreciate the hopelessness of his father's situation. Mikhail Kostoff's commander, Admiral Kolchak, was quickly going under, his government turning ever more corrupt and ruthless as he felt the Bolshevik noose tightening around his neck. And yet Vanechka could think only of hunting sables with the Siberian as his father and he boarded the last train east toward Manchuria and exile in America beyond.

"You should come with us, my boy," Mikhail Kostoff said to the sailor.

"Thank you, sir—but my place is here with my admiral."

They then exchanged salutes while Vanechka stood by, crying.

He later doubted that his father had felt much shame at this moment, for he'd come to despise the aloof Kolchak and blamed his rigidity for the defeat, but doubtlessly he had admired the sailor's loyalty. "God keep you safe," he said, forming the cross over the young man's head.

"And you, Your High Nobility." Then the Siberian knelt beside Vanechka and smiling, doffed his woolen cap to wipe the boy's tears off his cold-ruddled cheeks. "What's this, Vanka?"

Truly he didn't know: since watching the Siberian slaughter the stranger, he'd felt apart from him, feared him even. But now that they were saying good-bye, those feelings had vanished, and he loved the sailor dearly once more.

"You know very well we'll see each other again one day." The Siberian kissed the boy's forehead twice before whispering so only he could hear: "You are the last goodness left, old fellow. Not a

23

single day shall pass without my remembering you as the goodness that has gone out of my life."

Then he hurried from the car.

John Kost stretched at the hospital window. The dawn was clear, and across the bay the Berkeley hills were lucently green with spring grass. A big warship was putting out to sea, leaving a V-shaped wave to spread toward two towers of the Bay Bridge. Turning, he regarded the comatose William Laska. "I'm going in a few minutes, old fellow. I came here hoping to get a dying declaration from you. For that declaration to be any good you've got to believe that you're not going to recover. Do you believe that?"

The man's gaze remained fixed on the ceiling light.

At that moment a partrolman entered without knocking. "Morning, Inspector. Has he talked yet?"

"No . . . but he'd like to."

4

THE FAT LITTLE MAN in the sable-collared coat didn't detrain at
Ostankino Station.

Watching him from the opposite end of the car, the Chekist
half-expected him to bolt. But when—with a lurch, a rumble,
and then a clack over the first joint in the rails—the Leningrad-
to-Moscow train started moving again, the fellow was still on his
wooden bench, wedged between the wall and an old woman,
clutching his valise on his lap. He looked around, then out his
window. It had steamed over from the exhalations of the
passengers, and he rubbed away this fog with his coat sleeve.

The Chekist glanced at what the man was watching: a column
of Voroshilov tanks and katyusha rocket carriers lumbering
toward the Kremlin Armory for repainting, even though May
Day was three weeks away. This year's, then, would be the parade
to end all parades, a colossal wake for fascism. How'd he feel
about the coming peace? he asked inwardly. Like the Civil War
before it, this war had brought him advancement, vodka and
caviar, a box seat at the Bolshoi, Black Sea holidays. But did it
matter? He could advance no higher and was sick of Black Sea
holidays. And with peace the Politburo would do what it had

wanted for a long time: rein in the activities of the secret police.

The train began to slow again, this time for Leningrad Station. Here, the little man would have no choice but to abandon the crowded safety of the car. It was the end of the line, indeed.

Did the fellow have someone waiting for him? No matter— they'd both die then.

As the brakes locked and grated, the little man visibly clenched his teeth.

The Chekist smiled. He was a clear-eyed, robust man in his late forties, lacking the paunch and jowls of other Chekists his age. Of course, in the entire Mobile Group of Administration of Special Task, he was the only true veteran of the Cheka, Lenin's Extraordinary Commission for Combating Counterrevolution, Profiteering, and Sabotage; and it annoyed him that in Party parlance *Chekist* had come to mean any fool with the secret police, even if he'd been sucking his mother's teat during the Revolution.

The iron-ribbed roof of the station glided into view.

The Chekist decided to close on his quarry before he might team up with a comrade on the station platform. His plan was to make it look like an accident: a poor drunken apparatchik had tried to detrain from the wrong side of the coach while it was yet moving, stumbled and lost his balance, only to have his head pulverized by the wheels.

Politely excusing himself, another atypicality for a Chekist, he edged past an Eighth Guards lieutenant's knees and out into the aisle before the other passengers could rise and begin jostling each other for their luggage in the overhead storage. He was careful not to meet the little man's eye and perhaps alert him, but when he finally glanced in that direction, the man's place on the bench was empty.

"Damn." He unfastened the lowermost two buttons of his overcoat as he rushed down the aisle. The outer door at the car's end was ajar, so he didn't bother to check the lavatory.

Hundreds of Red Army wounded had just been off-loaded from another train, their stretchers in rows on the platform. No one could be seen running or even walking urgently among the bandaged men, so he crossed over to the far side of the car—and glimpsed a figure trotting out into the darkness beyond the overhang of the station roof. A short-legged man with a valise.

He jumped down onto the adjoining track and gave chase, his ankle-high boots drumming over the wooden crossties that despite the cold stank of piss and creosote.

His trenching tool was bouncing inside the deep side-pocket of his overcoat. He had a seven-shot Nagan revolver as well, in a belt holster. Yet he preferred to use his small German shovel. Before acquiring it, he had relied on a hatchet for this sort of work, and then an alpine ax, which had seen him through the most notorious assassination of his career, one carried out in a suburb of Mexico City against a fool who didn't know how to keep his mouth shut. But then a year later, he'd been sent to the front to deal with an overly cautious tank general. "Strict punishment" it was called. There, while waiting for the general to sober up enough to realize the enormity of what was about to happen to him, he witnessed something quite extraordinary in depersonalized modern warfare. A Nazi mountain trooper, out of ammunition and making a last stand in a muddy ditch, dispatched three Soviet soldiers with his razor-sharp trenching tool, opening their faces like ripe melons. A grenade finally got him, and its smoke was still hanging above the ditch when the Chekist strode over and retrieved the collapsible, exquisitely simple weapon. He tested the sharpness of the blade with his thumb, slitting his skin with only neglible pressure. Pensively, he sucked on the blood, imagining the general's horror when he saw that he would not, after all, be given the dignity of a bullet. The Chekist concealed the shovel in his overcoat pocket and had carried it there ever since. It had become the stuff of generals' nightmares, that shovel.

He now saw where the little man's tracks zigzagged up an embankment of wet, dirty snow. Above was another track. It curved south toward Kursk and Moscow Stations, the rails glinting like silver wires in the distance. He stopped to listen, then smiled. From afar he could hear huffing like a wounded

27

bear's. It was coming from the direction of the railway bridge over Rusakov Street.

At last he caught sight of the little man. He was hobbling as if he'd turned his ankle and had shifted his valise from his right hand to his left so he could grip the pistol he had drawn.

Now the Chekist had to make sure no shots were fired. That might bring in the militia, and it would be indelicate to involve the police even though they were an inferior branch of his own commissariat.

He hung back and kept to the building shadows.

A moment later, he thought the fellow was going to slide down the slushy embankment and limp for the Kremlin along Karl Marx and then Chernyshevsky streets. But a militiaman was posted in the wide intersection with Garden Ring, pacing the cobbles. Apparently, the little man had his own reasons for leaving the police out of this. He stopped once and regarded the spires of the Kremlin, more than a kilometer to the west, with what the Chekist would have bet was an expression of dire longing. The man's boss awaited him there, no doubt impatiently by now, but the little man peered back down the railway line before stumbling on again.

Within sight of the fogbound Yauza River, he veered away from the tracks. He struck out across a field, his shoes clattering over the rubble left by a German bombing earlier in the war. Holstering his pistol so he could hang on to some leafless shrubs, he sidestepped down a plunging slope and melted into the fog.

His disappearance didn't alarm the Chekist, who realized that he intended to follow the north bank of the Yauza down to where it dumped its chunks of spring ice into the Moskva River. From there he would undoubtedly turn for the Kremlin. But long before that an iron span loomed over his path: the railroad bridge he'd just decided not to cross, whose mist-shrouded trestles the Chekist now studied.

Then he too descended the slope, but farther downstream than the little man had, and finding a footpath along the riverbank followed it back to the railroad bridge. As recollected, the span rested on two large I-beams poised about three meters above the mushy ground. After making sure his pocket flaps were securely buttoned, he leaped up and grasped the bottom lip of one of the beams, then swung his left leg over the top of the truss. In a blink he was atop it, laying out his trenching tool and as a precaution, his Nagan revolver.

For a while there came no sounds but the groans and screaks of the ice being shoved along by the foamy current, but then a quiet huffing mingled with the noises of the thaw.

The Chekist clicked open the trenching tool so the blade projected at a ninety-degree angle from the wooden handle. He had about twenty feet of visibility through the fog.

The huffing, growing closer, was now offset by a faint wheezing. But he'd no sooner heard a shuffling of shoes than they drew to a halt.

Pressing his cheek to the clammy iron of the I-beam, he smiled as he imagined the transformation taking place on the dim footpath below. In the desperation of the moment the little fellow's instincts, dulled by a sedentary adulthood of dialetic and then more dialetic, were trying to shake off their long dormacy.

Then he could be heard scuffling along again.

The Chekist watched him materialize out of the fog, clasping the valise to his chest with his left arm, advancing as if on eggshells, probing the mists with the muzzle of his pistol. He expected danger from every direction. Except up. Except from the direction of God's good heaven. Blame it on a religious upbringing, the Chekist thought in the split second during which he swung down the blade, catching the man at the nape.

He collapsed as if his bones had turned to milk, and a fringe of his hair that had hung over his sable collar floated down after him.

The Chekist dropped to the footpath.

The little man had been nearly decapitated. His head was folded back behind his left shoulder, and blood was foaming out his nostrils. The sable on his collar was from an inferior animal, not worth saving even had the Chekist been of a mind to.

Turning to the valise, he removed all its contents, without taking time to inspect the various papers he transferred to his coat pockets. The leather case was then pitched into the river, where it rode the curdled ice for a few feet and then slowly sank out of sight.

Reluctantly, for there'd been times when he would have given much for such a nice 9mm pistol, he chucked the fellow's Polish-made Radom into the middle of the flow. Keepsakes had a bad habit of popping up as evidence in show trials.

Whipping open the little man's overcoat, he frisked him for his identity packet and found it in an inner pocket. This too he saved for later examination. He unbuttoned the man's wide-lapelled jacket and then his sweat-soaked shirt, exposing a soft white belly. An arcing flash of the trenching tool, and the gut was neatly split from groin to rib cage—all the way back to the spine. This way, the gasses of putrefaction that would build in the abdomen when the water eventually warmed could freely escape from the corpse, and the little fellow wouldn't suddenly bob to the surface in July to spoil someone's picnic. But just to make sure, the Chekist punctured both lungs several times by thrusting his folding knife between the ribs.

He cleaned both his shovel and knife on the man's overcoat.

After doing all this, plus filling the fellow's trousers and overcoat pockets with chunks of bomb-shattered concrete, he slid the body into the Yauza.

"I'd feel worse if you were my first, old fellow," he said, "but you're not even close."

John Kost parked front-wheels-to-curb at the end of a lane that pitched straight up the flank of Russian Hill. Grabbing a clothes box and a half-pint of vodka off the front seat, he eased out of the Dodge. The seersucker jacket inside the box was a gift from a North Beach tailor whose son had been accepted by the Navy only because Inspector Kost had doctored his rap sheet for rum-running, and the vodka a token of appreciation from a Cantonese package-store owner who'd been protected from the local tong by Kost when he was assigned to a Chinatown footbeat. He crossed the cul-de-sac to a three-story apartment building. Its roof parapet was capped with terra-cotta tiles as if to add some Spanish flair to the nondescript chicken-wire-and-stucco structure.

Fusty-smelling, the interior corridor dimmed back to a staircase. The thin plank doors he passed somehow suggested the lives behind them. In flats like these, bodies sometimes lay undiscovered for weeks—until the blowflies revealed them.

He bounded up the stairs three at a time to the top floor and strode down the corridor to the last door. He knocked.

Almost at once the door jerked open as far as the chain lock allowed, and he beheld Mikhail Kostoff's white mustaches and day's growth of matching stubble. The cystic goiter under his Adam's apple was getting larger by the week, but John Kost had promised himself not to mention it again. How do you convince a man to go to the doctor when he insists that the surgeons killed more Russian soldiers than the Austrians? It was useless to point out that these San Francisco physicians were not with the Imperial Medical Corps. Nor could he be persuaded to eat fish, which would help his condition. In Manchuria, the warlord he'd served as a bodyguard had poisoned his chief rival with the venomous extract of some local fish.

"What do you have there?" the old man asked in French after unlocking the chain.

"A summer jacket for you, Papa." Entering the two-room flat, John Kost handed his father the half-pint, then headed for the armoire outside the bedroom door—the room itself scarcely had space for the bed. Behind him, he could hear the brown paper bag being crinkled open.

"Amerikanets," the old man hissed, reverting to Russian.

"Yes."

"Why not Polish? Polish is best."

"There is no more Poland."

Mikhail Kostoff had nothing but contempt for the American attempt at vodka, but that contempt helped slow his rate of consumption. After bailing him out of the drunk tank three times in one month, John Kost had reduced his father's ration to a half-pint every two days. He also bought the old man's food for

31

him and paid his bills so that no cash could tempt his badly arthritic fingers.

"What do I need a summer jacket for?"

"Come August you'll look a fool in your burka." Opening the armoire, John Kost frowned at this mangy goat-felt cloak with its stiff, square shoulders. Once he had overheard some kids in Portsmouth Square calling his father Count Dracula. To hang up the seersucker jacket he had to slide over the faded Don Cossacks parade uniform. That it had survived all the stations of their flight from Russia—Omsk, Irkutsk, Harbin, Tientsin, and finally, San Francisco—made the lack of a single photograph of his mother seem all the more unjust. Even the old man's saber had made it and was now propped, fluffy with dust, in a corner.

"How much did it cost?"

"Doesn't matter, Papa." John Kost shut the armoire doors and turned for the kitchenette. "You want me to start the samovar for you?"

"Does not matter!" the old man cried, his hand fisted around the neck of the bottle. "Your extravagance will ruin us! First you move out on a whim—two rents! Now this! What's wrong with you!"

Not arguing that he'd moved out nine years ago to marry, John Kost plugged in the electric samovar.

"Don't bother," the old man said with sudden calm. "All that hot water and I drink so little. I piddle even less." These days his anger gusted, whereas in years gone by it had blown for days on end like the tawny grit that had descended on Harbin out of Mongolia.

John Kost took the kettle off the samovar's top and poured the old, concentrated tea down the sink. As there were just the two of them, he would use tea bags. Filling the kettle from the tap, he gazed north across the bay. Through the rusted bars of the bedroom fire escape his father had a splendid view—of Alcatraz. John Kost was on the verge of smiling when his face grew solemn again. He rested the kettle on the stained porcelain, cross-wiped his hands on his French cuffs, then hurried for the telephone on the otherwise useless calling-card stand. He carried it into the bedroom, stringing out the cord behind him on the floor. Waiting for the department receptionist to answer, he idly opened the top drawer on its usual contents: Mikhail Kostoff's baptismal cross and Cossack dagger.

"Police Department."

"Homicide, please—Assistant Inspector Aranov." He saw his father shake his head and turn off the water. "Sorry, Papa," he said with his palm over the speaker. He started to sit on the bed but then saw that the icon of Christ Pantocrator was already down off the wall and resting on the George Washington coverlet for the day.

"Aranov, Homicide." His voice was shot.

"Nathan, John Kost here—"

"Where the hell are you?"

"A moment—something just came to me. Follow along now. Patrolman Elliot responded without a backup, yes?"

"Right."

"Why'd he handle a domestic disturbance alone?"

"All the Potrero cruisers were tied up with other calls."

"Precisely. D'you have a copy of swing shift's radio log?"

"Somewhere here. . . ." Aranov could be heard rustling through some papers. "Here it is."

"Good. Now tell me—was it a busy night in general?"

"Hmmm . . . no. Not until right before the call to two thirty-three Carbon. Then the switchboard lit up." Aranov suddenly exhaled. "Oh, shit."

"Quite, Nathan. Shit. We have to find out who made those calls that deprived Elliot of help."

"I should've thought of that."

"If you thought of everything, as you nearly do, you'd put the rest of us out of work. Listen, I'm going to grab breakfast, a change of clothes, then—"

"No, John!"

"I beg your pardon?"

"Have you forgotten?"

"So it'd appear."

"Coffey's briefing on the United Nations Conference. He's already in your office."

"Oh, no." John Kost clasped his hand to his forehead. "Tell the captain I'm on my way!" He hung up and ran past Mikhail Kostoff and out the door, but then spun around halfway down the hall and barged back inside the flat to embrace his confused-looking father before darting out again, tossing over his shoulder, "Eat something with that vodka, Papa."

5

THE CHEKIST STEPPED OUT of the limousine. He stretched while the driver made his U-turn and accelerated back toward Moscow, then waited until the last rumble from the Packard had echoed out into the birches before starting down the muddy road. For the sake of his shoes, he kept to the yet frozen hump at its center. Moon shadow dimmed the ground out among the trees, but he imagined tightly wrapped greenery spiking up through the carpet of dead leaves, irresistible growth clawing for the sun. Ahead through the trunks he saw a cigarette coal brighten. "Turn that muzzle away from me, Funikov," he softly called out.

He was answered with a phlegmy chuckle, then, "I knew it was you as soon as the limo pulled up."

"All the more reason to get your muzzle off me."

Funikov chuckled even louder. He was slinging his Shpagin submachine gun over his shoulder as the Chekist walked up to him and asked, "Is the Little Boss still awake?"

"I'd bet my life on it."

A woman then, the Chekist noted to himself.

"And he left word for you to see him whatever time you got in," Funikov went on.

"Anything interesting happen while I was gone?"

"Yes, the Nazis parachuted in and kidnapped the fucking Politburo. And now we're all up to our chins in shit. I have orders to shoot you and then myself. Or maybe it was the other way around." He took a pull off his chrome pocket flask, then handed it to the Chekist, who wiped the neck on his sleeve before drinking. Funikov lowered his voice. "Major to-do this morning at the Big Boss's Kremlin office. Konev, Zhukov, Malenkov, the Little Boss—everybody."

"Molotov?" the Chekist asked.

"Everybody, I said. The Big Boss ranted on and on about how he can't trust the Allies."

"That's not a new tune."

"Wait till you hear the second verse. He said Churchill and Roosevelt are getting ready to stab him in the back, but he's thinking about beating them to it. The Little Boss clapped louder than anybody." Funikov shrugged. "So at last we know which way the wind's blowing, what?"

The Chekist handed back the flask and strode on toward the dacha, saying over his shoulder, "Tell them I'm coming."

"Why? I'd like to see you squirming in the mud, full of holes."

But behind him he could hear Funikov cranking up the American-made field telephone.

The blacked-out dacha began to take shape through the birches. Within walking distance was the far grander one of the Big Boss, who was apparently getting ready to sever his umbilical with the West. The Chekist had never cared for Iosif Stalin as he had Lenin, a fellow with a more predictable temperament once you got used to it. And Vladimir Ilyich had possessed a sense of humor, an appreciation for ironies.

But such things were beside the point. And the point this deep inside the maelstrom had always been survival.

The guard on the front porch waved him forward, but the Chekist hand-signaled that he'd enter through the back door.

Nor did he care much for the Little Boss. In many ways he detested the man. But he didn't delude himself into believing he could fill the shoes of even a profligate drunkard like Lavrenty Pavlovich Beria. These high deputies had a dimension admittedly lacking in himself, a talent for tiptoeing around Stalin's paranoia. Even Molotov, who was sliding into disfavor, had enough of it to keep his head. So far. In turn, the Chekist had something they all lacked: a genuine predaceousness, not a trumped-up one such as Stalin's reputation as bank robber. It made him invaluable. Lenin himself had said that this "howling in our young comrade's soul" saved the Revolution. Untrue. It had saved Vladimir Ilyich, which in his mind had been the same as the Revolution.

He snapped his fingers at the corner of the dacha, keeping most of his body behind the wall.

The man covering the back door clicked on his electric torch. The light quickly went out. The Chekist had been recognized. "Anything left to eat, old fellow?"

"This and that," the man whispered as the Chekist slipped past him into the kitchen.

The Little Boss's steward was drowsing at the table, his forehead resting on his fist. Behind him was a serving cart bearing the remnants of a late-night repast: smoked sturgeon, golden caviar, bread, sweet butter, and cheese. The bottle of Kakheti was empty, but no matter: the steward had set a carafe of vodka, which the Chekist preferred over the sweet red Georgian wine, and two crystal glasses on the shelf above the wheels. He reached for the carafe, filled a glass to the brim, and downed it. He poured a second to savor with his food, then garnished a heel of bread with caviar. As he chewed, his jaws began clicking, the result of being bludgeoned by a White Army interrogator long ago.

The steward startled awake.

"Easy, old fellow." The Chekist gripped the man's shoulder so tightly he winced. "Kindly announce me."

The servant had a mulberry dapple on his brow where his fist had been. "At once, Comrade Colonel."

The Chekist thought of helping himself to another glass, but then reminded himself that the Little Boss might be in the mood for one of his drinking bouts. A downward glance assured him that he had no blood on his clothes, just a little rust from the bridge.

The steward came back in. "He'll see you now."

The Little Boss had a smooth, round face that turned infantile when he took off his pince-nez eyeglasses; even the cleft in his chin failed to give it any angularity. He was sitting in a leather wing chair with such studied dignity the Chekist knew at once he was drunk, although it wasn't always such an easy thing to tell with Beria.

Across the thoroughly petit bourgeois parlor, on a suffocatingly soft couch, sprawled a young woman. The wine must have inflamed her pretty face, for by this much time in the company of Beria it was doubtful that she could register embarrassment—he was known to expedite his seductions with drugs. The parlor was overheated, and the Chekist was careful to betray no disgust at the ruttish odors mixed in the sultriness. The phonograph was going softly. Prokofiev. Was he back in favor then?

"Comrade Colonel," Beria said at last, his Georgian accent thicker than usual because of the alcohol, "may I introduce Mademoiselle Tabakova."

Lazily, she held up her hand to be kissed, but the Chekist only nodded. He had seen finer women in this parlor who, out of either desperation or ambition, had fancied they could better their lot by spreading their legs for Lavrenty Beria. Of course, he had also seen barely pubescent girls in this setting as well; the Little Boss had plucked them off the streets outside their schools only to rape them here, or in his office at the Lubyanka Prison, or even at his house on Katchalov Street, with his wife, Nina, at home during the entire debauchery.

"Mademoiselle is with the State Music Publishing House. But truly—she's a musician. A violinist like your father was."

"I see," the Chekist said coolly. The drift of her eyes told him she was working hard to keep his face in focus.

"Where'd your father play?" she asked.

"In Siberia, mostly."

Beria laughed. "The good colonel means his father was overheard by the Okhrana spouting reform and was exiled. Before that he was with the Moscow Conservatory Orchestra, wasn't he?"

"Correct, Comrade Commissar."

"I thought so." Beria turned to the young woman, regarded her tenderly for a moment, then said, "Let us have a word in private, will you?"

"All right." Tottering slightly, she rose and crossed the parlor, her bare feet as white as marble against the plum-colored Bokharan carpet. The Chekist didn't give Beria the satisfaction of leering after her, even though she had womanly hips that ordinarily would've sparked his interest.

The door latch snicked shut again, and Beria gave a sigh. "Well, how was your trip?"

"Interesting." It was his way of bringing up complications.

Naturally, Beria sniffed this out at once. He took his pince-nez from his dressing jacket and began dusting the lenses with his handkerchief. "Oh?"

"I was followed."

"From Moscow?"

"Yes, the entire trip."

"But the child made it safely to Leningrad?"

"Correct."

"And what of the man who followed you?"

"I wasn't sure at first if he'd been sent to assist me . . ."—a careful way of suggesting Beria had sent a second operator in the event the Chekist failed. But the commissar's expression shed no light on the issue one way or another. Alcohol made him even more inscrutable than usual, much like the other powerful Georgian in Moscow. "But then," the Chekist went on, "my tail went about his business so poorly I knew he wasn't one of our people."

Beria clipped his glasses onto the bridge of his nose. "Did he see where you left off the girl?"

"No, I made sure of that. Just as I made sure he was able to find me again in Leningrad after she was left off at the old monastery on Lake Lagoda."

"Good, good." Beria suddenly smiled, although the Chekist knew no affection was involved. "Was she well behaved?"

"Admirably."

"But I've also been told you have a good way with children."

"Thank you, Comrade Commissar. I prefer their company to adults."

"Like most Russians then. And what'd the woman do?"

The woman—a peculiar way of referring to her in light of their former relationship. "She was upset, of course, but said nothing untoward." She had said nothing at all while her daughter was ripped from her arms. But he decided not to add that her refusal to speak had affected him more than any amount of pleading would have. He would have to watch her in the future. She was an estimable woman, and such a woman could be counted on to pick her own moment of revenge.

"Now what of this fool who tailed you? Where's he now?"

"Somewhere under the Yauza's ice."

Beria's eyes widened. "Any idea who he was?"

The Chekist handed him the identification packet.

Beria reached over his shoulder and missing the switch on the first two tries, finally turned on the lamp. He studied the photograph for only an instant before closing his eyes.

"Do you know him, Comrade Commissar—if I might ask?"

"Yes, one of the barnacles clinging to that filing clerk." Beria meant Molotov, whom Lenin had called "the best filing clerk in all Russia."

"Did you find anything else on him?" Beria asked.

"Yes—these in his valise." The Chekist took the sheaf of documents from his overcoat pocket. He had begun to perspire under the heavy outer garment, but liked his trenching tool close at hand, always.

"What are they?"

"I don't know. I had no chance to examine them," the Chekist lied, for he'd gone through the exit visa applications before ordering the militiaman in Tagan Square to call him a car. It was safest with Beria to make him think you knew only what he wanted you to know.

"Stamped in Leningrad," Beria muttered—then froze as the implication hit him.

"Something wrong, Comrade Commissar?" He knew only too well what was wrong: Molotov's fat little fellow had somehow latched onto pieces of the paper trail left by the Mobile Group team that in mid-January had flown out of Leningrad for London and then on to San Francisco.

"Can you be sure he didn't contact any of his people before you dumped him in the Yauza?"

"Reasonably. Comrade Beria must remember that I had a four-year-old girl with me."

"Not good enough!" he exploded.

The Chekist refused to flinch. He himself remained expressionless while Beria's face was gripped by paroxysms. "Do you have any idea what this means!"

"No, Comrade Commissar," the Chekist again lied. His head was filling with scarlet, a boiling sensation that made him wonder with an almost sexual urgency what it would be like to pump a bullet into Beria's face.

"The people we have in place are now useless to us. With less than two weeks to go, they're useless. Damn you, man. Damn your carelessness!" Then, abruptly, Beria's rage dissipated and he sank back into the wing chair, although he added as if in a childish snit, "Well, you'll have to go to San Francisco—that's all there is to it."

"I'll go as ordered. But it's been only five years since the operation in Mexico City. American Naval Intelligence conducted an investigation independent of that by the incompetent *federales*." The Chekist smiled, although he was dangerously close to reaching for his Nagan. That Beria undoubtedly had his own revolver inside his dressing jacket meant nothing; it weighed like a gnat on his sudden lust to kill the man. "They know the

41

Mexicans arrested the wrong fellow for what happened to Trotsky."

"Then that's a risk you'll have to accept," Beria said. "Your plane departs at noon. Leave me now."

At first Nathan Aranov had considered it a kick in the teeth to be assigned to John Kost's unit. The rosy glow from passing the dick's examination with the highest score in PD history, then acing the oral review board, and finally being appointed to Homicide instead of Vice or Bunco like most rookie plainclothesmen—all this had burst like a big soapy bubble with the realization that he'd been put under a man whose real name was Ivan Mikhailovich Kostoff, a reactionary with a Cossack colonel for a father. He had grown up on a steady diet of pogrom stories; his own father, as a teenager during the First World War, had walked out of Russia with his rabbi, except that the rabbi hadn't made it out because he couldn't run as fast as Aranov's father. A bunch of Cossack peasants caught up with him, ripped off his trousers in the suspicion he was circumcised. He was. So they beat him to death with barrel staves. This story had made Aranov's first gym-class shower at Galileo High School a delight.

"Hey, Natty. . . ." Sergeant Ragnetti, whose desk abutted on Aranov's, was fiddling with the dials on his table radio. He kept tuning back and forth across the signal as if something were wrong with it. "What the fuck's this?"

"Country music."

"*Which* country?"

"This one, Vince—some new station for the war workers."

"Is that what them Okies listen to?"

"That's it."

"*Jesus*," Ragnetti said with an amazed expression that on another man's face might be taken for constipation. He was easily amazed and gave profound consideration to anything, no matter how trivial, that came close to nicking the unblemished surface of his tabula rasa. He had been another pleasant surprise for Aranov upon arrival at Homicide. Not only had the rookie been handed over to a Goliath of a Cossack, the inspector had then apprenticed him to a 270-pound Sicilian with bulldog jowls and an indelible five-o'clock shadow.

"Aranov!" Captain of Inspectors Patrick Coffey shouted from inside John Kost's office. "Did you phone him like I said!"

"He's on the way, sir."

And in the beginning there'd been days Aranov regretted ever having left Patrol. The blue uniform, hated at the time, had in reality been a costume, making it possible for him to act out the role of a San Francisco cop. But in the Homicide bull pen, clad in tweed like any encyclopedia salesman, he was painfully himself once again. John Kost was polite but distant. Ragnetti ignored him unless it was to order him to shag sandwiches and beer from a saloon around the corner. The other dicks, when there'd still been other dicks to share the bull pen with Ragnetti and him, behaved in no remarkable way toward him. But whatever they'd done so unremarkably, it had made him feel acutely Jewish.

Then one drizzly morning John Kost strolled out to the bull pen windows, where he sometimes stood to brood. After a while, Aranov felt the inspector's gaze on him. "Tell me, Nathan, in your opinion please, who was the greater operatic genius? Verdi or Puccini?"

With all the eyes in the bull pen fused on him, heat flooded into his face. Part of it was anger. He was sure the Cossack was baiting him. All kikes were supposed to be eggheads, and the inspector was going to prove it to his boys. And part of his blush came from being called down for doing something on the sly, as Aranov did go to the opera, the ballet too. He didn't know back then that John Kost did these things as well, that he took to the performing arts as much as he did to rich society women. But in those days Aranov had buried his penchants in the hope of blending in with the other dicks; he'd gone so far as to wear a rakish-looking fedora and to bone up on baseball, although nobody ever invited him to join in the baseball arguments. "Hell if I know, Inspector," he finally said with a stupid laugh.

John Kost's dark eyes shifted toward Ragnetti. "Vincent, what do you say?"

"Shit. . . ." The sergeant began pressing his fingertips together, isometrically, as if limbering up for a sparring match. The seconds ticked past to an accompaniment of Ragnetti's soft, rhythmic grunts, and Aranov was sure the First Homicide Bureau Opera Symposium had just died a natural death. "Shit, I dunno, John. I mean, it's like who's the better president—Washington or Lincoln? Without neither of them, America wouldn't be America. Without Verdi and Puccini, well, it wouldn't be opera."

"Exactly. . . ." Aranov heard a pedantic voice say—and was mildly surprised to recognize it to be his own. "Verdi was the father of Italian opera, the master architect of its dramatic form and use of melody. But Giacomo Puccini, with his lyricism and—oh, yes—his *verismo* sentimentality, humanized it . . . he. . . ." Then Aranov choked up. He couldn't believe that he'd just gone off his nut like this in front of the entire bull pen. Half of the guys already suspected he was a twink, even though they'd met his fiancée, Sylvia, at the Christmas party.

"Yeah," Ragnetti said through a grin, the first Aranov had ever caught on the man's swarthy face, "isn't that what I just fucking said?"

"I don't know, fellows." Looking perplexed, John Kost took his raincoat off the wooden tree. "You two have put it a bit too neatly for my taste. But we can hammer it out over lunch. . . ."

"Jeez, Inspector," Aranov automatically said, "I got to finish up the narrative on that—"

John Kost simply tossed him his coat.

That afternoon the threesome never made it back to the Hall of Justice from Carlo's. Ragnetti picked the dishes, explaining each one's specific boon to health: "Here, eat some of this, it'll give you *cogliones* like a bull ox."

"What're they?"

"Take a fucking peek under your napkin, Natty."

The service might have been faster had not John Kost insisted—even while the Verdi-Puccini debate raged—that the waiter, a San Francisco Opera understudy when he wasn't slinging pasta, take time out to sing selections he believed corroborated the point he was trying to make. In the midst of one of these points, Ragnetti interrupted him, pointing with his fork at the nude painting in the adjoining barroom: "Hold on, John. Look at the lovely bombs on that hooker, Natty. . . ." And incongruously, in that moment with the sergeant rambling on about bombs, Aranov realized what John Kost had done. Blaming his smarting eyes on the Chianti they'd been quaffing, he raised his glass to the inspector. "You listening to me, Natty? I'm talking *bombs.*" And because he was a gracious man, John Kost pretended not to understand Aranov's surge of gratitude. Instead, he zeroed in on Aranov's previous boast that he'd memorized the entire libretto to *La Tosca*, which the young plainclothesman then made good on while Ragnetti came close to laughing himself sick, hollering midway through the lightning recitation for old Carlo himself to come listen. "After memorizing the Mishnah," Aranov said breathlessly but happily when he'd finished, "*Tosca* was a cinch."

He now sat up: John Kost had just swept into the bull pen on the way to his office. He hadn't come directly, as promised, for his fresh change of clothes said otherwise, and he'd shaved, reminding Aranov that he himself had not. John Kost gave a passing wave to his two men as he began placating Coffey: "Captain?"

"Where you been, for Chrissake!"

John Kost left the door open, perhaps because he knew how much Ragnetti and Aranov enjoyed these performances. "Please, let me apologize. I'm terrible. Utterly worthless—"

"Tell me something I don't know," Captain Coffey said, but already a smile was creeping into his whiskey voice. "Now get back out there, John, so I can get this medicine show on the road."

"Of course, Captain."

"And send that gumba bastard of yours down the hall for Hurley and Mulrenan."

Ragnetti was already on his feet, feigning masturbation, when

John Kost came out of the office. The inspector remained straight-faced. "Vincent, would you please—?"

"Yeah, yeah." Ragnetti ambled out for the two plainclothesmen. Hurley and Mulrenan had originally been assigned solely to Homicide, but then with the war had been shunted from bureau to bureau as needed. Coffey called them his "flying squad," which Ragnetti had meliorated to "flying fucks." Within a minute, the sergeant was leading the insouciant assistant inspectors back into the bull pen. Neither Hurley nor Mulrenan acknowledged Aranov. Their noses were still bent out of shape because the "Hebe," their junior in Homicide seniority, hadn't been tapped for the flying squad instead of one of them. John Kost probably had not helped the situation by telling them that with a bare-bones roster he couldn't do without Aranov, even though hearing about the confrontation later from Ragnetti had made Aranov feel genuinely proud of himself for the first time in his life, almost convincing him he was something more than a pastiche of a cop.

"All right, all right," Captain Coffey said, yawning as if he instead of the graveyard-watch detective had been up since yesterday, "every last one of us feels like the devil about this kid killed in Potrero. . . ." With a cranky narrowing of his eyes, he turned to John Kost. "What was his name?"

"Wallace Elliot, sir."

"Yeah, Elliot. But life goes on. So here's the business at hand. . . ." Coffey took a three-by-five card from his shirt pocket. "This last summer near Washington, D.C., the big-four Allies got together at Dumbarton Oaks. Any of you guys read about it?"

Silence in the bull pen.

"Anyways, the U.S., Russia, England, and China decided to hold another conference, this one in our fair city to"—he referred to the card—"'to create an international security organization empowered to take such action as may be necessary to maintain or restore international peace and security.'" He glanced up. "Any questions so far, gents?"

There was none.

"Now," Coffey went on, "I'm sure you can imagine the headaches of having more than a thousand world bigwigs in town. So from this time on, all scheduled days off, holidays, and vacations are canceled." A groan went up, which he tried to glare down.

"Excuse me, Captain," John Kost said, "but it's my understanding the Conference doesn't begin until April twenty-fifth."

"That's right—seventeen short days from now. But the delegates are already hitting town. Matter of fact, John, a good part of your delegation flies in to Hamilton Field tomorrow."

"*My* delegation, sir?"

"Listen, gents—there's going to be Secret Service, FBI, State Department Security, Army and Naval Intelligence swarming all over this thing. But if one of the delegates gets plugged or mugged, who's going to take the heat? Good old San Francisco PD, that's fucking who. And believe me, every pickpocket, whore, and grifter who can come up with the train fare is on the way here. So each of you is being assigned to a delegation. And the biggies too. We saved a disciplined unit like Homicide for the major league countries."

"We ain't Homicide anymore," Hurley said for Mulrenan and himself.

Coffey ignored the comment. "A few of you speak foreign languages, which was gravy for us. But otherwise, you were picked for a particular country because the chief thought you'd get along with those folks. We got some background scoop and your delegation's schedule for you. . . ." He turned to a sergeant from Administration who'd just arrived on cue with five manila folders piled on his forearms. Coffey took the topmost folder, read the name on it, and called out, "Aranov. Great Britain."

He stood uncertainly, wondering how to broach the problem this additional assignment created for him.

Thankfully, John Kost spoke up: "Excuse me again, Captain, but Nathan's ramrodding the Elliot homicide."

"So? You got the suspect, don't you?"

"Well—"

"Based on Aranov's preliminary report, it seems open-and-shut to me."

"We wouldn't want to rule out anything at this point."

"Then don't, John." Coffey's lips tightened as Aranov continued to balk at coming forward. "Son, just take the goddamn folder from me. We all got our cross to bear until these gasbags run out of steam in June and go home. You can go ahead with the Elliot case when you're not chitchatting with Anthony Eden."

"But sir," John Kost persisted, "when will Nathan sleep?"

"When he's listening to Anthony Eden."

No laughter followed. At last, Aranov dragged up for his folder.

"Ragnetti—China."

"What happened to Italy? I speak Italian, not Chink."

"Italy's not coming to the Conference. Something about a guy named Mussolini queering the invitation for them. Heard of him?"

"Hell," Mulrenan butted in, "the sarge used to brag on the son of a bitch until Pearl Harbor."

"Bullshit!" Ragnetti said. "I never said nothing for that bald fuck—and don't say otherwise!" He turned back to Coffey. "Jesus, Cap—I got nothing in common with a bunch of Chinamen."

"We know. But the chief heard the Chinese have great respect for ugliness."

That finally got a laugh from the bull pen.

"Inspector Kost—Soviet Union."

"Captain, may we have a word in private?"

"No, John—I got four more of these minstrel shows to do before lunch. And you've already put me forty-five minutes behind schedule. If you got a beef, tell me now."

"It's not my beef, sir, but it might be the Soviets'."

"How's that?"

"My father fought with the White Guardist forces," John Kost said in a rush. "He was Admiral Kolchak's right-hand man. The Bolsheviks shot Kolchak. Dumped his body in the Angara River—"

"Ancient history." Coffey reached for the next folder. "Hurley—France."

"There's no such thing as ancient history to a Russian. I'm asking you to—"

"John! Come up here and take the damned thing!"

6

A JUDAS WINDOW WAS the only breach in the Soviet consulate's massive front door. It was glazed with a mirror on John Kost's side. He sensed he was being watched from within, yet nearly a minute passed before his knock was answered by a woman in a starched white apron. "Inspector Kost, San Francisco Police," he said in English. "I have an appointment with the vice-consul." She gestured for him to follow, then after several turnings deposited him in an anteroom bare of furniture but for two hardback chairs. Withdrawing, she left him to wonder how long he'd have to wait before the Soviets decided he was adequately impressed with his own unimportance. Framed in gold and red, Lenin glowered down from the wall.

Surprisingly, a young man promptly slipped through a side door and offered his smooth hand. "Inspector Kost?" he asked in heavily accented English.

"Yes."

"I am Grigor Pervukhin, Vice-consul Martov's secretary. Thank you for being on time. He would like to see you at once."

John Kost trailed him down a corridor into a comfortably appointed sitting room. "Some tea?" Pervukhin asked.

"Please."

The secretary doled out some tea concentrate into a glass, which he then diluted with hot water from the samovar's spigot. His delicate manner was unexpected; it smacked of the intelligentsia, something John Kost would've thought undesirable in the reign of a coarse Georgian whose favorite expression was reportedly *Yob tvoyou mat'*! Fuck your mother. "A nice day for the drive up, yes?"

"Exceptional," John Kost said.

Pervukhin slopped a little tea over the lip of the glass as he heard footfalls behind him. "Ah, Vice-consul, may I present Inspector Kost."

Martov was a handsome, white-haired man of perhaps fifty years with a self-satisfied smile. "A pleasure, Inspector."

Again, nothing but English—John Kost was relieved that Captain Coffey had apparently not mentioned his White Guardist background to the Soviets. "Good to meet you, sir."

They shook. Martov had a forceful grip.

"Your tea," Pervukhin said, giving John Kost his glass. The custom hadn't changed from his father's day in this regard: men drank their tea from glasses, women cups. "Anything for you, Vice-consul?"

"Nothing, Grisha, thank you. That will be all."

The secretary did everything but bow as he backed out of the room. Martov was smiling engagingly for a fellow who, in being the number two official here, probably headed the intelligence operation. "This duty for us, Inspector, must be a great inconvenience to you."

John Kost shrugged. He wanted it understood from the beginning that he did indeed have more important things to do. "How many cars will you be taking to Hamilton Field?"

"Only mine. Will you ride with us?"

"If you wish."

"Please—I had a dream last night my driver got lost in the redwoods of Marin County."

John Kost took a sip of tea, realizing that he hadn't been

51

invited to sit. Martov was eager to get going, then. "How many of your delegates are arriving today, Vice-consul?"

"Thirty delegates and experts, in four aircraft."

Experts in what? he wondered. "Won't it be a bit of a squeeze in your car?"

Martov folded back his starched shirt cuff to check his wristwatch. "Your Army Air Corps has kindly offered to help us in that regard with several cars and drivers."

John Kost made his own time calculations. The arrival was slated for four o'clock; that meant the procession would be filing into town at rush hour. "Will these people be coming back here to the consulate?"

"No, the St. Francis Hotel."

They would have to negotiate the downtown streets—John Kost gave an inward groan. "I'll have to make a call. I want our Traffic Bureau to have a motorcycle escort waiting for us on the south end of the Golden Gate bridge."

"Is that necessary?"

"If we don't want to be delayed."

"As you think best, Inspector. Please help yourself to the telephone in here while I have my car brought around."

Nathan Aranov ducked under the bedsheet on the clothesline, startling the tall, rawboned woman on the other side. She took the clothespin out of the corner of her mouth: "Who're you?"

Aranov parted his jacket, revealing the badge clipped to his belt. "Sorry I scared you."

"You sure did." She patted the back of the flowered bandana wrapped around her yet damp perm. "You catch that jerk who was sneaking around my windows night 'fore last?"

"No."

"Figures." She turned back to hanging up her wash.

"But that's what I want to talk about. My name's Nate."

She didn't volunteer hers, but he knew it to be Mabelline Shipley from the April 8th activity log. During the minutes in which Wallace Elliot had been responding to 233 Carbon Street, she had been one of several callers for service, and hers had been

52

one of the more urgent requests that had deprived the patrolman of a backup.

"You ever had this problem before?" he asked.

"Nope. Just don't stand there—hand me some stuff."

Aranov reached down into the sopping basket, his face reddening as he touched a pair of panties. Feigning a yawn, he handed her a tea towel, followed by several white stockings, most of them almost worn through at the heel. "You ever call the cops before?"

She shook her head, then said with one side of her mouth tight around a wooden pin, "Don't like to be a bother."

"I understand. I wish there were more people like you."

Obviously realizing that she was being buttered up, she gave him a sidelong glance.

"Where do you work, Mabelline?"

"How d'you know my name?"

"A log's kept for all incoming calls to the department. Who employs you?"

"Navy. Mare Island."

"That's a long ways up bay, isn't it?"

"Navy's got a water taxi for us."

"What do you do for them?"

"I wait on the soda fountain at the exchange. Why?"

"Just wondering." If she worked for the Navy, she had undergone an FBI clearance check, even though it had probably been a cursory one. Enough, Aranov decided. "Well, if this happens again, don't hesitate to call us."

He felt her eyes on his back all the way to his car.

As the vice-consul's mussel-shell-black Cadillac slowed for the Golden Gate tollbooth, John Kost cranked down his backseat window and dangled out his star. The attendant gave a two-fingered salute and waved the Fleetwood sedan through. The wind flowing across the bridge was stiff enough to rock the heavy car and make the driver keep both hands on the wheel. Martov had introduced him simply as Ruml. Gaunt-faced and unsmiling, he had secret police written all over him, despite his modest height. The Soviets liked their agents gargantuan. Right off, John

Kost had noticed the bulge in his double-breasted coat. "Your captain," Martov said pleasantly, "he mentioned that you are attached to the Homicide directorate."

"Yes."

"How many men do you have under you?"

"Well, ordinarily six. But only two at present—the war."

"Of course, the war. But even six seems a small number to command, isn't it?"

"Not in investigations. Control is tighter because the work's more exacting."

"I see." Martov checked his watch again, an expensive-looking gold job. Probably Swiss.

John Kost faintly smiled. Was the vice-consul what his father called an apple: Red on the outside, but still White inside? The man's questions about the Homicide Bureau now made him feel free to ask, "Who're we picking up today? Ambassador Gromyko and his staff?"

"No, he will be flying in from Washington later in the month with the foreign minister."

John Kost hid his surprise. "Molotov's coming to the Conference?"

"Yes, as the head of our delegation. It will be announced by our embassy tomorrow morning."

The tires clipped over the expansion joint at the north end of the bridge, and although the way into Marin County on Highway 101 seemed clear, Ruml looked to the rearview mirror and asked for directions.

John Kost waited for Martov to translate before saying in English, "Tell him to keep going straight. Hamilton Field's about fifteen miles up the road on this side of the bay." He realized that Martov still hadn't said who was arriving today.

"All right, Doc," Vincent Ragnetti said between puffs to get his big cigar going. "I got a message to you from the inspector." He ordinarily didn't smoke cigars, but he invariably bought one at the newsstand along the short walk from the Hall of Justice to the morgue. Still puffing, he shot a glance at the sheet-covered corpse on the autopsy table. "Correct me if I'm wrong—but this is called a *fresh* post, right?"

The doctor just glared at him. A fine-boned guy with thinning hair, he could have passed for Natty Aranov's cousin.

"So, Doc, the inspector asks this—how can forty-three hours be fresh? It ain't fresh for fish, is it? Would you buy fish two days old? So how can it be fresh for a postmortem? You hear what I'm saying?"

"*You* listen. It's not enough that I'm the only forensic pathologist left in San Francisco. In the last two days I've had to deliver three babies, remove a ruptured appendix, and pinch-hit for a radiologist whose kid just got killed in Italy. Oh, and I also got three hours sleep on the sofa in my office. So"—his forefinger poked Ragnetti in the gut, hard—"you tell your boss to go screw himself. Dead people, even dead cops, are low on my priority right now!"

Ragnetti was making a fist when, without warning, he chuckled. The little sawbones had balls. "Settle down, Doc. We cleared the air. That's all what's happening here, okay?"

The pathologist spun away and was nearly to the table when he turned on the sergeant again: "Wait a minute, are you Ragnetti?"

"Yeah," he said around the smoldering cigar, sounding pleased, "you heard of me?"

"You bet. Grab the stool in the corner there."

"Why?"

"Just grab it and come over here." The pathologist took the stool from him and placed it in a niche between two poured-concrete pillars. "Sit and shut up."

"It's all cramped in there."

"Right. Sit—I'm not sewing you back together again." He pointed to the suture scar on the underside of Ragnetti's chin.

"That was you?"

"Yeah."

Sheepishly, the sergeant squeezed his shoulders between the pillars and slid down onto the stool, firmly lodging himself into the niche. "I forgot to eat that day," he said on a gust of smoke.

"Sure." Then the pathologist bundled the sheet off the autopsy table and tossed it in a corner.

Ragnetti's skin slowly lost its deep olive color as he regarded the uncovered corpse, the vicious-looking throat wound that was purple around its jagged edges. Until this instant, it hadn't sunk in that he was here as the PD's witness to the dissection of a cop. His eyes became moist and sad, but he felt no nausea, and for that he was thankful.

He did fine through the opening of the torso, and then the removal, weighing, and slicing up of the various organs. But when the pathologist, after making an incision across the crown of the head, folded down Patrolman Wallace Elliot's face as if it were a rubber mask, only to fire up his circular-bladed bone saw and begin cutting into the skull to get a gander at the dead brain, Ragnetti's eyes fluttered up into his brow.

John Kost watched the four olive-drab C-47 transports swoop in low over San Pablo Bay. One by one, they touched down on the far edge of Hamilton Field, and unexpectedly, the ominous red stars on their fuselages gave his stomach a squeeze. Vice-consul Martov seemed not to notice the aircraft taxiing in across the mirage-rippled plain of asphalt. Instead, pointing, he asked, "Is the big building across the water there San Quentin Prison?"

"I'm afraid not," John Kost said. "That must be part of the Mare Island Naval Base. We went past San Quentin on the way up. I should've pointed it out."

"No matter." Martov smiled without meaning—unless he was thinking that sooner or later his activities here might land him in an American prison. This shackjob of an alliance wouldn't last forever, and it was already showing the strains of nearly four years of cohabitation: a few minutes before John Kost had spotted Robert Cade, an FBI special agent with the San Francisco field office, lurking among the newspeople. A 35mm camera was slung around his neck, although still in its leather case, and he'd forsaken his usual straw boater in the interests of anonymity, as if his grossly fat neck didn't give him away. Tactfully, John Kost had ignored him.

"Our people will be quite exhausted . . . ," Martov said, his eyes snapping toward a large U.S. Army Air Corps truck that had just pulled up to the apron. Two files of military policemen in white helmets, gloves, and leggings leaped down onto the pavement, careful not to stab one another with their chrome bayonets. "Their flight began in Moscow yesterday," Martov went on, "and took them over the Arctic to Canada, Montana, and finally here." Then, holding on to his hat, he turned to the midlevel greeter the State Department had sent out to welcome the Soviets. He was shouting a question at the vice-consul, but it was lost in the roar of the props. The American ground crews began jogging for the planes, which were slowly wheeling so their left-side passenger doors would face the small crowd. Tires were chocked and the Red Air Force crews assisted with setting the off-loading ladders. Inside the hatchways were red-tasseled portieres that made the GIs smirk and mutter what were probably whorehouse allusions. At last, engines were cut and the propeller blades spun down into visibility.

The first man out of the foremost plane in line wore the gold star of a Hero of the Soviet Union. He saluted, then embraced the American colonel waiting for him. "Major Taran," Martov explained to John Kost, even though the State Department man should have been the focus of his conversation. "Taran is one of our most courageous pilots. Leading this historic flight over the North Pole was our way of honoring him."

"I see," John Kost said, although he didn't really see how a day and a night behind the controls of a C-47 was much of an honor.

Apparatchiks in rumpled clothes began streaming out of the other transports, a surprising number of them women. John Kost supposed they were secretaries to the delegates and was tempted to ask about their presence in such numbers, but then realized that Martov would only regurgitate the General Line about no disparity between men and women in the Workers' Paradise. Well, at least not in terms of graceless dress and severity of demeanor.

Yet, a young woman exiting the third C-47 was the exception, and even though the VIPs were climbing out of the lead plane his eyes stayed with her. Her chestnut-colored hair had been wrenched back into the obligatory bun, but it seemed unnaturally constrained, as if ordinarily it flowed around her thin shoulders. She was slender, as had been his teenage wife, and he found something sensuous in the grace with which she came down the ladder and shaded her eyes with a hand as if searching for someone in the crowd. Her face was so striking he suspected that, as with women of the stage, its loveliness—an illusion of powder and mascara—would lessen with each step he took toward her.

But he had no chance to test this, for Martov, the State man, the press corps, and the MP honor guard had started for the lead aircraft. Following, John Kost saw Special Agent Cade snapping quick shots—not of the VIPs, as were the bona fide news photographers, but of the lesser Soviet dignitaries, some of whom were already trickling off toward the Army Plymouths awaiting them on the street behind the flight line.

Inside a cordon hastily formed by the MPs was a scramble of handshaking and comradely cheek-kissing presided over by a Red Navy admiral with one of those mercurial Slavic faces that was petulant one moment and radiant with charm the next. It turned decidedly harsh when the newsmen began hollering questions at him. "I have no comment," he said in Russian, then impatiently asked Martov where their transportation could be found.

The press thought he had offered some traditional Russian benediction until the vice-consul translated, and by that time the admiral and most of his party were halfway to the cars. The MP lieutenant, at Martov's insistence, refused to let the press chase them down. The young officer would've been ignored but for his men's bayonets. In the midst of the caterwauling from the outraged newsmen an Army Air Corps band struck up the "Hymn of the Soviet Union," and all the Russians froze wherever they stood, gazing around for their national emblem in vain. John Kost had seen a private, believing the ceremonies to be over, load both the Soviet and U.S. flags in the back of a jeep and drive away.

"Admiral Konstantin Rodionov of the Navy Commissariat,

and Anatole Lavrentev, assistant to the peoples' commissar of Foreign Affairs," Martov said when the anthem was done, "may I present John Kost, our liaison with the San Francisco police. The good inspector speaks Russian, I'm told."

Thank you, Captain Coffey. John Kost shook their hands.

Admiral Rodionov's smile had flickered at Martov's obvious warning that their remarks would be understood by the American, but now it grew steady again. "Where were you born, Inspector?"

"Moscow, sir."

"And to whom do you report?"

"Captain of Inspectors Patrick Coffey."

"What sort of fellow is he?"

"Satisfactory, sir—of Irish proletarian stock."

Rodionov and Lavrentev laughed, then piled into the back of the Cadillac, leaving Martov to explain, which he did in Russian now, "I've got to ride in this car, Inspector, and ask you to go in the one behind with Madame Martova and her associates."

John Kost hiked an eyebrow: he hadn't seen them greet each other. "Your wife?"

"Yes," the vice-consul said offhandedly, "she'll serve as hostess for our delegation. Kindly have your driver take the lead so you can guide us."

"Very well."

Martov caught him by the arm as he turned to go and whispered, "The admiral liked your joke."

"So it seemed." John Kost trotted back to the olive-drab Plymouth, got in, and said to the corporal driver, "John Kost, San Francisco PD."

"Roberts, sir."

"All right, Roberts—wait until everybody's loaded up, then pull out in front of the Cadillac. Do fifty miles an hour on the highway until I say otherwise. There should be little traffic until we hit the Golden Gate."

"Wartime speed limit's thirty-five, sir."

"Indeed—except when transporting Bolsheviks. It's in the Vehicle Code." John Kost turned around to introduce himself to the passengers in the backseat, and his face went deeply still. Three women were gazing at him. Wedged between the other two was the chestnut-haired one, clasping herself in her willowy arms as if she were cold, although it was a warm day for April on the bay. He had been wrong. She was even more lovely at arm's length, with lucid gray eyes and a fine Varangian nose. Yet, she seemed so distant, so indifferent to him, he found himself eager to dislike her.

He explained who he was, and the women made no comment.

A tap on a horn from far behind told him all the cars were loaded. "Go, Roberts."

The women hadn't introduced themselves, but John Kost had no doubt which was Martov's wife. A man who fancied an expensive Swiss watch wouldn't settle for a plain wife. As Roberts accelerated around the Cadillac, John Kost glanced to the sun-visor mirror to take in her expression as she watched her husband slip past. But he found her eyes locked on his in the dusty reflection.

He sat back as they sped through the main gate, promising himself he wouldn't look at her again until they reached the bridge. He would ration his glances. But then she curtly asked in Russian, "How far to the center of the city?"

"About thirty versts now. And you are?" He looked to the mirror again: she'd closed her eyes and was resting her head against the top of the seat, exposing her smooth, white throat.

"I'm Elena Martova."

The other two women also introduced themselves, but by the time they came to the Golden Gate he'd already forgotten their names.

7

THE ARMY DRIVER LOOKED far too young to be much of an informer, but the Chekist made up his mind to say nothing that might set him apart from the other three Russians in the speeding Plymouth. As soon as his plane had taxied up to the apron, he'd noticed the photographer with the fat neck—FBI, most likely, by virtue of which Soviets he'd chosen for subjects. And the Chekist was sure more FBI would be waiting at the St. Francis Hotel. He would have separated himself from the others at the airfield had it not been a military base surrounded by a concertina-topped fence.

The man beside him in the backseat asked the driver in Russian if he might smoke. His name was Govorov, a so-called security specialist with the Commissariat of Foreign Affairs.

"What's that?" The young soldier tossed a nervous grin over his shoulder.

"He wants to know if he can smoke," the Chekist finally said, afraid the driver might pull over, thinking something was wrong, and fall behind the rest of the convoy.

"Tell him—sure."

"*Da*," the Chekist told the others, who after all these hours were yet intimidated by his presence. That he had bumped a Balkans expert named Boris Pugachev from the flight two minutes before the Moscow departure had been enough to convince them he was secret police, an impression he did nothing to counter. He had taken more than Pugachev's seat; he now had his identity as well.

"You speak English pretty good," the driver said.

"Thank you." He had learned it thirty years ago from British gunnery instructors aboard the *Aurora*, the now venerated cruiser that had fired the first shot of the October Revolution: a blank round that merely signaled the Bolshevik guns in the Peter and Paul Fortress to begin the actual bombardment on the Winter Palace. This particular had been excised from the legend. Like so much else. Four years later his former shipmates had mutinied with fifteen thousand other sailors at their Kronstadt base. They had been slaughtered to the last man by Trotsky's Red Army and the Cheka's firing squads.

The cabin had filled with cigarette smoke, and he cracked his window.

"Aren't you dying in that coat?" the driver asked. The Chekist smiled. The innocence that spawned American idioms amused him. It was unlikely the young soldier had ever seen men freezing to death in their frayed coats, as he himself had near Irkutsk during the final stages of the Civil War.

"I am fine, thank you," he said after a moment, although the coolness coming in the open window made him aware of the sweat on his face.

Govorov shifted to get more comfortable, his elbow brushing against the trenching tool in the waist pocket of the Chekist's ankle-length summer overcoat. The Chekist leveled his gaze on the security specialist, who blanched and then tried to mollify him with a stricken smile. Govorov didn't move another muscle in all the time it took to cross the Golden Gate Bridge and enter the city behind the two police motorcyclists, whose sirens had little effect on the traffic.

The convoy turned off Lombard Street and joined the automobiles crowding Van Ness Avenue. Horns brayed back at the sirens. Incredible, laudable even, and the Chekist chuckled under his breath at the anarchism of it all. Struggling to keep in line with the rest of the convoy, the driver eventually crept left onto Post Street. Wherever the traffic stalled, soldiers and sailors, many of them drunk, jaywalked between the Plymouths, pounded on the car bonnets with their fists.

"Driver, please let me out here."

"It's another couple blocks to the hotel."

"The walk will be pleasant. And I want to get some cigarettes."

"Good luck, pal. There's a shortage in town."

"Well, old fellow," he said, reaching for the canvas grip, which he'd refused to store in the trunk, and stepping out, "you must understand that I am a determined sort." He shut the door and turned, only to bump gently into a woman and her child. Apologizing, he knelt to peck the small girl on the forehead. "You are fortunate, madam, to have so pretty a daughter. If you have a pretty child, you have everything, what?"

Then he stood up and melted into the flow of pedestrians.

John Kost sat in the front seat of the vice-consul's Cadillac, half-listening to the sporadic conversation in the back between Martov and his wife. He wanted only to return to the consulate, pick up his car, and then check on William Laska at the hospital. An hour before, while locked in traffic on Van Ness in an Army car with three untalkative Soviet women, he'd bought an evening paper from a newsboy. The boxed late bulletin at the bottom of page one had leaped out at him: "Hospitalized Suspect in Hunter's Point Cop-Killing Improves." The source had been "a police spokesman," Captain Coffey no doubt, but the text failed to tell how Laska's condition had improved. Was he conscious now? Could he finally speak?

"Are you hungry, Lena?" Martov murmured in Russian. Elena Martova sat completely across the backseat from him, watching San Francisco drift past as if it were the high seas. "I asked if you're hungry, my dear," Martov tried again.

"I don't know. Perhaps."

63

"It'd be shame to eat at the consulate and miss even a mouthful of this city's wonderful food."

"Do as you like."

Martov leaned forward to tap Ruml on the shoulder. "Russian Tea Room."

Ruml nodded sleepily, and before John Kost could ask to be let off at his Dodge, the vice-consul insisted he accompany them to the restaurant. "We should get better acquainted, Inspector," he said. "I'm afraid we'll be seeing much of each other in the coming weeks." Then, in the same affable tone, he added for his wife's sake, "Inspector Kost's the son of an expatriate Cossack general."

She went on looking out the window.

"A Don Cossacks colonel," John Kost corrected him.

"Oh? I'd heard he was with the Tsar's Own Convoy . . . and later with the Siberian White forces."

"A long time ago, Vice-consul."

"So it was."

"John's an English name, yes?" she asked, abruptly changing the subject. "Were you born here then?"

She sat catercorner from him, and he turned slightly to meet her eyes. "I was christened Ivan," he said, "in Moscow."

"You don't look like an Ivan."

"And what should one look like?"

"I don't know." For the first time, she smiled, a weary smile but one so strangely appealing he had to glance away; she had seemed on the verge of crying when she'd smiled instead. "One of the diminutives might suit you better."

"Vanya then?"

"No. . . ." She thought about it a moment, then startled him with, "Vanechka." She had said it in a whispery voice, as his mother did in his dreams.

"Yes," Martov chimed in as if thoroughly enjoying the exchange, "he's gentle, the way a Vanechka should properly be, wouldn't you say?"

Instead of answering her husband, she said to John Kost, "May I ask your patronymic?"

64

"Mikhailovich."

"Very well, Ivan Mikhailovich. Mine's Valentinovna."

Ruml double-parked in front of the Russian Tea Room.

John Kost got out, frowning when he saw that the dusk shadow had crept almost to the top of the Coit Tower. He had to find out about Laska's condition. Walking around the Cadillac, he opened the door for Elena Martova. At first, he thought by the blank look in her eyes that she was going to refuse the offer of his hand, but then she took it, gave it a hard squeeze that left him puzzled, and broke away from him to drape her arm through Martov's.

Walking behind the couple, John Kost noticed that she had a limp.

As Nathan Aranov waited in a lounge booth at Cliff House, gazing down upon Seal Rocks and working on his second scotch sour, he told himself that he no longer cared about the Elliot homicide, even though it involved a cop. He absolutely lusted for sleep, of which he'd had none in two days now. It was the worst thing about the job: the periodic sleep deprivation. Of course, after five or six hours of shut-eye, he'd awaken to the conviction that the case was everything again, and then he would think of this present lapse in dedication as the reason he'd never be a twenty-four-karat cop like John Kost. Even on his best day, he was just a fourteen-karat cop.

He yawned.

The sun had been gone twenty minutes, but an amethyst luminosity still lingered over the Pacific. Offshore, Seal Rocks seemed to be shining with snow, although it was actually guano. Too early in the season for seal watching, he reminded himself, but to the north he could follow the skimming of a pair of minesweepers back and forth across the entrance to the Golden Gate.

A half hour before, while driving home from a painfully cordial meeting at the British consulate, he had been advised by dispatch to phone the inspector at the Russian Tea Room. John Kost had sounded preoccupied: "Nathan, I know you're close to collapsing, but can we meet somewhere for a few minutes? The three of us?" Sure, why not? Aranov lived only four blocks from Cliff House, so he'd suggested the seaside restaurant.

And now Ragnetti slid into the bench seat across from him. "What's this about?"

"I think John just wants to touch bases on the Elliot thing."

"Oh." Ragnetti whistled over the bartender and ordered a pitcher of beer. "You want to split a large order of fried clams, Natty?"

Nothing common or unclean, an instilled voice reverberated—his long-dead father's. Recalling his father made him wonder if the rest of the evening was going to slope away into sadness. Damn this fatigue. "No, thanks."

"Still make it a large order, bub," Ragnetti said to the bartender. He drained his first mug, poured another, then gazed down on the surf-wet rocks. "Where's the seals?"

"Too early in the year, I guess."

"You figure they do their fucking underwater?"

Aranov smiled. "I don't have a clue. How're the Chinese treating you?"

Ragnetti grunted, then stuffed his mouth with fried clams, which had just arrived in a wicker basket. The steamy, golden tangles looked good enough for Aranov to try one. "You sure you don't want a separate order, Natty?"

He shook his head as he chewed guiltily.

"I had a late lunch in Chinatown with the little bandits," the sergeant went on. "It started off friendly enough with all them jabbering to each other like long-lost cousins. Then something happened. Search me what, but they all starting ragging this one little fuck with a Charlie Chan mustache. I thought they were gonna peck his eyes out. Well, to make a long story short, it turns out this guy was the only Commie in the bunch and—" He glanced up as John Kost appeared at the table with his usual vodka neat in hand. "Hey, John. . . ." He scooted over, making room for him.

"Thanks for coming, boys."

66

"Let me guess, John—one of them Rooskies you broke bread with happened to be a real doll-face, right?"

For once John Kost didn't rise to Ragnetti's ribbing about his women. He stared down into his drink for a moment, then up at the sergeant again. "How'd the postmortem go?"

Ragnetti's face grew taut. His squeamishness at autopsies was notorious, but his fearlessness otherwise saved him from being kidded about it, that and the fact every cop secretly had something that unnerved him. Corpses didn't bother Aranov, but he trembled like mad when faced with situations that could reduce him to one. Supposedly John Kost's demon was sharp steel: early in his career he'd been stabbed clear through the thigh.

"No surprises," Ragnetti said, polishing off another glass of beer. "Elliot died of the throat wound."

John Kost turned to Aranov. "I saw this afternoon's bulletin about Laska. Did you put it out?"

"No, I called Coffey because you were up in Marin, and he gave it to the papers."

"No matter. Is Laska conscious?"

"Not fully. But while I was there, he mumbled his wife's name."

Then, for no reason, John Kost smiled. "Emma?"

"Yeah, Emma." Sometimes Aranov felt as if he still didn't know the man. "But that was it, John—Laska shut up again."

"He knows what he did—thank God. Put a wire recorder in the room and tell the patrolman to switch it on if Laska even so much as groans."

"Already done," Aranov said, and basked in John Kost's approving look.

"I think we should come to a decision," the inspector went on, "as a team, I'm saying. Is Captain Coffey right? Is this an open-and-shut file? A simple voluntary manslaughter with suspect in custody and incompetent to stand trial at present?" John Kost held up his glass for a refill, which surprised Aranov. Bolting down booze wasn't his habit. "Nathan, you first."

"Well. . . ." He paused, trying not to sound as if he were back at the academy reciting from the *Penal Code*. "Voluntary

67

manslaughter depends on some sudden quarrel or heat of passion, doesn't it? Laska shot both his wife and Elliot from a sitting position. Also, Elliot had enough time to draw his wheelgun. What I guess I'm saying is this—whatever Laska did, it wasn't sudden and it wasn't passionate."

John Kost appeared to consider this, then motioned for Ragnetti to speak.

"As usual, Coffey don't know shit."

"And then there're the wiped doorknobs," Aranov added.

"Indeed. Who'd take the trouble?"

"Some fuck who knows he's got his prints on file, John," Ragnetti said. "That's who. I mean it—I never seen a cherry stop to worry about leaving his latents all over the place."

"Then we're looking for someone with a prior booking?"

"Not necessarily," Aranov said. "Maybe we ought to enlarge on what Vince says about somebody with prints on record. That could be a schoolteacher, a government employee—you name it."

"Then let's do just that," John Kost said as if the conversation had begun to annoy him. "Tomorrow, Nathan—check with our ID Bureau, Sacramento, and the FBI. Find out all the criteria for fingerprinting and see if it cracks some ice for us." Aranov relented with a roll of his eyes. Pry information out of three obdurate technicians, plus do fifty other things he had on his follow-up list, not to mention those tasks the British delegation would drum up for him. When would he ever sleep again? Or see his wife? Sylvia was probably going through his life insurance policies at this very second. "Nathan, what about the calls on Sunday evening that tied up Elliot's backup units?"

"All legitimate calls for service, as far as I could tell."

"Any longshoremen reporting parties among them?"

"Nary a one. No known Reds either."

John Kost looked displeased. "Why were you thinking that?"

"Thinking what, John?" Aranov asked a bit anxiously.

"About Communist involvement?"

"I don't know. It was just in the back of my mind. The books in Laska's place, maybe. Just a hunch." Aranov now felt lame for having brought it up. He felt something like a witch-hunter, even though the international president of the Longshoremen's Union, Harry Bridges, was a known Communist and under almost continuous FBI surveillance. John Kost had always made it clear that, unlike other White Guardist expatriates, he wasn't obsessed with Bolshy conspiracies. "I don't know, John," Aranov repeated inanely, "a hunch."

"It might be worth looking into," John Kost said, but without conviction. "I'll handle that myself. Anything else?"

Aranov had the sense something vital was being overlooked, but that feeling was a companion to every investigation, so he deferred to Ragnetti with a shrug. The sergeant was leaning with his bristly cheek almost touching the window glass, gazing deeply at the nearly black Pacific. When Aranov looked back across the table a few moments later, John Kost was gone. He had a glimpse of the inspector's back as he hurried around the big redwood bar toward the entryway. "What's with him tonight?"

"She is," Ragnetti said knowingly, without glancing away from the sea.

"Who?"

"His wife." Ragnetti's voice had turned warm and low. He also had a shy little smile that betrayed his pleasure in being the chief authority in the department on John Kost's moods. "His dead old lady. Except she wasn't old. She was only nineteen."

"What're you talking about?"

"I seen him like this before. Not in a while. But it happens now and again."

"Why? Was it something I did or said?"

"Nah." Ragnetti waved off the notion. "It has nothing to do with you or me, so don't take it personal. A new woman does it to him sometimes. One what reminds him of his dead wife." Then he added significantly, "But it's mostly his routines. They been knocked out of kilter, see? He's just one of those guys who needs his routines. You know, to help him forget. To help him shrug off her ghost."

"Her *ghost?*"

"Sure," Ragnetti said.

The Chekist stood on the prow of the fishing boat as it churned away from the boathouse near the Hyde Street Pier. His hands were clasped behind him, and he was smiling into the chilly evening breeze. If he closed his eyes, the velveteen air became that of the Baltic Sea of his youth—

"Comrade Colonel. . . ." Tikhov, the resident, or chief of intelligence operations in San Francisco, was standing behind him, offering him vodka in a tin cup. He and his deputy manning the helm in the wheelhouse both wore rag-wool sweaters like ordinary seamen.

"Thank you," the Chekist said. "Tell me, are there any worthy fish in this bay?"

The man's frantic smile must have begun to ache on his face, for he rubbed his cheek with one of the eyepieces of the binoculars he'd strapped around his thick neck. "Yaroshenko and I have been here only since late January, Comrade Colonel. There's been no time for fishing."

"A pity. You should take some recreation now and again." The Chekist turned away if only to keep the huge fellow guessing. It was clearly driving Tikhov to distraction: being treated with affability one moment, then shunned the next. Excusing himself, the resident lumbered back into the wheelhouse to rejoin his deputy, the absolutely terrified Yaroshenko.

From aft came the murmur of the diesel, nothing like the profound rumble of the *Aurora's* engines, and from closer by the sloshing of the car tires hung over the gunwales of the *Lorelei* as side fenders. He'd read the name on the sternpost before boarding. A pretty name that had cost him so much trouble and still might cost Tikhov and Yaroshenko their heads, for why hadn't it been painted over or the boat scuttled after the recent brush with disaster? Pure sloth, although there was no such thing to the Little Boss. Sloth was only proof a fellow was an agent of foreign capital.

The daylight was going fast, the haze on the water growing a darker purple.

As if uneasy about leaving the Chekist to his own musing,

Tikhov came forward again and needlessly began pointing out landmarks. "That there, of course, is the Bay Bridge, Comrade Colonel. It passes through Yerba Buena Island, which is linked by an isthmus to that larger island. Treasure Island. Both have significant naval facilities. But of course, what war-making facility isn't significant, yes?" With a faint smile, the Chekist listened to him babble on while the *Lorelei* puttered into the broad channel between Treasure and Angel islands. It was the music of panic, Tikhov's babbling—shrill, *rapido* and *agitato*, with sudden little felicities that only seemed to be chuckles, for in reality they were sobs, pleas for leniency.

"Enough," the Chekist finally interrupted him, tossing his empty cup over the side and watching it sink, "stop here."

Tikhov signaled Yaroshenko to idle the engine and join them on the prow. The man brought with him two fishing poles, one of which he handed to Tikhov, whose hands were trembling on the reel as he dangled a hookless weight over the side into the water.

The Chekist eased down onto a gunwale. He was no longer smiling. "Give me an accounting of what went wrong."

Tikhov's lips were moving but his words were lost in a roar as the sky directly above them flashed black. A blast of wind rocked the boat and momentarily blinded the Chekist, but when he could see again, Tikhov and Yaroshenko were sprawled across the deck, having dropped their fishing rigs. He himself remained sitting upright, watching the U.S. Navy dive-bomber complete its wave-top bank and head southeast.

Tikhov and his man rose. "I should've known," the resident said sheepishly. "Their Navy conducts a mock raid on Treasure Island every day. See for yourself, Comrade Colonel. . . ." He handed over his binoculars. "It's supposed to prepare their sailors for the noise and confusion of battle."

"There's no preparation for that," said the Chekist, adjusting the lenses down from the bovine width of Tikhov's eyes.

"My conviction exactly, Comrade Colonel."

"Is it also your conviction to completely forget where you are?"

71

Tikhov started to say something about instinctive reaction, but then his words grew halting and finally trailed off into silence.

The dive-bomber was now closing on what looked to be a landlocked destroyer escort. The plane pulled up sharply, and although it dropped no bomb, a shower of red sparks erupted from the ship's aft gun tub, and what appeared to be a land-mine detonation scattered the sand off the port bow. As if this was not enough for one engagement, signal flags were switched on the mast and the stern began arcing dummy ash cans out across the twilight.

The Chekist laughed softly. "Do the Americans have so little war they must wage it on themselves?"

"Yes, Comrade Colonel."

The dive-bomber could dimly be seen in the north, coming around for another attack. The Chekist waited until it was overhead, until he could smell the aviation gas fumes, then reached inside his overcoat and drew his revolver. He fired on the plane from behind, squeezing the trigger four times before lowering the Nagan to his side.

There followed a long moment in which Tikhov and his man stood speechless, but finally the resident croaked, "What've you done!"

Yaroshenko was racing for the wheelhouse to engage the murmuring engine when the Chekist lofted the revolver and blew out the salt-stained window with two quick reports. The man skidded to a halt and held up his palms.

"Not only do you two forget where you are," the Chekist cried above the crump of another explosion from the island, "you have no idea what's possible and what isn't!" He then controlled his voice, although his eyes remained incensed. "If you honestly think a Nagan revolver can hit a dive-bomber, let alone bring it down—why are tens of millions of us rotting in the ground between Moscow and Berlin!"

Tikhov's eyes tracked the plane as it finally droned away to the south. "What do you require of us, Comrade Colonel?"—a whisper.

"You!" He was pointing at Yaroshenko. "Get rid of this boat tonight. Sink it in deep water and come ashore in the dinghy!"

"Understood, Comrade Colonel."

"Tomorrow evening one of our C-47s flies back to Moscow from Hamilton. Be on it." He spun on Tikhov. "And you—go into hiding as soon as we dock."

"May I return to the consulate for my things?"

"Absolutely not. Stay out of sight. I'll instruct you how to contact me for further orders. I may have one more thing for you to do before your return to Moscow." At last, the Chekist holstered his Nagan. "Meanwhile, I must try to clean up your mess. So give me an accounting. And hold nothing back if you know what's good for you."

Mine is a wanton loneliness, Father Aleksei, because it comes in the midst of tenderness from others. But that, like most personal truths, is beside the point, isn't it? In the past week I've done two things that warrant the Sacrament of Penance. As the nations of the world gather in this city to bring about an abiding peace, I've been able to think only of the inconvenience this Conference causes me. And then I've slept with a woman outside the Sacrament of Marriage. I think I must sleep with her again tonight. So if I came to the physician of my soul now, I would depart unhealed . . . Seated behind the wheel of his Dodge, John Kost suddenly took the keys out of his trouser pocket and started the engine he'd killed just the moment before. The combustion noises blotted out the polyphonic singing drifting from the Church of St. Basil the Great. Amazing—that these vesper voices could also whine for him to fix traffic tickets, to arrange bail reductions, to doctor rap sheets. . . .

As usual, Lydia Thripp's Clift Hotel apartment was overheated, but she looked so radiantly glad to see him he decided not to complain. "To what do I owe this?" she asked. "I thought the weekend. . . ."

"I apologize for not phoning first."

She frowned up at him, perhaps thinking he'd broached the

forbidden issue of fidelity. He hadn't, nor had he ever felt the need to ask for it—as he would've with a woman he'd fallen in love with. He was already regretting having come, but going home to his empty three rooms was out of the question.

"Something to drink?" she asked.

"Wonderful. Please."

Before heading for the kitchen across the expansive flat, she opened the living room curtains for him, giving him the view of the Bay Bridge he liked so much. Part of the vista was blocked by the St. Francis Hotel—as of this afternoon a nest of Red vipers, as his father would say. But he tried not to think about the unhappy woman whose face and laconic conversation in the Russian Tea Room today had brought him down to this state.

Lydia returned with a crystal carafe of vodka and two small glasses on a tray. "You look exhausted."

"Yes, I must be."

She leaned over and kissed him.

He tried to relax, telling himself that his lack of passion would be taken for weariness. But now that he was here with her once again, he realized that the need hollowed out by his loneliness wouldn't be fulfilled tonight. His thoughts turned away from his own satisfaction and toward hers, penitentially, for he promised himself that he'd never come here again to make love to her. For her sake as well as his, he would make a gentle parting.

He was too spent for talk, so within minutes he found himself in bed, facing her across silk sheets made affordable by the ceaselessly compounding wealth of her dead industrialist husband. Lydia Dmitrievna had been born in Petersburg to a comfortable bourgeois household diminished by the war and then ruined by the Revolution. Like John Kost, she'd arrived in San Francisco with her father, penniless, dependent on the generosity of the other émigrés. Yet, her father had so exhausted his welcome in Russian homes that he did something Mikhail Kostoff would never have considered even in his most desperate hour: he widened his pandering into American circles and eventually arranged his daughter's marriage to a shipyard owner thirty years her senior. Mallory Thripp had been a New England–bred reactionary, an abrupt, humorless, powerful man who collected White Guardist sycophants—cloves of garlic to ward off Bolshevik bloodsuckers. But he'd somehow marshaled the good graces to die at age fifty-nine.

Lydia had let slip an interest in John Kost long before her husband's death, but he'd gracefully deflected her advances until Mallory Thripp was buried and mourned. That way he hadn't unduly burdened Father Aleksei.

He now looked down upon her in the soft crimson light. Over the bed she'd hung her matched set of marriage icons, Christ and then Madonna and Infant, both lit by beeswax tapers in red glass cups attached to the gilt frames. She was quite handsome, but didn't have the plaintive features, the sensual underlip his wife had had—or that Elena Martova had. And so it was easier to do what then followed.

He curtailed his own motion, but remained poised above her, motionless but for the rise and fall of his chest.

She lifted her head off the pillow to find his mouth, her breath coming in small gasps as she widened the touch of her kiss to include his chin, his brow, his eyes. And then she began her own slow thrusting, testing a few rhythms before fixing upon the one with the greatest promise.

"I love you, Vanya," she said with breathy suddenness.

He replied by kissing her shoulders, then hunching lower so he could reach one of her breasts with his mouth.

He had suspected that her excitement would be close to the surface tonight if only because of the unexpectedness of his visit. She liked the unexpected. And it gladdened him how promptly she found and explored her own pleasure. Later she would probably weep—he could hide nothing from her, but now it was good to watch her in such happiness.

He rolled over onto his back, and sleep came even more deliciously than his ejaculation, a sensation of falling in place. He was deep within it when from far above came the jangling of a telephone. Lydia kept saying that it was for him. It was Nathan Aranov. Clumsily, he took the handset from her. He listened for only a few seconds before saying, "I'm on the way. Call out Vincent and the captain."

8

Assistant inspector aranov had entrusted him with a wire recorder. The strange machine so intimidated the rookie patrolman he'd felt the need to test it on the hour until 0200, after which he grew too drowsy to care about recording a stanza from Poe, playing it back to listen to a voice that sounded far too high-pitched to be his own. He'd memorized the whole of "Annabel Lee" for a high school recitation, but in the three years since had forgotten all but the first stanza:

> It was many and many a year ago,
> In a kingdom by the sea
> That a maiden there lived whom you may know
> By the name of Annabel Lee;—
> And this maiden she lived with no other thought
> Than to love and be loved by me . . .

The wire recorder worked okay, but the prisoner hadn't let out with a peep in all the time the patrolman had sat beside his bed. Would this tick off Assistant Inspector Aranov, who'd think he had somehow kept William Laska from talking? Aranov seemed like a regular guy, but the patrolman was on probationary status for another eight months, which meant he could be terminated for any reason or no reason at all, and he wondered if a bitch-up like this could get him booted off the department. He wasn't sweating the draft, because he was a sole-surviving son, but like hell he wanted to lose his job with millions of GIs coming home soon to scrounge for work.

When first ordered to report to the hospital for the guard detail, he'd felt funny about the prospect of being shut up all alone in a room with a guy who'd murdered a cop. But with his head whitely bandaged, Laska didn't look much like a cop-killer. He looked more like Gunga Din. And except for his staring eyes, he looked dead. Maybe he was dead, but his soul didn't know it yet.

The patrolman started upright in his chair.

How long had he been dozing?

Everybody had warned him about sleeping on the job, even though the same guys who'd cautioned him did it regularly. Maybe it hadn't been hypocrisy, but just a way of telling him to be careful until he was off probation. They'd also warned him not to diddle the Tenderloin whores while in uniform, he recalled with a half-smile.

Rising on a yawn and a stretch, he crossed the dark-green linoleum to the basin and washed his face with cold water.

Truth was, he was a patrolman in name only. Barely a month out of the academy, he had yet to be assigned to a training officer either on a footbeat or if he had any luck, in a cruiser.

He strolled back to the chair, wondering if it'd be okay with the floor nurse if he turned on the overhead fixture to help him stay awake. The only light in the room was glancing in under the door, and the near darkness kept making him nod off. But he was afraid to bother her. She had acted as if he were an awful nuisance when he'd signed in, saying that on account of the war she had to cover two floors instead of just one.

He started listening to his own breathing. It came in and out of his mouth, shallowly.

After a while, he found himself chatting with his two dead

brothers. They talked to him as if it were no big deal that they were dead. In fact, they never brought it up.

That jolted him awake again. "Shit."

He thought of saying something to the prisoner. But talking to a guy with a bullet stuck in his brain seemed spooky. What if Laska woke up and went crazy or something? Then the patrolman might have to shoot him, and the academy instructors had warned him that, whatever tomfoolery he did in the course of his long career, he was never to discharge his revolver inside a hospital. Never.

Then he sensed he was no longer alone.

He believed that his eyes were open, but the room was so dim and his mind so dreamy he wasn't sure. Had his relief arrived? It didn't seem likely. His ten-hour watch was scheduled to end at 0600, and if that were truly the time, the room should be gray with daylight. "Nurse?" he finally asked.

But the figure standing at the foot of the bed didn't answer.

Shaking off his drowsiness, the patrolman began to make better sense of the figure—a tall man who bore himself as if he belonged here. The man was dressed in a smock that hung all the way to his ankles. The doctor who'd removed his tonsils had worn that kind of long smock, but that had been fifteen years before, and in all the time since he hadn't seen another physician dressed that way.

But something more than an old-fashioned smock was wrong about this intruder. He seemed poised on the verge of doing something unpleasant.

"Who're you?" The patrolman slowly came to his feet. He reached under his blue coat and was beginning to unfasten his holster flap when he remembered where he was. Hospital. His hand dropped to his side.

The smock began floating toward him, ghostly silent as it came.

He hesitated, wondering what a saltier cop would do, wondering what would happen to his job if he drew down on what turned out to be some old fuddy-duddy of a doctor. And as he wondered, he suddenly thought that a bird had flown only inches

79

past his face, its tail feathers gusting wind into his eyes, making him blink, hard.

He had been driven against the wall. But by what?

He tried to touch his throat, for he felt both pressure and a growing numbness there, but his fingers bumped against something flat and metallic imbedded in his neck. Screaming was out of the question—his throat was filling with warm liquid. He was drowning in that wet warmth. Seizing the metallic thing with both fists, he tried to pull it out of him. But he no longer had the strength. He could feel his knees buckling and his back sliding down the wall.

"Here, old fellow," the man said, kindly almost. And he yanked it out.

"What in the name of Christ is this about!" Captain Coffey asked for the third time since barging into the hospital room.

John Kost glanced up at him from the foot of the empty bed. He supposed the captain's question had been directed at him, but he didn't reply. It would be tactless to say anything to the man who'd written off Wallace Elliot's homicide as open-and-shut.

On the scene thirty minutes now, John Kost had noted all the essentials. The boy-cop slumped against the wall, his throat crudely opened. William Laska's covers draped across the linoleum. The wire recorder sans reels. He could even visualize how the intruder had made his way up to the fifth-floor room unseen: the fire escape would've done. And surprising Laska's young guard had been no great feat. A child in blue. But how had he made off with the longshoreman? Certainly he hadn't climbed down four ladders packing a stout man across his back, only to drop ten feet from the final platform to the ground.

Aranov slipped into the room, started to speak, but was then distracted by the deputy coroner's ministrations to the half-stripped corpse. "Zip on anybody seeing a laundry basket in the hallway tonight," he said at last. "I also checked down in the laundry room itself. Supervisor said all the baskets are pushed up together against the wall like they should be."

"What about unfamiliar staff in the building tonight?" John Kost asked.

Aranov shook his head, then appeared to realize that he was still in his fedora and the woolen muffler Sylvia had knitted for him. He took them off.

Coffey hadn't caught Aranov's gesture. "What was that, son?"

"Nothing, Captain," he said with scarcely contained irritation. "No one saw anything out of the ordinary until the nurse checked in on the prisoner and found. . . ." He didn't finish: to describe the garish red thing beyond his shoulder as a homicide probably struck him as being inadequate.

John Kost asked, "Where's Vincent?"

"He said he wanted to give the parking lot a look-see, then start working the neighborhood."

"The lot's on the front side. . . ." John Kost was on the verge of stringing some elusive connection together, but Coffey interrupted his train of thought.

"You think maybe this was a mob hit, John? Laska was big for the union, so maybe he crossed somebody he shouldn't."

"Perhaps, Captain," John Kost said, even though he knew the suggestion was absurd. He couldn't recall any of the West Coast families ever having made a move against a California cop, let alone two in quick succession. In his experience, mobsters had been deferential in their dealings with San Francisco PD. Yet, how could he explain to Coffey what he truly believed: that there was a directness, an audaciousness to this that didn't fit the oblique American criminal mentality? The intruder killed routinely and with absolute impunity. How else could he afford to stylize his work with a blatant signature like the broad-bladed instrument he'd used to slash the young cop's throat? But was he the same man who'd watched William Laska shoot his wife and Patrolman Elliot, and then wiped two doorknobs before departing 233 Carbon Street?

"What d'you think, John?" Coffey pressed.

"I'm sorry, sir—?"

"Is this mob work or not?"

81

"I'm ruling out nothing at this point." Then he called through the open door, "Anyone from ID still here?"

"Yeah." Delbert ducked inside from the corridor. Even he was pale. "I'm packing up, Inspector. Need anything else?"

"Just an answer—what'd you find?"

"Some textbook latents off the faucet and the window hardware." Then the technician shrugged. "Which means they belong to the victim or the hospital staff. Latents that pretty are never from the suspect."

"Do you have the elimination prints yet?"

"Right—all the doctors, nurses, and orderlies who worked tonight on this floor. I'll come back tomorrow to catch the day and swing-shift personnel."

"Good, thank you," John Kost said. "By chance, have any of the surfaces in here been wiped?"

"No. Just the usual cumulative smudges. Will that be all?"

"Yes—again, thank you." John Kost stood as a gurney was rolled in to remove the body to the hospital morgue, where the autopsy could more conveniently be performed in the morning than at the city charnel house. He wanted to turn his face from the sight of slack-limbed youth, bare and bloody-chested, being lifted by three orderlies and the deputy coroner onto the thin white mattress. But his fascination with death wouldn't let him look away, not until the body was covered with a sheet that proved instantly pervious to the red of the throat wound. "What was his name, Nathan?" he quietly asked.

"Fenby. Lon Fenby."

"Christ," Coffey said from the other side of the room, his eyes glistening. "What's this all about?"

John Kost tried not to sound accusative: "We'll never find out unless we get enough time to work it."

Coffey's gaze slid past his face to the blood-streaked wall. He said nothing.

"Captain—relieve my men and me of our Conference duties. At least until we get a handle on this."

"No can do, John." Coffey looked genuinely miserable. "We

got nine unprotected delegations as is. And you especially are needed. I was going to brief you on this tomorrow, but some crank is sending letters to the Russian consulate. Says he's going to dynamite Molotov to kingdom come as soon as he steps off his plane later this month."

"A week then. Give us an uninterrupted week."

The captain began rubbing his nape. "Two days."

"What good are forty-eight hours when we need a week?"

"Take it or leave it."

John Kost took stock of the look in Coffey's eyes, then exhaled. "All right, I'll see what I can get done in that time."

"Two days for your *men*. I can't spare you at all. I mean it."

John Kost gave up with a flap of his arms against his sides.

"How about a news blackout on this, Captain?" Aranov asked.

Coffey took out his handkerchief and wiped his face even though it looked dry and cool. "Probably a good idea—wouldn't you say, John? At least until we know who we're up against?"

John Kost answered him with a nod. He had drifted to the window, two large, metal-encased panes that cranked outward from the latches on the center-post. He ran a forefinger along the disturbed dust of the sill—then froze for a moment before bending over to inspect the swarm of red tadpole-shapes there. The absence of satellite droplets around the main spatters told him that the blood had impacted on the sill from less than a foot above it. And one glancing spatter was visible on the glass of the right-side pane, which could only mean this section of the window had been opened at the time.

Hurriedly now, he sprung the latches and began cranking.

"What is it?" Aranov asked from behind.

Leaning his head outside, John Kost stared down the darkened backside of the building. Then, wheeling, he ran out into the corridor and begged a flashlight off a patrolman.

Aranov caught up with him at the elevator doors. "John, what is it!"

"This fellow," he said, hammering the down button with the heel of his fist, "is like no one we've known before. We must remember that, Nathan—for our own good." He gave up waiting for the stainless steel doors to part and instead bolted down the stairwell.

Aranov's voice echoed down after him: "Is it us? Is the son of a bitch after cops?"

"In Elliot's case, maybe. But this young fellow tonight? No, he was simply standing in the way to Laska." He stopped at the second-story landing for breath, and Aranov flew down the steps three at a time to catch up with him. "Also, I'm not sure this is the same man who wiped the knobs at Laska's place."

"Why? Isn't the link clear?"

"No." He waved for Aranov to follow him again.

They rushed past the first-floor nurses' station, loose change jingling in their pockets, and out the back door. Behind the hospital was a patch of grass and a jacaranda tree, its branches on one side espaliering up against the building. Ragnetti was standing on the lawn, gaping up into the foliage at something. An elongated shadow. "Listen," he said, drawing John Kost's attention to a sound like raindrops popping on a tarp.

He flicked on the flashlight and swept its beam upward.

Aranov let go of a breath as if he'd been punched in the gut, and Ragnetti whispered. "Oh, fuck."

William Laska was dangling with his left ankle trapped in the crotch between two limbs and his right leg folded down in front of his wide-eyed face. He was completely nude, his hospital gown having been ripped off him by the higher branches, where it was fluttering in a stale breeze off the bay. His bandages had unraveled into two streamers that were rolling across the grass. Having come to rest in a tangle of dead twigs, his head was cocked to the side, and this made it easier to trace the gash that began near his Adam's apple and ended nearly at the back of his neck in a glimmer of exposed vertebrae. The last of his blood was sparking redly out of his head and throat wounds and plopping onto a circle of bare earth around the trunk.

John Kost could see the captain staring down at him from the fifth-story window. "What d'you have?" Coffey called to him.

The Chekist waited for the black Cadillac to disappear around the corner before he strolled across Market Street. He stepped inside the telephone booth the timid-looking driver had briefly entered. Leaving the folding door open so its overhead lamp wouldn't come on, he grasped the handle of the square case the driver had left there. Then, checking for traffic and seeing none at this early-morning hour, he crossed Market again and took the first southward alleyway into the din of the warehouse district. In and out of the pooled light on the loading docks, workers darted, wheeling stacked goods out of trailers and returning from the warehouses with their empty hand trucks rattling. He avoided these men, but not in a furtive way that might draw police attention to himself. So far, it seemed that for a city so large San Francisco had extraordinarily few patrolmen. Except in the central district most of them seemed to be motorized, one or two fellows to a black-and-white automobile. This made evading their patrols simple; he just listened for the purr of a slowly approaching car, or watched for the flickering of a spotlight.

As he neared the waterfront a stink of brackish water and rotting fish made him take shallower breaths.

Within sight of the bay, he climbed an exposed wooden staircase—pausing once, surprised by his weariness—to reach a door set high on the smutty brick wall of the abandoned building. It had once been the headquarters of a shipbuilding firm that had since moved its offices and shops a mile down the peninsula to Islais Creek Channel. He inserted the key and turned the lock. Inside was a tiny cubicle of an office—dark, and he left it that way. So as not to bang his shins, he shuffled over to the desk, on whose top he rested the square case. He doffed his summer overcoat, draped it over the back of the swivel chair, and sat. As promised, a liter of vodka was waiting for him in the top right-hand drawer. But he'd been left no glass, and drinking from the neck of a bottle reminded him of desperate attempts at drunkenness, three or four fellows shivering around a smoky fire, gulping amnesia in the face of the truth that death is always as close as the frozen hairs in your nose.

He laughed to himself and drank anyway. Had they been such terrible times, really?

Yes, he gradually decided, the sense of those days pouring into him along with the vodka's warmth. In the minutes before the Chekist had shot him dead, Admiral Kolchak turned to him, the stalwart young Baltic Fleet sailor who'd so completely ingratiated himself to the general staff of the Siberian White Forces, and asked as if blind to the revolver trained on him, "Do you honestly believe my elimination will vastly improve things?"

"I have my doubts, Aleksandr Vasiliyevich," he answered, using the admiral's forenames to let him know that they were now equals. "But the only way to settle those doubts is to eliminate every last one of you. *Then* I'll know."

Kolchak had laughed. "Get it over with, my boy. And never fail to add that I died well."

"I won't," the Chekist now said quietly between pulls on the bottle. He lit a match to find a wall socket, then opened the case, revealing an American-made wire recorder, fumbled around for the cord, and finally inserted the male plug into the receptacle. Taking the doughnut-sized reels from his jacket pocket, he snapped them onto the recorder, hoping that the electricity had been reconnected to the office, as promised. He rewound the steel wire, then punched the play button. After a moment, a boyish voice recited:

> *It was many and many a year ago,*
> *In a kingdom by the sea*
> *That a maiden there lived whom you may know*
> *By the name of Annabel Lee . . .*

It was a tender voice, artlessly innocent, and was definitely not William Laska's. That only left the policeman's.

The stanza was repeated six times with precisely the same metronomic inflection—and then the profound silence that sometimes follows poetry.

86

He was no longer visualizing the young policeman in the hospital room. He was sifting across Kotlin Island like smoke, watching once again the last of his former Baltic Fleet comrades being herded out of their bunkers, gasping as they staggered up into the rubble that a few hours before had been Kronstadt Naval Base. Among them was his petty officer off the *Aurora*, the anarchist Zakusov, who in recognizing the Chekist in the ranks of the secret police suddenly smiled as if the gulf that lay between them was not fatal, as if none of this was worth hard feelings. Such was the peculiar sweetness of the old anarchism that a man could foresee goodness from his own destruction! And when the rifles of the Cheka were hoisted and leveled on his jumper, he cried from Pushkin:

> *Sweet mournful days, charm of the dreaming eyes,*
> *Your beauty is dear to me that says farewell!*

Zakusov, unmindful of the present, had been counting on him to do something, someday. That much was clear. But what? The Chekist had been asking himself ever since.

He took another sip of vodka.

9

Braving the morning cool of her balcony patio, Lydia Thripp had set breakfast on the white wrought-iron table. Of course, the sumptuous dishes hadn't been prepared by her own hand; they'd been covered with silver and carted up from one of the Clift's two five-star restaurants, the French Room today, and left for her to serve personally. Domesticity happened to be the ambience she desired to create on this occasion, and with that aim she'd given her servant the day off. The door chimes sounded for a second time, but she lingered to inspect the table, then primp the blooms of the potted fuchsias encircling it. She had draped her ermine stole over the back of her chair in case she felt a chill. Finally, serenely, she went to the door.

It was always a minor shock to see how much more he'd aged since their last meeting. But then she was able to delude herself into beholding him as he'd once been: straight of back, virile in a weathered sort of way. The deep crow's-feet astride his hazel eyes had come from endless hours of squinting into the sun from the flying bridge of a battleship.

"Lydia, my dear. . . ." Removing his peaked hat, he lightly kissed her cheek. "You look ravishing."

"Charles." She saw his Marine sergeant at parade rest in the corridor, his eyes discreetly fixed on the fleur-de-lis wallpaper opposite him. He would wait there like a faithful dog until Charles emerged again. "I hope you're hungry this morning."

"Famished."

She knew this to be a polite fib. Peptic ulcers made him distrust food. On their way to the patio, she briefly inclined her head against his arm, and smiling, he reached across his decorations to touch her hair. In some ways, advanced age had feminized him, made him appreciate small shows of affection as much as the act itself.

"How very nice," he commented on the table, but his eyes said that his thoughts were elsewhere.

"Coffee?"

"I'm sorry?"

"Would you care for some coffee?"

"No, thank you—as much as I'd love a second cup."

She took the silver cover off his plate. "And how's the Twelfth Naval District been treating my Charles lately?"

"Oh, pretty fair. The pebble in the shoe isn't with the Navy right now. . . ." His voice rumbled apart into a bronchial cough.

"Then who's it with?" She filled his crystal goblet with milk, her expression both concerned and vaguely preoccupied. A woman listened sympathetically, but never intently. "I hate them already. Who's giving you fits?"

"The damned coloreds."

"Not that again."

He nodded dismally, then began picking at his crab Newburg omelet.

The July before, the Port Chicago Naval Magazine on Suisun Bay had suddenly gone up in an explosion raucous enough to make her porcelain figurines pirouette on their glass shelves thirty-five miles southwest of the blast. When the smoke had cleared, more than three hundred sailors were missing, Negro ammunition handlers mostly. Shortly after, at nearby Mare Island Depot, other Negro seamen had refused to load ammunition until their safety could be guaranteed, and a large number of them had then been court-martialed for mutiny. Charles considered the entire affair a stain on his record, something Lydia pretended not to understand.

"Those NAACP lawyers are trying an end run on me," he went on. "They're in Washington, lobbying the Advocate General's office behind my back."

"What's their argument?"

"The same bunk that came out in the mutiny trial—that these were just scared kids who didn't know what they were doing. I wonder what Mallory would've thought of all this. Well—to hell with them." Abruptly, he smiled around the cigarette he'd just lit. He had also scooted his plate out of the way. "You know John Kost pretty well, don't you?"

"We go to the same church." She kept a bland expression but secretly hoped that Charles's Office of Naval Intelligence snoops hadn't seen the inspector coming here at unseemly hours. She'd long suspected that ONI was watching her, although she had no proof. "May I have a smoke?"

"Oh, forgive me." He lit a Chesterfield for her with a gold-plated lighter. It was embossed with the White House. "Would you say he's pretty reliable?"

"Well, he's a good Christian—"

"I was thinking more along political lines."

She took her ermine stole off the back of the chair and with his help wrapped it around her shoulders. "How's that?"

"Does he see things the way we do, my dear?"

"I suppose. He's a police officer, isn't he?"

"I'm afraid I need something more than that. You know—his attitudes, his convictions."

She blew a little pall of smoke up against the blue morning sky. "I'm not quite sure what you mean, Charles."

"His father was a White officer, wasn't he?"

"Yes, he mentioned something about that once. The old man's really quite repulsive, so it's hard to believe he was an officer of any consequence." She knew all too well that during the Civil War Mikhail Kostoff had been highly placed to Admiral Kolchak, and before the Revolution even to the Tsar himself as commander of His Imperial Majesty's Own Convoy of Cossacks. But all of a sudden she sensed danger in appearing too well versed about John Kost's background. "The poor inspector. He's so embarrassed by his father."

"But the point is—given his family, he's familiar with the Bolshevik menace, wouldn't you say?"

"Oh, yes. That much I can vouch for."

"Good." The admiral drifted off into thought for a moment, then remembered himself and smiled warmly again. "Can you keep an important confidence, my dear?"

Her frown came quickly. "You offend me by asking."

"Now, now . . ." He reached across the table and patted her hand. "It's just that national security's at stake and I have to be careful. You can understand that, can't you?"

She could. But not about to let him off the hook so easily, she gave him a peevish shrug.

"Lydia, some pretty unsavory Bolsheviks are coming to this Conference. People who have no damned business in this country—war or no war. Vyacheslav Molotov for one."

"*The Hammer,*" she murmured, her eyes briefly fixed on a fuchsia blossom that had begun to wilt. "My father knew him when his name was Scriabin. Before the Revolution."

"Then I don't have to remind you what this breed of animal did to your family, to all the other reliable Russians. But regardless of the stupidity of letting dozens of Kremlin agents pour into San Francisco, I've got an inkling here's a dandy chance to get a peek at their intentions toward us after the war. Not from their public declarations, of course. They're born liars. But I'm sure they'll be talking turkey among themselves. And I'd love to have a mouse in Molotov's pocket." He took the sprig of parsley off the edge of his plate and twirled it between his nicotine-stained fingers before asking, "John Kost speaks crackerjack Russian, doesn't he?"

"With an American accent, though—like me."

His smile turned positively lewd. "A good-looking cuss from a lady's point of view, wouldn't you say?"

"I suppose."

"Can you arrange a meeting? Dinner here would be just grand."

"I don't know, Charles. He's terribly busy, I hear. The Conference and all."

He chuckled. "I know. I've been using all my grease at the PD to make sure he stays busy—and right on top of the Soviet delegation. What do you say, my dear? Can you help a tired old sailor and set this up for the four of us?"

"Four—?"

"Yes, I'd like to bring along Dennis Jennaway, my Intelligence boy."

"Truly, Inspector Kost, I didn't want to bother you this morning." Again Vice-consul Martov was sharing the Cadillac's backseat with his wife, and again Elena Martova was sitting as far as possible from him. "But your own captain—Coffey, isn't it?—"

"Yes."

"—he suggested this as the best way for Madame to learn where it's safe to go, what neighborhoods to avoid."

"San Francisco's a safe city," John Kost said, sounding piqued. Once more he found himself in the front seat with Ruml, who was in the same suit and dingy shirt he'd worn to Hamilton Field. And judging by his sharp odor, the driver had been in these clothes ever since. "You've never felt in danger here, have you, Vice-consul?"

"No, no—a lovely city. But isn't it unfortunate, that policeman of yours being murdered Sunday night?"

Elena Martova asked her husband what he was talking about. From the corner of his eye, John Kost saw Martov give her a flick of his head as if he didn't care to explain right now, and she glared at him. A tendril of hair had fallen across her brow in violation of her otherwise strict coiffure.

"Are many policemen shot here, Ivan Mikhailovich?" she asked, sounding genuinely curious.

He wondered if gangster films had left this impression with her. But under what circumstances could she have joined the

92

privileged few who reportedly screened them? Rumor had it only Uncle Iosif and his bosom cronies saw Western movies. "No," he said, "not many are shot."

Rested now from her long flight, she seemed more interested in the city, although she had yet to ask him about anything except cop fatalities. Did she know about the murders of the young patrolman and Laska in the hospital last night? And how had Martov learned so much about Mikhail Kostoff's White Guardist past? He decided it was useless to speculate; Russians seemed furtive even when blameless. He peeked at his wristwatch: a quarter to noon. Half the day already spent, and on the vice-consul's orders Ruml was driving away from downtown so Elena Martova could see Golden Gate Park.

"What culture is available to Madame, Inspector?" Martov asked.

"Well, the usual seasons have been curtailed because the Opera House will be used for the Conference . . ."

"Yes, the bodies will be packed in there, don't you agree? You'd think a more spacious building would've been chosen."

He held back the urge to say that, unlike their Moscow counterparts, San Francisco architects didn't confuse colossal proportion with good design. *Why is this couple annoying me so?* He faced the windshield as he said, "The work sessions will be held in the Veterans Building next door to the Opera House, Vice-consul. So I imagine there will be enough room." He decided to veer the subject back to culture. "A number of special symphonies are planned around the city—"

"Who's conducting?" Elena Martova interrupted.

"Let's see . . . Vladimir Golschmann on the twenty-eighth of this month. And I believe André Kostelanetz will have the honors on May eleventh." Again, he caught Martov giving her a censuring look, which mystified him. What harm in asking who was conducting the San Francisco Symphony?

He was prepared for her to ignore her husband once again, but then she asked Martov about the small, building-cluttered island out in the bay, and he told her Alcatraz was the American equivalent of the Lefortovo—the most secure prison in the

93

Moscow area, John Kost recalled—and was filled with political prisoners and trade unionists. She then inquired about the larger wooded island beyond, and Martov leaned forward to ask John Kost its name, as if he didn't honestly know.

"Angel Island, Vice-consul."

"Is it inhabited?"

"Only by the government."

"For what purpose?—if I may ask."

"Oh, it used to be the immigration port of entry. But now the facility's being used to process prisoners of war."

"Is this where you came into the United States?"

"Yes."

"It'd seem to me," Martov said, sitting back again, "the authorities of that day were pleased to welcome the head of Nikolas Romanov's personal escort."

John Kost turned halfway around and answered the vice-consul's ironic smile with his own. "My father was with His Majesty's Own Convoy for less than two years. Most of his service was spent in line Cossack regiments, fighting first the Japanese at Port Arthur and later the Austrians—both of whom seem to be Russia's enemies once again."

"Japan's not yet our enemy, Inspector." Then Martov quietly chuckled and begged forgiveness: "I was only making a clumsy observation on the reactionary attitude of the American government of that time."

"In that you're correct. My father and I were held on the island for three weeks under suspicion he was a Bolshevik."

"Really?"

"Really."

"That must have rankled," Martov said.

"How old were you?" Elena Martova asked, distraught-sounding enough to make him glance at her in surprise. Even Martov didn't seem to know what to make of this sudden change in the timbre of her voice.

"Ten years," John Kost said.

"Were you frightened—you know, being locked up like that?"

Something in her eyes disarmed his irritation, but left him no

94

less confused. "I don't remember, Madame," he lied, for it had been an awful time laced through with uncertainty and boredom and longing for the city that glimmered across the watery night. "In any event, they gave me the run of the immigration compound. And I had my father's company, of course."

"Would you have been terrified to be completely alone, Ivan Mikhailovich? Alone among strangers, I mean?"

"I suppose. But I wasn't alone."

"Did you leave the East from Vladivostok?" the vice-consul asked, ever the intelligence gatherer.

"No, from China."

"Interesting. I imagine you were too young to acquire a taste for Chinese food?"

"We were mostly in Manchuria. It isn't noted for its cuisine."

"A pity. I adore good Chinese food and want Lena to try some. Will you have luncheon with us?"

John Kost nodded without enthusiasm. But a moment later when Martov told Ruml to forget Golden Gate Park, which they'd just entered, and head for the Cathay Gardens, he glimpsed a chance to snatch a few minutes of work on his caseload. "Do you mind if I suggest the Three Dragons, on Grant at Washington?"

Martov bit his lip, then asked, "What kind of cuisine?"

"Cantonese."

"Is it better than Cathay Gardens?"

"I think so." An untruth, which John Kost compounded with: "It's where the locals go."

"Very well then," the vice-consul said, "the Three Dragons it is. And while we're learning the ins and outs of your city, can you suggest a suitable Orthodox church for Madame?"

John Kost frowned, sure that he was being baited again.

But the Martovs stared blankly at him, waiting for an answer. Naturally, the émigré community had heard how in the first desperate years of the war Uncle Iosif had invoked all the

95

trappings of traditional Russian nationalism, including Orthodoxy. But if a genuine reversion in the Party's attitude toward the Church had existed at all, it died at Stalingrad with the Red Army's going off the defensive.

Martov laughed quietly at his surprise. "I myself am profoundly atheist, but Madame persists in the old ways."

John Kost looked to her. "You're a believer?"

"Yes," she said after a moment. This hesitation did nothing to convince him of her sincerity, but he wondered about the unhappiness in her voice and eyes. "I'd like to be confessed before Pascha."

"Father Aleksei hears confession before vespers. Is this evening convenient?"

She glanced to Martov, who nodded indulgently. "You two go without me," he said. "I'll be busy with your State Department people until midnight at the very least. And I only attend services when I'm of a mind to submit an article to the *Enemy of Religion.*"

John Kost sensed that Martov had referred to the Soviet antichurch journal for Ruml's sake, not hers. Yet, she was studying her husband's face as if it were monstrous and deformed, and not coolly handsome, as it was. "May I pick you up at the consulate at six-thirty then, Madame?" John Kost asked. "The service begins at seven."

"Please," she said.

As Ruml pulled up in front of the Three Dragons, John Kost realized that he'd committed himself to another Conference chore he might just as easily have begged off. But he also admitted that he wanted to share some time with Elena Martova, alone.

"Should I stay in the car, Comrade Vice-consul?" Ruml asked with a surly grin that begged otherwise.

"And go hungry all afternoon? No, I think you should join us. What do you say, Lena?"

She said nothing.

John Kost got out and opened her door for her. This time, she

96

disregarded the offer of his hand and limped resolutely for the restaurant's entrance without waiting for the others.

The foursome were no sooner handed their menus than she excused herself for the powder room. John Kost watched her walk away. Although smart-looking, her black gown was several years behind American fashion, and its long lines accentuated her limp. When he looked back across the table, he realized that Martov had caught him staring, but the vice-consul revealed no offense. On the contrary, he seemed to have read the question in John Kost's eyes, for assuming the inspector would understand, he said in French, "It happened five years ago. . . ."

Ruml, who'd been slurping tiny cup after cup of green tea, shifted his dull gaze to Martov's lips. It was obvious he understood no French and resented his boss's lapsing into it, but he then turned his attention to unwrapping his chopsticks.

"She was with the Bolshoi, you know," Martov went on.

"I didn't," John Kost said, although he'd suspected from that first glimpse of her at Hamilton Field she was a dancer.

"And the Maryinski Theatre in Leningrad before." Martov then added, pedantically, "The Kirov, as it's now called."

"I know."

The vice-consul gave him his self-contained smile. "Yes, you would. At any rate, going from one company to another was hard for her. Hard for anyone. . . ." He hoisted the teapot for refilling, as Ruml had drunk it dry, and explained that while the Maryinski stressed lyrical classicism the Bolshoi placed a higher value on virtuosity and dramatics. "The Bolshoi demands fireworks. And fireworks can burn, yes?"

"What happened?"

Martov poured himself tea from the fresh pot. "She came down out of grand jeté on her right heel. Her Achilles tendon tore off part of the heel bone. The doctors tried to repair it but. . . ." He shrugged. "And I, to my everlasting discredit, was not there that night to console her." Then, noticing her return to the table, he lowered his voice: "Please say nothing about this to her. Nothing about ballet."

John Kost was struck by how pale she was. Had she been sick in the lavatory? Taking her chair, she looked at the teacup Martov set before her as if she didn't know what it was. "After luncheon, I need a rest," she said to the vice-consul.

"Are you certain?"

"Yes."

All of a sudden John Kost had to be away from the Martovs, the brittleness that enveloped them, and was thankful he had a lead to follow up on. Rising from the table, he said he wanted to make sure his favorite chef was on duty.

Martov looked nonplussed. "Will you be ordering for us?"

"No, I'll leave that to you. Everything is good. Pardon me."

The headwaiter tried to block his progress toward the kitchen. "What you do, John Kost?" he asked, snapping the sleeves of his red monkey jacket over his shirt cuffs. "You never come Three Dragon now, you big gumshoe. You never come for bellyful wonton no more."

"But I'm here today, aren't I? Please see to my friends. I told them this was the best restaurant in Chinatown."

"Then you lie, John Kost." Laughing, draping a fresh towel over his forearm, the man scurried toward the Martovs' table.

John Kost passed through gilt double doors, leaving the lamplit twilight of the dining room for the steamy neon brightness of the kitchen. Two cooks in greasy whites were sweating over a battery of sizzling woks. Behind them at a butcher-block table stood an old man with a shaved head, ankle-deep in spinach stems, celery butts, ginger rinds, and duck feathers, his knife flashing. But John Kost looked past these Chinese to the man in an apron and galoshes hunkered over the sink. There was more silver in the fellow's jet-colored stubble than he recalled, and his body was no longer sinewy and robust in the muscular way glorified by the Party labor posters of the thirties.

"Uichi?"

The man glanced up, but then went back to scraping dried sweet-and-sour off the plate he was clenching in his rubber gloves. "John Kost, as I live and breathe." His voice was smooth, educated even, and his English accentless.

"May we talk?"

He turned off the taps and wiped his damp face on his T-shirt sleeve. "Not inside here."

10

HOW'D YOU FIND OUT I was back?" Uichi Nishio asked as they stepped into the alley. Passing the clothing rack on the way out, he'd fished a pack of Camels from his field-jacket pocket and now offered John Kost a smoke.

"No, thanks. The War Relocation Authority sends a monthly list of returned Japanese internees to the PD."

"Figures." Nishio slowly shook out his match. "The bastards include my place of employment?"

"Yes."

"How about the broad I'm straddling?"

"That too, my friend." John Kost smiled at this flickering of the old Uichi, the Longshoremen's rabble-rouser who'd stood his ground at the hastily built brick barricade on Rincon Hill during the '34 riot, bellowing profanities through the tear gas at the cops. "How was the camp?"

"Tule Lake?" He hocked up some phlegm and spat on the cobblestones. Yet, the hand holding the cigarette was trembling, sending up a squiggle of smoke, and his suntanned face seemed more jaundiced than healthy. "I got out for damn near a year. Harvested sugar beets for small farmers up in Idaho. Regular kulaks, these guys. But then they didn't like the way I talked politics, so I wound up right back in the middle of the Hoshi Dan boys again. They didn't like the way I talked politics either."

John Kost asked, "Who were they?"

"Fascist Japanese up at Tule bellyaching to go home to Tojo. Lovely chaps." Nishio pulled his T-shirt down by the neckline, showing an indentation in his collarbone. "The bastards did this with a mattock handle. Broke my elbow too. But I was already out cold so I didn't feel that. And then the Army nearly ran me over with a tank during a little civil unrest. Yeah, a fucking *tank*. I was just coming back from the shitter, but I guess the tank didn't know that." He laughed humorlessly.

"It wasn't right, Uichi. Any of it. But it was to be expected, I suppose."

Nishio shrugged. His eyes had grown dim again.

"Well," John Kost said, "the government's taken you back. What about the Party?"

"No invitations yet. . . ." Supposedly on Moscow's insistence, Nishio and several other nisei Communists had been booted out of the Party by the American general secretary following Pearl Harbor. Stalin had never trusted Japanese Reds. So Uichi Nishio had been trundled off to an internment camp on the California-Oregon border under American suspicion of being pro-Axis, even though he had written John Kost that he'd gotten off the MP-guarded bus singing the "Internationale."

"Harry Bridges been to see you?"

Nishio harrumphed. "Yeah, he came down the other night and helped me dry dishes."

"He couldn't have built the Longshoremen's Union without fellows like you."

"I guess, John. Thanks." Nishio looked down as if embarrassed, but then his expression slowly soured. "So what d'you want?"

John Kost simply said, "William Laska."

"I hear he shot a cop. Did the cop deserve it?"

"Not this time."

Nishio smiled.

"Do you know Laska?"

"Yeah, I know Will. And I must be the only guy in town admitting it right now."

"You were comrades?"

"Until 'thirty-five."

"What happened then?"

"He dropped out of the Party. His wife, Emma, too."

"Why did—"

"Hang on a minute. . . ." Frowning, Uichi tossed his Camel into a rain-flooded pothole. "What am I doing here? Squeezing Will into the gas chamber?"

"No."

"Can you promise me that? You never lied to me in the past, but can I count on you now?"

"Absolutely," John Kost said with conviction, particularly since at this hour Laska was being dissected on an autopsy table. "I'm just trying to understand the man. Why he'd murder his wife and one of our people, then try to take his own life."

"Christ, John, who can explain a thing like that?" But Nishio upturned a garbage can, sat on its rusty base, and reflectively lit another cigarette. "Will and I got together while he was still in school and I was involved with the Wobblies, who—like most genuine unions—were falling apart fast. He was a real egghead back then, but I think he looked up to me because I was self-educated. . . ." He went on to explain that Laska had finally been expelled from Berkeley for political agitation; he'd met his wife there.

"What was she like?" John Kost interrupted.

"English lit major. Some guys said Emma was a plain Jane, but I always thought she was kind of pretty."

"I meant politically."

"She later developed into a solid comrade. But her Marxist education was pedestrian. Not like Will's."

"Any trouble between Will and Emma you recall?"

Nishio smirked. "Not that Will ever found out."

"You mean you had relations with her?"

"Come on, John, what do I have to do? Draw a picture?"

"This might be important—was she an adulteress?"

"Your bourgeois morality's showing. And that was the point a lot of the married couples were making back then—they weren't going to be bound by that kind of claptrap. He'd go his way. She'd go hers. They'd get back together when they felt like it. No great shakes."

"But the Laskas—what came of their experimentation?"

"It ended."

"How d'you know?" John Kost asked.

"One afternoon she said no to me. Another comrade got the same business. So that was that—'this too shall pass.'"

"I mean, was there some kind of row between Will and Emma that led to her decision?"

"I'm sure not. And I was living with them at the time."

"Did he ever beat her?"

"No, no." Nishio chuckled at the idea.

"Was he abusive toward her in any way?"

"He just wasn't the kind. He was hardheaded, but not brutal. And besides, I think he really loved her. You're getting me off track."

"I'm sorry." John Kost leaned against the back wall of the restaurant, hoping in that way to appear less voracious for Nishio's information. "Go on."

"Anyways, the IWW collapsed, so Will and I gravitated toward Harry Bridges, not that we knew a damn thing about stevedoring. It's just that the docks were the center of the struggle in those days, what with the bosses throwing out daily job assignments like meat scraps to starving dogs, and we trusted Harry on account of his international perspective. Everything was going great, just beautiful, then wham—Will and Emma up and quit the Party. No amount of pressure got Will to change his mind. And then the U.S. general secretary of the Party himself told us to quit wasting our time on Laska."

"This was in 'thirty-five?"

"Right. It bowled me over. I mean, to Will Laska, Stalin was God. I thought Joe was pretty swell too until he got in bed with Hitler. But with Will it was different. . . ." Nishio paused as if to remember. "He was never a guy with much humor in him. But when this fire for Stalin took hold, it was like it dried up all the laughter inside him. Even Emma looked at him with new eyes. Know what I mean?"

It was a sudden, errant thought, but John Kost decided to voice it: "If Will Laska had believed Stalin himself wanted him to do it, would he have willingly shot his own wife?"

"Jesus—what questions," Nishio said. "What the hell do you think?"

"I'm not convinced a fellow could be persuaded to do such a thing, even a fanatic."

"You think not?" Nishio then softly recited, "'God said to Abraham, "Take your son, your only son, Isaac, whom you love, and go to the land of Moriah, and offer him there as a burnt offering upon one of the mountains of which I shall tell you."'"

"We, the poor opiated, are warned that nobody's better at quoting scripture than Satan."

Nishio laughed, but then cut it short. It had been good to see him laugh, even briefly. "You know, you're surprising me how you're looking at this, John."

"How's that?"

"I mean—a counterrevolutionary liberal bourgeois like you should be the first to see that if for some goddamn reason Joe Stalin wanted Will Laska to shoot his wife, willingness would have nothing to do with it." Uichi Nishio got up off the overturned garbage can and stretched. "Well, it's a tidy explanation, ain't it though? Except for one thing. . . ."

"Yes?"

"Will Laska quit the Party ten years ago. The fires of worship died out long before last Sunday night. But it's a dirty shame— you know, John? About Emma, I mean. She had a sweetness. A real sweetness."

Over the long afternoon the Chekist had watched a line of foam slowly recede on the chained bayside doors. And the water in the berth had faded from pale jade to absinthe and finally, in the last few minutes, to an oily black. He somehow sensed that it was raining outside the windowless boathouse, but could hear nothing over the slopping of tiny waves around the mussel-encrusted piles. Taking an electric torch from his overcoat pocket, he lit his way down a rickety ladder and stepped into the skiff that was moored to its foot. He had already dragged the block and tackle into position overhead and lowered the cargo hook almost to the water. Casting off, he slipped the oar into the stern rowlock and began sculling with his right hand, clasping the light with his left. He had been waiting for low tide so he could row under the horseshoe-shaped dock. Now, dropping to his knees, he flattened the angle of the oar and glided back into the brackish-smelling confines under the planking.

A metal drum was floating on the spume-coated backwater, tethered to a piling.

He slipped his trenching tool from his coat pocket and severed the rope. Grabbing the line off the surface, he threaded it through the bow eye and began wending his way back out through the piles, towing the drum alongside.

He tied the skiff to the ladder, then attached the block-and-tackle hook to the rope still girdling the drum. Eight pulls on the line and he had it up on the dock. He pried open its lid with a tire iron and gently wriggled his hands down into a dunnage of rags and week-old copies of the *San Francisco Chronicle*. Locating the two small crates by feel, he stacked them on the planking.

Taking a moment to adjust his eyes to the Roman letters, he read the shipping label glued to the top of the uppermost box:

FROM: ATLAS POWDER COMPANY, WELDON SPRING, MISSOURI
    TO: RECEIVING OFFICER, MARE ISLAND NAVAL DEPOT

And then the black stenciling on its side:

MK1 MOD 0
CHARGE, DEMOLITION

He would take care to preserve all the markings on the crates, which from now on would be stored separately from the cast explosives and chemical detonators.

"Well," he murmured, patting the boxes, "here's to whatever, old fellows. Even to a better world, should we happen to bumble into one." He glanced upward. Rain, definitely. He liked the tinny drumming on the boathouse roof.

Father Aleksei stole out into the breezeway that separated St. Basil's from his residence. Overhead, the runoff was rattling into the rain gutters, humming down the tin pipe before gushing phosphorescently into the alley. So the lowering mist at dusk had decided to do something. The air was sweet and moist, and he almost thought he was going to be left alone these few minutes before vespers—when footfalls slapped the wet cement behind him.

"Father, I apologize for the intrusion. . . ." It was Ivan Kostoff, the policeman who could never quite be convinced that repentance is best evidenced to God by the amendment of one's ways. Yet, this same Ivan Mikhailovich, who loved and honored his dotard father in the face of the old man's indifference toward him, rarely missed a mass and was impulsively generous to both the coffers of the church and anyone down on his luck. He also had a running spiritual sore that the Holy Spirit could unexpectedly penetrate like sunlight breaching clouds, and when Father Aleksei sought to catch an eye out in the nave, it was invariably his, and often that eye was moved to tears, to contrition and sanctification. "I've brought a woman, Father. . . ."

"What do you mean you've brought a woman?"

"To be confessed before Pascha."

"Oh, Lydia Dmitrievna then?"

"I'm afraid not. A stranger. I met her just yesterday."

Something in how he'd said this made Father Aleksei ask, "A believer?"

"So she says. Is it convenient now?"

106

Shaking his head, the priest walked past him and slowly down the breezeway toward the back door of the church. Privately, he hoped Ivan Mikhailovich could yet be persuaded to marry Lydia Dmitrievna, even though she was a decade his senior and her looks were starting to fade. But that way, God willing, two sinners might be saved by a single sacrament—two snipe felled with one shot, so to speak. The confessions of both dizzied him with tales of promiscuity: Ivan Mikhailovich because he was still groping for reflections of his dead child-bride in other women, and none had proved to be anything like that strange and beautiful and often sullen girl; and poor Lydia Dmitrievna because she couldn't disassociate sex from having food in her mouth, from surviving in a dangerous world filled with men far more powerful than herself.

But he would be the last to suggest marriage to Ivan Mikhailovich. First, despite his many love affairs, the inspector might truly hold his vows to be eternal, as the church counseled; and secondly, the priest had done everything but arrange Ivan Mikhailovich's marriage nine years ago, only to see him a widower within six months. And in little signs that alarmed Father Aleksei it was clear that Ivan Mikhailovich had never recovered from her sudden death. Was he avoiding needless risk as much as a policeman should? Father Aleksei had his doubts.

"'I've brought a woman,'" he dryly muttered to himself, looking off toward the icon stand at the edge of the altar screen as he swept into the nave. Yet, as soon as he dimly saw her waiting there, her eyes fastened on the cross and gospels before her, he sensed that of the dozens of confessions he'd strained to hear in the past week, this one would unfold as it had been intended in the beginning: *a washing of tears.*

"Lord, have mercy. . . ." Hers was a glorious, musical, purely Russian pronunciation. What was this believer doing here in San Francisco? There'd been no new émigrés in years. "Have mercy upon me, O God, after thy great goodness; according to the multitude of thy mercies do away mine offenses—" Her voice suddenly broke.

"You mustn't despair." He smiled at her as she wept into a

107

handkerchief—a cosmopolitan Petersburg face but with doleful Slavic eyes. "Now tell me about this thing that so painfully separates you from Him."

"I don't know if I can . . . no, I can't."

"You won't open yourself to—"

"What am I to do, *Batushka!*"

He thought to take her hands, but she was twining her fingers around the triple bars of the cross. "First you must—"

"If I go through with this thing," she interrupted, her eyes shining, "evil will triumph."

"Then eschew evil."

"No, no—if I do, my heart's joy will die. Where can I turn!"

John Kost had just lit a taper on the memorial table when Elena Martova burst into the smoky alcove and snapped, "I wish to go." Then, with her wet eyes catching the blaze of dead souls, she turned and hobbled through the worshipers waiting patiently for vespers to begin. He caught up with her in the vestibule only because at that instant Mikhail Kostoff came through the door and blocked her escape.

"Forgive me, daughter," he said, looking shrunken and batlike in his burka as he sidestepped into the jamb, striking his brittle skull with an alarming knock.

"Papa. . . ." John Kost grasped him by the arms and held him until he seemed sure to stay on his feet. "Are you all right?"

"Yes, yes."

Elena Martova then remembered herself and began begging his forgiveness.

"Petersburg, yes?" Mikhail Kostoff interrupted, waving off her apologies and smiling warmly: he'd finally gotten a good look at her.

"Yes, does it still tell in my voice?"

"Like birdsong to these old ears." He reached for her hand and smartly bringing his heels together, kissed it. With his lips yet pressed to her skin, he glanced up into her eyes. "You're frightened, aren't you?"

Her face went to stone.

"Is it because of the boy here? If that's so, I'll take a knout to him. He has my stature, and I've often been told by women my height frightens them at first. He should learn to gentle his height, as I have."

"No, your son is *très sympathique*."

Mikhail Kostoff beamed: he'd often railed that men and women could properly communicate only in French. But when he then asked her *en français* how she liked San Francisco, it quickly became apparent that her French was rudimentary. Hiding his disappointment behind the same tender expression, he said, "It's been a pleasure, but I mustn't be late." He went on into the nave, and John Kost was sure the magic of her first impression had let go of him when he suddenly turned and smiled once again. "Beware of this boy. He's half-Gypsy, you know."

Impetuously, she limped after him, embraced and kissed him apparently on the bulge of his goiter—John Kost couldn't quite tell from where he stood. But as he withdrew, the old man seemed aware of his deformity for the first time. He began rubbing his fingers over it, yet he was also clearly pleased by her beneficent kiss.

Through a downpour John Kost trotted around the corner for the Dodge while she waited on the steps under the narrow overhang of the blue-domed belfry. He rushed to start the engine and then return to the front of the church before she got soaked. His headlamps sweeping over the steps, he frowned at the sight of her. She was stooping, trying to close her collar around her throat with her fist. He didn't want to feel sorry for her. Not in the least.

"I don't want to go back right away," she said, getting inside, filling the interior of the car with the smell of her wet clothes. "May we drive awhile?"

11

Won't the vice-consul be worried if you're late?"

"So?" Removing her kerchief, Elena Martova shook the rain off it, then reached for her American-style purse and began digging through its contents. She took out a pocket-sized note-book and a compact before finding the cigarette case she obviously wanted. Full of nicotine impatience, she lit a smoke for herself with a mother-of-pearl lighter before he could offer to help. In the flaring he could see where her facial powder had been streaked by either her tears or the rain. "Show me your city, Ivan Mikhailovich. No, wait—I want to see lights on the ocean. I love the way they shine across the waves."

"The war will have to end for that, I'm afraid. There's a dimout along the shore."

"Then let the war end," she said with forced brightness. It seemed as if she'd shamed herself by crying and now wanted to make up for it with some desperate good cheer. "Would you care for a cigarette?"

"No, thank you."

"Because it's Russian?"

"I don't smoke." He accelerated away from the curb. The rain was striking the street at a slant.

"You're not much like him."

"Like my father, you mean?"

"Yes."

"I suppose not." The gutter on the low side of Van Ness Avenue had turned into a rivulet. Swiftly, he forded the dirty stream before too much water was sloshed by the front tires up into the engine compartment.

"Is it true what he said?"

"Which thing?"

"You know, about your mother being Gypsy?"

"So I've been told."

"Don't you remember her?"

"Not really." He leaned forward: the wipers weren't keeping up with the deluge; also, the inside of the windshield was fogging over. "I mean, I can recall bits and pieces about her. Her hair was black." With his handkerchief he wiped his half of the glass. "She was killed in Moscow when I was only five. Shot in some kind of riot."

"I'm sorry." For a while, she said nothing, smoking intently, but then she proved her determination not to be glum. "With those courtly manners of his, your father has probably broken a lot of hearts in this country."

"He's been impotent for over twenty years. . . ." For a moment he paused, surprised with himself for having said such a thing to a stranger. "I suppose he lost the faculty when he finally realized that he'd left Russia forever. I wish he hadn't lost it. For both of us." He glanced over: her eyes were bright with curiosity. "He might've married well, and we could've eaten better at the beginning. As it was, he got up at three in the morning and loaded milk crates into delivery trucks. He did that for two years. After that he manned an elevator in a two-star hotel. When I finally got a police job, my first check bought him back some of his dignity. He retired to his memories."

"You love him a great deal, don't you?" she said. John Kost braked for a signal but didn't look at her when he'd come to a stop. "Unwilling love comes from God," she went on when he gave no reply.

Keeping to Van Ness, he cut through the civic center, where trucks of all sizes were parked outside both the Opera House and the Veterans Building, and the sidewalks were impassable with crates and stacks of plywood. "This is where the Conference will be," he explained. He was turning onto Market Street when his Motorola squawked with some routine Patrol traffic, startling her. "My police radio," he said, tapping the microphone that was mounted low on the dash.

"What was said?"

She looked anxious, so he smiled. "Nothing of importance. A patrolman was telling our headquarters he'll be out of his car on a follow-up investigation."

"Something to do with your man who was killed last Sunday?"

"No, homicide investigations are my responsibility. Had it been one of my assistant inspectors—yes, it probably would have something to do with that case."

"How many assistants have you?"

The second Martov in two days to ask him that. He slid open the ashtray so she could stub out her smoke. "Two."

"Are you and your men any closer to learning why the murderer did this horrible thing?"

"Somewhat. Surprising fellow, this William Laska."

She reached inside her purse for another cigarette.

Eventually, he drove out onto the Bay Bridge, thinking in an aimless sort of way of going as far as Berkeley and then back to town. He hadn't liked the way she'd clammed up at his mention of Laska, although he could assume that she and most of the consular staff knew both Laska and his wife had been Party members. Pyotr Martov himself was most likely waiting for the other shoe to drop—and for John Kost to throw Laska's Communist past up to him.

The siren on the bridge began to wail.

"What is it!" she asked, putting out her fresh cigarette.

He pulled over to the rail and killed his headlamps, as did the three other cars he could see on the bridge. The bulbs hung from

112

the overhead bracing went out, and the rain-blotched lights of the waterfront cities died in clusters. Complete darkness hovered against the car windows, but only until his eyes adjusted to the night; then the shoreline loomed black against the sheen on the bay.

"What is it, Ivan Mikhailovich!" She was breathless now.

"Air raid blackout."

"Are they coming?" She was now sitting as far forward as she could, craning her neck to have a look out the windshield, but the trestlework was frustrating her view.

"No, it's nothing," he said. "An exercise."

She fell silent, so silent he had to ask after a moment, "Are you all right?"

"I was in Leningrad, visiting my mother," she said with a quaver in her voice, "the first day the Nazis bombed."

"Please—relax." Reaching across her lap, he cranked down her window, letting the cool air gush in around them. "Listen, no airplanes. . . ." All that could be heard were dripping noises on the asphalted span from the water collecting on the trestles above. He prayed no American plane would drone over just when she seemed on the verge of calming down.

She seized his arm before he could sit upright again and began twisting his wrist in her hands. Tenderly. Then, just as he was closing his eyes to dampen his rising sense of unreality, he felt her lips brush his chin. They were warm but dry.

"Elena Valentinovna—"

She found his mouth, and he felt his own lips part to accept the tip of her tongue, which came into him as he'd known it would. His free hand went to her waist, but she nudged it lower so that his fingers came to rest atop her thigh.

Outside, the sounds of the rain became a roar.

His hand was groping for the hem of her dress when something snapped his desire. Later he wasn't sure if it had been the abrupt slackening of the rain or the first audible pitch of the siren announcing the all clear, or even the mistrust that was smoldering inside him—whatever, he moved away and started the engine.

Nothing more was said on the drive back to the consulate.

He let her off without accompanying her to the door, which glided open for her before she could knock, and closed again as soon as she was inside.

He opened the wind-wing and dumped out the ashtray.

Two blocks on his way back downtown, with the rain thinning to a sprinkle, it came to him out of the blue—the thing neither he nor Aranov had accounted for at the crime scene on Carbon Street. A meaningless glance into Elena Martova's purse while she'd been fishing for her cigarette case had somehow jiggled the intermittent short out of the connection he'd been trying to form for the past three days.

He made a U-turn and sped for the nearest call box.

Typing with his index fingers on a shopworn Remington that tossed letters wherever it pleased on the page, Aranov was two hours into a supplemental investigation report and facing another three—when the telephone frazzled his caffeine-singed nerves. But this surge of adrenaline swiftly faded under the weight of his exhaustion, and groggily, he reached for the handset. "Homicide, Assistant Inspector Aranov."

"Nathan, John Kost here—"

"John. Glad you phoned. It'll save me a memo, and I still have three to do. You mind if I start working this angle in the morning? I'll need some clearances, I'm sure, probably from the captain, and maybe even higher up the ladder. I really don't know how to get the ball rolling on this one."

"What angle, Nathan?" John Kost sounded impatient. "What are you talking about?"

It hit Aranov with a mild jolt that he had yet to explain himself. Maybe it would be best to discuss this with the inspector after both of them had gotten some decent shut-eye, but when would that be? Then, despite his vacillation, he heard his own voice grating on: "I think we ought to work through the State Department . . . you know, on the assumption one or both of our men were killed by somebody who got in the country on a diplomatic passport." There, he'd said it: the thing he believed.

"And your rationale for this?" John Kost asked.

Aranov stared at the Remington, his eyes blank, then struck the zero key, hard. "It's kind of a hunch. Call it instinct . . . a collateral perception. . . ." He strained to think of a more cogent argument, but his forehead had begun to ache from the effort of tracing the evolution of the idea. Yesterday evening at Cliff House, hadn't Ragnetti said that the suspect who'd wiped the doorknobs inside Laska's place had done so because he knew his prints were on file? And then there'd been all those socialist books. But was that all there was to it? Now that he was staring his doubts in the face, the possibility was beginning to dawn on him that this notion might lead nowhere. The two ID technicians he'd managed to get hold of today, Delbert from his own department and the state's expert in Sacramento, had expressed doubts, in light of the immunity issue, that diplomatic personnel were fingerprinted upon entering the country. The FBI and State Department Security, either of whom should be able to clear up the matter, had yet to return his calls. But that didn't get him off the hook of John Kost's question: *What's your rationale?* "You've got to agree there's something strange, I don't know—something *foreign* about all this."

"Maybe," John Kost admitted. "Your suspicion that Laska belonged to the Party is on target. An informant of mine confirmed it this afternoon—"

"All right!" Aranov waited for a little self-congratulation to warm his tiredness, but none came. "I thought so. You sound like you got something for me to do."

"If you will, please. . . ." And as soon as John Kost explained what he needed done, Aranov slammed his fist on the desk blotter.

"Christ! How could I forget to check that! Stupid fuck!"

"We both forgot—it was too simple. We were focusing on what was there, instead of what's missing. Are Elliot's effects back in-house from the coroner's office?"

"Hell, yes, I checked them into evidence myself!" Aranov groaned at his own ineptitude.

"Go easy on yourself, old fellow. I'll be there in ten minutes."

All the way to the evidence room Aranov upbraided himself for not remembering what the missing item meant to a patrolman. It was the chronicle of his beat, his alibi against disciplinary action, his crutch against sounding either like an amnesiac or a moron on the witness stand. It was his personal Rosetta stone with which he could translate the existential events of the streets into criminal convictions. "Let me see Elliot's stuff, Sammy," he said to the evidence and property clerk, a middle-aged colored man with lank hair he undoubtedly processed with lye, who took one look at Aranov's expression and half-ran into the vault.

Aranov leaned his forearms against the shelf topping the lower half of the Dutch door, trying to catch his breath. He wished he had thought of this instead of John Kost.

"Kindly sign the chain-of-evidence manifest, Mr. Aranov."

He scribbled out his signature. "Stand by a second, Sammy, if you don't mind—I may need another witness to this in the future."

"My pleasure." Sammy folded his arms across his chest, assuming his official-witness stance.

Aranov dumped the contents of a glassine bag onto the counter. Keys. A brass whistle. A wrinkled handkerchief. Less than a dollar in silver change. A flat sap. A mint toothpick yet in the paper wrapper. A black basket-weave leather wallet, which Aranov left closed. A note from Personnel that Elliot's badge had been removed for inclusion in the memorial case for officers killed in the line.

"His bloody clothes and Sam Browne gear's still in the back, Mr. Aranov. You want to see them too?"

"In the morning. I want to take them up to ID first thing in the morning." Then he growled, "See, I went through his clothes at the scene. I went through every last goddamn pocket. Touched every button. But maybe, just maybe, Sammy, I didn't bitch up the partial latent left on Elliot's right breast pocket button."

"Why'd there be a fingerprint other than Mr. Elliot's on that button, Mr. Aranov?"

"Tell me, do you see Elliot's spiral notebook?"

"No, sir, I sure don't. . . ." Then the clerk's eyes widened with understanding.

The rain had quit pelting the bedroom window, but the glass was still pocked with water. The streetlight in front of the consulate was catching these droplets and magnifying them into mottles that fell across the blanket with which she'd covered herself on the settee. Although Martov's face was in the shadow, Elena could feel his eyes on her. His white hair showed against his headboard, and his arms were sprawled across what years before would have been her side of the bed. She prayed he would say nothing and let the night pass as they had agreed: a connubial pretense for the sake of the staff, especially for the consul general, a genial fool who survived on appearances.

But then Martov cleared his throat. "Lena?"

She rolled over on the settee, giving him her back.

He chuckled, his habit when stung or dismayed. "I know I lost the right to ask such things a long time ago, but please—why are you here? Truly now, who sent you?"

His asking only strengthened her determination to leave him bewildered about why, after four years of separation, she'd suddenly shown up in San Francisco. Another man, a braver man, would deserve an answer. Such a man might even deserve a bit of lovemaking if only as a small kindness to help him sleep.

But not this man.

Then, without warning, her own courage was tested by a wave of fear. It had come over her involuntarily, like chills.

Starting to cry, she bit the inside of her cheek until she tasted blood. With that her tears quickly subsided, and she trusted that she wouldn't fall apart as she had twice tonight: first with the priest and then with the inspector, Kostoff. It had been a panic pure and simple with the priest, and she'd come with a hairsbreadth of telling him everything she knew. But suspicion had rescued her at the last second, distrust born of dealing with clergy who'd stayed in Russia and compromised with the new order. Or was it that the stakes were now so high she shrank even from trusting God? *The Devil take me if that's true!* She wouldn't

117

shrink from God, but neither would she become like her mother, who'd remained devout against the onslaught of atheism only because she'd not been about to relinquish such a powerful ally for her daughter's career. But could the woman be blamed? Her own mother had been a half-mad peasant of the Dukhobor sect, the Spirit Wrestlers who refused to shed blood for any reason, but readily shed their clothes and stood naked before the tsarist authorities to protest the slightest affront to their beliefs.

Then she laughed under her breath as the absurdity of her own past rushed back in on her: mother and daughter praying to the Creator of All to smote Galina Ulanova so Elena Valentinovna might become prima ballerina of the Maryinski! Yet in the end she and not Galina had been struck down, and the mother who'd taught her to petition God for the downfall of others had starved to death in Leningrad. She laughed again, but bitterly now—at the righteousness of God's sentence.

"Is something wrong?" Martov asked drowsily.

"No. I don't want a conversation."

He sighed. "I wasn't striking one up."

Her behavior with the inspector had been even more inexcusable than her scene with the priest. That she'd found Kostoff attractive and strong willed and tenderhearted in ways that had been drudged out of Soviet men, and that the air raid siren and the sudden darkness on the bridge had terrified her—these did nothing to justify what she'd done. It'd been a lapse into the sinful habit that had lowered her to his point, pleasing a man she didn't love in the hope he might help her, take up her predicament as his own. There were no such men where she had come from, and she doubted their existence here or anywhere.

Tonight would mark her last collapse into weakness, and she vowed that from now on if even the most crippling terror seized her, she'd show nothing, then use it to marshal the same degree of cunning that was being used against her.

Bedsprings clacked as Martov turned on his side finally to sleep.

Martov tossed again a few minutes later, but then she slowly realized that more than a few minutes had passed.

118

It was dawn and she'd been dreaming again of Galina Ulanova. Why did the dream never vary? Why always the same crash to pain that, in combination with some slight noise, jarred her awake?

Galina at twelve years is standing at the foot of her bed, looking down upon her with mute goodwill if only because Lena is the youngest student at the Leningrad school and misses her father terribly. Throwing off her covers despite the cold, genuflecting on her bony knees, she begs Galina's forgiveness even though this dream-night is clearly years and years before the onset of the bitterness that drowned their girlish love in hatred and jealousy, and she says that soon she'll do something perfectly brilliant to please both dear Galina and her *maman*, who loathes poor Galina. A thing of immaculate love. "You'll see, you'll see!" And then she is staring at her toe shoes: left foot forward and turned out to the left, right foot pointed back and out. She hurls herself into a grand jeté, soars up into flat white clouds cut from wood, suspends in an arabesque before plunging down through mist so real it tickles her eyelashes. Below, the stage is as small as a button, but it rises with frightening speed. At first she thinks the flooring has given way under her right heel, but then, prostrate, hearing the rustle of the alarmed audience, she feels the pain and screams.

Elena flung the blanket over her face.

12

I CAN USE A DRINK, John," Ragnetti said, piling into the backseat of the Dodge.

Aranov stretched before getting inside. "Me too."

Both of them glanced back at the green canopy over Wallace Elliot's grave, the hundreds of blue-suiters scattering through the cemetery monuments toward their cars, before looking expectantly to John Kost again. "I sure as hell don't want one of these three-ring circuses when it's my time," Aranov said. "Promise me it'll be simple. No rifles. No taps. No nothing from the department."

"Don't tempt God with bullshit like that."

"I'm serious, Vince."

"Be serious then, but don't tempt God. Talk like that makes me want to mash your lips."

"Then mash them."

Ragnetti let the challenge slide with a breathy grunt. "You got a nip for us, John?"

"Glove compartment."

Aranov took out the brown-bagged half-pint, Mikhail Kostoff's two-day ration. John Kost hadn't found the time to deliver it this morning, and now the old man would start hitting the phone booths, clicking open the Bakelite coin returns in the hope of nickels all because his bastard son refused him the solace of limitless vodka. "Ugh," Aranov said, passing the bottle back to Ragnetti, "that's kerosene."

"Kerosene, the little fuck says—after three snorts already."

John Kost did nothing to stop their bickering. He found it reassuring, a stab at normalcy, and most likely they did too.

Ragnetti tapped him on the shoulder with the butt of the half-pint. "Here. We got us another one of these to go through for that Fenby kid?"

"No, his department service will be held off until the chief decides when to announce his death to the press. Could wind up being weeks."

"What d'you say, John? Let's drive someplace where we can see the ocean."

"Sure." Ragnetti's request made perfect sense to John Kost. After seeing the claustrophobic smallness of that coffin, he needed to see something vast. They all did. Starting the engine, he joined the black-and-white centipede of squad cars creeping out of the cemetery.

"You know," he said after a while, "there's something to what you said last night, Nathan."

"About what?" he asked a bit sullenly.

"Cops being creatures of habit. Let's bat this around for a minute—Elliot was killed for his notebook, he jotted down something while making his rounds. He himself probably didn't even know if it amounted to a hill of beans. Comments?"

"Come on, John," Ragnetti said, reaching over the front seat and snatching the bottle out of his grasp, "what could be so big they'd gun him down for it? And then croak the pigeon who pulled the trigger for them?"

"That's what we have to find out."

"Elliot had a drinking buddy," Aranov mused out loud, "an auxiliary who partnered with him on weekends. I'll phone him as soon as we get back to the station and try to get a handle on Elliot's routine."

"Good." John Kost had already thought of doing this, but didn't say so now to Aranov as he began winding up Twin Peaks Boulevard toward the wooded summits. Since the beginning of the war, most cruisers had been one-man cars, except for Friday and Saturday nights when part-time officers reinforced the regular Patrol force. "Then we can divvy up Elliot's beat into thirds and start hitting the bricks. I have lunch at the Soviet consulate, but I should be free by two-thirty. Don't wait for me, I'll meet up with you two in the field."

"John, can I ask a question what may sound funny?"

"Shoot, Vincent."

"Do the brass really want us to crack this one?"

John Kost parked in a muddy overlook and rolled down his window for some breeze. The seascape was so bright and loud and airy it was hard to imagine that anyone could be buried on such a day. "Yes, Vincent," he said at last, "the brass want us to crack this one—and do everything else under the sun while we try to work it. But we have no reason to question their motives."

Ragnetti parked his unmarked 1941 Dodge on the north side of China Basin, giving the shiny black hood an affectionate swipe of his jacket sleeve before hoofing it out toward Pier 46.

Elliot's auxiliary partner had just told Aranov that the slain patrolman usually checked this dock, the northern limit of his waterfront beat, between ten-fifteen and ten forty-five when on swing shift—his last watch rotation before his murder.

Also, Pier 46 was where William Laska had worked.

Ragnetti rubbernecked at the merchant ships with his hands in his trouser pockets like some harbor buff, even though he knew the stevedores had his number and the word *cop* was being passed from white-capped longshoreman to longshoreman faster than he could walk. "Fuck 'em," he muttered, smiling.

He was feeling pretty good. Getting away from a police funeral felt a lot like getting out of mass, not that he had anything against religion. It kept his mother happy, even though Vice had popped her parish priest for playing I Peek–You Peek in a public toilet in Lafayette Square. That was something the old woman had never learned about and never would if he could help it. The monsignor still didn't have a clue either. Ragnetti had scared the piss out of the delinquent father, threatened him with a hundred years in San Quentin with a Holy Roller for a cellmate, but in the end had shitcanned the criminal complaint with the collusion of his buddies in Vice. He'd just figured it was up to God to kick a priest's ass, not some fairy judge who probably did a little I Peek–You Peek on his own.

He noticed a stevedore his age perched on top of a guano-splattered capstan, steadying himself by bracing his boots against the big, greasy cable that sagged up the bow of a freighter. The man was trying to eat his lunch, but the gulls were at him, hopping right up to him, twisting their heads from side to side to have a look-see at the ground for crumbs. He kept shouting them away, but the birds were fearless, and his protests had no sooner been carried away by the breeze than the gulls were back, swooping and squawking around his head, trying to bomb him with gray squirts—hoping maybe he could be rattled into dropping his lunch.

"That won't work," Ragnetti said, rocking on his heels.

"You got a better idea, bub?"

"Sure?"

"Like what?"

"My mother showed me this. . . ." Ragnetti drew his Detective Special and emptied all six rounds up into the flock. Only one gull of scores was hit, but it folded its wings around itself and dropped like a stone into the water. The rest dove and skimmed low across the choppy surface of the bay, having decided the pickings were probably better over on Alameda Island.

The longshoreman was now on his feet, and his sandwich was in pieces on the pier. "You nuts or something?"

"Cop." Ragnetti ejected the spent casings and reloaded from the ammo loops on his size forty-eight belt.

"Same thing."

"Yeah," he said with a grudging smile as he holstered the Colt, "same lousy thing. Anything else bothering you around here?"

"Nothing I'd care to tell you about."

123

They both laughed.

Ragnetti waited for a lift truck to tool past, then sauntered over to the stevedore and rested his left shoe on the cable. He was wearing his white spats today. Afraid of being accused of dressing like a guinea hood, he only wore them to cop burials. Somewhere along the line it'd gotten into his head that as long as he wore this very pair, which had been his father's, to department funerals, he himself would die in bed as his old man had. "Did you know a cop named Elliot?"

The stevedore stared off the end of the pier at the gull, which was floating breast up. "He's dead, I hear."

"I didn't ask you what if he's dead. I asked if you fucking knew him."

"I knew of him."

"Any trouble with him? You're talking like a joe who had a run-in or two with him."

"I just told you I didn't know him. I knew *of* him."

Ragnetti decided to back off a bit; this guy was the sort to turn into a hardnose if rubbed the wrong way. "What do you do around here? Other than wolf down lunch on time and a half, I mean. Ain't everything over six hours time and a half?"

"What's it to you?"

"Maybe I'm interested in getting in this line of work."

"How long you been a cop?"

"Seventeen years," Ragnetti said.

"Forget it—you're ruined for real work by now." He bent over and picked up the pieces of his sandwich, slapped them back together. "Take my advice and stay in what you're doing, bub."

"Name's Vince."

"Mickey."

They shared a testy handshake, then Mickey gestured with his sandwich toward the inlet to the basin: "See that there forty-footer?"

"What? That motor launch coming our way?"

"Yeah. I'm waiting for it. The Navy sends it down from Mare Island to drop off forty-millimeter ammo for the ack-ack guns on any of the merchantmen heading out. It'll pick me up, then we'll load the shells out in the stream."

"What stream? I don't see no stream."

"Out there in the bay. Away from the docks. You can't load hot cargo off any of these city docks."

As the launch coasted up to the pier pushing a big hump of tan foam before it, Ragnetti saw that the three-man crew was colored. He asked the stevedore about it.

"They're not bad kids," Mickey said, closing the snaps on his lunch box, "if you know how to handle them."

"That so? I never got on much with them." The steersman, a nice-looking Negro despite his prissy horn-rimmed glasses, was giving him the evil eye. He smelled a cop, for sure. "What's your fucking problem?" Ragnetti hollered over the grumble of the launch's motor.

The colored sailor looked away.

"See what I mean?" He chuckled to Mickey, then turned at the approach of footfalls on the planks.

"Somebody fire off a gun around here?" demanded a big guy with pens and pencils in his denim shirt pocket. He was holding a longshoreman's hook in his right hand.

"Let me check," Ragnetti said, cupping his hand over his genitals. "Nope—dry as a bone. But then again I'm a bachelor and don't get much chance to use it."

"I'm serious." He looked it too.

Ragnetti showed his badge. "Homicide. Sorry for the disturbance. I was running the ballistics test on a murder weapon."

"What's the number on that badge?" He had put down the hook and taken a pencil and a pad from his pocket.

Ragnetti advanced until he was toe-to-toe with the man. "You want my number?"

"Yeah, I'm dock foreman here." A good sign. Although his face didn't show it, he was goosey enough to feel the need to explain who he was. There'd be no gripe to the brass. Yet he did start jotting down Ragnetti's number.

The sergeant suddenly batted the pencil out of his hand.

"Jesus," Mickey murmured apprehensively.

"You don't need that. Name's Vincenzo Ragnetti. . . ." He spelled it for him. "Homicide. And my boss is John Kost. His boss is Pat Coffey. And his is that worthless fuck we call chief. You still want my number?"

The foreman didn't say; his jaws were locked.

"Here's my fucking number—I'm coming back tomorrow and I want a list of every swinging dick on this pier who worked with William Laska. Then I'm going to talk with each one of them. If somebody shits on me, says he don't know Laska when he does—and I find out, *and* I always find out—I'm getting me a bus and taking you all downtown until I start getting straight answers."

"How come none of our boys can go see Will up at the hospital?" the foreman asked, but with the steam gone out of his voice.

"Then you know him?"

The foreman wiped the corners of his mouth with his fingers. "Sure, everybody down here does. Everybody."

"Well, he's not feeling so good. That's why you can't visit him." Ragnetti gave the brim of his hat a squeeze, then said over his shoulder as he started back for his car, "Swell shooting the breeze, Mickey. And if you got any more problems with our feathered friends, don't be afraid to give me a ring."

Putting down his dessert fork, his éclair untouched, John Kost frowned up at the Louis Quatorze clock on the mantel. It was two thirty-five and so far Pyotr Martov had given no sign he intended to adjourn luncheon to the sitting room, even though fifteen minutes before, the cocktail table in there had been furnished with a bottle of cordial and six tiny glasses. Including Elena Martova, seven people were at the vice-consul's table, so John Kost guessed that she'd be excluded when Martov finally got down to business—if he ever got down to business.

Despite last night and everything that had passed between them on the Bay Bridge, Elena refused to avoid his frank glances. On the contrary, she had begun to study him as conspicuously as he was staring at her, and during one of her husband's florid toasts to eternal Soviet-American friendship John Kost felt almost sure that her eyes were laughing at him. Yet, on the whole, she seemed withdrawn and contemplative, if only because it was proving cumbersome for her husband or his secretary, Grigor Pervukhin, to translate her replies to the overly attentive American men. "What amuses them so?" she had asked Martov at one point, confident perhaps that only he, Pervukhin, and John Kost would understand.

"Their fantasies, Lena," he had said quietly in Russian, winking at John Kost through the vapor off the soup tureen.

Flanked at the table by the agent in charge of the local field office of the Secret Service and the State Department's Security Division chief for the Conference, bland-looking fellows who talked in monotones, John Kost found himself hearing without listening, thinking all the while about the homicides.

Upon their brief return to the Hall of Justice after the funeral, Aranov and he had been told by the ID technician Delbert that a partial latent fingerprint impression had indeed survived Nathan's opening of Elliot's notebook-pocket button. And this fragile impression, consisting of body oil, was neither Aranov's nor Elliot's. Nor was it Laska's. But Delbert had stressed the word *partial*: of the twelve identical comparison points required by a court to match a print to a particular human being, only nine could be made from the smudgy crescent of friction ridges left on the brass button. Although this shred of physical evidence was meaningless in prosecutorial terms, it was still worth following up, and somehow since last night he had warmed to Aranov's idea about a foreign cast to the killings. While Nathan's rationale was no doubt exquisitely analytical, his own was purely visceral.

He was familiar with no one at the State Department, and certainly the simpering bureaucrat at his elbow would take no pains to help him investigate a wartime ally. But he knew that the FBI might have what he needed: the prints of the Soviet consular staff and the delegates to the upcoming Conference. As far as latching onto an FBI contact, he had only to look across the table at Robert Cade of the Bureau's San Francisco office. He had last seen Cade at Hamilton Field, pretending to be a newsman. The fat-necked G-man was commonly known in police circles, and probably in diplomatic ones as well, to be Hoover's counterintelligence ramrod west of the Mississippi. He had just lit up a cigar, although he'd failed to ask Madame Martova if she minded.

John Kost caught his eye.

Cade nodded and asked, "Any luck on your latest gig?"

"Some."

"Well, if we can be of any help—just sing out."

"I will, Robert."

Realizing that Martov and Pervukhin had been hanging on every word of this exchange, John Kost turned and asked the Washington-based State Department man how he liked California, resolving to tune out immediately whatever the fellow said.

But Martov chimed in, altogether too eagerly, "An amazing variety of country in one region, wouldn't you say?"

The State man agreed, completely.

"Seashore, mountains, fertile valleys, desert," Martov waxed on, then pointedly looked to John Kost. "And I want to make sure my wife sees as much of it as possible before she must return home. Especially the Yosemite. I was fortunate enough to be there last May, when the waterfalls were at their fullest in years." Next, he caught the State man's eye. "Do you suppose a trip can be arranged?"

The fellow hesitated, probably thinking of the directive that restricted free Soviet travel to the environs of San Francisco, but then he said, "I see no reason why not, Vice-consul."

Elena asked Martov what was being said, but he ignored her and went on in English, "Good, excellent—then it is settled."

"Let's see now," the State man said, "today's the twelfth of April. When would you and Madame care to go?"

"Oh, I cannot be spared anytime in the near future. Preparations for the Conference, you understand. But that should not stop her from going. How about tomorrow morning?"

The State man's jaw dropped, but then he found the presence of mind to say, "Of course, in accordance with the terms of our agreement one of our people will be glad to accompany Madame

Martova. But I doubt very much, sir, we can locate a Russian-speaking escort and have him here in less than . . .what?" He tapped his wristwatch. "Eighteen hours?"

"Ah." Martov held up his palms as if relenting, but then his eyes widened on John Kost. "Wait—the inspector here speaks Russian. And I think a fellow in his capacity would be acceptable to your ministry, yes? I am sure he will be kind enough to help us out. I would never forgive myself if Madame missed the Yosemite."

John Kost had no intention of junketing two hundred miles east into the Sierra Nevada, not with four homicides still on the books, two of them cop-killings. He felt even less inclined to go when he recalled how unsettled—both embarrassed and hungering—last night on the bridge had left him. But Martov's proposal raised an unpleasant question: Had her seduction attempt been on his orders? He quickly decided that now wasn't the time to argue. "I'll take it up with my superiors."

"Please do, Ivan Mikhailovich."

Cade lofted an eyebrow at the vice-consul's use of John Kost's Russian forenames. But Martov didn't notice—Elena had grabbed his jacket sleeve and was demanding a translation. He bent close and whispered to her.

After a moment she said, "I'll go nowhere."

"Later," he snapped, then smiled around the table. "Gentlemen, will you take a liqueur with me?"

Rising on this cue, John Kost shrugged to Elena as if to assure her that this trip would never be realized, but she tossed down her napkin and hurriedly limped from the dining room without meeting his eye. She had his wife's carriage, and he followed the sway of her girlishly thin hips with such stark longing he suddenly became self-conscious. Fortunately, Martov had been busy backslapping the three federal officials toward the sitting room, and if Pervukhin had caught his indiscretion, he gave no sign. Once again John Kost was amazed to think that a fellow this sensitive-looking had survived the purges engineered by Stalin and carried out by Beria—both Georgians of the crudest stripe. In Martov and Pervukhin he sensed that he was dealing with two apparent dilettantes who'd somehow survived while thousands like them had perished. He would remind himself of this achievement whenever he began to feel comfortable around them.

"Well," Martov said, motioning for Pervukhin to shut the door, "I ordinarily don't handle security matters. . . ."

A coy smoke screen, John Kost thought—unless the Soviets were far more adept at this shell game than he'd imagined, and Martov was not the secret-police resident. Just before the door was shut, he glimpsed the maidservant clearing the wineglasses with care, touching them only by their stems. Then Pervukhin handed him some Grand Marnier.

"Gentlemen, allies," Martov toasted, "to the Conference, a world at peace."

"Sure," Cade said, draining his glass first.

Martov then began going over Molotov's itinerary, the foreign minister's high-level meetings in Washington and New York before flying on to San Francisco. Once again, John Kost's mind began to drift. A jacaranda tree was in bloom outside the window; perversely, his inner eye kept showing him Laska dangling from it nude. But then mention of his name drew his gaze back to Martov's face: "And so, Ivan Mikhailovich, our primary concern is the reception Commissar Molotov will have in your city. Has there been any progress in regards to that lunatic reactionary who writes letters promising to blow up the commissar?"

John Kost had promised Captain Coffey he'd get as much mileage as possible out of this windfall, so to heighten the anticipation in the room he took his time reaching inside his jacket for the carbon copy of the arrest report. "Perpetrator's in custody as of last night."

"Really, Inspector?" Martov and Pervukhin seemed a bit surprised, while Cade and the Secret Service agent looked absolutely incredulous. Threatening-letter writers weren't easy to track down, particularly for local-level cops, whom the feds held to be the unskilled laborers of law enforcement. The Secret Service's vaunted Protective Research Section had been expected to crack this one, not lowly SFPD.

"Nice collar, John," Cade said tonelessly. "How'd it come together for you?"

"Just teamwork and legwork," he lied. Actually, some Civil Division plainclothesmen had been serving a landlord's eviction notice on the suspect—it seemed he stayed up most the night screaming profanities out his window—when the CD men noticed a pair of scissors and magazine text all diced up on the kitchen table. Under the copy of *Collier's* were the beginnings of a mosaic to the Soviet consul general promising a violent end to one V. Molotov. The happenstance nature of the arrest had then been doctored out of the report and replaced by some invented probable cause that the suspect's profanities had been hurled against imaginary Communists on the street below, while in fact they'd been boasts of his alleged prowess with Negro women.

"Very, very good," Martov murmured, still scanning the report. "This will be pleasant news to pass on. It has been a major concern of my commissariat's—the violence here."

Cade rolled his eyes, then smirked at John Kost.

As soon as the Americans had said their good-byes and were outside on the sidewalk, the agent laughed. "You lying Cossack bastard. . . ."

"I beg your pardon?" John Kost feigned indignation.

"How'd you really nab that prick?"

"Just like the report said."

"Right—and we got Dillinger by figuring what kind of movie he likes." Cade put on his outdated straw boater. "Square with me, Kost."

"For what reason?"

"We're pals."

"The hell you say."

Cade laughed even louder. "Okay, okay—what are you after this time? It took me a while, but I finally got on to you. You like to barter. It's in your blood."

"Did you know Laska belonged to the Party?"

Cade stopped beside his car, a Hudson DeLuxe, and leaned against the rear fender. "Yeah, we got a thing or two on Laska in the files. All old stuff going back to Wobbly days."

"I want to thank you then, Robert."

"What d'you mean? Does that ancient shit figure in this?"

"I'm not sure. But had one of your people been shot down in cold blood, I'd give you the courtesy of letting you decide for yourself."

Cade exhaled. "All right already, the file's on the way as soon as I get back to my office."

"Thank you."

"Anything else?"

John Kost was staring at the Hudson Deluxe. It had just occurred to him that he'd seen it Sunday night in the darkened parking lot of the hospital. And the driver had worn a straw boater. So regardless of what Cade had to say about Laska's being ancient history, the Bureau had an ongoing interest in him. He had probably hoped to beat Homicide to the hospital with his own set of questions for Laska, but John Kost's arrival had spoiled that plan. But he confronted Cade with none of this for the time being. "Yes, there's something more I want, Robert— comparison-quality photostats of the fingerprint cards of every Soviet citizen who's been in this city within the past month."

"Can't help you there."

"Why not?"

"We don't take them. Neither does the State Department."

"Are you sure?"

"Positive."

John Kost didn't bother to hide his disappointment. "Dammit."

"We feel the same way about it."

"Wait a second. . . ." John Kost had just recalled how the Soviet maidservant cleared the wineglasses so any impressions left by the American agents wouldn't be destroyed before they could be lifted for eventual storage in Beria's Moscow archives. "All right, so you don't openly print diplomats. Does that mean you have *no* latents for any of these people? Especially suspected secret police?"

"I didn't say that."

"Then what are you saying?"

132

"I'm saying it isn't Bureau policy to violate diplomatic immunity, *Ivan Mikhailovich.*"

He glared at the agent. "You want to know how we really got the word-paster?"

"You bet—just for my own peace of mind, because I don't think you fog-brained gumshoes pack the smarts to pull off something like this."

"Then know you shall, Robert—the minute I receive all the latents you've got on the Soviets." John Kost walked on toward his own car.

Keeping to Divisadero Street on his drive south, he radioed for the dispatcher to arrange a rendezvous in Potrero District for him with Ragnetti and Aranov. It was almost three-thirty. Luncheon had taken an hour longer than expected. Listening as the dispatcher tried to raise his men, he would've guessed from her husky voice that she'd been crying. It meant nothing to him until he saw a middle-aged woman sobbing on a bus bench. He turned on the AM radio and was dismayed to hear nothing but patriotic music from one end of the band to the other. Just like after Pearl Harbor. He grabbed his microphone again. "Central One, have I missed some special traffic?"

"Stand by, all units and stations." Then the emergency-alert tone came over the radio. "All units and stations," the Communications sergeant said, "according to a bulletin issued by International News Service at fourteen forty-seven hours, Pacific War Time, President Franklin Delano Roosevelt is dead."

John Kost pulled over to the curb and set the parking brake. On the AM radio, Kate Smith was singing "God Bless America."

13

QUIETLY, the Chekist knocked.

He counted to ten before catching the faint groan of feet crossing the floorboards within: Tikhov was drinking, then. The door creaked open a handbreadth, and a bloodshot eye leered out at him with cyclopean distrust. "Greetings."

"Good evening," the Chekist said, entering.

Holding his Tokarev down at his side, Tikhov lumbered back to the unmade bed and stuffed the pistol under the mattress. "I was sleeping," he said, brushing down a rampant cowlick with his fingers.

"I see."

"It's impossible to get a good night's rest in this madhouse."

"Maybe it's the company you keep."

"No, I swear!" Tikhov took his handkerchief from his rear trouser pocket, wiped his face, and then, more carefully, his massive hands. "Nobody's been here. And I've been out only once since Tuesday—earlier this afternoon, as you ordered me by telephone."

"Then you haven't heard?"

"Heard what, Comrade Colonel?"

"Roosevelt's dead."

"Really now." Tikhov didn't seem particularly surprised.

"How have you been eating?"

Tikhov's pupils flitted toward the lower drawer of the writing desk. "I bought a few things. Crackers. Spam. I've gotten fond of Spam, you know. Some fruit. D'you want anything?"

The Chekist ambled over to the desk, but opened the upper drawer instead of the lower. As expected, within were several bottles of vodka. "Yes, I believe I will."

"I'll get you a glass." Tikhov ducked into the lavatory.

Humming some Mahler, the Chekist raised the blackout shade, revealing a view of the Coit Tower through the rusty screen. The minaretlike spire evoked memories of Azerbaijan, of his first meeting with the head of Cheka operations there, Lavrenty Beria, whose "proscription lists" had left that Soviet republic far less Moslem than it had been before. At least Tikhov had chosen this room with a little thought: the window looked down on the small hotel's entry. He closed the sash, and a distant sighing of automobile traffic, unnoticed until that instant, died away.

"Here, Comrade Colonel—" But Tikhov, offering a glass, froze as he caught the Chekist's expression.

"Where's the phone?" he asked, snatching the glass out of the man's grasp. "I thought you got a room with a telephone."

"Oh, yes." Tikhov scrambled over to the bed and reached under it for the phone. "I put it here while I slept—to be sure I wouldn't miss your calls."

"You must be a sound sleeper."

Tikhov grinned. "So it is with my family, peasants used to country quiet."

The Chekist poured himself three fingers of vodka. "Don't patronize me. Your father was a shopkeeper in Gorky."

Tikhov's grin proved strenuous and vanished. "That's quite true, Comrade Colonel, but my grandfathers on both sides were—"

The Chekist raised a hand for him to shut up. Snapping the coverlet over the sheets, he then eased down onto the bed. It was surprisingly comfortable. Kicking off his shoes, he fully reclined, but plumped the pillow under his head so he could still drink. His overcoat he kept on. Its ankle length had made him feel conspicuous, so he'd cut a half meter off it and done a passable job of sewing up a new hem, but he couldn't do away with the garment and still carry his trenching tool concealed. "What'd your songbirds report?"

Tikhov turned the desk chair around and sat. "Noon today, one of the detectives was asking questions at China Basin. He wanted a list of stevedores who'd worked with Laska."

"Which pier?"

"Forty-six."

The Chekist winced. "Bloody hell. Was it the one called Kost?"

"No, the Italian."

"Kost sent him then. He pulls the strings."

Tikhov eyed the Chekist's glass, but probably knew better than to beg a drink for himself. "They're getting overly curious about Laska, yes?"

The Chekist gave him a shrug even though he realized this to be true. Alarmingly true. Independently, two informants had now hinted at John Kost's dissatisfaction with the conclusion that Laska, as the finale to a drunken row, had shot his wife, Elliot, and then himself. And if Kost came to understand Laska, and the man's manic devotion, which nonetheless had failed him at the last instant, the entire operation was as good as down the sewer. How needlessly complicated this ever-widening circle of death— and all because the name *Lorelei* had appeared in a little notebook!

"Then, Comrade Colonel, what must we do about Kost?"

"You tell me."

"I don't understand," Tikhov said.

"Is he a capable sort?"

"I suppose. He's Russian, you know."

"So are you." The Chekist smiled at the man's truckling nod. "What really do you know about him?"

"Not much, I'm afraid."

"Oh?"

"On your orders I've been stuck inside this room."

"Quite right."

Tikhov appeared to relax a little. "I do know he's a class enemy to the unionists, a religious fanatic—"

Again, the Chekist held up a hand. "Please spare me. I want to know something of the *man*."

But before Tikhov could answer, the phone rang from beneath the bed, and the Chekist reached down for the handset. "Hello," he said in English.

"Is Paul there?" a female voice asked woodenly, as if the words had been memorized.

"Speaking."

She switched to Russian: "I haven't much time."

"Where are you?"

"A restaurant. Another Chinese restaurant."

"And your husband?"

"At our table. I can only be gone a few minutes."

"Understood, my dear. Did you see our fellow today?"

"Yes, he came to luncheon. But I couldn't get him away from the others. And there's something else . . ." Her voice came close to breaking. "Something that puzzles me. . . ."

"And what's that?" the Chekist asked consolingly, hoping to calm her.

"My husband's sending me away tomorrow morning. To the Yosemite with our fellow."

The Chekist said nothing for a moment; he too was puzzled.

"Why would he arrange such a thing?" she asked.

For her benefit, the Chekist chuckled. "Your dear husband has no idea what's going on and probably wants to put you on the shelf until he can at least find out why you're here. Don't let his uncertainty infect you, my dear. He's not one of us, not even remotely, so he's bound to behave as he sees fit."

"But what should I do? Pretend I'm ill?"

"No. . . ." He was beginning to see advantages in her going. "Enjoy the Yosemite. How will you travel—by automobile?"

"No, train. He handed me the tickets this afternoon." She paused, and the Chekist could hear Chinese voices mingled in

137

the background hiss of the connection. "Do you think this man and my husband are working together?"

He almost laughed. "I quite doubt it. Our fellow's rumored to be a second-generation White Guardist."

"It's no rumor. I met his father last night. Definitely White Army."

"Well done, my dear. What campaign?"

"The Siberian. So his son wouldn't be working with my husband, would he?"

The Chekist didn't reply. He was running a mental roster of Siberian-front White officers through his head, but could come up with no Kost. An equivalent of Constantine, it was a common Russian name, but surely he should be able to recall the names of Admiral Kolchak's entire staff. "Did you happen to learn the old boy's Christian name and patronymic?"

"Mikhail Mikhailovich."

He swung his legs over the side of the bed. "*Kost?*"

"No, Kostoff. Mikhail Kostoff."

"Vanka," the Chekist whispered with an odd smile that made Tikhov tip his head, questioningly.

"What was that?" she asked.

But again the Chekist's attention had turned inward. *Kostoff,* yet another variant of Constantine, but less American sounding than Kost to the ears of a young émigré hoping to blend in.

"Are you still there? I must get back to the table. Hello?"

"Yes," he said quietly, "I'm here."

"What should I do?"

"Why, go to the Yosemite. Befriend our fellow." He said this in such a way she would have no doubt what he meant. "Learn what you can. And when you come back, check our drop once again. I'll have another telephone number taped there for you. Good-bye for now."

"Wait, please—"

He knew precisely what she was going to ask and tried to forestall her tears, her pleas, by saying warmly, "You mustn't worry about her, my dear. We Russians have always found it easier to love a child than a grown-up. She's on a lake, you know.

When it warms up, they'll be taking her down to the shore for a wade now and again." He hung up without saying good-bye, then lay back down. After a while, he fixed his eyes on Tikhov's porridge-complected face. "Did you know John Kost is Colonel Mikhail Kostoff's son?"

"I think I've heard the name." The man rubbed his chin. "Yes, I suppose I did. Is it important?"

In a single fluid motion, the Chekist reached inside his overcoat pocket, came out with the trenching tool, and struck Tikhov on the left elbow with the flat of the blade, not hard enough to shatter bone, but with enough force to give him an electric jolt of pain that spun him off the chair onto the floor. He reared back again, but Tikhov groaned, "No, I beg you!"

The Chekist was amused by the irony of a man who could probably kill him with a single blow balled up on the floor, cowering.

Lowering the trenching tool, he lay back down. He would sleep the night through, the first adequate rest in over a week now. When had he taken the train to Leningrad? It seemed like months ago. He would need his strength. Tikhov and his fellow incompetents had made this a thousand times more difficult than it had to be. "Can you get an automobile somewhere?"

Cradling his elbow, the man nodded. "And ration stamps. They're as important as the car itself."

"I want you to drive to the Yosemite tonight. How far is it?"

"I don't know. Three hundred kilometers? Maybe more."

"Whatever—be waiting for them. Do you have papers for an American identity?"

"Of course." At last, reasonably confident he wasn't about to be executed, the man could stand it no longer: "May I have a drink please?"

"Why certainly, old fellow."

Reaching for the bottle, Tikhov eyed the trenching tool as if it were a cobra. "Am I going because the woman can't be trusted?"

"*Au contraire*, she'll do precisely as she's told. The insurance against her doing anything else has been deposited near Leningrad. But let's be clear about one thing—you're going because *you* cannot be trusted."

Tikhov's eyes were fixed on the Chekist's, but then after a moment he took another swig of vodka. "I understand what I'm to do."

"Good. Be sure of your chance." Agitation had begun to tighten the Chekist's face when he suddenly closed his eyes and pretended to sleep. But behind his eyelids Siberian snows were lowering onto the station at Irkutsk; they were dissolving the train chugging east toward Manchuria, burying the last natural feeling he could call his own. *Without liberty I cannot imagine anything truly human.* Who'd said this? The revolutionary journalist Herzen? No matter, perhaps—this was no season to be human.

"Comrade Colonel?" Tikhov asked hesitantly. "What should I do about the woman? I mean—if she gets in the way up there?"

John Kost found Aranov asleep at his desk, his arms criss-crossed over his typewriter, his face down on them. He hung his hat and coat on the oaken tree and went to his office. Flopping into his swivel chair, he sorted through his messages, which included a perfumed envelope that immediately annoyed him. From Lydia, of course. He balked on the verge of opening it, blaming himself for going to her Tuesday night and reawakening her expectations. Also on his desk was a manila envelope marked CONFIDENTIAL. It was from Robert Cade: the FBI's file on William and Emma Laska. As expected, it ended in 1935 with an agent's report that the couple had apparently renounced their Party memberships because of differences with Stalin's increasingly repressive policies. There was no evidence of any follow-up surveillance on the Laskas, which John Kost had expected, and he learned little from the file beyond what Uichi Nishio had already told him: Emma's maiden name, Goldblatt.

"Thanks for zip, Robert," he said, rising with a yawn and going back out into the bull pen.

Ragnetti's peg on the status board indicated that he'd not yet gone off duty and was still in the field, doing what John Kost himself had been doing since lunch at the Soviet consulate:

working his network of informants, the shabby little lives from which betrayals could be squeezed for the price of a drink, a few kind words. At four that afternoon, he had met with Ragnetti and Aranov at Jackson Park, just south of China Basin. Both men had been out of sorts. Neither had made any progress, and then the news of the president's death had done nothing to improve their moods. Ragnetti had turned positively rebellious toward Captain Coffey's approaching deadline: "How about I call in sick, then keep working these cases on the sly, John?"

"They'll only send me to your mother's house to deliver you to the Chinese delegation."

Aranov had seemed close to being in shock. "FDR," he'd kept saying, as if the fact wouldn't quite register.

Someone's clearing his throat now drew John Kost's attention to the door. It was Patrick Coffey, looking over the tops of his bifocals. "Got a minute, John?"

"Sure."

Coffey led him down the corridor to his office, one of the few with a panorama of the bay. He closed the outer door and then the one to his private lavatory. "A nip of the creature?"

"Please." It gratified John Kost to see the coroner's reports spread over the desk; Coffey was putting in extra hours too.

Taking a bottle of Irish and two shot glasses from his file cabinet, the captain said, "We had another pair tonight."

"Two of our people!"

"No, no—sorry to rattle you. Sweet Jesus, no." Coffey poured for both of them, then hoisted his glass with a palsied hand. "To Franklin Roosevelt, God rest his weary soul."

"God rest him." The whiskey hit John Kost's already raw stomach like carbolic.

"No, Johnny, a couple pachucos knifed each other down in Castro District. Died in each other's arms. Open-and-shut. I let Hurley and Mulrenan handle it. You and your boys already have enough to do."

"Thanks," John Kost said.

The captain's eyes clouded as they passed over the jumble of reports on his desk. "Look at this fucking mess. How you doing on your own?"

John Kost knew better than to tell him too much too soon. "Plodding along."

Coffey nodded. "And how's things going with the Russians?"

"All right—other than the vice-consul's insane idea that I take his wife to Yosemite."

"I know. He already phoned the old man. . . ." Coffey refilled their glasses.

"And what'd the chief say to Martov?"

"He told him you'd go."

"What!"

"Hey, we had to use a lot of grease to get your party into the Ahwanhee Hotel. Did you know that joint is booked two years in advance?"

"Dammit!" John Kost rocketed to his feet, spilling most of his whiskey across the carpet. "Where's this pressure coming from!"

"Easy, Johnny."

"I'm trying to find out who killed two cops! Do you hear me, Pat!"

"Sit down—you're wasting good booze!"

Breathing heavily, struggling to get a hold on himself, John Kost pressed his fingers to his brow and began rubbing the icy ache there. Gradually, he began to feel ashamed of himself, of his presumptuous anger. Coffey wanted these cases closed as much as he did. "I'm bushed, Pat. My men are too." He sank back into the chair.

Smiling again, Coffey said, "You haven't blown like that in a long time. Last time you did it you tossed your badge in my coffee cup. Gonna do that now?"

"No, I'm afraid you'll keep it."

The captain lowered his voice. "The pressure's coming from all sides to brownnose the Russians. But mostly from the State and War departments. This is hush-hush, but when I say departments, I mean the secretaries are personally leaning on the old man—Stettinius and Stimson."

"Why does this mean so much to them?"

"Japan."

"You've lost me."

"Next year, maybe sooner, we're gonna invade Japan. I'm only repeating what I've heard on the links at the Presidio from the military boys, but this invasion—in terms of casualties and sheer logistical effort—will be like starting the war all over again from day one. Christ, the Japs got an entire army of two million in north China that's never been in the fray. So when Hitler gets licked, which is any day now, Roosevelt wants. . . ." He caught himself. "Truman will want Russian manpower turned against the Japs. Our government—and I mean its highest levels, Johnny—wants SFPD to do all it can to jolly the Reds. Our department's relations with these sneaky bastards haven't always been the best—you know that. But Martov, who we guess is the real power here, likes you. So do you think the old man's going to let me reassign the first copper these Bolsheviks haven't turned their noses up at?"

Coming to his feet again, John Kost sighed. He was done with swimming against the tide, but he took one last shot: "What patsies."

"Who?"

"Our government. Do they honestly believe Uncle Iosif will enter the Pacific war for our sake? If he comes in at all, it'll be to grab as much as he can before Japan hits the canvas." John Kost turned at the door. "While I'm showing Madame Martova the sights, will you do a favor for me?"

"Name it, Johnny."

"I asked the FBI for some fingerprint latents. If they don't arrive by tomorrow afternoon, can the chief use some of that grease of his on the Bureau?"

"I'll see what he can do."

"Thanks."

John Kost returned to the bull pen intending only to fetch his hat and coat before heading home. But then he made the mistake of sitting for a moment's rest in Ragnetti's chair, at which point plodding down to the basement garage and then driving more than twenty blocks to his Marina District apartment seemed to be too much to ask of his body. Idly, he switched on the sergeant's table radio. Beethoven's Sonata Number 8 in C-Minor, Opus 13.

"Nice," Aranov murmured, still collapsed over his typewriter. But when John Kost asked him if he had called Sylvia to let her know he'd be late, he didn't answer. And only moments later he gave out with a soft nasal snore.

"Indeed, Nathan."

He took Lydia's envelope from his shirt pocket and finally opened it: *My darling, I'm giving an intimate dinner party next Tuesday and you absolutely must attend, or I'm completely ruined in this city. I'll expect you early at 6:00 to help me with the cocktails. All my love, L.D.*

"Damn, damn, damn. . . ." He then rested his eyes behind his hand.

He realized that he'd drifted off only when Ragnetti crept in sometime before dawn and taking their coats off the tree, gently covered both Nathan and him.

14

"Martov was curious about something." Elena Martova had yet to refer to her husband as Pyotr Aleksandrovich, let alone a nickname as affectionate as Petrusha.

"And what's that?"

"Are you married?"

John Kost looked out the lounge car window. Raindrops were stippling the glass. Ahead, as the train began to round a curve, he could see the locomotive broadside, its stack disgorging oily smoke that mingled at once with the low clouds.

She locked her fingers around her vodka glass. "If you are, then we've been remiss for not inviting Madame Kosta to join us on at least one of our outings."

"I'm a widower," he said at last.

"Oh, I'm terribly sorry for asking."

"Don't be."

"Was she Russian?"

"Russian-American, yes."

He thought that was the end of it, but then she asked, "Was this recent?"

"No, eight years ago."

"So young."

"Nineteen. Anything else?"

She covered her mouth with a hand in a gesture of apology, and he almost regretted having snapped at her. "I'm being rude, Ivan Mikhailovich. I'm so sorry. I meant only to say that it must've been sudden."

"Yes." He didn't like the moisture that had just welled up in her eyes, but then realized that his irritation was with himself: he wanted very much to tell her about his wife. He attempted a smile, but knew at once that it was needlessly ironic. "I don't care much for suddenness."

"Neither do I. If I may ask, how . . .?"

"Childbirth."

"And the baby?"

"Stillborn." Then he added, "A girl."

"I'll pray for your wife tonight, Ivan Mikhailovich. Your little daughter too."

He looked directly at her as he said, "She wasn't my child."

A lurch of the car roused Ruml, who sat upright and ran his hands over his gaunt face. He gaped around at the other tables, which were taken mostly by military officers and their women, before smiling foolishly at John Kost. "Trains make me sleepy." Elena had been encouraging him to drink heavily ever since they'd switched trains at Modesto.

The steward, wearing a black armband for FDR, announced that the end of the line was ten minutes ahead and the bar was closing. Ruml offered to help Elena to her feet, but then had to grasp the table's edge to get out of his chair. John Kost took her arm and walked with her back to their coach car, where the other passengers were already taking their luggage down from the overhead storage.

Reaching up for her suitcase, he felt his shoulder holster chafe against his underarm. He disliked carrying a revolver, partly because of the discomfort and partly because it left a tumorous-looking bulge in the cut of his jacket. Whenever he could, he tossed it under his car seat or left it in his desk. Several times he had raced to a call only to realize afterward that his handgun was

146

still back at the Hall of Justice in a nest of paper clips. Ragnetti gave him the devil for it, but he argued that he didn't want to visualize the world through the sights of a revolver. Vincent had only grunted.

They detrained onto a rain-splattered platform. John Kost and Ruml each used the hand not gripping luggage to help her make a dash for the overhang of the station roof. When she faltered on her bad ankle, they lifted her completely off the planking, and she laughed. "Smell that!" she cried, her Russian turning the heads of the other passengers—woodsmoke was leaking from the stovepipe of the stationmaster's house on the slope above them, and the dank air was pressing the balsamic pall down onto the platform.

The hotel bus awaited them on the far side of the station.

"Oh, how charming!" She climbed aboard while the men handed the luggage to the driver. Hers was such a desperate happiness John Kost knew it wouldn't last long. To him the bus looked rattly and uncomfortable, adding to his ill humor, but they'd not gone more than a mile into the darkly wooded valley when he said without glancing at her, "Please do pray for my wife's daughter, Elena Valentinovna."

At the close of the American national anthem the audience remained standing for the *marcia funebre* of Beethoven's *Eroica*. Listening intently, for he genuinely loved the adagio second movement of the symphony, Pyotr Martov shut his eyes, inadvertently triggering the sense he'd been suffering from all day: that he had stumbled into a dark room filled with low growling and didn't know whether to move or stand still. His sensibilities were so caught up by this feeling he didn't realize that the movement had ended until he heard the rustle of the other mourners sitting. Unbuttoning his black coat and easing down into his aisle seat, he then scanned his program: an afternoon of pedestrian classics to honor the late president, who no doubt had had rather pedestrian tastes. But Martov was interested in hearing the piano soloist once again. He'd been treated to a performance by Artur

Rubinstein years before in Warsaw and had found him refreshingly unrestrained for a Jew.

"Excuse me, sir." It was the usher, bending over him. "Are you Vice-consul Martov?"

"I am."

"A gentleman wishes to see you in the foyer."

"Thank you."

The gentleman would be his secretary, Grigor Pervukhin.

Only this morning, at their first breakfast together without Elena present, had Martov felt safe enough to divulge his growing worries to the young man. But then, on the brink of telling all, Martov shrank back into doubt. What if Grisha were on Beria's payroll as well as the foreign ministry's? In that case, Martov would be playing directly into the hands of the secret police if he showed the slightest interest in what obviously was a Mobile Group operation under way here. "Grisha," he finally said between small bites of black bread. "I've been hearing some rather disturbing things about Molotov's wife."

"From whom?"

"Oh, this person and that." Paulina Molotova, a Jewess, was known for her outspokenness, and by her mention Martov hoped to gain some idea of how Pervukhin felt about their mutual superior.

"Beria again."

"What's that?"

"Beria's up to his old mischief," Pervukhin said, but not before checking over his shoulder. This expression of contempt for the secret police chief made Martov feel free to share—in a whisper—his anxieties of the past week. Why was Elena here? Grisha responded to the question with a sullen shrug. Where were Tikhov and Yaroshenko? And why had Pugachev, a Balkans expert known to Martov, failed to register at the St. Francis Hotel? "I must do something to keep us out of harm's way, my dear Grisha. But what? What can I do if I know nothing?"

At this point Pervukhin set down his tea glass and admitted that he'd heard from Tikhov.

"When?"

"Tuesday evening. Late. He ordered me to drop off one of our American wire recorders at a phone booth on Market Street."

"Did you see who picked it up?"

"No, Tikhov insisted that I drive away from the booth at once." And then, looking boyishly miserable, Pervukhin confessed to running other errands in the past for the resident without the vice-consul's knowledge. "I felt I had no choice, Pyotr Aleksandrovich."

After a moment Martov couldn't help but to smile at him. "You didn't. But from now on we must tell each other everything, all right?"

"Yes, everything," Pervukhin echoed. Then he asked hesitantly, but asked nonetheless, "Are you sure you didn't ask for your wife to come here?"

"What?" Martov laughed at his anguish. "If so, why did I spend an hour this morning tearing through everything she didn't take to the Yosemite with her? Grisha, my dear Grisha—are you so easily touched to the quick?"

"Yes," he had said, "I am, Petrusha."

And now Pervukhin awaited him across the foyer of the Civic Auditorium. But before Martov could make his way to him, the American press corps, pouncing on any and all foreign officials with tasteless questions about FDR's passing, closed around him. Looking appropriately somber and deciding to play it safe, he repeated only what Molotov had already given *Pravda*, even though it translated awkwardly: "It is our desire that American and Soviet friendship continue to flower as a genuinely majestic monument to the great president Roosevelt, who departed so untimely to his grave. The Soviet people and the Red Army will never forget the help that the United States, under Roosevelt's leadership, rendered our country in its heroic struggle against the Hitlerite enemy. Now if you will excuse me, gentlemen. . . ." He bowed his head and ignoring the parting questions slung at his back, crossed the foyer to his secretary. "Outside, Grisha," he said, although it was raining.

Pervukhin unfurled his umbrella over their heads. "I learned something."

"Good." Martov glanced back: the more determined newsmen had followed them as far as the awning over the main entrance. "Let's put a block or two behind us before we talk."

"Very well."

Pervukhin had already told him that five weeks before, on Tikhov's instructions, he'd delivered a sealed envelope to a stevedore on Pier 46. Martov had immediately asked if this had been William Laska, but Pervukhin said no, it had been another man. This afternoon he had gone back to that pier to question the same fellow.

"Go ahead," Martov finally said when they'd reached Market Street and its murmurous traffic.

"Tikhov was there yesterday, asking his own questions." Pervukhin dabbed the rain off his face with his sleeve. "And so was one of Ivan Kostoff's men from the Homicide directorate."

"At the same time as Tikhov?" Martov asked, suddenly fearful of something he'd never imagined—that the PD inspector had ties to Beria. If so, he was doubly glad he'd sent Elena and him to the Sierra until he could make sense of the situation.

But Pervukhin quickly put this groundless fear to rest: "No, the policeman came much earlier."

"Did you ask your stevedore if Tikhov had another Russian with him?"

"I did—but no, he came to the pier alone."

"Damn," Martov said. "Where's Pugachev? And what's he up to?"

"I dropped by the St. Francis again, as you asked." Pervukhin shook his head. "No one's seen him since the ride from Hamilton Field."

"Did you get a description of him?"

"Yes, he's quite tall with fair hair and—"

"My God!" Martov cried, in his distress giving in to old habits. "Pugachev's a midge of a fellow. The only short Cossack I know. And his hair's black!"

Ruml planted his elbows on the table and leaned forward as if trying to bring the inspector's face into focus. That John Kost was backlit by an orange glow from the fireplace seemed to be frustrating his efforts. "Ivan Mikhailovich," he said thickly, "this is very, very good potato soup." John Kost at first suspected that Ruml was making a stab at a joke, for set before him was a frosted glass containing a triple vodka neat, not a bowl of soup; but then as the man fumbled for the salt shaker and liberally sprinkled his drink, he realized that Ruml's befuddled mind had leaped ahead to dinner, on which they were waiting, and it was time to put him to bed.

"Excuse us," he said to Elena, rising.

"Of course. Have a pleasant rest, Viktor Fyodorovich," she said.

"It will be a pleasure . . . in a place that has such very good potato soup." Staggering to his feet with John Kost's help, he upset his chair behind him. It banged against the floor, the racket drawing frowns from the other guests. Moments after the sound had echoed up into the high ceiling, Ruml reeled and reached over for it, nearly pitching himself onto the floor and dragging John Kost with him.

"Easy, old fellow."

"Is it broken?"

"I don't think so."

"If it's broken, I can fix it with some glue and a bit of wire. I'm quite good at fixing chairs, you know."

John Kost felt something being pressed into the ticket pocket of his jacket—Elena was slipping him a key. "Would you please bring down my overcoat?" she asked. "And yours as well if you want to take a walk with me. I want a clear head before I eat."

"As you wish." He wondered if their supper reservation could be reshuffled anytime before midnight, and a glance out the window onto the sleet-glistered meadow convinced him that even worse weather would come with nightfall. But he had vowed to himself not to argue with her; it would only sharpen his resentment at having been ordered to accompany her in the first place. The other patrons were now glaring at Ruml and him. He turned the man toward the stairs, supporting him under the arms.

"Are you sure the chair's all right?"

"Yes, yes—it's fine." He put Ruml's hand on the banister as if for a blind man.

"I like making chairs too. Much more than what I do."

"What d'you do, Viktor Fyodorovich?"

A sly smile broke through his intoxication. "Why, I drive, of course, Ivan Ivanovich. . . ." Wrong patronymic, but no matter when weighed against more than a quart of vodka since breakfast. "I drive the vice-consul's big Cadillac. But driving's not as good as making chairs and things."

John Kost rested on the landing for a few seconds, dizzy from the exertion and his own load of vodka. Ruml wasn't a large man, but his drunken weight was as dead as clay. "Why not?"

"Well, when you make a chair, you have a *chair* when you're done, yes? But when you make a trip, what do you have at its end? Truly, what do you have?"

"A memory?"

"Ekh . . ." Ruml let go a sour outbreath. "Try sitting on a memory, Ivan Ivanovich."

"Where's your key?" John Kost asked, leaning the man against his door as if he were a cello.

"Somewhere here. . . ." Ruml began frisking himself. "Where's the bloody . . . ?"

John Kost found it in one of the man's trouser pockets, underneath a used handkerchief. Turning the lock with one hand, he clutched Ruml by the collar with the other so he wouldn't tumble inside the room when the latch gave.

The door glided open, and a darkened room awaited them.

John Kost hesitated for some reason, perhaps because of the dusky stillness beyond the entryway, but then said, "Here we go, Viktor Fyodorovich. Short steps to the bed now. But let me get the light first." During all this clumsy waltzing with Ruml, he was able to confirm something he'd suspected since meeting him: the man was packing a handgun in a shoulder holster much like his own. At last he let go of him, and Ruml collapsed onto the mattress with such force he thought for an instant the bed frame had been cracked. He pulled off Ruml's shoes, then rolled him on his side so he wouldn't aspirate if he vomited.

"Viktor Fyodorovich?"

No answer.

The last thing John Kost wanted to deal with tonight was an armed drunk, but when he reached inside Ruml's coat for the automatic pistol there, a hand shot up and pinioned his wrist.

"Leave it," Ruml said, his eyes still shut.

"Let go of me," John Kost said firmly enough to make Ruml part his groggy eyelids and relax his grasp slightly.

"But you too have a gun—yes, Ivan Mikhailovich?"

"Yes."

"Then leave mine alone. That way we stay equals. Friends."

John Kost considered this for a moment. "What if I put them both in the hotel safe?"

"What of it?"

"Why, we'd still be equals and friends. Otherwise the bellboy or anybody could steal yours while you sleep."

Ruml's hand slowly fell away. "The safe, you say?"

"Yes, both weapons—until we check out."

"I don't know. Will it be all right in there?"

"Absolutely."

"And you promise no treachery?"

"On my honor as a Russian, Viktor Fyodorovich."

"But it's also said you have Gypsy blood."

"On my honor as a Gypsy then."

The man gave a raspy chuckle. "Well . . . do as you think best. You're probably right about its being stolen. But please don't deceive me. I've started to like you, so don't deceive me. The safe, then?"

"Yes."

"The altitude makes me too sleepy for my own good."

John Kost removed the pistol and making sure the corridor was empty, examined it on the way to Elena's room. The same model of Mauser Laska had used. An increasingly common war souvenir in the U.S., so why not in the Soviet Union as well?

He took the garde-corps overcoat from the closet in her room, then noticed her suitcase. It lay open and unpacked on the bed, as she'd insisted on having cocktails as soon as they'd checked in. He went to it, but refused to let his hands linger over the apparel they burrowed past. They seemed too delicate to be Russian made but so strongly suggested her presence he kept glancing at the door as if she might come through it at any instant. Then, in one of the elastic-topped pouches, he found her own insurance against deceit, a coal-blue Tokarev with a spare eight-round clip. Strangely, finding the pistol set his mind more at rest. Now it would be easier to deal objectively with her if the need arose. She wasn't helpless, after all.

He slipped Ruml's Mauser and her Tokarev into the flap pockets of his dinner jacket, then turned for his room and his own overcoat. He also kept Ruml's room key so he might check on him later.

The waiter was demanding something, and panic was blotting out what little English she understood. Terrified by his stern expression, she was looking for the first pretext that would allow her to rise from the table and put the curious gazes of the other patrons to her back. The thought of saying in Russian or French that she didn't understand had occurred to her but been dismissed; she was afraid that this would only draw even more attention to herself. Then, thankfully, Ivan Kostoff returned to the table, not by way of the stairs he'd so laboriously climbed with Ruml, but from the direction of the front desk. He spoke to the waiter, who nodded but continued to wait.

"What does he want?" she asked.

"To know if we need another round. I said fine. Is that all right?"

"Yes—no." She felt foolish now, but the smile she then feigned was so tremulous she gave up on it. She had to be away from this bright room, these Americans. "I mean, I'd like to take a walk. . . ." She could tell that he'd been hoping that she had forgotten this notion, but her need for cold air was even more urgent than before. "Does that present a problem, Ivan Mikhailovich?"

"That'll depend on our supper reservation." He asked the waiter, who looked utterly disconsolate until Ivan unobtrusively passed him some money, then the man gabbled off something with a smile before withdrawing.

"What'd he say?"

"We can eat at eight," the inspector said, rising to help her into her overcoat, "but he thinks all the beef dishes will be gone by then."

"It's Lent. What would that matter to us?"

"Ah, yes—Lent." He led her through the lobby and outside onto the covered porch. The rain had decidedly turned to sleet, but he hesitated only a moment before stepping out into the stinging fall. She caught up with him, and side by side they hurried for the protection of some cedars, black and pyramidal against the twilight. But their dense boughs fended off the sleet, and the path he found for them wasn't muddy yet.

"Poor Ruml's out for the night," he said.

"I can't stand him."

"Is that why you spent the day getting him drunk?"

"Yes, the sooner he passes out, the sooner I'm rid of him. Oh, look here—what fine oaks! This is like Ielagin Island in winter, don't you think?"

He didn't answer.

"But surely you must've gone to Petersburg. Your father was at court."

"Yes, my father."

His face so quickly darkened she regretted whatever she'd said to bring this on. "Well, there are some lovely islands north of the city: Ielagin, Kretovsky, Petrovsky—"

"I put Ruml's pistol in the hotel safe," he interrupted, the words running away from his mouth in vapor. It was getting colder, and the dusk was going fast.

"Good."

"Yours as well."

His gaze stayed out among the oaks. The trunks of the older ones had been deformed by burls that were taking on human form in the fading light. "And what about your gun, Ivan Mikhailovich?"

"In the safe too. We're quite harmless to one another now." They had come to a river, its clear waters rippling over a bed of round stones. The sleet had given way to snow, a wet and clinging snow that half-veiled the cliffs of the valley's south wall. Tucked against the foot of this precipice were a few late snowdrifts, sprinkled with pine needles.

"Why did you go through my things?" she asked.

"It was necessary."

"Oh?"

"I was afraid Ruml might help himself to your pistol if he awakes and finds his gone."

"What made you think I had one?"

He didn't answer.

"It doesn't matter," she said. "I didn't want to bring the thing, but Martov insisted."

"Did he expect trouble?"

"Always—and then does nothing if it comes."

He started to ask something when a crackling of dead branches spun them both around. "What is it?" she whispered.

He said, "Deer," in the same instant a doe pranced out of a willow thicket and then upstream along the bank.

"Where's her male?"

"The bucks keep their own company until the rutting season."

"I see."

They walked on. She wiped the melted snowdrops off her cheeks. It was cold enough for her gloves, but she only faintly missed them. Then, just as she was beginning to calm down, she felt herself sinking into the sense of helplessness that had made her behave so badly with the priest and this man two nights before. But how could she ask Kostoff to help her when she saw so clearly how it would destroy him? Was it comfort enough to imagine that, if she asked, he might indeed take up her predicament as his own? It was a delicious fantasy, but had already begun to dim when he said, "You're shivering. Let's go back."

"No." She had made up her mind to stay outdoors until she had a grip on herself. The cold was familiar. It somehow made her feel less frightened. "Do you have any brothers or sisters? Your father seems a man who'd want to surround himself with children."

"Really?" He looked surprised.

"Yes. You as well, Ivan Mikhailovich."

Ahead, across a winter-brown meadow, the path zigzagged up onto a ridge of boulders. Something about these heights put her off, but neither did she want to go back to the hotel.

"I had an older half brother," he said.

"Had?"

"Killed at Tannenberg."

Taking his arm, she told herself to stop examining him for qualities that would make a good ally. That's what her desperation was making her do: grovel for an ally. Wasn't God enough? "I'm sorry to keep bringing up such painful things."

"I never knew him."

"Of course, you were so very young."

"No, not that." He paused and glanced at her with an unconvincing smile. "My father and mother never married, Elena Valentinovna."

"I'm sorry," she said, ashamed of herself again.

But all at once he seemed to need to talk, to purge himself of what her indelicate questions had unleashed. "I didn't even know about my brother until we left China. The American immigration official in Tientsin asked for my patronymic, and somehow mention of my brother came up. Mikhail Mikhailovich were his forenames. Just like my father's. . . ." They had started up into the lichened boulders, but his eyes had turned inward. "You see, like most bastards, I was christened with my maternal grandfather's name. As luck would have it, his name was also Mikhail."

They halted atop the ridge, taking shelter in the lee of a boulder. She continued to grasp his arm. "But your father must love you a great deal—he brought you out of Russia with him."

"You should see the ridiculous things people carry out of their burning houses."

157

"Forgive me, Ivan Mikhailovich, you don't see this clearly—"

But suddenly he broke free of her grasp and covered her mouth with his hand. He'd obviously heard something, and she now caught the same sound in echo. Metal acting against metal.

She tried to ask him what it was, but he shook his head for her to keep quiet.

Something thudded into a tree above them, closely followed by another object ringing against the stone close to his face. He flinched, then threw her to the ground and fell across her body.

"Someone's shooting at us," he whispered, "shooting with a silenced gun. Stay down!"

15

Isn't this great?" Aranov asked, watching Ragnetti hunt-and-peck his way through a supplemental report. The sergeant's eyes were on the page and he didn't ask what Aranov was talking about. Behind him, rain was sheeting down the window glass, dissolving the streaks of pigeon guano. Once again, Aranov checked the date and time stamped on the envelope, then said, "The blood alcohol return from the lab's been sitting in John's basket for two goddamn days."

Ragnetti finally looked up. "What're you doing going through his traffic?"

"He told me to—"

"*What?*"

"—just until he gets back from Yosemite."

"Oh." Ragnetti's face was ashen and his lips a faint blue, signals that he was run-down. But suddenly his neck showed heat. Aranov knew what was wrong at once, having anticipated it. The scepter of police rank was paperwork, and here John Kost was entrusting it to the low man on the totem pole. Not that Ragnetti cared for pencil-pushing.

"John told me he wanted you free to zero in on the fieldwork," he fibbed, hoping Ragnetti would be mollified.

He seemed to be, insofar as he went back to typing.

Aranov ran his thumb under the seal of the lab envelope, getting a paper cut that made him growl. Everything he came into contact with seemed either to slice, bite, or burn him. He could feel a blister on the roof of his mouth with his tongue, a souvenir from a gulp of scalding coffee. And dozing at his desk last night had left him with a stiff neck. Sucking on his thumb, he read the laboratory analysis of William Laska's blood alcohol level, the sample drawn from him as soon as he'd arrived at the hospital after shooting his wife and Elliot in what was supposed to have been a drunken rage. "Jesus Christ, Vince. . . ."

"What?"

"Laska was good only for a point oh five percent." Scarcely enough for a mild glow, and only halfway to the minimum legal standard for intoxication, .10 percent. At any hour of the day or night most of the plainclothesmen on this floor would have at least .05 in their veins, Aranov mused.

"You sure?"

He handed him the half sheet of onionskin.

"Shit," Ragnetti said after a few seconds, "this crazy fuck did it sober."

"And I don't think he was crazy either."

"Then what's that leave us?"

"Discipline. He was given his part to do and he did it."

"You mean like he was on a team or something?"

"That's my hunch," Aranov said, dialing a number in Daly City John Kost had scribbled down for him before departing for Yosemite. "Somebody was in the place with Laska to make sure he didn't fuck up under pressure. Then that guy, or maybe somebody completely different—I'm not sure—he chucked old Will out the hospital window when it looked like he might recover enough to tell us exactly what happened that night—"

The handset in Daly City was picked up on the third ring. "Hello?"

"Robert Cade?"

160

"Speaking."

There was dinner table chitchat in the background, a quiet clatter of forks and dishes, but the causticity in the FBI agent's voice kept him from apologizing for the interruption. "Nate Aranov from John Kost's office."

"Oh, yeah."

"John asked me to phone you this evening if we hadn't received the materials he requested."

"In the morning, for crapsake," Cade said. "I got my own clearances to take care of. Washington clearances."

"But you do have latents on these people?"

Cade didn't reply.

"Then may I show up at your office at nine?"

"Show up when you please—I got no guarantee I'll have the clearances anytime before quitting time, if even then."

"I see . . . I see. . . ." John Kost had given him permission to rattle Cade's cage a bit if no latent fingerprints had arrived by five. It was now pushing six—and no latents. "Well," Aranov went on, sounding disappointed but not surprised, "I see I'm not getting anywhere. Fine."

"What d'you mean by that?"

"It's obvious you folks prefer dealing with somebody who has more clout than an assistant inspector."

"Listen, Aranov—let's quit being cutesy with each other, okay?"

"What d'you mean by that?" he said coolly, echoing Cade.

"You guys are working a Soviet angle on these cases, right?"

No one could accuse Robert Cade of being stupid. Boorish and sarcastic, yes. But not stupid. "What makes you think that?"

"Oh, I guess we're not through with being cutesy." Cade fell silent, and Aranov kept mum too, unsure how much John Kost wanted revealed at this point, even to the FBI. Especially to the FBI. "Tell you what, Aranov, to prove to you I'm not dragging my feet, why don't you drive down to my place right now . . . ?" He gave the address in Daly City. "As soon as I'm done eating, I'm shutting myself up inside my study with a Tom Collins and the photos I took of the Rooskie delegation arriving at Hamilton Field. We can go through them together and try to come up with a roster of their players. It's a start, right? Then maybe we can begin pulling together on this thing, instead of apart like we've been doing. What d'you say?"

Aranov hesitated, wondering if Cade intended to play him for a patsy, suck him dry for information and give nothing substantive in return. It was the FBI's forte. He was worried that the older and more powerful man would buffalo him into giving the Bureau the reins to the cases, and John Kost would return only to find Cade snug and warm in the middle of what was rightly the PD 's investigation, even if foreign nationals might be involved. Then Aranov's uncertain eyes lit on Ragnetti. "All right, but I'd like to bring my partner."

"Sure, whatever. See you guys in a half hour."

Cade hung up, and Aranov looked across cluttered tops of their adjoining desks to the sergeant. "How about going down to Daly City with me?"

Ragnetti rubbed his nose with a knuckle, then went on pecking.

"Cade has some photo work that might interest us, Vince."

Ragnetti ripped the page off the platen, balled it up, and bounced it off Aranov's chest. "Can't you do anything on your fucking own?"

He reminded himself that the man was overworked and in need of sleep, but still the remark stung. Before Ragnetti could notice the sudden moisture in his eyes, he got his hat and coat and hurried from the bull pen.

Fuck Vincent Ragnetti.

His first thought, as he sprawled over Elena Martova with snowflakes crashing wetly against his neck, was that she'd lured him outside the hotel to die. But her grip on his shirtfront was so wrenching he realized that she herself expected to die. Droplets of blood were seeping from a scrape on her chin.

He lifted his chest off her back, hovered above her on his palms. His arms began to tremble.

The dusk was only minutes from being gone. But those

minutes would flow like molasses, and the man out there would have more than enough light to do what he had to do. He was probably squatting along the forest's dripping edge, berating himself for having let go with two rounds from such distance, for having expected a cheap victory. A handgun, particularly one fitted with what was most likely a Maxim sound suppressor, was a belly-gun. And now he would have to gather his courage and close in for the kill against alerted—and possibly armed—prey.

He felt her stir beneath him, and when he glanced down, she was trying to hand him a chunk of granite. She wanted him to have it to throw at the man when he finally came at them. He found her offering so childlike he half-smiled and whispered, "I don't want him to think we're that desperate."

"Are we?"

He shrugged with the same hint of a smile, and the stone fell from her cricked fingers. She then wrapped her arms around him, but he was afraid he wouldn't be able to move if he needed to. Gently, he shook off her clutch.

"Don't kill him," she said, "please don't kill him."

"Wait here."

"Why?"

"Just do it. No matter how close he gets, stay in this spot. No matter what you hear, stay—unless it's my voice telling you to run. Do you understand?"

She nodded.

He brushed her cheek with his hand, then crawled away, keeping to the flooded hollows among the boulders. He headed downriver. He planned to outflank the man, capture him if possible, kill him if it came to that. Had she begged him not to kill him because she was a believer? He wanted to think so, but wasn't convinced. And this doubt made him wonder if she knew who was out there. Of course, his second suspicion when the bullets had first flown around them was that it was Ruml risen from his stupor, triggering a silencer-fitted pistol he'd squirreled away someplace. But given how much the man had drunk since midmorning, how severely his reactions had been dulled and his vision multiplied, that he was their assailant was more wishful thinking than anything else.

No, he'd bet that Martov's driver was still passed out in bed. This was someone else, someone deadly sober.

He inched along on his elbows and knees, gritting his teeth at the clatter from the broken granite he disturbed. The snow was turning to sleet again, drenching his head and his trouser legs. But at least these pellets, bouncing off the boulders around him, were making a soft, covering sound as they raked the valley.

By now the man would be advancing on where he'd seen the couple fall. He would be nearing Elena with his pistol held before him.

To prevent this, John Kost rose to a crouch and began trotting noisily toward the closest stand of cedars. A bullet spun out of the sleet with a sound like tearing fabric. Then another popped against stone inches above his head, striking at such a flat trajectory it failed to ricochet.

He dropped.

The man was within a few yards of him, breathing hard. But he was being drawn away from Elena. That is what counted, and John Kost decided to cinch it. He let go with a grunt like a man who's been hit and is trying to hold back the scream boiling up his throat.

Pressing his hands against the ground, he felt vibrations. The man was running headlong his way, probably having made up his mind from the lack of answering gunfire that John Kost was unarmed.

There was no chance now of outflanking him.

The Merced River. He would lead him toward the river. At bankside he would make his stand wherever the cataracts were loudest. Somewhere along the Merced he might be able to even the odds. He would only have one chance.

Scrambling on all fours, he didn't stop moving until he reached a fallen log. He kept expecting more bullets. But none came, and this gave him hope that the man had only a single clip of ammunition. Topping the ridge on his belly, he slid down the far side to the edge of the plunging current. The waters looked

164

dark and heavy now, another sign nightfall was imminent. If only he could elude the man until then. Elena and he might live if the darkness came as swiftly as it had in Siberia, a wash of black velveteen that fell over the twilight just when it seemed eternal.

He came into willows, tripping over roots as he hurried, realizing that the noise from his thrashing would never let him set up his own ambush.

Shedding his overcoat and dropping it to bob away on the riffles, he then began wading downstream along the shallows, ever farther from Elena. The snow-fed waters burned around his lower legs, and he kept turning his ankles on the slick, round stones that cobbled the riverbed.

After a hundred feet or so, alders jutted out of the bank, splayed bonily against the sky, the iron-gray trunks so dense he knew at once he would find no better place. And he could hear the man following, wheezing, his shoes scuffling over rocks.

He reached down, grabbed some pebbles, and one after the other, plunked them into the shallows below. Then, squeezing his hand inside the ticket pocket of his dinner jacket, he squatted behind the stoutest alder in the stand and waited.

A bird sang so unexpectedly, so shrilly, he believed for the first time that he was going to die. Pollutions of self-doubt began to muddle his thinking, made him want to bolt whatever the consequences.

Fortunately, the man was not long in coming.

Motionless, John Kost watched his approach through the willows: lumbering, fending back the budding switches with his forearms. Then he slowed even more to sidestep and duck and jostle his way through the first alders along his path.

Even before John Kost glimpsed it through the latticework of branches, he had known it would be a Slavic face, broad at the cheekbones with an oriental cant to the eyes. He rose and said amiably in Russian, "Good evening."

The man started, but then slowly grinned when he saw no gun trained on him.

"Take your hand out of your coat," he said in Russian-accented English, leveling his silenced pistol on the sliver of John Kost's face showing around the tree.

"As you say. . . ." But from his jacket ticket pocket John Kost brought out a single-shot derringer, a stubby pearl-handled job Ragnetti had taken off a whore and then given to his forgetful inspector with orders to carry it at all times. He fired. The .22-caliber report was nothing, a crack that was swallowed by the river sounds, and the bluish muzzle flash was even less intimidating. But the man's left shoulder jerked as if a puppeteer had tugged a string fastened there, and his gun hand flew to the wound to stem the flow of blood.

"I was never much of a shot," John Kost said, angry with himself for missing the man's heart so widely, even though it was a weapon meant for ranges no wider than a bed. For some reason he was glad he hadn't killed him, but then a surge of bile-tainted fear made this reason seem superfluous.

"Damn you!" the man cried, discharging his pistol three times. But the bullets thwacked harmlessly into the tree.

Before the man could think to work around the alder, John Kost flew at him, seized him by the gunshot shoulder—making him bellow—and spun him out into the river. His beefy torso overreached his feet, and with his arms flailing for balance he disappeared under the surface.

But he staggered right up, water cascading off his chin, and fired once more.

The bullet sizzled past John Kost's ear, and he hunched to the side. He aimed his empty derringer at the man, who did his own shimmy to get out of the way.

Eight now, he reminded himself. Eight cartridges had been expended. But God only knew how many rounds this fellow's pistol held. A Tokarev could hold nine, with one in the chamber. Some Mausers, eleven. A Browning 9mm, fourteen. The list was endless. "Enough now," he said in Russian.

"Nyet," the man growled, his eyes shining through the dimness.

Dropping his derringer, John Kost dove after him, stroked and scissors-kicked through achingly cold water until he collided with

166

the man's legs, then fettered them at the knees and overturned him, expecting all the while for a bullet to hammer into his back. But instead of lead ripping through him, he felt two powerful hands close around his throat. He tried to pry the thick fingers off, but couldn't get a purchase on them. Yet, he realized with a dull satisfaction that the man had been forced to let go of his pistol in order to throttle him.

The cold seemed to be lifting his scalp off the top of his head. Gagging on a lungful of icy water, he pushed off the bottom with his legs to break the stranglehold. But the man held fast as they both tumbled farther out into the current, and he started digging his thumbs into John Kost's windpipe, despite having to tread water to keep his own mouth above the surface.

Taller by half a foot, John Kost could still skim the bottom with the toes of his shoes, but this only reminded him that he and his attacker were being swept downriver.

He repeatedly jammed the heel of his right hand against the man's nose. Black smears of blood ran from the assailant's nostrils into his gaping mouth, but he refused to let go. John Kost's headache was beginning to fade, not toward painlessness, but into insensibility. It had been a long time since he'd fought someone of equal strength, he realized with an incurious feeling that he was only an observer to this. Finding his anger again, briefly, he tried to gouge out one of the man's eyes, but the huge fellow simply arched his back and turned his face out of reach.

Then, instead of grappling with him, John Kost clasped him around the ribs. Even though something within him begged him to hoard every molecule of air, he purged his lungs in a frenzy of bubbles that drifted up past his eyes.

Together they began to sink, slowly at first, but then with rising speed. The bewildering pulsations of the current took hold of them, and John Kost had no idea which way was up or down. But all at once his back was skidding along the rocky bottom and the vise of hands let go of his throat: the man was now struggling to be free of him. Doubtlessly, he was thinking only of the air at the surface, so he seemed not to notice when John Kost quit girdling him and grasped him instead by the jaw and the crown of the head.

He gave a twist with all his remaining strength, and a faint crack was telegraphed through the water.

The man went limp, his arms flowing up with eerie grace as if he were bringing a choir to crescendo.

Dora Cade took Aranov's fedora and raincoat from him as if she didn't like touching a stranger's clothing. Her cold blue eyes seemed impervious to amusement, yet Robert Cade kept chuckling at his wife's small talk as if her listless questions were Milton Berle punch lines. "Yes, it's still raining," Aranov replied as he watched her mope down the hallway with his belongings. He wondered with a spasm of guilt if he were being given a glimpse of Sylvia a quarter century from now.

A very old woman with eyes the same blue as Dora's, although clouded by cataracts, sat stoop-shouldered at the dining room table. A bamboo cane was hooked over the back of her chair.

Cade didn't introduce him. "Mother Fletcher, d'you want a drink?"

She startled, frowned, then told him to repeat himself.

"Would you care for a drink?" he said, raising his voice.

"Yes." She crabbed her face away from him and said nothing more.

And again Cade's chuckle chipped away at the awkward silence. He had always seemed so formidable to Aranov it was embarrassing now to catch him kowtowing to his peevish wife and apparent mother-in-law.

"First door on the right is my study," Cade said over his shoulder as he headed for the kitchen. "I'll meet you there in a minute. What happened to your partner?"

"Couldn't make it."

Dora Cade passed Aranov in the hallway, but didn't meet his gaze. Flicking on the ceiling light, he thought he'd heard the door wrong from Cade, for there wasn't a book to be found inside the small room. But then he noticed an escritoire and file cabinet pushed up against the far corner. He sank into one of two overstuffed chairs that were separated by a coffee table, all of which looked to have been retired from frontline service in the living room.

A glass in each fist, Cade swept in and handed him a gin collins without breaking stride on his way to the cabinet. "Kick the door shut for me, will you?" he asked, the old sarcastic bite back in his voice: the women were behind him now.

Aranov took a quick swallow from his drink, then got up and shut the door. Cade was unlocking the bottommost file drawer. "So John got snagged into going to Yosemite anyways, huh?"

"Looks that way." He was unsure what *anyways* meant. He made himself stop rubbing his thumbs along the lip of the glass: it was producing a squeal.

"I think he'll have his hands full with that Martov dish. She kept making eyes at him all through lunch yesterday."

"John can take care of himself. . . ." Then it hit him that he was posturing, jockeying for some utterly worthless dominance with the agent—something he'd promised himself on the drive down he wouldn't do. Cade, who'd baited him before, had a knack for this game and would circle in on any challenge like a shark that had just tasted blood in the water. "Is this Martov woman nice looking?" Aranov asked conversationally, forcing himself to sound less contentious.

"Kinda pouty-faced. . . ." Cade took from the drawer a photograph envelope and unwound the twine fastener. He examined the contents for a second, but didn't take them out. "But yeah, she's turned a couple heads in her time." For some reason, he retied the twine and tucked the envelope under his arm before folding down the escritoire's writing surface. He reached inside for a glass jar packed with cigars. "Smoke?"

Aranov was tempted, thinking maybe a cigar would make him appear more sure of himself, but then said, "No thanks." He'd only look like a ten-year-old with his first cigarette.

Cade lit up, asking between fulsome sucking noises, "How d'you feel . . . you know, about the Soviet Union?" As an afterthought, likely with his wife in mind, he parted the fox-hunt-motif curtains and cracked the sash to let out the smoke.

Rainwater could be heard trickling off the eaves into the foliage of a carefully trimmed privet Aranov had noticed along the front of the ersatz-Tudor house. "Give me an idea."

For the first time, anger flashed through him. It felt good. He jiggled the ice cubes in his glass. "What's that supposed to mean?"

Cade sat down, the envelope still clasped under his arm, and smiled as if to say that no offense had been intended. "With the war, there's been a lot of well-meaning confusion about Russia. Soviet-American friendship and all that bunk. I'm just asking you where you stand."

"Does it matter?"

Cade picked a flake of tobacco off his lower lip, gazing at it before flicking it away. "I'd say so."

"Then I feel the same as John Kost about it. We're working a case that's tough enough without us letting our political beliefs get in the way."

"Then you don't give a shit about the Soviet Union one way or the other."

"I didn't say that."

"But you did say you feel pretty much the same as Kost does. And Jesus, he was suckled on hate for the Bolshies."

Aranov was on the verge of admitting that he had inherited his father's reflexive dislike for most things Russian outside of its music and food, but then he realized that this would please Cade, and he had no intention of catering to the agent's biases. Instead, he said, "I mean I don't let my opinions color my work. I leave my blinders back at the stable."

"Christ!" Cade said with exasperation, but still smiling. "That's all I'm asking—your opinion of Stalin and his boys!"

"I don't think that's any of your business." He hid his flushed face behind his upturned glass, even though he was proud of himself.

"All right, have it your way. But in that case I don't understand why you drove down here."

"You said something about some photos."

"What the devil d'you need them for? You sound lukewarm about Soviet involvement."

"My feelings toward the Soviet Union and the possibility of Soviet involvement are two different things," Aranov said evenly.

Clenching his cigar between his teeth, Cade shrugged as if he didn't understand.

Aranov began counting off on his fingers his reasons for zeroing in on the Soviets in town: "First, William Laska was a Red, a dedicated one until he suddenly quit the Party in 'thirty-five—which strikes me as a fishy termination from the get-go."

"Could be." Cade gave another cat-and-mouse shrug. "We never ruled out that possibility."

"Second, two doorknobs in Laska's place were wiped clean of latents, which tells me somebody sat in on what happened there. Third. . . ." Hotly, Aranov went on for another minute until it dawned on him that Cade had pulled him on like a boot; just when he had felt sure the situation was under control, he'd been suckered into saying too much. No longer could he hold back his anger, which was mostly directed toward himself now. "Go to hell, Cade. You had no intention of helping us in the first place. What're a couple of blue-suiters to you!" He slammed his empty glass on the coffee table and came to his feet.

"Easy with the furniture—Dora'll have my ass." Cade looked genuinely mystified. "What's with you alluva sudden? You have a case of the nerves or something? You tired?" He opened the envelope once again and began spreading eight-by-ten photos over the tabletop. "Sit down already so we can go over these together. Okay? Come on, Nate."

He glanced at the glossy black-and-whites taken on the flight line at Hamilton Field, recognizing John Kost in one of them backdropped by a military transport with a Soviet star on the fuselage. Wavering, despising the indecision that kept him from storming out of the house, he asked himself what John would do. Finally, he lowered himself into the chair, crossed one leg over the other, and gripped his kneecap. He wished that Ragnetti had agreed to come. None of this would have happened if Vince were standing in the corner, scowling.

"That's more like it," Cade said. "Christ Almighty, you're touchy tonight. I'm only trying to establish some common ground here. Somebody down at your place bad-mouthing old Bob Cade to you?"

"No," he mumbled, "I'm just tired, like you said."

"Okay, okay—let's get down to their list of players." Cade picked up a photograph, turned it so they both could see. "We both know who this is," he said, his index finger tapping a distinguished-looking sort with silver hair and Douglas Fairbanks, Jr., taste in clothes. "Right?"

"No, I don't know," Aranov admitted.

"Pyotr Aleksandrovich Martov, the vice-consul."

"Secret police?"

Cade deflected the question with a breathy laugh and: "No more than any other vampire in that haunted house."

"That's not an answer. Is Martov an operator or not?"

Cade stopped smiling. "No, not in the sense you mean. Oh, I'm sure he does light espionage on demand. Even the maid shags ground balls for Commissar Beria. But we're almost positive Martov's not the resident here."

"Who is?"

Cade ignored the question as he picked up the next photo. "Okay. From the left, this joker's Novikov, head of British relations. . . ."

Aranov continued to stare at him, taking satisfaction that the agent was now the one to be ill at ease.

Zarapkin, Cade pointed out, head of American relations.

Golunsky, international affairs expert.

Krylov, another international affairs man, but his true purpose in coming to San Francisco was somewhat suspect to the Bureau. In a hotel-lobby discussion with New Zealand's delegation, overheard by an FBI agent, he had let slip a rather baffling notion that the United States had dominion status in the British Commonwealth.

"Who is the resident here, Cade?" Aranov pressed.

172

Sobolev, Balkans expert.

Lieutenant General Vassiliev.

Vice Admiral Rodionov.

Seeing that his discourse was being ignored, Cade tossed down the photograph and sighed. "Either of two guys on the consul's personal staff. The best bet was somebody called Yaroshenko, if only because he was the less obvious of the pair. A real marshmallow by the looks of him."

"What do you mean *was* the best bet?"

"Last Wednesday evening Yaroshenko was driven to Hamilton Field and put on one of the C-47s returning to Moscow."

With a sinking feeling, Aranov realized that this Russian might well have been the man inside Laska's triplex, but now was thousands of miles beyond American justice. Still, he wasn't about to give up when Cade had finally honestly begun to trade information. "Who's the other possibility?"

"Some grizzly named Tikhov. He definitely looks the part, but whether he's chief or just one of the Indians—we've caught him with his fingers in the cookie jar more than once. Not that he ever found out."

"You mean you did nothing about his espionage activities?"

"And risk offending our courageous socialist allies?" Cade said. "You gotta be kidding. That'll have to wait until this war's over and both sides can put on the gloves again."

"Where's Tikhov now?"

"Out and about town, probably."

"Don't you have him under constant surveillance?"

"*Constant?* What with the Bay Region crawling with a couple thousand foreign nationals, half of them who mean this country no good? Not to mention the regular crap my handful of people got to deal with?" The agent began rummaging through the photographs again. "Here, I want you to get a good look at one of these jokers. . . ."

It rankled. Aranov couldn't keep his mind off the possibility that the fingerprint wiper—and the murderer of William Laska and the rookie patrolman, Lon Fenby—had soared away into last Wednesday's dusk. "You're absolutely sure Yaroshenko got on that plane to Moscow?" he asked, accepting what, by virtue of the photograph's graininess, was a blowup.

"Confirmed. You want to see that snapshot too?" Cade started to rise, but Aranov muttered no, it was all right.

The first thing to strike him about the subject of the enlargement was his ankle-length tan overcoat. It looked like a turn-of-the-century motoring outfit. The photo left the face indistinct, but the keenness of the eyes came through. They were pogrom eyes. "Who's this?"

"No idea."

"What? He entered the country without a name?"

"Oh, we got a name. For what it's worth. Boris Pugachev, assistant to Sobolev, the Balkans expert."

"I'm assuming you took this picture Tuesday afternoon at Hamilton Field?"

Cade nodded.

Then Pugachev had arrived in San Francisco with more than enough time to case the security at the hospital. "Where's he now?"

"We lost him."

"Didn't he check into the St. Francis Hotel with the rest of the delegation?"

"Nope, the son of a bitch vanished."

Aranov felt the hair on the back of his neck prickle. All at once Yaroshenko seemed less interesting, and he would've bet his life that the killer was still in San Francisco.

Cade explained that Pugachev was registered at the St. Francis, but the same enlargement Aranov was holding had been shown to most of the staff, and nobody could recall having seen the Soviet in the long coat. Nor had an admittedly part-time FBI surveillance team caught him going in or out of the consulate over the past three days. The agent then revealed the depths of the Bureau's quandary when he began hinting that it'd be nice if John Kost used his Conference assignment to find out about Pugachev. "I got one more thing to do," Cade went on when Aranov refused to commit in the inspector's stead, "and that's to drive up to Hamilton in the morning and question the Army drivers. Care to tag along?"

"No, I've got to iron out the final arrangements for Anthony Eden's arrival with the Brits. That's why we're going tonight."

Cade tapped the ash off his cigar. "You've got to be kidding."

"I'm not." He stood up. "Want me to break it to Dora?"

16

Sʜᴜᴅᴅᴇʀɪɴɢ ᴏɴ ᴀ ɢʀᴀᴠᴇʟ ʙᴀʀ out in the river, John Kost flexed his chilled hands, hands that had just killed a man.

The sleet fell like sparks against his neck, but he could no longer feel the water flowing around his legs. Racked by heaves, he had been unable to crawl completely out, having used his last energy to beach the corpse. It was sprawled beside him with its arms outstretched.

Splashing. He reared his head to listen, but it flopped heavily back down into the gravel. Shallows separated the bar from the bank, and the splashing sounds were coming across them toward him. The man he'd killed had a backup, and now this new threat was fast approaching. He staggered to his knees, clenched himself in his arms, and tried to bring the apparitionlike figure into focus. The night was misty, although he sensed that the mist was clinging to his eyes and not the river. Would he ever see clearly again?

The figure continued to wade toward him, hobbling over the stones, leaving a trail of luminous foam.

His only escape lay behind him: the river, black and rolling.

But he could never force himself back into it. If he did, he'd never come out. Bullets were to be preferred over the Merced.

He fumbled for rocks, but his numb fingers refused to come together around them.

The figure stopped while only midway across the shallows, and then Elena's voice drifted out to him, "Ivan Mikhailovich . . . is that you?"

He shut his eyes. She had left her hiding place to find him. Even though she'd had no idea which man had survived, she had come looking for him. "Yes . . . here . . . come."

She sloshed the rest of the way out to the bar and knelt beside him. Then she saw the body. "What's this?"

He wanted to say that it was a gaping rupture with his past, that he'd never taken a life before and now nothing would be the same again. But after a moment he just gave a helpless flap of his arms. "I thought he was breathing a while ago."

"Was he?" she asked hopefully.

"No." He gnashed his teeth together to keep them from chattering; the noise had been making him feel even colder. "I must keep moving," he heard himself say as if in a dream, and as in his dreams he was speaking Russian. "I've got to get back to the hotel."

"Oh, dear God." She tussled out of her overcoat and draped it over his shoulders. The warmth from her body quickly faded from the wool, but while it lasted, the sensation was blissful. He took a step, and his knee came close to buckling. She threaded her arm around his waist, but despite her surprising strength he knew she'd never be able to hold him upright once he started to topple over. He had to stay on his feet if only because he wouldn't be able to rise again.

They halted after only two steps. "Wait. I need some more feeling in my legs. I need—"

"Hide the body," she whispered.

He thought that he'd heard her wrong. Too convulsed to try to understand such a strange request, he ignored it. But with her help he plodded over to the corpse and groaning, bent over to begin rummaging through the man's pockets. He found a wallet and a pack of cigarettes; but once again his fingers were useless. "In here," he said, "a billfold. Get it for me."

She whimpered, but did what he asked.

"Do you still have your lighter?" he asked. "You had it in the lounge."

She dug into a pocket of the overcoat she'd wrapped around his shoulders and came up with it.

"Get it going." He couldn't take hold of the mother-of-pearl lighter, so he grasped her wrist and waved the flame back and forth across the already waxen face. A purplish lump betrayed where the neck had been snapped. "Who is he?"

She shook her head.

"Please—!"

She began to cross herself, then spun away from the sight and vomited, dropping the lighter and the wallet to the gravel. The flame sputtered out.

"Go ahead," he said softly. She wasn't as inured to corpses as he was. It made him feel better about her. Reaching down, finally able to manipulate his own hand again, he grabbed the lighter and thumbed the striker wheel. Then he picked up the billfold. She'd just stopped retching when he said, "He has a California driver's license, but he was Russian. We talked to each other in Russian. Are you sure you—"

"No! I don't know him!"

He slipped the pack of smokes from the man's coat and showed it to her. Pushkin cigarettes.

She looked away. He shut the lighter's lid and began walking stiff legged toward the bank, toward the hotel beyond with its steam heat. But ten feet into the shallows, she seized him by the sleeve. "What are you going to do?"

He didn't stop moving. "I'm going to get warm. Then I've got some calls to make."

"What for?"

"To report this, for the love of God!"

"No—please!"

"Woman, I'm freezing to death!"

She let go of his sopping jacket. "Yes, yes—of course. We'll get you warm. You'll see what I mean as soon as you're warm. You'll see then."

He clambered up the bank and began groping his way through the alders. To his back he could hear her voice sliding into a resolve that disturbed him: "I'll get you warmed up. Nice and warm. Then we can come back here and properly hide the body." Suddenly she fell with a crash into a tangle of undergrowth.

Turning, he pulled her to her feet. "*Properly* hide it?"

"Yes, please."

"God save us, do you do this often enough to know the difference?"

"What are you saying? I would never kill anyone. I would die before I'd kill somebody!"

"All right, all right—"

"Nothing's all right!" Was she weeping? He wasn't sure, for having given up her overcoat she might have begun shivering. He tried to hand it back to her, but she refused the offer with a snap of her head. "But I'm begging you—hide the body and say nothing!"

With the ridge of boulders behind them and the last meadow stretching whitely toward the hotel lights, he began trotting, his waterlogged shoes squelching with each stride. The effort made him light-headed, and his limbs were tingling as if termites were boring through the cramped muscles. But it was good to see the amber windows grow larger against the storm clouds. Limping alongside him, she snatched at his sleeve, then again just as quickly let go when she seemed to remember his misery. "Before we get back, promise me!"

"What?"

"Promise you won't call."

"I can't."

"You must!"

He was beginning to feel warmer. The exertion. He ran faster. "Why? Give me a reason why!"

When there followed no answer, he glanced over his shoulder: she was crouched low to the ground, doubling her legs in her

179

arms and sobbing. He went back, although his body yearned for the glowing hotel.

"I'd never ask anything like this for myself," she said, weeping. "Not for myself."

"For whom then?"

"My daughter. My little daughter." She looked up at him, but it was too dark to make out her expression. "I'm a hopeless sinner. But why should she suffer for my stupidity? That's the injustice of it—that she should suffer for what I've done."

He exhaled into his cupped hands. "What've you done?" He suspected that she was smiling bitterly through her tears.

"You don't trust me, do you?"

It was uncanny, how much she sounded like the other woman who'd asked him precisely the same question. "I don't know. I'd like to." Once again he helped her up, then slowly embraced her when she pitched weeping against his chest. The warmth of her was intoxicating; selfishly, he would have sucked it all out of her, had he been able; her warmth was life itself. "I won't do anything until we talk," he said. "I promise. Now quickly—to the hotel."

"Yes, I'm sorry. Let's get going!"

"Ah!" His legs had set like concrete, but he willed them forward again. "Run ahead. Go through the lobby to the door on the north side. It's locked to the outside—I already checked, so you'll have to let me in."

"Which way's north?"

He pointed.

John Kost reclined in a tub filled to the taps with steaming water, quaffing vodka from a water glass. She had warmed the bellboy-delivered bottle in the bathroom sink, then poured a bumper for each of them before sitting atop the vanity with her long legs drawn under her damp slip. She looked distracted, hunted even, as she took a sip and held the liquor in her mouth for a long moment. Her hair, freshly toweled and fanning down over her shoulders, was flecked with dead cedar leaves she had yet to comb out; and her skin was shiny from the cold. She swallowed and set down her glass. "I want to make sure Ruml's asleep before we talk. Do you still have his key?"

"What makes you think I kept it?"

"I would have," she said, so frankly he realized that she had a grip on herself again.

While he was tempted to go with her, nothing on earth could have persuaded him to forsake the hot bath. It was like being hooked up to a blood transfusion. "Trousers, one of the front pockets—if it's still there."

She began picking through his pile of wet clothes in the corner. "Yes, here it is."

"Be careful," he said.

"Ruml's nothing." She smiled, and he found himself reaching with a warmly dripping hand to clasp the side of her face, a gesture more imploring than affectionate. For an instant she laid her hand atop his, seemingly aware of his nudity for the first time. Then she quickly left, closing the bathroom door behind her, and he sank deeper into the tub. A glimmer raced across the ceiling. He realized that it was from his baptismal cross, and he began idly twisting its gold chain to direct the spot of light here and there as if looking for something.

The cold was stubbornly leaving his body. It lingered as a prickling in his fingers and toes, an ache in his forehead. Another sensation lurked far below his wrinkled skin, a heaviness that defied precise location, the slow clotting of his remorse perhaps. Or the fear that kept needling him to go down to the safe for his revolver. And despite his obvious physical needs, he was worried that this delay in reporting the death, although it stacked up to justifiable homicide by a peace officer, would look bad to the Park Service and Mariposa County authorities who'd ultimately investigate it. And whom really had he killed? William Laska's and Lon Fenby's murderer?

The driver's license bearing the name of James Zyla of San Leandro was no doubt a forgery. Zyla. A Ukranian name. A plausible enough alias for a fellow with a Russian accent. He only hoped the forger, to make the cover more convincing, had instructed his Soviet client to do two things: execute the signature for James Zyla—the handwriting might then be compared to the signatures on the visa documents of the Soviet staff; and use his own thumb for the thumbprint.

The doorknob rotated, and he sat up.

Elena stepped back inside. "He's asleep. The room stinks of him." She sat again on the vanity, drained the last two fingers of vodka from her glass. "What do you need to know?"

"You can start with your daughter. What's happened to her?"

Her eyes moistened, but her voice remained clear. "She's been taken hostage."

"Where?"

"Back home."

"In Moscow where you say you live?"

"No, in Leningrad." She frowned at his insinuation that she might not live where she claimed to, but then shook her head as if correcting herself. "*Near* Leningrad . . . somewhere on a lake. Lagoda maybe. I don't know exactly."

"How old is she?"

"Four." She reached for a tissue. "Just four."

"Is she in danger?"

"No . . . yes . . . how can I ever know?"

He nodded, but not sympathetically. Sympathy could wait until he felt sure she wasn't lying. "What's your husband doing about this?"

"What can he do? We're powerless, both of us." She shielded her eyes with the tissue, and he gently coaxed her into pouring herself another drink. Waiting for her to gather herself, he pondered something that once asked would instantly turn this into interrogation. Over the past week Martov had seemed remarkably gregarious for a father whose daughter was being held hostage on the far side of the globe. Composure is one thing, indifference another. But this revelation about her daughter did help explain her eagerness to win John Kost's favor, although he still had no idea how she expected him to help her.

"I'm sorry, Ivan Mikhailovich, go ahead now."

"Who is holding your child?"

She looked right through him and said nothing.

"Elena Valentinovna?"

"I can't see shit." Robert Cade leaned over the steering wheel of his Hudson DeLuxe. Away from his wife, the agent had resorted to his old self. Maybe it was his straw boater. As soon as he put it on, he stopped being Dora's husband and became the two-fisted gangbuster he probably fancied himself to be.

They were heading back to town from Hamilton Field after interviewing the Army Air Corps driver who'd taken the Soviet in the long tan overcoat into San Francisco Tuesday afternoon. The PFC had looked scared to death upon being ushered by two MPs into the presence of an honest-to-God federal agent and a police detective, but Aranov had tried to put him at ease, assuring him that he'd done nothing wrong—even though Cade kept whispering, "Goose him. Keep him on the edge of his chair."

"Yes, sir, I remember that guy," the young private said as soon as he was shown the blowup of Boris Pugachev. "You bet, I took him and three others in my car."

"Why do you remember him?"

"That coat."

"Did you drive him all the way to the St. Francis?" Cade horned in, disregarding his own promise to let Aranov field the questions.

"No, sir, I dropped him off a couple blocks before the hotel. Somewheres along Post Street. About Post and Taylor, I think."

"Why?" Cade's eyes tapered as he sucked another cigar to life.

"Sir?"

"Why'd you let him off early?"

"The guy asked me to. Said he wanted to get some cigarettes."

"What'd you say?"

"I told him good luck, what with the shortage. Jeez, the Owl Drugstore down on Market got a couple cartons in last week and there was a line all the way around Third—"

"No, I mean—what'd you say about him getting outta the car too soon?"

"Nothing." The kid squirmed a little, maybe sniffing the next question before Cade got it off.

"Weren't your orders to take these people from this base to the St. Francis Hotel?"

"Yes, sir, but I figured these Russians were free to go anywheres they wanted. Like guests or something."

Seeing no point to this other than Cade's penchant for intimidation even when there was no need, Aranov took control again. "I assume he spoke English to you."

"Yeah, real good. Kinda like he was an Englishman or something. You know, 'old fellow' and all that."

"He was polite then?"

"Real polite."

"Did the others say anything to him when he announced he was getting out before you reached the hotel?" Aranov asked.

"No, sir."

"Was there any discussion among them on the ride in?"

"Not what I recollect." The private paused. "Wait—one of the others asked if he could smoke."

"In English then?"

"No, I mean he had this guy in the long coat translate for him. I said it was okay with me. Other than that, I don't think they said much."

"Said much or said nothing, which is it?" Cade asked.

"Nothing, I suppose, sir—they was a quiet bunch."

"Which direction did our man walk after he got out of the car?"

After a moment, the private had shrugged helplessly.

Now, as Cade accelerated off the rain-slick Golden Gate Bridge, Aranov told himself all misdirection was behind him, that he was on the verge of learning why four citizens of his city, two of them cops, had been murdered since last Sunday night. While there was nothing evidentiary linking Pugachev to the homicides, and it was certain that he had not come to town until Tuesday afternoon—more than forty hours after Wallace Elliot and Emma Laska had been shot, Aranov trusted that if he found this elusive Soviet, the scales would fall from his eyes. The only stumbling block was Cade, who had dibs on the lead.

"Want me to drop you off at your car?" the agent asked sleepily.

"Please." Aranov's Dodge was in the underground garage at the Hall of Justice, where he'd parked it after following Cade up from Daly City. "About this Tikhov joker you mentioned. . . ." He purposely didn't finish.

"What about him?"

"You say you caught him with his fingers in the cookie jar?"

"Yeah, he's been known to step on his dick within camera range."

"In town here?"

"And other places around the bay."

"Any of those places worth staking out?"

Cade rolled down his side window three inches, blinked against the inrush of rain as he tossed away his cigar stub. "Maybe. But I don't have the manpower. And neither do you, if I can believe Coffey's bellyaching."

"I'm the manpower."

"Like when?"

"Tomorrow, as soon as I'm finished with the British. Just give me a list, and I'll cover the sites as best I can."

Cade sighed. "What happens if this turns out to have nothing to do with your cases? You like your water hot?"

Aranov realized that the last thing bothering the agent was whether or not a SFPD gumshoe got caught out on a limb by his own brass. No, Cade was worried that on an outside chance Aranov might somehow stumble across Pugachev, whose disappearance was the Bureau's bailiwick. "If I hit paydirt, I'd swear I was only backing you on the gig."

Again, Cade sighed. Some faint inner Anglican voice was probably reminding him that he was dickering with the Devil incarnate. "You promise to call me before you do anything?"

"The first opportunity."

"I mean it, Aranov."

"So do I."

The final sigh, one of resignation. "Got a notepad?"

"Always."

"Write down these addresses. . . ."

When Aranov had recorded the last of them, he said, "Now, what about the latents?"

"What fucking latents? How would I get latents on the Soviets here?"

"You tell me."

Cade laughed wearily. "What does it matter? You said yourself the doorknobs in Laska's place were wiped. Tell me what you got in the way of a comparison, and I'll see what I can scrounge up."

If only for pride's sake, Aranov felt like withholding something from the agent: the partial latent that had been lifted off Elliot's notebook-pocket button. "Jacks to open in this game, Bob?"

"You're damned right. Let me see your openers."

"Then I fold. Forget the latents for now. You can take it up with John when he gets back."

"Who is holding your daughter?"

She stared down on John Kost from the vanity top. Her face expressionless, but she *knew*. "A man. A terrible man."

"His name."

"Isn't it enough to know that he tried to kill me?"

John Kost had every reason to believe that he and not she had been the target. Otherwise, the man passing himself off as James Zyla would never have taken the bait and followed him down to the river; he would have closed in on her straightaway. But perhaps she genuinely thought that she had been the mark, and it was best to drop this and find out the identity of the obviously powerful man in the Soviet Union who was holding Martov's and her daughter—and just as importantly, his reason why. *If* anyone was doing such a thing, he reminded himself, realizing that over this momentary silence between them her eyes had grown calculating, as if she felt herself sliding down into complexities too deep for her cunning. He somehow trusted that she was new to this business. It was the only thing he fully trusted about her. "You leave me no choice," he finally said, squeezing the hot water out of his washcloth onto his chest.

"What're you saying?"

186

"Tell me everything, or I'll make those calls."

She got down off the vanity and slipped her cigarette case from a pocket of her overcoat, which he'd hung on a hook upon shedding it. Streaking up the back of her foreleg from her crippled heel was a long crosshatched scar. A botch of a suturing. "You promised not to," she said. "You promised we'd talk."

"I've killed a man under color of authority. Do you understand what that means?"

Her gaze slid past his. "No."

"If I hide this, I'm in trouble."

"But why? You were protecting me."

"Yes. But it won't look that way if I fail to report it. Elena—"

"You don't want to know everything." She lit her cigarette and slowly exhaled. Then, wiping a clear swatch on the foggy mirror with her palm, she examined her own face for an instant. Examined it as if for leaks.

"You're lying."

She turned toward him, questioningly.

"Lying about the girl."

"How can you say such a thing!"

"Easy. Tell me why Martov's so unconcerned. He's the most collected father of a kidnapped child I've ever met."

She lowered her voice again. "He's a better actor than I."

"That's probably true. I don't think lying comes easily to you. I think it grinds inside you."

She tossed her cigarette into the toilet. "Oh, God! Please, I'm thinking of you!"

"Oh?"

Kneeling beside the tub, she said, "Would you share a secret that kills? Would you, Ivan Mikhailovich?"

"It seems my life's already in jeopardy. So, yes, I would. I'm safer knowing than not."

"Don't be so sure."

"Let me decide."

A mask fell over her face, and from this he realized that she'd finally made up her mind to speak, although he also sensed that her resistance hadn't completely collapsed. Not yet. Rising, she opened the sink faucets, then sat on the toilet cover and folded her hands together. As the water gurgled down the drainpipe, she leaned toward him, the wet smell of her hair strong, and whispered, "Martov and I will be forced to do something . . . something at a reception following the opening ceremonies of the Conference. . . ."

"Go on."

"We're to see that Anthony Eden is murdered. . . ." She closed her eyes. "God save us, that's what we must do."

A chill jerked his shoulders, but he calmly asked, "What do you mean by *see* that Eden's murdered?"

"To help out. To make sure it's properly done."

Again, that word. "Why the British foreign minister?"

"How should I know? I don't know anything about politics. All we've been told is that our baby will die if we don't help!" Tears once again, copious, seemingly sincere.

"Who wants Eden dead? Who has your child?"

At last she came out with it: "Vyacheslav Molotov."

The commissar of foreign affairs and Stalin's handpicked delegate to the Conference. That the Soviets were capable of such vicious machinations wasn't hard for him to believe, but his mind raced to blend these farfetched elements into something resembling a motive. Eden was Winston Churchill's heir apparent, and the Kremlin certainly had no affection for the reactionary prime minister who'd repeatedly warned the more credulous Franklin Roosevelt to be wary of the Russians. These cracks in the alliance had already been detected by the American press and could be expected to widen as the war wound down to an uneasy peace. But coerce the vice-consul and his wife to murder Anthony Eden? Was the Kremlin that artless? His gut feeling was that Elena Martova was lying from start to finish; but the dead man on the gravel bar lent a wisp of credence to her story. And if Wallace Elliot had somehow stumbled on such a plot, no wonder he and then the longshoreman who'd killed him had been eliminated by Molotov.

He stood up and stepped out of the tub. He had begun to feel vulnerable in it. She handed him a towel, her eyes on the bath mat. "Why do you think this fellow tried to kill you tonight?" he asked, drying off.

"Martov objected to this, as much as he dared. I think my death was meant to warn him. . . ."

"That he must carry through no matter what?"

"Yes."

"How will Eden be killed?"

Starting to weep again, she lifted his baptismal cross off his chest and kissed it.

"Woman—*talk* to me!"

She nodded that she was trying to control herself, and after a few seconds she said in a hush, "At the close of the reception—"

"Where?"

"Pacific Highlands."

"You mean Pacific Heights?"

"Yes, I'm sorry—that's it. Martov rented a big house for entertaining. After the reception Martov is to delay Eden on the sidewalk before he gets into his car. I'm to stand beside Martov so everything will look natural. Eden will be shot from the darkness."

"By whom?"

"We don't know."

"Somebody with the consulate or somebody flown in just for this?"

"I said we don't know."

He wrapped the towel around his waist, then took the bottle and his glass into the bedroom. She followed him, limped to the far wall, and bending over, turned up the steam radiator, which began clanking as if someone below were hitting the pipes with a hammer. He eased down onto the bed and poured himself another bumper. He wasn't drunk, and he needed to be. "What will you do now?"

She sat beside him, brought his glass to her lips by clasping her hands over his. "I've got to go on as if nothing's happened up here."

"James Zyla will be missed."

"Yes, but his bosses won't know anything for sure. Not if he's

189

properly hidden. They trust no one. They might think he went over to you Americans. Or made his way to Mexico, as a secret-police man did from Washington a few years ago."

"One by one these possibilities will be eliminated."

"Yes, eventually." She took another sip from his glass. "But before that you'll think of something. Won't you?"

Without thinking, he picked a cedar leaf out of her hair.

"I have only you to help me, Vanechka. You'll think of something clever, yes?"

"What about your husband?"

"He's pathetic."

"You don't mean that."

Her grin was malicious, but did nothing to weaken his desire for her. "The truth is the truth."

"Why me then?" His own voice sounded to him as if it were curling out of a seashell, softly roaring out of the thing he must quickly control. "Why do you come to me?"

"You're kindhearted. You of all the men I know. Even Martov has remarked on it, although he says you're too kind to be much of a policeman—"

He came to his feet.

She asked him what was wrong, but he didn't answer that this casual, almost contemptuous mention of her husband had made him stop wanting her. In silence he dressed in the suit he'd worn on the train, then said as he went to the door, "Please go to your room before I come back."

17

JOHN KOST RETRIEVED his service revolver, but made up his mind
to leave the two pistols in the safe until morning. He had no idea
how Ruml figured in this, and in Elena's present state she wasn't
to be trusted with a handgun, lest room service fall victim to her
jittery trigger finger. In the privacy of the manager's office, he
strapped on his shoulder holster, then put on his jacket over it.
"Will that be all, Inspector?" asked the night clerk.

He stared at the telephone. One quick call to the park
superintendent and it would be done. He'd be off the hook,
exonerated, but instead he heard himself say, "Yes, that's all for
now, thank you."

"Very good, sir."

He felt overheated, claustrophobic even, and against his better
judgment he strolled outside. Something indefinable was falling
through the driveway floodlights: snow, sleet, whatever; it melted
on his bare hand before it could be examined. He was almost
sure her eyes were trained on his back from the second story. But
then he reminded himself that his room and not hers was on this
side of the hotel. Still, he fought the urge to turn around. He
looked straight ahead as he walked down the glazed drive—afar,

a waterfall gushed like milk from the north wall. Not yet thoroughly warm, he missed the overcoat he'd cast adrift on the river. It was tumbling downstream on the current, sleeves lazily flailing. On that image he drew to a halt. Remorse. He felt none, even though he'd seen cops with hard yellow calluses on their souls flounder in a sea of contrition after killing a man. Atheists asking for priests. Believers insisting there was no God. And nearly all of them had wept at one point or another. Tomorrow maybe he'd feel what they had. But not tonight, for all he could think of was: *You don't trust me, do you?*

What had made her say that? Had God put that echo in her mouth?

The room had been white, whiter than this snowy meadow, although it had also smelled of blood and disinfectant. An intern had woken him out of a sound sleep and hurried him into the room because there was no time left, and if only because she herself had guessed that there was no time, she gave him a lidded glance from her sweat-dark pillow and tried to define the thing that had kept them apart: "You don't trust me, do you?" And because they had been through this countless times before without resolution, because his jealousy and selfishness had made it resistant to resolution, he mumbled only that he loved her, but that had not been enough and she'd died alone, in her final moments asking for the boy who'd given her a baby and vanished.

He turned for the hotel, squarely into the floodlights, and walked back as if at each stride he might break into a run.

But she didn't answer her door.

He jiggled the knob, then tried his own room key in that lock, but of course it wouldn't work. Then it struck him that his wild pounding had frightened her. He called out her name. It shamed him how desperately he used her name. He was breathing so hard from the run inside and then up the stairs he almost failed to hear the snick from across the hallway.

He spun around. No one was there. But then he noticed that

192

his own door was ajar. He moved toward it as in a dream, ponderously, ineffectually.

She was sitting on his bed, still in her slip.

"I didn't phone," he said.

"I know."

"I wanted to."

"I know that too, Vanechka."

He chain-locked the door behind him. When he took off his jacket, she eyed his revolver, but said nothing. He shucked off his shoulder holster and put it in the nightstand drawer. Meanwhile, she had poured a vodka and now carried it around the bed to him with mincing steps as if afraid of spilling some.

"I don't need anything more to drink," he said.

She let the glass drop to the carpet.

"Come here. . . ." His hands luxuriated in the smoothness of her silk slip as they ran up and down her spine, again and again as far as the beginning of the curvature of her buttocks—he had no wish to express his lust so soon. "My hands are cold."

"Your touch is lovely."

"But my hands—"

"Vanechka . . . Vanechka. . . ."

That she'd been a dancer told in her body: her back was strong and supple. Her hands glided in crisscross around his waist and then slowly up his flanks to clasp his shoulders, but not in a way that seemed practiced. A slight awkwardness to this gave him comfort.

"I'm going to trust you," he said.

"Don't speak of it, Vanechka."

"But you must never betray me . . . promise me you won't betray me."

She kissed him on the chin, then left a trail of kisses that ended wetly at his mouth. "You're all the help I have."

"Promise," he said like a willful child.

"I promise."

Sleet began tapping against the window—entwined, they'd been moving toward the bed in a desultory sort of way when the sound made them stop to listen. But then he found the switch on the nightstand lamp, and the darkness that followed made it seem as if some glaring eye had been put out, that the pine walls of the room had become impenetrable. The man on the gravel bar had never existed. The white room reeking of disinfectant had never been.

He delayed entering her as long as he dared, but not so long she might think him to be a voluptuary. "I could love you," she said, then gave a defensive shudder as he went into her.

How forbidden it seemed, the intimate *thou* in Russian.

He came sooner than his pride liked, but felt no embarrassment. It had been like this with his wife before she'd grown too large with child, and he prayed now it would be this way with Elena as long as they had each other. With Lydia and the others he had sometimes purposely cut short the act by suddenly slowing the rhythm of his haunches as if he'd been glutted. He had known it was hopeless: his yearning—or at least the memory of that hunger—had not been stirred, and without it his sadness swelled with each undulation.

But now another arousal came on the skirts of the first. The yearning did not have a glib release.

"I could love you," she said again.

"I love you already, Lenochka."

Tikhov hadn't telephoned at ten P.M. Now it was half past two and still no word from the Yosemite. The Chekist regretted not having gone himself. Sitting beside the open window of Tikhov's hotel room, he listened to the rain fall across the North Beach neighborhood.

Suddenly, he took his Nagan off the nightstand. Footfalls were approaching. A sailor and a young whore came running up the steps into the hotel, laughing. The seaman held his peacoat over their heads like a dark-blue awning.

What had he been thinking about? Ah, yes—loyalty.

For personal loyalty he had no regard. It was utterly useless in terms of survival, and even damaging when attached to a living icon such as Stalin, who actually relished scything down those who venerated him. No, the Chekist had learned early that blackmail was more certain to win a superior's respect than protestations of fealty. The simple proof of this was that no state security fellow had survived the entire roster of secret police chiefs—except himself.

With Beria he followed the same regimen that had seen him safely through all the others: diligent security work buttressed by a threat made with all civility at the outset of the new boss's administration. Such insubordination was made possible by a windfall he'd come across on the first morning of the February Revolution while ransacking the Okhrana's Petrograd headquarters. Among the archives of the tsarist secret police, in one of the few remaining sections not set afire by the mob, he discovered the master pay voucher for its prime informers. It was no surprise to him that his superior at the time—and then most of this fellow's successors—had played both sides against each other in the long and skewed course of the Revolution. What surprised him was each chief's mangled expression when confronted with photostatic evidence of his crimes against the Proletariat Struggle.

He had imagined that these bright fellows would have come up with a cover story in the event of being unmasked. Clandestinely working for the Party, that sort of thing. He himself would have, and then stared down his blackmailer. But Beria had been the most shaken of all, and through his pallor the Chekist had glimpsed the heart of a true coward, a man capable of kidnapping and raping a pretty adolescent who'd come to his armored train to inquire about her brother's disappearance, and then marrying her when he realized how his reputation with the puritanical hierarchy of the Party might be enhanced by becoming a family man!

What Caligulas I have served!

Of course, any threat would have been pointless had the original pay list remained inside Russia. But on an early mission to Teheran the Chekist had entrusted it to his cousin, an incorrigible entrepreneur he'd helped emigrate to Persia for this very purpose. If his kinsman didn't hear from " Vanka" every six months, he was to post copies of the voucher to persons guaranteed to cause the Chekist's current boss a good deal of trouble. Foremost on this list was Iosif Stalin.

He had been given something of a scare when early in the war Soviet and British troops had occupied Persia, but so far his cousin hadn't been troubled by the occupation forces.

Still, no matter how secure the voucher with its numerous entries of L.P. Beria of Baku District made him feel, he assiduously stuck to the other portion of his regimen: he was the best operator in the Mobile Group. Tikhov, a lesser light, had obviously failed, and now he had to assure himself that the ever-widening ripples of the man's failure would not lap over his own careful efforts. If Tikhov had been detained and questioned instead of killed outright, there were immediate problems to deal with.

Holstering his revolver on his belt, he went to the closet across the darkened room and slipped his overcoat off the wire hanger. As usual, one pocket was heavy with the trenching tool.

Then he cracked the door, listened for several seconds, and finally went down the stairs and out the back of the hotel.

It was less than a kilometer to the basin between the Hyde Street Pier and the Army Port of Embarkation at Fort Mason, and he was no sooner within sight of the boathouse than he realized that Tikhov had failed more egregiously than he had expected: a Dodge sedan was parked in the alley by which he was approaching the waterfront.

Although empty, it was the same model of unmarked vehicle he'd seen driven by Vanka Kostoff. And the engine-compartment bonnet was still warm.

Halfway down Geary Boulevard toward bed and Sylvia, Aranov had suddenly decided not to go home. He would start sitting on Cade's list of places Tikhov had haunted while gathering intelligence on his country's wartime ally. The first was the public john up in Mt. Davidson Park, where the Soviet had met with an American contact some weeks before, but all Aranov accomplished there was to roust two queer Marines who were less embarrassed by his stern warning than he was.

Twenty minutes later he parked in an alley near the Hyde Street Pier. East of the dock was Fisherman's Wharf, dark now that the tourists were gone for the night. But on its Fort Mason side stood a boathouse, its plaster dingy from a decade without fresh paint; before the completion of the bridges had mothballed most of the automobile ferries, it had served as a repair shop for their lifeboats. Tikhov had come here in early March, alone and on foot from the Soviet consulate. The FBI's tail had expected the Russian to meet somebody, but Tikhov simply went inside the structure and then left ten minutes later. "Was it a drop?" Aranov had asked Cade on the drive back from Hamilton Field, but the agent said, "Unknown," that he and his men had torn the place apart and found nothing but the butt of the Pushkin cigarette Tikhov had smoked there.

Yawning, Aranov now swung his legs up onto the passenger side of the seat, then eased back against the door. Rain was ticking on the roof. A few bars of music, the composition yet unrecognized, kept coursing through his boredom. He trained his tired gaze on the boathouse's facade. It wasn't long before this picture bleared gray around its periphery and slowly filled in.

A check of his watch a few minutes later jolted him with the realization that it wasn't a few minutes later, but rather a quarter to three. And the rain had stopped. Stars were backdropping the Golden Gate Bridge, although the eastern sky was still opaque with storm. "Shit." He'd have to get some sleep before facing the British if only to have the clarity of mind to make sure his grammar was up to snuff. God, how they made him feel self-conscious about his English. About everything.

But first he would try to glean some idea why Tikhov had found his boathouse worth ten minutes of his time.

The front door lock was so rusted he was sure no key would ever open it again, but Cade had told him that the swivel plate was no longer screwed to the jamb; the entire lock and hasp assembly could be pulled aside.

He fished his flashlight out of his jacket pocket and sidled inside. The beam fanned out across an oily-looking surface being rippled by tiny swells. A ladder led down to the high-tide water, and lashed to a rung was a six-foot boat, its wood splotched with black mold.

He began pacing the U-shaped deck, whistling the snatch of the composition he still couldn't name. The melody was vaguely ominous, the rhythm characterized by a pronounced ebb and flow. Sylvia would know its title right off.

He didn't so much look into each nook and cranny as try to intuit why the Soviet had come here. Had he merely been trying to lose the G-man tailing him? In that event, how had he known about the useless lock? Certainly, he hadn't rattled all the locks along the waterfront like some blue-suiter door-shaking his beat for burglars.

He stopped walking.

Beneath him, something was being gently knocked against a piling by the swells. What would make a sound like that? A floating timber? It seemed metallic.

Giving up on the idea of making this suit last until the end of the month, he dropped to the filthy deck and peered over its lip, aiming his flashlight beam into the dark recess beneath the landward end of the boathouse.

A fifty-gallon drum was tied to a piling.

Cade had said nothing about a drum.

Before he got a stiff neck, he lifted his head and propped his chin on his flashlight, thinking. Was it a buoy or some other maritime appliance? He knew nothing about these things. But how'd it get back there without the efforts of a Navy frogman?

Then his eye lit on the boat.

Other than a block-and-tackle rig, it seemed to be the only usable piece of equipment on the premises, a significance in and of itself. "Sure," he said, rising, hurrying around toward the ladder, "sure as hell."

But then a sharp and unmistakable sound from outside made him wheel toward the door. It had been the hood of his Dodge being slammed shut. He had checked the oil and radiator at the start of each shift for too many years not to know the crunch of its latch.

He nudged open the door a few inches with the muzzle of his revolver.

No one was standing around his car.

Was somebody inside it then? Christ, was some idiot trying to steal his car?

He started up the alley, keeping clear of the building walls as Ragnetti had told him. Vince had shown him on a shooting lane sidewalk at the range how glancing bullets tend to hug the hard surface they've just struck. He also remembered what the sergeant had said about never lying down in a gunfight, about a hole in the shin beating one in the noggin any day of the week.

Twenty feet and still no movement inside the Dodge, no tattletale rocking of the chassis.

Holding his flashlight flush to his revolver, he turned on the beam and angled it down through the driver's side window, swept it around the felt-upholstered interior.

Empty.

His hands were shaking so badly it was a few seconds before he could open the door and reach for the microphone. "Central One—" But then he felt the severed end of the mike cord tap against his thigh.

Nor would the engine start. Rushing to the grill, he popped the hood. The distributor cap was missing.

Shoes scraped cement behind him, and he spun around once again. Standing at the boathouse end of the alley was a tall figure in a tan overcoat. The length of the coat had been trimmed up to knee length, but Aranov had no doubt whom he was facing. Alone.

18

By the time Aranov had drawn his revolver and sprinted to the end of the alley, the man in the overcoat was gone.

He sucked in a breath and held it. He listened for some sound of Pugachev fleeing, having already decided that it had been the missing assistant to the Balkans expert. Keeping to the building shadows, his eyes straining against the darkness, he became aware of his own pulse. It was spilling into his ears. He could hear nothing but this liquid hammering.

And he was winded. Without having run more than fifty feet, he was winded. Maybe it had something to do with the glottal thickening in his throat.

He wanted to stay securely in the shadows, but forced himself to leave the alley. Clenching his Colt down at his side so as not to spook any late strollers, he glanced up Hyde Street, hoping against hope to see a patrol car creeping down the hill. But the glossy street was empty.

Beneath his feet, the street car cable was ringing like a fire alarm.

Where was the nearest call box? He'd never worked Central Patrol. He was turning around in search of one when across

Hyde, out among the foliated shadows in Aquatic Park, he caught movement. A man was sifting through the alternating pools of darkness and lamppost light toward the Fort Mason docks, marked by the towering smokestacks of the troopships.

He had promised Cade a call if he came across Pugachev, but he also knew that if he took the time to hunt up a box and then have the station phone the agent with the message to link up with him here, the Soviet would once again melt into the city.

He started following Pugachev, telling himself not to be so scared. At this moment ordinary guys the world over were going through worse. He often lay awake at night, with Sylvia peaceful beside him, and imagined what other men his age must be going through, the shellings and the stench of burnt flesh and all the other trappings of global war. This was nothing compared to that. Actually, it was a long-shot payoff not to be squandered just because he had cold feet. He could handle the fear. So Ragnetti could eat those words about his not being able to do anything on his own, words from a man who went to jelly when ordered to write a search warrant affidavit or sit in on an autopsy.

He trotted into the park with his jacket flying loose, trying not to think about anything except whittling down the distance between Pugachev and himself. He avoided the cement walkways because the grass was quieter, although the fallen rain soon soaked through his socks, chilling his ankles. "Cold feet," he muttered.

Instead of continuing to the bayside guardshack at Fort Mason, Pugachev turned up Van Ness Avenue, taking long strides but with no air of urgency as he skirted the embankment along the east side of the base. Then, with a hint of martial precision, he right-faced onto Bay Street, passing through the funnel of light shining down from a dimout-shielded streetlamp; it blanched his tan overcoat, and for a split second he was a figure of pure white, a bloodless thing drifting along the waterfront.

Why wasn't he running?

Aranov decided to hang back more, to keep watch all around

himself in case a car suddenly pulled alongside. Pugachev might have a backup. He snugged his revolver back into his holster, but didn't button his jacket. He had begun to sweat, even though he felt cold under his damp clothes.

Never looking behind, Pugachev kept to the streets that lined the bay.

In passing, Aranov glanced up Fillmore Street toward the heart of the old pale, which he'd fled at eighteen in favor of the middle-class Richmond District. But something now made him want to turn up Fillmore—with all its tawdry familiarities: Saturday sundown with the grimy shops re-opening until midnight; the "world famous" electric arches blazing on like carnival lights over the intersections; and a crap game already going in plain view through the front windows of the United Cigar Store—and forget about Pugachev. But he didn't.

Pugachev was still heading west.

Approaching the Yacht Harbor, Aranov looked across the narrows of the Golden Gate and up at the black hump of Mount Tamalpais, and then down at sailboats in the basin before him, most of them in canvas chrysalises for the duration.

When he faced forward again, the Soviet had vanished.

He started to run along Baker Street, figuring that with the bay to the north and the Presidio's wire fence to the west, Pugachev would have turned south into the neighborhoods of the Marina District. But the street before Aranov was so convincingly quiet he spun around and backtracked toward the jetty that crooked out to the St. Francis Yacht Club. Why had Pugachev waited all these blocks to give him the slip? He hurried on toward the darkened clubhouse and was stepping over the chain barring the private road when a voice said calmly from the jetty boulders behind him, "Here, old fellow."

His hand flew to his holster as he reeled toward the voice.

He realized only a moment later that he had drawn, crouched, and shouted for the unseen man to freeze.

But he could make out nothing except the ten-foot poles of the Presidio's Cyclone fence filing down to the bay's edge. A thousand cicadas skirled inside his head, and he feared he was going to get sick. The strength in his legs were gone. He eased down on his knees.

A clang made him flinch. The sound made no sense until he found the nerve to go up to the fence and switch on his flashlight. Pugachev had somehow severed the wire ties that held the fencing to the poles. Then he had crawled under, for the tidal mud was disturbed and shoe prints struck west as far as the reach of Aranov's beam.

"He doesn't want a shadow anymore," he whispered to himself. "You've got him on the run."

Loosening his grip on his Colt before his hand went numb, he squirmed under the fence—and tore his trousers. He grimaced, imagining Sylvia trying to thread a needle. She hated to sew. He'd take the trousers to a tailor, a friend of the family, and brave the griping that he never showed at the synagogue anymore.

He followed the shoe impressions across the tideland the length of Crissy Field, the Presidio's airstrip, all the way to the southernmost buoy of the submarine net that stretched across the narrows—where the tracks were erased by the storm-heightened waves.

He had lost Pugachev again, this time probably for good.

The relief he felt shamed him.

Giving his back to the bay, he gazed inland, hoping to see no one. He didn't.

Then, from behind, he heard sloshing, as if someone was charging toward him out of the shallows. Turning, he cocked the hammer, although there was no need with a Detective Special and he'd never done this before, and tried to pick out his target against the concrete fenders around the bridge towers. In the split second before the blackness howled into him, he realized that the blow had not been to his mouth or even to his head; he felt it as a buzzing in his molars and then an overpowering urge to sneeze the smell of blood out of his nostrils. Mount Tamalpais, on which his eyes happened to be fixed, was matted by blue-tipped fires, but these faded into an emptiness so deep he was sure he was falling through it like a hailstone.

He dreamed a little boy's dream. He dreamed he had been captured by Indians and thrown over the back of one of their ponies. He was being jostled along a trail, being carried deep away into the Apache night. He opened his eyes, but couldn't trouble himself with focusing them. Even while he'd dreamt, his wound had been a burning demarcation along his left shoulder that kept his numbness and nausea from spilling into each other, but now it was the fountainhead of a warm, drowsy indifference. The pony rocked beneath him.

Crissy Field, it came to him.

He had been standing at the end of the runway, out near the submarine net. And now it seemed reasonable that the bleared structure he was seeing upside down was the old brick fortress nestled under the southern anchorage of the Golden Gate Bridge.

Pugachev.

His name was Pugachev, and he was packing him toward the point where the ocean mingled with the bay. He could now see where his blood had stained the Soviet's wet overcoat. But somehow the flow had been stanched, maybe by the pressure from the way in which he lay over the man's shoulder.

Surely a guard was posted on Fort Point.

Yes, an Army sentry would hear him.

He was taking a breath to cry out when it hit him that Pugachev imagined him dead and would finish him off if he proved not to be. Nor was there much hope his Colt was lodged in his holster; he'd had it in his hand when struck. But he would think of something. He'd shake off this strange indifference and knuckle down to business. With a faint grin he thought of John Kost and Ragnetti, looked forward to seeing their jaws drop when they learned how he'd kept his wits and come through a scrape this grievous. They'd talk about this for years.

Yet, it was grotesque: the calm way Pugachev was bearing him toward disposal. And again that infuriatingly nameless tune began coursing through his head.

Pugachev halted and slowly pivoted toward the steel-colored waters. They were gurgling and chuckling with turbulence. Aranov couldn't see his face, but was sure he was surveying them for something. Was it the patterns of foam crisscrossing the surface?

Suddenly, Pugachev took four running steps toward the shore, hunkered down, and then sprang up again.

He felt himself being catapulted into the sky. He hung like a cloud between the stars and the bay for an impossibly long time, then tumbled down into a shocking iciness. The salt water inflamed his wound, made him want to dig at it with his fingers, but instead he lay flat with his arms outstretched and his face down.

He waited.

Warmth trickled up around his neck and chin. A renewed gush of blood, he realized. His spent air burned the back of his throat. It tasted like ammonia.

He wanted to hear Pugachev walking away from the shore, but the foam bubbles were crinkling too loudly in his ears.

When he could no longer stand it, he rolled his face to the side and inhaled, taking in more brine than air because of the swelling of a wave. When a gag racked his shoulders, he was sure Pugachev would shoot him.

But no bullet came.

He stole another breath, a richer one, then began silently counting. He made it to thirty-seven before he had to lift his head again.

Pugachev was nowhere to be seen.

He started crying. But it scared him: how pathetic he sounded. So he stopped.

Then it dawned on him that he'd been taken by the current while playing dead. He checked the shoreline: it was at least fifty yards distant and receding. Swift as a millrace. But he was confident he could swim back to the spumy line of boulders. And besides, he'd heard that the tide flowed into the bay along the south rim of the Golden Gate; so for the short term at least he wouldn't be swept out to sea. If anything, he would just be shunted around the mile-wide channel until the crew of some ship heard his cries.

Bracing himself against the pain, cutting short a moan with a growl, he experimented with a breaststroke, but found that the left side of his body wouldn't respond. When he grasped his left hand with his right, it felt as if it belonged to somebody else. *Christ, how bad is it!* He started to explore the gash with his fingertips, but then shrank from it. He was afraid he might throw up. Shivering was taking enough of a toll.

He bumbled onto his side and began pulling with his right hand while attempting half a flutter kick. But the runway lights at Crissy Field had come on in the last few minutes, and he could see that the shoreline was fading into the south faster than he could walk. Walk on water. The image of himself serenely hoofing along the waves like Jesus threatened him with giddiness. He warded it off by punching himself in the face, twice.

A fighter landed on the airstrip, and the lights went out again.

His clothes were weighing him down, although he knew that he could never shed them without the use of both arms. But he was able to reach down with his good hand and flip off his shoes.

The swells were getting higher. From their troughs he could see only the stars directly overhead; even the summit of Mount Tamalpais dipped beneath these pounding ridges. Some curled and broke as they drove on toward shore, slapping his head until it lolled drunkenly.

"Hello the bridge! Help!" He giggled hysterically. "Help, bridge . . . help me."

Then, sobering again, he made up his mind to conserve his strength in the hope the current would return him to the submarine net. He began floating on his back, an effort more exhausting than he'd expected, for he had to scull constantly with his right arm to keep his mouth above water.

Then the answer seeped into his dazed consciousness—the composer and title of the composition that had been haunting him these past hours. "Of course," he said, laughing in the same helpless way as before, "Mendelssohn's *The Hebrides* Overture."

206

It was now roaring around inside his skull like a prayer beseeching the exaltation, the intoxication and surge of release that surely come with the knowledge that one's going to die. But if he truly felt any exaltation, it was but an echo of his terror, garbled by his desire to live, to go home and sleep the rest of the night through with his wife, to get up in the morning and go to work with John and Vince, to sleep twelve thousand more nights with Sylvia.

He reared up, looking for the submarine net.

It would be marked by a string of buoys. He'd grab the cable running atop the barrier and wait for one of the net tenders to chug along.

But after only a few minutes of straining for a glimpse of buoys, he had to admit that the current had gradually borne him north, then northwest, and finally west. He could feel the pull of the Pacific on his leaden body.

As the underside of the bridge floated into view, Mendelssohn filled him, vibrated within him, and he tried to conjure himself, his spirit maybe, into the imperishable flow of notes.

He vowed to survive in some way as the ocean spread darkly before him.

The Chekist returned to the automobile shortly after four in the morning, his sopping and bloody overcoat bundled under his arm. In no way had the Dodge been disturbed, so he believed it hadn't been discovered by any other policemen.

Ignoring the discomfort of his saltwater-soaked clothes, he crawled inside and rolled down the side windows. Rather than take the time to replace the distributor cap and manipulate the electrical wiring in such a way that the ignition would work without the key, he simply shifted the transmission out of gear, leaned himself into the doorpost, and pushed the car to the end of the alley. Then, after checking the far ends of the street for any unlikely traffic, he muscled the Dodge onto the dock beside the boathouse and going to the rear bumper, shoved the car over the planking's edge. The raucous splash failed to affect him, and he watched with a quiet face as the Dodge nosed in and sank. He was thinking about depths. To accommodate ocean-going ships the slip had to be at least six meters deep.

The car would not soon be found.

The explosives might be another matter—unless they were moved at once. He picked his overcoat up off the dock and started for the boathouse.

19

SOMEONE WAS TRYING to raise him.

John Kost lowered his eyes from the foggy street to his Motorola speaker. Out of the usual Monday-morning jumble of radio traffic, Communications was trying to raise him. He parked at the next corner beside a call box, then realized his mistake when the dispatcher's nasal voice continued to repeat his call sign. Only in the past several months had the department gone to a two-radio system; before that a fellow was alerted by radio and then went to a call box for his assignment. He'd reverted to old habits. "Go ahead, Central One," he said hoarsely into the microphone, "but I'm almost to the Hall of Justice."

"Negative on return to station. Meet with the beat unit at the St. Francis—Code Two."

"Copy. Responding from Washington and Brenham."

During the night, tule fog, dense and clinging, had slithered down the rivers that drained into the bay. Corrupted by a stench of rotten water weeds and sludge, it was the least ethereal of the city's fogs, the least soothing.

"Code Two," he said, pulling away from the curb. Code Three was reserved for life-threatening circumstances. Lights and siren.

Code Two lacked that urgency, and when applied to Homicide, it became an informal code for the discovery of a dead body.

There, he thought, it's over—he's been found at last. However grim, finding him would be a relief, a fresh grounding in reality, for between them neither he nor Coffey could recall a cop's evaporating like this and then materializing again hale and hearty. And the shock of it had already been played out in Yosemite on Saturday morning, when he'd been paged from a somber breakfast with Elena and Ruml at the Ahwanhee: "John, this is Vince. Listen, Natty didn't show for the Brits this morning." John Kost had asked if Aranov might be ill; had anybody checked with Sylvia? "She ain't seen him since yesterday morning. . . ." At that instant, clenching the receiver, he had felt the chill of the river seep into him all over again. "I'm taking the first train out of here. Don't let them stop hunting for him. Don't let them decide he's drunk or off with some woman. Promise me, Vincent." Ragnetti had.

Black bunting for FDR was draped along the front of the St. Francis Hotel. Finding Nathan here might vindicate the man's idea on how to crack the cop-killings; it was, after all, where the Soviet delegation was staying.

He ran through doors and into the lobby, where he was met by the manager.

"Police?"

"Yes. Which room?"

"No room—it's in the first elevator there."

The pneumatic doors were open and through them he could see a patrolman, who was facing the rear of the car with his revolver drawn. As John Kost hurried toward the car, the second blue-suiter came into view, and he too was preparing to shoot. "Put that down, you old fuck!" he shouted.

Bringing out his own Colt, John Kost burst inside the car, then cried, "Papa!"

Backed up against a corner, Mikhail Kostoff was in the full regalia of His Majesty's Own Convoy of Cossacks, his long bloodred coat swirling around his bandy legs as he fended off first one patrolman and then the other with his sword. John Kost

could tell from the skew of his black fur cap and his watery eyes
that he was very drunk.

"Papa," he said in Russian, "sheath your *shashka*."

"Why must I—"

"Do it!"

Mikhail Kostoff glowered at him, but then with a loud scrape
did as he'd been told. Not deigning to look at the patrolmen, he
turned his face and crossed his arms over the cartridge pouches
sewn onto his coat. Long ago, John Kost had thrown away the
cartridges just in case he chanced upon a Berdan carbine
someplace. He was dangerous enough with his cold weapons, but
could not be relieved of these without a complete collapse of
pride.

"It started at the front desk, Inspector," one of the blue-suiters
explained, holstering. "He barged up and told the clerk to phone
this Russian admiral—"

"Rodionov?" John Kost asked.

"Yeah, that's him. Well, your old man wanted to challenge
him to a duel in the lobby."

"True, true," Mikhail Kostoff said with dignity.

John Kost motioned for him to be quiet. "What happened
then?"

"Well, when the clerk refused, your father drew that knife of
his—"

"Dagger, you fool," Mikhail Kostoff harrumphed in his broken
English.

"—and planted it in the top of the counter. When we arrived,
he was making for the elevator. He took out that sword of his, and
it turned into a Mexican standoff real quick. Him calling us geeks
and all."

"*Geeks?*"

"Yeah, can you believe it?"

A weary smile flickered over John Kost's lips. "No, no, old
fellow—my father wasn't insulting you. *Gik-Gik* is a Cossack
battle cry."

"Oh." Then the patrolman dropped his voice a peg. "I knew he
was your old man, Inspector, on account I had a couple run-ins

with him before. That's why I asked the manager to phone and have Communications send you, personal."

"My father and I appreciate your tact. . . ." As John Kost removed a five-dollar bill from his wallet, both patrolmen began to protest, but he waved off their insincere objections and tucked the bill in the pocket of the blue-suiter standing closest to him. "This is for lunch, gentlemen. The least I can do." Smiling, they filed out of the car, and John Kost punched the button to close the doors. He scooted the operator's stool across the floor to his father, who eased himself down.

"Where'd you get the money?" he asked, burying the pang of guilt that came with the realization he hadn't left off a half-pint ration for his father since last Monday. The old man lived for the arrival of those *merzavchiks*, or little rascals, as he called them. "Are you listening?"

"Don't use such a tone on me."

"I'm simply asking, Papa."

"I entrusted that wretched coat you gave me to a friend"—his way of admitting he'd pawned the seersucker jacket. A colonel of the Tsar's Own Convoy did not *hock* his clothes.

"And why're you in uniform?"

"The reception today." Then the old man's eyes brightened as he said, "For the British ambassador."

John Kost doubted if the ambassador would risk offending the Soviet Union by attending any function hosted by the threadbare vestiges of Romanov Russia, but he didn't say so to his father. "What's this craziness about a duel with Rodionov?"

"Crazy indeed!"

"Dueling's illegal in this state, Papa. Punishable by seven years imprisonment."

"Ekh!"

"Did you hear me?"

"What's illegal about killing a Bolshevik? If that were so, I'd be in prison until the Second Coming."

"You are not killing anybody in my city!"

Mikhail Kostoff rose. His voice was quavering. "Have you forgotten what they did to your mother? Have you forgotten!"

"What!"

"Murdered her! That's why my manservant had to steal into Moscow to rescue you!"

John Kost threw up his hands. "Then Rodionov's personally responsible?"

"How dare you split hairs over such a thing!"

"Because that's what we do in this country, Papa. We split hairs."

The old man glared at him a moment longer, then closed his eyes and began rubbing his goiter with his fingers. "Her singing could break your heart," he whispered at the brink of tears. "Even if you didn't know a word of Russian, her songs could make you weep. I saw this happen once with an Italian who spoke no Russian at all."

John Kost's expression softened. "What time's your reception?"

"Six—I'll need you to drive me. We've booked the Excelsior." A Class B hotel situated next to a brewery: the ambassador was definitely not coming.

"I want you to get some sleep before then."

The old man nodded as if he were already drowsy. "I'll see."

"Here, take my arm," John Kost said, opening the doors. But his father shook off any offer of support as they threaded their way through the crowded lobby.

"What're you looking for?" he asked, hanging up his hat and raincoat.

Ragnetti was going through Aranov's desk drawers. "I don't know. An address. A matchbook. You name it." He didn't look up when John Kost sat on a corner of the desk, but asked, "Something cooking at the St. Francis?"

"My father."

"Oh." Ragnetti needed no more explanation.

"I put him to bed and poured the rest of his vodka down the sink."

"He's getting pretty old for this shit, isn't he?"

"Yes." John Kost's eyes gravitated toward the bull pen windows, the whitish midday sky beyond. "Just before he dropped off he asked me to cover the street with straw."

"How's that?" Ragnetti slammed shut a desk drawer and opened another. His mouth was closed, but John Kost could tell by a rippling under the skin that he was gritting his teeth.

"Used to be in Russia when a fellow was dying, the servants covered the street outside his bedroom with straw. You know, to muffle the racket of the carts and carriages."

"John? A minute please?" From the door Coffey gestured for him to follow. John Kost caught up with the captain halfway down the corridor.

"Yes, Pat?" Again, his heart was racing. Expecting at any moment to hear about Aranov was wearing him out; he'd have to put it out of his mind and sleep soon, or collapse. But neither did he want to be rung out of a sound sleep to hear that the coroner had a DB in need of identification. "What's up?"

"A rhubarb—that's what." Coffey rocked his head from side to side as if trying to loosen a stiff neck.

John Kost noticed the boater on the hat rack even before he stepped inside the captain's office. Cade tossed off a quiet hello, but it was apparent by the tight-lipped way in which he puffed on his cigar that he was spoiling for a fight.

"Bob here," Coffey said, falling into his chair, "is of the opinion we're holding out on him."

John Kost asked, "In what regard?"

"Aranov's regard," Cade said. "Nobody bothered to tell me crap until your missing bulletin crossed my desk this morning."

"What's wrong with that?" John Kost felt like swatting the cigar out of his face. "Why'd you expect a special notification?"

"Because I was *with* Aranov on Friday night."

"Good God, do you know where—!"

"No. And considering what we were working on together, it don't sound good for him either. I told the damn kid to phone me before he did anything stupid."

John Kost's hopeful look faded. He sat. "Explain."

"It started with him bugging me Friday evening for the Photostats of the latents you wanted on the Soviets. Which we don't have—but I'll get into that in a minute. I invited him to come down to my house for a skull session." The agent glanced to Coffey. "I already told Pat here all the goodies I shared with Aranov. But in a nutshell, your kid had it in his head the Russians might've had something to do with the Elliot and Fenby homicides. . . ." He paused and grinned sarcastically at John Kost. "And thanks a bunch for telling me that a second cop's been knocked off."

"That was my doing, Bob," Coffey said.

"Whatever. I'm talking about a general attitude here, Pat. That's what galls me, okay?" Cade shifted in his chair toward John Kost again. "Because Aranov said he was working a Soviet angle and I found his ideas kinda interesting, I gave him what we had on their key operators in town."

"Who are?"

"Well, we believe the resident was some joker named Tikhov."

"*Was?*"

"Yeah," Cade said, "he dropped out of sight early last week. Tuesday, to be exact. Our boys keeping an eye on the consulate haven't seen him coming or going since."

Coffey leaned across his desk and handed John Kost two San Francisco PD arrest booking photographs, a full face and a profile. John Kost's eyes remained blank, but his thumb was denting the photos. After a moment, he asked, "Is this Tikhov?"

"None other," Cade said.

"Any AKAs?"

"No aliases we know about."

"Why'd our department mug him?"

"Because you people collared him in late January for five oh two. He was photographed and fingerprinted before he could make it clear that he had diplomatic immunity and your Traffic Bureau had no business hauling him in for drunk driving. Ten minutes later a car from the consulate picked him up. The arrest record was blotted out and—"

"You picked up the arrest photo and fingerprint card before they could be destroyed as well," John Kost finished for him.

"Bingo," Cade said. "Our boy was tailing Comrade Tikhov

215

when your Traffic cruiser caught him weaving all over Market Street. And listen, John, I wasn't being cutesy about the latents, even though to be precise about this we had your department's fingerprint card on him, not latents. But I just wanted to have an understanding with you people before you all went stampeding after Tikhov, blowing our surveillance on him and—"

"Do you have Tikhov's card with you now?"

The agent gestured toward Coffey, who held it up.

"Captain," John Kost said, "that should go to ID right away."

"Why's that?"

"Nathan"—how that name suddenly stung—"he thought of having the button on Elliot's notebook pocket dusted. ID got a partial latent off it."

"Elliot's then?" Cade asked John Kost. "Or Laska's?"

"Neither."

Coffey grabbed his phone. "How come I wasn't made aware of this, Inspector?" He rarely addressed him by rank.

"I apologize. I'm behind in reviewing my men's supplemental reports. Yosemite, sir," he added with his own touch of anger. Then, while the captain dialed ID, he asked Cade, "Was Nathan out looking for Tikhov Friday night?"

"Not exactly. I gave him a list of places we'd seen Tikhov cavorting. But actually he was looking for another joker in the Soviet deck. . . ." Cade reached across John Kost and took one more photograph off the captain's desk, an eight-by-ten blowup of an obvious Russian in a long, light-colored summer overcoat. A Soviet-marked C-47 transport was in the background.

"Taken at Hamilton Field last Tuesday?" John Kost asked.

"Yeah."

Despite the graininess of the photo, there was a tantalizing familiarity about the middle-aged man's face, his penetrating and intelligent gaze perhaps, but John Kost attributed the sense to having seen him at Hamilton. "Who's this?"

"That's the big question. . . ." Cade went on to explain how on Tuesday one Boris Pugachev, the alleged assistant to the Balkans expert, had asked his Army driver to let him off on Post Street before the convoy arrived at the St. Francis. Pugachev had never checked into the hotel, nor had he been seen by the FBI since, which led John Kost to suspect that he had local help in lying low. Cade then noted, "This guy speaks excellent English, by the way, and seemed damned sure of himself."

"What about the list you gave Nathan?"

Cade started to answer, but a knock at the door made him clam up. "Come," Coffey said.

Delbert from ID shuffled inside. "You wanted to see me, sir?"

"Right." Giving him the fingerprint card, Coffey ordered him to compare it to the partial latent taken off Elliot's uniform button. "I want an answer in ten minutes."

"I'll try."

"Piss on trying, Del. Just do it."

As the technician hurried out, John Kost asked Cade, "Two Soviets have vanished in a week's time for no apparent reason?"

"Make that three. Well, sorta. A consular staffer named Yaroshenko flew out of Hamilton on Wednesday evening in one of the returning Red Air Force transports."

"Secret police?"

"Sure. There's even some divided opinion he may have been the resident. But I don't think so. Just looking at him, you could tell he didn't pack the weight Tikhov did."

"What about that list, Robert?" John Kost asked.

"One of my boys and your man Hurley are already out going over the places one by one, inch by inch. Okay?"

And then John Kost could think of nothing more to ask. Tikhov's drunken and flashbulb-startled eyes were trained on his. He went through the photos one more time, but it was only an excuse to lay them facedown on Coffey's desk.

A silence fell over the smoky office, broken a few minutes later when the captain brought out his bottle of Irish and poured them each a shot. Nobody made a toast, not even a joking one. They just drank. John Kost's glass shook a bit in his grasp. He needed sleep. He needed a clear head before he tried to come to any conclusions.

The captain's phone rang. "Coffey." Listening, he began massaging his brow. "You sure now?" Another long pause. "All right then—thanks, Del." He hung up and gave himself another splash. "It's as good as Tikhov's latent on the button." Then he whistled. "Christ Almighty."

The thing is so cumbrous he must drag, not carry it across the shallows, and the current, swift and heavy at midchannel, nearly snatches and sweeps it away. He prays continuously, contradictorily: for help to do this, and then for forgiveness in having done it. Grunting for breath, he pulls it out of the river, up through the flagellating branches of the willows, and finally onto the hard spring snow. Between the cliff wall and the drift is a thin, bluish crevice. He widens it by scooping out the snow with a pewter ice bucket he's brought from the hotel, flinging the bucketfuls over his shoulder. By the time he's cobbed out a grave big enough for the thing, the masking cedars around him have gone from black to green—it will soon be dawn. He hurries, although his fingers are stiff with cold, and at last lowers the thing into the hole. With his handkerchief, which he has coiled into a sash, he tries to tie up the dangling lower jaw, for no one should have to wear such a look into the interlude in which all the dead, the good and the pestilential alike, await the possibility of expiation. No one. But it's no use. The rigor mortis is cresting and won't begin to subside for another six hours: the gape is set in concrete. He takes from his shirt pocket a slip of writing paper and the ink pad he pilfered off the front desk. He is reaching for the dead right hand to fingerprint it when suddenly the extinguished eyes clap open. He cries out, churns backward on his heels to flee—but not before a butcher knife flashes out of the grave and sinks deep into his thigh. . . .

John Kost awoke to a wavering red glow.

He saw that he'd thrown off his covers and was pressing his palm against the old stab wound, just as he had years before to slow the bleeding while he used a sofa cushion to fend off the further slashes of the woman who'd made up her mind to erase a lifetime of indignities, real and imagined, by killing a cop. Any cop would have done.

The indented scar in his thigh was pulsating. It had its own memory.

218

The glow was flickering from two red-glass taper cups, each mounted to an icon. The icons were obviously a marriage set, and in his bewilderment he imagined—with a twinge of regret—that once again he'd blundered into Lydia's bed, that once again he'd rearmed her expectations. Yet, these icons were hung on the wall across from the bed, not over the headboard as were hers. Directly above him, a drawn window shade was letting in some pale light. Then they were his icons. He was in his own bed.

Rising up on his elbows, he caught sight of the kneeling figure of Elena Martova just as she finished crossing herself before the icons. She was nude, and the lean beauty of her back so evoked his wife's he whispered, "Lenochka," if only to remind himself not to lapse into that other name.

"Did you sleep well?" she asked, her face still averted.

"Yes," he lied. "Come back to bed."

With the candlelight glancing around her hair, she half-turned. The sadness in her profile brought it back to him, how he'd no sooner arrived home at three this afternoon, ravenous for a few hours' sleep, than she'd appeared in his yet open door, her face powdered and blank, her gloved hands tight around her purse. "What're you doing here?" he blurted.

She looked hurt as she stepped inside. "Do you want me to go?"

He hesitated, then shut the door and engaged the rim lock with a snap that made her startle. "Of course not. But what if Martov had you followed?"

"He didn't."

"How d'you know?"

"He just didn't," she repeated, pulling off her gloves and superstitiously placing them on the console table *in love*—in the shape of the cross.

"Did you walk?" he asked, trying not to make this sound like an interrogation.

"It's only a few blocks."

"I know how far it is." He helped her out of her overcoat. "Do you do this to spite him?"

"No. He has nothing to do with us."

"Then why, Lenochka?"

"You're going to help my child," she said with a brusque smile that refused to admit the possibility of failure.

"And if I can't?"

"Don't talk that way." She looked sharply round. "Are you alone right now?"

He wondered what could move her to even a paltry jealousy; they'd made no claims on each other. Or had they tacitly, now that a corpse was buried in a snowbank? "Who else would be here?"

"Your father."

"We live apart."

"Why?"

"He finds fault with me."

"You only imagine so."

He noticed the scrape on her chin she'd gotten at Yosemite and wondered how she had explained it to Martov. "Aren't you going to ask me how I found your flat?" she asked.

"It had occurred to me."

"Your driver's permit," she said as she began strolling around his living room, examining the Spartan furnishings. "I saw it at the Ahwanhee when you laid out your wallet papers to dry." She caught his eye. "You don't spend much time here, do you?"

"Very little."

"Why's that?"

"I don't have much time away from my job," he said, irritated with himself that in the midst of such exhaustion and remorse he could be aroused by her. There was something distastefully primeval about killing a man and then celebrating it with fornication.

"Is that it then? Your job?" She smiled.

"Yes." Already she suspected that he took his comfort not here but in the company of women like Lydia Thripp. Why did she seem so bent on a possessiveness neither of them would ever be free to cultivate? It made him watch her shrewdly as she limped around his living room.

But still he wanted to take her again.

He was prepared to wait, but suddenly she approached him, no longer smiling, and took his hand. She touched it to her cheek in such misery he realized that this afternoon she needed the liberation of orgasm more than he. "God help us," he whispered, "but you'll ruin me."

"No. Only I will be lost, Vanechka. I'm already lost." She found his lips with hers, shared the warmth of her hunger.

He would not nurse his own pleasure but—with great care and restraint—attend hers. He tossed her coat onto the sofa, and it slid off like a dead body.

His caressing hand fell from her cheek and found the small of her back; he pulled her into him. In the darkness of his bedroom, he stiffened against the chill that came from entering her; he resisted the excitement that threatened to turn his own hunger self-serving. Patiently, using the meager light slanting down from the window above his bed, he studied her face, waiting for that look of soft pain to wash over it. His ejaculation, when at last he freed it, was really nothing, a flash that turned sluggish, a lessening of pressure, damp matches. But afterward, for the first time in days, he'd dropped off to sleep.

Now, as he waited for her to rise from prayer and come to bed again, he realized that none of this had brought them closer to trust. "What time's it?" he asked.

"Around five, I think."

"I've got to get going."

"I too." But instead of dressing she lay down beside him. She kissed his baptismal cross, then embraced him. Absently, she began tugging at his chest hair with her fingers. After a while, she asked, "What're we going to do?"

"I don't know."

"Perhaps your government can—"

"One of my men is missing."

She drew back from him a little. "What do you mean?"

"Aranov, one of my assistants, vanished while on duty Friday night."

She let go of him entirely. "Surely there's some harmless explanation."

"No."

"Does he drink too much from time to time, does he—"

"He's the most responsible fellow I know." He paused, sickened to imagine that she might already know about Aranov's disappearance, might even know what had become of him. But he wasn't willing to believe this, not with her eyes warm and steady on his. "Do you know anything about a man named Tikhov?"

"At the consulate, you mean?"

"Right."

"Just the name. I've never met him. . . ." That might be true: she'd arrived on Tuesday, the same day the resident had dropped out of sight. "You know," she went on, "Martov asked me about him too."

"Why would he ask you about someone on his own staff?"

"I have no idea, but Martov was curious if there'd been any talk about him on the flight here."

"Was there?" he asked.

"No. What makes him so interesting?"

"No one can find him and. . . ." His voice trailed off.

"Yes?"

"He's said to be the head intelligence man at the consulate." Once he had gone so far as to broach this, he decided to risk the next question: "Lenochka, I've got to know something if I'm to help you. . . ."

She looked at him, waiting.

"By all that's holy, tell me—is your husband with the secret police?"

She laughed derisively.

"Then the answer's no?"

"No, Vanechka, and no again a thousand times. I'm sure the Cheka enlists bolder men than Pyotr Martov."

"Men like Boris Pugachev?"

She stopped laughing, and her eyes darted back to his cross. "Who?"

"I realize he wasn't on your plane, but at the Moscow airfield did you notice a tall fellow in a long tan overcoat?"

"No." Then, as if to break the troubled mood that had fallen over them, she kissed him and said, "All I know is that you're an exceptional man. You do exceptional things."

"Like what?" he asked with a skeptical smile.

"You married a woman who was carrying a baby not yours. And you would've loved that child as your own, yes?" When he said nothing, she touched his lips with her fingers. "I'm sorry. I know it's hard for you to talk about this."

"I've got to pick up my father," he said. "I think we should leave separately."

20

Rᴀɢɴᴇᴛᴛɪ ꜱᴀᴛ ᴛʜɪɴᴋɪɴɢ at his desk for a long while after John Kost told him what had been said in Coffey's office, so long his fresh cup of coffee had gone cold by the time he remembered to take a swig. He wasn't thinking so much about how these missing Russians, Tikhov and Pugachev, might figure in Aranov's disappearance as he was about the boss. John had come back from Yosemite with a screwball look in his eye. Part of it could be explained by Natty's vanishing into thin air, for sure, and part by that black cloud John went into from time to time, which left him dopey and glum until he made up his mind life in general and the Homicide Bureau in particular were worth screwing with again. But it was some other part of John's present lousy humor, one Ragnetti couldn't quite put his finger on, that had him worried—like why had he gone home at midday for a nap? It'd seemed like the captain of a ship handing over the bridge in the middle of a typhoon. Natty was *gone*. Sure, they were all in need of more shut-eye than what they were getting; but when was the last time John had gone home in the middle of the day?

The phone made Ragnetti jump. He glanced around the bull pen to make sure no one had seen this evidence of his ragged nerves before he reached for the handset. "Ragnetti, Homicide."

Nobody said anything at the other end, but he knew somebody was there because breath was whistling in the line.

"Who's this? Talk." Again no reply, so he said, "Well, whoever you are—if I had a feather up my ass we'd both be tickled." He hung up. All at once, the faded green walls of the bull pen were closing in on him and the clatter of a typewriter from down the hall in Burglary was making his flesh crawl. He got his hat and with plodding steps, started for the elevator. He didn't care where he was headed as long as it was away from the Hall of Justice.

Should he finally drop by and visit Sylvia Aranov? He had passed up the chance to tag along with John Saturday night when he rushed from the train to her house. Sylvia didn't like him—he just knew she thought of him as low company for Natty. But maybe that wasn't the real reason he hadn't called on her: he was afraid she'd look right through him as if his skin were wax paper and see the thing that was smudging up his insides, making him feel like puking all the time. It had started as a little smoldery coal, and he wouldn't have given it a second thought had Aranov showed up to baby-sit the British the way he'd been supposed to on Saturday morning. But Aranov hadn't showed, and now— deep inside his ears, over and over again—he kept hearing his own voice chewing out Natty for never doing anything on his own. Those words hadn't been one hundred percent true, for Aranov had grown some balls since reporting to Homicide, a bookish little Hebe whose eyes had watered if anybody so much as said boo to him. But he'd always needed John or Ragnetti himself to pat him on the head for each and every thing he did right. Who ever gave Vince Ragnetti a pat on the head?

A guy like Natty had no business being a cop in the first place. He just wasn't large enough. In the old days, the personnel captain went down the line of recruits punching each on the arm as hard as he could, and those who budged or cried out got the boot; Ragnetti punched him back and that got a good laugh, even from the captain.

Startled, he realized that he was behind the wheel of his Dodge, cruising down through Chinatown toward Market Street.

"Jesus." He could recall neither the elevator ride to the basement nor firing up his car and pulling away from the Hall of Justice. Like a magnifying glass or something, the afternoon haze seemed to be making the light even more blinding. Sitting up, clearing his head with a shake, he made up his mind to go to Mt. Davidson Park and check on how the search by the auxiliary police was going. Maybe having someplace to go would keep his mind from blanking out, and kicking around where Aranov had gone might help him dope it all out.

Yet, he no sooner arrived at the park than he made a U-turn and headed back toward the north end of town, using the huge gas tank in Marina District as a kind of beacon. He didn't feel like talking to the auxiliaries, who wanted to be real cops so bad they could taste it. He'd decided on a new destination: the Hyde Street Pier, where the PD motorboat was supposed to be dragging the berth with grappling hooks. But then, while cutting across Marina District toward the waterfront, he had a mental picture of one of those hooks coming up with Natty in its claws. He almost retched before he could crank down the window for some breeze.

It was John Kost's fault. If he'd told Aranov to clear everything through his sergeant the way the book said, none of this would have happened. Ragnetti would have said no to working with the FBI because they were conceited pricks who grabbed more than they gave and weren't above sending a flatfoot out to clear a minefield for them.

Pulling over, he went into a corner grocery owned by an old Italian he knew from his mother's church. He asked for a fifth of California Chianti and got it gratis, as expected. While the owner uncorked the bottle for him, in violation of the beverage control laws, Ragnetti told himself that the dryness of the wine would soak up any more bad pictures inside his head. He asked the old man how the Seals would do this year.

"Ah, *non me ne frega niente, Vincenzo*," he said—I don't give a fuck. He was pissed at the team because a cop had made him give up a foul ball he'd caught, as was the park rule. Ragnetti was in no mood to hear out a complaint. So he walked out.

He'd left without saying good-bye, it hit him a couple blocks

226

later. But suddenly it didn't matter. He had a new destination, someplace that had been popping into his mind all afternoon. And each time it popped up he'd felt like a bum. But now he had to go there. For Aranov's sake, maybe.

He parked down the street from the apartment, but not so far that he couldn't see the bay window and the door. The 1939 Dodge sedan was still parked out front, so he sat back and began sucking on the bottle of Chianti.

After an hour or so, he tried the AM radio, but the stations not broadcasting a nationwide hookup by the new president—a whiny-sounding little fuck who had no chance of filling FDR's shoes—were playing hillbilly music. The only decent station had just launched a Puccini opera, but for some reason Puccini reminded him too much of Aranov.

He switched off the radio.

The murky-orange sun was just dipping behind the Presidio's trees when John Kost came out of his apartment dressed in a tux. He got into his Dodge without glancing up out of his thoughts and started the engine, smoke gusting out of the tailpipe. A few moments later, over the police band, Ragnetti heard him ask Central One if there was any traffic for him.

"Negative," the dispatcher said.

As expected, John made the first right turn and headed downtown. But Ragnetti didn't follow him. He finished the Chianti and waited. The wine had finally made him feel up to Puccini, and he turned the radio back on.

It was not long before a woman came out of John's apartment. She *did* look up and down the street before clipping across the asphalt in her high heels toward the corner. She had a limp, but was still a knockout with long legs and a tiny waist. He felt an ache of futility that he would never in his life have a woman like that. But then this ache of envy went away as he thought of Aranov.

He turned the key and gunned the engine. Reaching for the volume knob, he brought Puccini to full blast as he sped away.

The screech of tires from the departing car so unnerved her she changed direction at once and didn't head back toward the consulate until it was dark. Who had driven the car? Was Vanechka right after all—was Martov having her followed? These thoughts made approaching the mailbox around the corner from the consulate an agony.

At the last second, certain she was being watched, she panicked and passed it by, hurrying on into the evening.

But leaving it unchecked seemed as dreadful as going up to it, so she came around the block again and keeping her gaze steadfastly forward so as not to draw suspicion to herself, suddenly genuflected and groped beneath it. Rising, she came away with an envelope that had been taped to its bottom.

She began breathing again.

John Kost stepped out of his car into a miasma of raw beer. He frowned up at the brewery looming over the Excelsior Hotel, its rusted stacks pouring an incandescent effluent into the nightfall. "The British ambassador, indeed." He followed the orchestral strains into the reception hall, which he no sooner entered than a cry of recognition went up. Giving a curt bow of acknowledgment as the living solution to émigré difficulties with city hall, he then began searching for his father, who'd not been in his unlocked flat when he'd arrived at a quarter to six to pick him up.

Semyon Obolensky swept up to him, grinning widely. The librarian of the San Francisco Symphony was decked out in a frock coat as if to suggest that he'd been one of the Tsar's familiars. "Ah, Ivan Mikhailovich! Splendid you could make it!"

"Yes, have you seen—"

"The prince will be here tonight!"

"How nice." John Kost didn't feel moved to ask which one; there had been over two thousand of them at the start of the Revolution, and three times that number had cropped up in exile. "Have you seen my father, Semyon Petrovich?"

"His High Nobility arrived shortly before you did."

"Thank God," John Kost said.

"But a bit worse for wear, I'm afraid. He's upstairs repairing his uniform." Then Obolensky added, "He must've stumbled a time or two on the march over . . . Here, wait!" Snatching two vodkas off a passing waiter's tray, he offered one to John Kost, but then held it back when the inspector reached for the glass. "Only if you eat something with it. You look spent down to the last kopeck, Ivan Mikhailovich."

"I am." But then he asked, altogether too innocently, "Is the ambassador here yet?"

"Didn't you hear? An hour ago he sent his most profound regrets." Obolensky pointed with disdain at a young but balding man standing awkwardly in the corner, waiting for someone to speak to him. "*That* is Mr. Profound Regrets, the assistant to the assistant deputy consul, or something like that. He's not even from the embassy in Washington, mind you."

"How embarrassing," John Kost said.

"Particularly for the prince."

"Yes, the prince."

When the conductor of the rented orchestra, which was still warming up, waved for Obolensky's attention, John Kost made his escape. He knew it was time he did indeed eat something, but no sooner did he approach the buffet table than a portly man there exclaimed to his equally fat wife, "Why, if it isn't young Kostoff, Mother!" The Kropotniks were Lydia's godparents, and in better days he'd been a councillor of state and a confidant to the Grand Duke. He was now a liquor wholesaler.

John Kost pressed his lips to madame's cream puff of a hand. "Good evening."

"My dear fellow," Kropotnik said in French, munching on a cracker tottering with black caviar, "I've had some misfortune with your Traffic Bureau."

"I'm sorry to hear that." He would have been looking to make a gracious retreat, except that he needed to know if Lydia would be attending tonight. He meant to bow out of her dinner party tomorrow evening, but wanted to tell her in person. "What kind of misfortune, sir?"

"Well, one of your fellows put something between my windscreen and the wiper blade."

Madame tittered at the presumptuousness of doing such a

thing to her husband's automobile. On her corsage was a miniature of Nikolas II, framed with brilliants. John Kost didn't have to look closely to know they were glass. "By chance, do you have the citation on your person, sir?" he asked.

"Why, yes—I believe I do. Is that what it's called? A 'citation'? Why, that makes it sound like an honor."

"The word doesn't translate well."

"I see." Kropotnik produced the ticket and stroked one of his waxed mustaches while John Kost examined it. "I can't make any sense of it. Can you?"

"Well, sir, the officer alleges you keep parking the wrong way in front of your office on Fourth Street."

The man scoffed at the very notion. "How's that possible, Ivan Mikhailovich? An automobile goes both forward and backward at the driver's will. So tell me, how's it possible to ever park in the wrong direction without defying the laws of mechanics?"

"I quite agree." John Kost tucked the citation in his cutaway coat. "Please let me take care of this inconvenience." The Kropotniks beamed, and he asked, "Is Lydia Dmitrievna expected tonight?"

"Oh, no—she's out of town, isn't she, *ma chère?*"

"Yes, quite, Father."

"Did she happen to say when she'd return?" John Kost hoped that she had somehow forgotten about her own party—unlikely but possible.

"Tomorrow morning, she said. And where was she going this time, Father?"

Kropotnik shrugged with a smile, and John Kost saw no further reason to belabor the conversation. "Please excuse me, I must check on my father."

"Yes, do," she said with concern, but also with enough condescension in her tone to make him suddenly loathe her. Without the likes of his father, who wore the order of St. George for genuine gallantry on the field of battle, the Kropotniks and their ilk would not have lasted as long as they had in pomp and opulence. The Devil take the Kropotniks.

I really can't be trusted in polite company tonight, he thought, feeling the vodka rise to his face. *I'm spoiling for a quarrel.*

Kissing her hand once more, he then started for the staircase before Obolensky could find him again. He was halfway up the balustrade when a French horn plaintively declared the first notes of "The Cavalry of the Steppes." "Here you are!" Obolensky whispered from behind. "I thought I'd lost you." He nodded toward the orchestra. "A rather gauche old war-horse, wouldn't you say?" Yet, when the librarian caught sight of John Kost's eyes, he added, "But moving in its own way."

John Kost looked past the librarian and could see muzzle flashes winking across a wheat field. It had happened somewhere between Moscow and Irkutsk—an ambush by Red partisans. "Tadeusz," his father had cried to his Polish manservant, "take the lad to the rear!" And with Vanechka clinging to his back, the old servant galloped his nag toward the edge of the twilight—but not before the boy saw Colonel Kostoff, the most fearless of men, the most glorious of men, force his mount to rise up on its hind legs in front of his soldiers. Then his Cossacks brandished their carbines over their heads and charged—

"Ivan Mikhailovich?"

"What?—please, Semyon Petrovich, I'd like to be alone for a while." Then, to spare himself the embarrassing consequences of his own rebuff, he continued up the stairs, taking them three at a time. As he came into the echoing porcelain sterility of the men's lavatory, the orchestra abruptly quit "The Cavalry of the Steppes" and struck up "God Save the Tsar." The prince—whichever prince—had arrived. Framed by a long rank of urinals on one side and the toilet stalls on the other, Mikhail Kostoff was standing at the window. The pebbled glass was dark; the sun was completely gone. The notes of the anthem seemed to hover around him as if he'd coaxed them here with him from the imperial enclave at Tsarskoye Selo, a swarm of bees for whom he'd not yet found a suitable apiary. Somehow, the stoop was gone from his back, and his goiter seemed less protuberant than usual. Yet, his salute was pathetic.

"Papa," he said when the music was done.

The old man turned toward him. His face was shining wetly. "Go away please."

"I came to your flat at quarter to six, as promised."

"Go. This has nothing to do with that."

"I know, Papa. I know very well."

The old man nodded, then gave him his back.

John Kost no sooner reached the top of the stairs than Obolensky stood in his path, looking hangdog. "Honestly, I'd rather cut my throat than bother you again, Ivan Mikhailovich—but some fellow insists on seeing you in the lobby."

"Who?"

"I didn't talk to him myself. The doorman asked me to find you."

"Thank you, Semyon Petrovich. And forgive my rudeness a while ago. I'm very tired."

"I saw that right off. No offense taken, Ivan Mikhailovich. But you should rest—"

Thinking it to be someone from the department with news about Aranov, John Kost nearly ran from the reception hall.

But it was not a cop who awaited him. It was Ruml, whose face remained unsmiling as he said, "The vice-consul apologizes for disturbing you, Inspector"—no familiarity had apparently survived the trip to Yosemite—"and asks for a moment of your time." He pointed through the glass doors at the black Cadillac parked across the street.

John Kost could see the silhouette of Pyotr Martov's head in the backseat. He crossed his arms over his chest, but did so only to make sure his revolver was snugly in its holster. "All right."

21

Lᴇᴛ ᴍᴇ ᴀᴘᴏʟᴏɢɪᴢᴇ, Inspector," Pyotr Martov said, "for taking you away from your affair. But I doubt I would've been welcome inside, wouldn't you say?"

John Kost didn't. He had purposely closed the tail of his coat in the door so it wouldn't latch.

The vice-consul sat in the opposite corner of the backseat with his arms outstretched like a boxer. The only touch of the old nonchalance about him was the cigarette glowing in his right fist.

Ruml drove away from the curb. The traffic was sparse, but he managed to pull in front of another car. A horn barked. He ignored it.

So far, no explanation for this summons had been discussed, but John Kost felt certain enough of Martov's reasons to see no purpose in asking. Besides, there was an implicit agreement in this sort of thing that the cuckolded husband have the opening shot when and where he wanted it. But he also wondered if Aranov had taken this same ride Friday night. Ruml was no doubt armed, and Martov probably as well. Yes, he realized that the two Soviets were sitting catercorner across the interior of the Cadillac, and if the tempers got out of hand, he might be able to delay their gunfire simply by interspacing himself between them—before tumbling out the door. "Where to, Comrade Vice-consul?" Ruml asked.

"Just drive awhile, Viktor Fyodorovich . . . no, wait—take us to that ridiculous place Elena Valentinovna and I went the other night. I'm in a ridiculous mood."

Ruml turned north onto Montgomery Street.

"How'd you find the Yosemite, Ivan Mikhailovich?"

"Chilly."

"A pity." Martov stubbed out his pungent Russian cigarette in his armrest ashtray. "Well, again, with my apologies, I had no choice but to disturb you tonight. The schedule's been advanced on something rather important."

"How's that?"

"This kind of talk goes smoother over vodka." Martov eased back, light and darkness flickering over his deadpan face. He yawned behind his hand.

John Kost didn't care for his insouciance. Is this how a good Communist reacted to another man's making love to his wife? By now he had hoped for some shouting to break the tension; his nerves were tuned for a confrontation. But after a preliminary coolness, which may or may not have had anything to do with Elena, Martov had lapsed into his usual amiable self. "She's a peculiar woman," he broke the silence at length. "Once she makes up her mind in matters of the heart, there's no changing it." He gave John Kost a composed but ambiguous smile, then turned to look out the window at nothing, the street was dark. "But I suppose one must expect differences of the heart if one marries a woman fifteen years his junior. . . ."

When another silence followed, John Kost realized that nothing more would be said about her tonight. But Martov had felt moved to reveal that he *knew*, even though something—or someone—was making him hold back his anger.

Meanwhile, Ruml had double-parked in front of Mrs. Testa's, a North Beach night spot.

"Have you been here before?" Martov asked.

"Yes." John Kost got out, pretending to spring the latch.

234

"Stay with the car, Viktor Fyodorovich," the vice-consul said.

At the reservations desk, a matronly transvestite in a taffeta gown spread his arms to embrace John Kost. "Why, Inspector, how long has it been?"

"Too long, my dear Mrs. Testa." Without hesitation, he returned the embrace. This had been the only nightclub friendly to the beat cops in the bohemian colony; accommodation and self-effacing humor seemed more in harmony with this way of life than radical politics. "I believe you may already know Pyotr Martov of the Soviet consulate."

"Of course, *enchanté* again, Vice-consul. This way, gentlemen."

"Not too close to the musicians, please. We'd like to talk," John Kost said, following Mrs. Testa through a slit in a pair of maroon velveteen drapes. Martov added, "But not so far from the show we will have trouble seeing it."

John Kost's gaze swept up to the klieg-bright line of female impersonators, then back down to the candlelit tables, searching out any Slavic-looking faces in the meager Monday-night crowd, perhaps even Pugachev's. But he saw nothing other than the usual gawkers and out-of-towners, here to flaunt their sophistication. Apparently Martov had brought along no backup other than Ruml.

"What will it be, friends?" the waiter asked. Doe eyes in a pasty face.

Martov glanced to John Kost: "Dare we ask for *pertsovka*, Ivan Mikhailovich?"

"Sir, *this* is San Francisco—two peppered vodkas coming up," the waiter said with affected indignation, making Martov laugh uproariously. "Will Smirnoff's do?"

John Kost nodded.

"I could happily die in this city," Martov said in Russian, still chuckling. But then he sobered when he caught John Kost's look. "Why so glum, Vanya?" He paused. "Do you mind if I call you Vanya? Ivan Mikhailovich's too bourgeois and Vanechka's too cloying."

"I'm very tired. What d'you say we get down to the business at hand?"

"And what business is that?"

"You mentioned the schedule."

"Oh, of course—our hospitality ship's arriving a day earlier than expected from Vladivostok, and the consul general has asked me to make sure there will be police security on the pier for it."

"Hospitality ship?"

"Yes, it's loaded down with vodka, caviar, cigarettes—you know, provisions for our entertaining."

"Do you intend to hold receptions aboard it then?"

"Well," Martov said, "I'm not sure about that. It won't be tied up to the wharf, but will moor to a buoy out in the bay. Its dinghy will ferry our people to and from the pier."

"Which pier?" John Kost asked.

"Thirty-nine."

"And when does it come in?"

Martov checked his wristwatch. "The captain radioed from the vicinity of the the Farallon Islands about two hours ago."

A quick mental calculation convinced John Kost that, if it didn't have to wait too long for a pilot to negotiate the minefields, the Soviet ship could be docking within the hour. "I'll phone and see what can be done."

But Martov gently held his forearm to the table. "Stay put a moment, dear Vanya—our drinks." The vice-consul accepted his glass from the waiter and immediately hoisted it. "To the memory of your mother."

John Kost flinched.

Offering the same inexplicable smile, Martov asked, "Have I said something wrong?"

"No. To my mother, then."

Both men drained their glasses. "Oh, my," the waiter muttered, taking away their empties for refill.

"Do you mind talking about her?" Martov asked.

"What's there to say?"

"It's just that I find it curious when you say you know so little about her."

"She died when I was five."

"May I ask how?"

"Shot. A food riot."

Martov gazed off toward the lithe young men in their brassy wigs, but seemed not to see them. "I'm very sorry. Those were terrible times."

"And where were you during those terrible times? With the Red Army?"

"Oh, no," Martov said. "I was with the Maryinski Theatre."

John Kost had to hide his surprise. "As a dancer?"

The vice-consul shook his head. "Assistant to the regisseur. It was much later when I joined the Party and went into foreign service." John Kost wanted to know if this is how he'd met Elena, but he didn't want to bring her up and perhaps undo the truce they'd settled into. "What was your mother's name, Vanya?"

He stared at him a moment before saying, "Alla. Her name was Alla."

"And she was a Gypsy?"

"Yes, a singer."

"Really?" Martov appeared fascinated. "In Moscow?"

"Yes."

"Which restaurant?"

"The Yar."

"You don't say? I dined there more times than I can remember. There or the Strelnya. And you mustn't be so closemouthed about such an interesting mother. Many of the Gypsy singers I knew were women of both culture and substance—not to mention means. She must've been quite striking, if I might judge on the basis of your looks."

John Kost ignored the compliment. "I don't know. I have no photograph."

"*No?*" Martov said as if this were the most distressing thing imaginable. "Why, all those grand old restaurants had photographers on staff for benefit of the patrons. Certainly a portrait or two has survived somewhere. Let me make some inquiries in your behalf."

"To the secret police?"

Martov's smile didn't falter as he said, "There are other sources of information. Ah, here we go now—" The waiter had arrived with the second round, which the two men then put away with dispatch equaling the first. "We would like some champagne," the vice-consul said in his somewhat formal English, "but we are willing to drink vodka until the champagne is truly cold."

"And pray tell, what is *truly* cold?" the waiter asked.

"I want to see needles of ice floating in it, my dear fellow."

John Kost said, rising, "I have to call the station as soon as possible. It's going to take a while to get a patrolman out to the pier."

"Very well, but hurry back. I'm beginning to forget myself in your company, and a man would go mad if he didn't forget himself from time to time. What?"

Instead of dialing the Hall of Justice, John Kost took a list from his wallet. The ink had been smeared by the Merced's waters, but the telephone numbers were still legible. He asked the operator to connect him with a Daly City number, then deposited the toll when she told him the amount.

"Hello," an impatient voice answered.

"Cade?"

"Yeah, who's this?"

"John Kost. I have only a moment, so listen. Did you know a special Soviet ship will be anchoring off Pier Thirty-nine sometime in the next two hours?"

For a few seconds nothing but background static came over the line. "No, I didn't." And then in an fierce whisper: "Fuck the Office of Naval Intelligence!"

"For not knowing?"

"Hell, no—for knowing and not telling us. As usual."

"Well," John Kost said, checking over his shoulder as an uncannily pretty impersonator sashayed down the corridor toward the men's rest room, "in my father's words, this ship's going to make for excellent 'conspiratorial premises.' I wouldn't be

238

surprised if Mr. Pugachev even goes aboard from time to time. As you know, I'm a little shorthanded right now. Can your people stake it out?"

"You bet, even if I got to watch the tub myself."

"Good. I'm going to put an auxiliary cop on the pier for an hour or so—just to keep the Soviets happy—and then pull him off. He'd just scare away any interesting company."

"Right, get him outta there as quick as you can. Deputize some bastard from the Braille Institute if you got to."

"Until later then, Robert."

"Hey, John . . . ," Cade said with unaccustomed camaraderie.

"Yes?"

"Thanks. I'll be waiting for the sons of bitches."

"Be careful. They could be waiting for us."

After phoning the Central Station watch commander and instructing him to post a guard on Pier 39 until one hour *after* the arrival of the ship, he returned to the table. "It's arranged."

"Excellent, thank you." Martov's eyes were in a jovial squint. "The Yar, you say!"

"Yes. Your boss, what with his tastes for dance and the violin, must've frequented the place, I'm sure."

"My boss?"

"Yes, Vyacheslav Molotov. He's your superior, isn't he?"

"Oh, well—distantly, I suppose, in that he's head of the commissariat. I'm afraid many, many bosses stand between me and Comrade Molotov."

"How many?" John Kost asked.

Martov buried his frown in his glass. "A considerable number."

"What of the delegates to the Conference?"

"What of them?"

"To whom do they report?"

"I have no idea what you're getting at." Martov held up his glass in the waiter's direction.

"Yes, you do. You know exactly what I'm getting at."

"I find this discussion rather indelicate."

"I don't give a damn," John Kost said, then smiled at the vice-consul's sudden discomfort. "You picked me up tonight because you need information. You need to know how much I know. Am I right?"

Instead of replying, Martov wiped his lips with his handkerchief as if there were a bad taste on them.

"And I have a feeling we're concerned about the same thing, you and I. Otherwise, you wouldn't be bothering with me."

Martov's voice was nearly a whisper. "What has Elena told you?"

"Nothing. You yourself have so much as told me this."

"Pardon me, Inspector Kost"—it was Mrs. Testa—"telephone. An emergency, your fellow said. Go ahead and take it in my office."

"Thank you." Without excusing himself, he got up and strode for the phone. The mouthpiece was heavily scented with the perfume Mrs. Testa was awash in tonight. "Kost, here."

"Yeah, John," said the Central Station watch commander he'd talked to only a few minutes before, "Communications just put out an urgent ATC on you."

He started taking deeper breaths. He already knew what the attempt-to-contact was about. "Yes?"

"I think they've found Aranov."

He had the sensation that he was sinking through the floor, and his own voice seemed to be coming from far above him as he said, "Please send a cruiser around for me. I'll be waiting out front."

On Ragnetti's desk was a three-inch stack of supplemental reports Hurley and Mulrenan had half-assed on the pachuco homicide down in Potrero District. But he shoved the paperwork aside and folded his hands atop his blotter. He was mildly drunk, but it took a lot more than a fifth of Chianti and four Rainiers to make it apparent. He wanted somebody to talk to, but then again he had nothing to say—at least until he made up his mind what it meant, this thing between John Kost and the Russian woman who looked for all the world like John's dead wife, same chestnut hair and skinny build. He had known at once that she was the looker from the consulate who'd sent him into the tailspin last week, but never could he imagine his selling out to the Reds, war or no war. But maybe he wasn't thinking too clearly right now. John seldom did when it came to women.

Telephone bells jangled his thoughts. "Homicide, Ragnetti."

Once again—that live silence.

"Jesus fucking Christ," he growled. "I gotta put a tap on this son of a bitch so I can get an address where I can beat you to death?"

"Settle down," a nervous voice said.

"Well, well—I finally got somebody to talk."

"You alone?"

"What's it to you, bub? Maybe you want me to tell you what kinda underwear I got on?"

"I want you to shut up a minute, Vince, so I can talk. I don't got long."

"Do I know you?"

"Yeah, you know me. But that don't matter none. Is this line safe?" the caller asked. The rasp of a lift-boom winch in the background told Ragnetti that he was in a booth somewhere near the waterfront.

"What d'you mean safe?"

"Can anybody else listen in?"

"Yeah, it goes through the switchboard. Want me to call you back on our secure line?"

"No way, Vince, and I ain't meeting with you in person either so don't even ask. Gimme the number and I'll call you right back."

Ragnetti did so, then hung up the handset as if dropping a water balloon from a rooftop. He didn't care for snitches, even ones he himself had developed. With a loud sigh, he hoisted himself to his feet and strolled into John's office. One of the lines in there didn't go through the Hall of Justice's PBX. This phone rang, and he picked it up, sneering, "This who I think it is?"

"Probably, but don't go saying it out loud."

"You been having any more trouble with sea gulls?"

"Naw, you did a good job on them," the longshoreman Mickey said. "Listen, I'm just on a fifteen-minute break—"

"Okay, okay."

"—and I'm only saying this because I'm all for the war effort, you know, and I figure you're a regular joe who won't go blabbing."

"Blabbing about what, already?" Ragnetti asked.

Mickey hesitated, then said in even a quieter voice, "Two weeks ago—Christ, don't ask me what night of the week—that ammo launch from Mare Island, the forty-footer I showed you, it pulls into the basin near midnight. Except it don't dock like it usually does to take me or some other stevedore aboard."

"Up to Pier Forty-six?"

"Right—except it *don't* dock that night," Mickey said.

"I'm following you."

"So anyways, a couple minutes later this fishing boat comes into the basin too and ties up alongside the launch."

"This queer or something?"

"Christ yes, nothing civilian's suppose to get within ten feet of that Navy launch. But you're getting me off the track again—the two boats are no sooner lashed together than this spotlight comes shining off the Embarcadero and freezes on them."

"Spotlight?" Ragnetii asked, confused.

"Yeah, it turns out one of your cops had snuck his cruiser in between some crates to catch a couple winks, I guess, when he musta noticed the boats too." Mickey paused. "You getting all this, Vince?"

Ragnetti had closed his eyes. "And that cop was Elliot."

"You got it."

"What makes you so sure?"

"Well, afterwards—"

"After what?" Ragnetti butted in.

"After the fishing boat and the launch left the basin."

"Together?"

"Naw—separate. Afterwards, Elliot walked out on the pier and asked me what all that business had been about. I told him I didn't have a clue. I didn't neither."

242

"Did you tell him what you just told me? That no civilian boat is supposed to get close to that launch?"

"Well, Elliot started leaning on me, like the son of a bitch was always doing. . . ."

"Okay, okay," Ragnetti said, realizing that he'd get no further than Elliot had by getting nasty with the guy. "Does this launch got numbers or something painted on it?"

"No, too small for a number. But you can't mistake it. It's called the ack-ack boat and has the same crew what you and me saw last Thursday coming in from Mare Depot."

"All nigger?"

"Yeah."

Ragnetti asked him if he had any names for the crewmen, but Mickey said that he sure didn't, then: "Wait, I think the other colored call the coxswain Tillie." He added that he didn't know if that was a first or last handle, or a nickname that had something to do with his working the tiller. "But Vince, don't you wanna know the name of the fishing boat?"

"You got it?" Ragnetti asked in surprise.

"Sure, that spotlight was right on the stern. *Lorelei.* She was called the *Lorelei.* I got to run now."

Ragnetti frowned as the ringing of his own phone drifted in from the bull pen. "Hold on. Square with me."

"I been"—a little indignation for the first time.

"No, I mean about why you're telling me this. And enough of the 'regular Joe' bullshit. We both know I'm a prick."

Mickey let out a breath that sounded like a wave crashing on the beach. "I dunno. I went on graveyard shift right after we talked last Thursday, Vince. And a couple dark mornings out on the pier I got this real bad feeling—like what I seen that night had something to do with Elliot getting killed . . . and maybe with Will Laska going crazy and doing what you guys say he did to his wife."

"I think you're right," Ragnetti said warmly, tossing his snitch a bone.

"You not gonna try to see me at work . . . are you?"

"No, I promise. But if you come across something more, I want you to get in touch with me."

"Sure, good-bye."

Ragnetti hung up and was reaching for John Kost's memo pad when he suddenly fisted his hand and slammed it against the desktop. For the first time ever he was going to withhold a lead from John. It made him feel like a bum. He thought of taking it directly to Coffey, but the captain would only farm out the follow-up to Hurley and Mulrenan, who couldn't follow a hooker's bare ass to bed without getting lost.

His own telephone had stopped ringing, but Delbert from ID was storming around the bull pen as if he'd been told to clear the building because of a fire. "In here, for Chrissake," Ragnetti said, taking John's fifth of vodka out of the bottommost desk drawer.

"Don't you answer your phone, Sarge?"

"Never. Care for a drink?"

"Later. After you and I go through Nate Aranov's car down at the Hyde Street Pier." After a long moment Delbert asked, "You hear me, Vince?"

Upon John Kost's arrival at the boathouse, the surface of the berth had looked like verdigris. But then the crew of the wheeled crane that had been backed out onto the dock switched on two powerful floodlights, and the waters turned as translucent as an emerald. Now, at last, a cable was being fed down into the depths.

"You make out the car yet?" Ragnetti asked.

John Kost shook his head.

"What'd you say?" Ragnetti hadn't been looking at him.

"No, Vincent, I can't see anything." He thought he could hear Ragnetti breathing shallowly as if he were getting sick, but then realized that it was the wheezing of the gasoline air compressor.

"The diver," Ragnetti said, "when he came up after the first go, said he couldn't see nothing inside the Dodge."

"Were the windows rolled down?"

"Yeah," Ragnetti said, blowing his nose.

"What was it like here Friday night?"

"Cold, rainy."

John Kost thought about this for a moment, then said, "He'll be in the trunk, if at all."

Ragnetti didn't offer his own opinion. He folded his handkerchief in quarters and put it back in his trouser pocket, then peered down into the water again.

John Kost was studying him when the slamming of a car door turned them both around. Coffey was plodding down the short dock toward them, absently running his gloved fingers along the scabby plaster of the boathouse wall as he came.

"Gents," he greeted them, then crossed his arms and took stock of the scene: the crane operator giving his levers tender nudges now and again; the compressor crew making sure the diver got air; the ID and coroner's men standing by with cigarettes going, saying nothing. "Where'd they finally get a crane?"

Ragnetti said, "John finagled one out of Thripp Shipyards."

"They going to charge us?"

"No," John Kost said quietly. "On the house."

And then Coffey fumed, "From now on nobody but nobody works a stakeout alone! Do you hear me, John!" The PD's motorboat, which had been puttering around the entrance to the slip, began probing the night with a spotlight. It blazed down the length of the dock. "Turn that son of a bitch off!" the captain hollered, then lowered his voice. "They're like kids with those goddamn things. Anybody go by to see Sylvia today?"

"Not today," John Kost said. "She doesn't want us calling again unless we have news. She says it's too hard on her each time one of us comes up to the door."

"Still, she's a tough cookie." Coffey was pointing at a dark object that had just broken the surface. "What the devil's that? Harbor seal?"

"The diver," Ragnetti said. "He must have the car hooked up." A clunk followed as the crane's winch was engaged and its reel started taking up the cable.

"Amazing what those things can lift," Coffey said, his eyes pinched-looking in the wash of the floodlights.

A shadow took shape deep in the pale-green water, wavering as it rose.

"Amazing," the captain repeated.

The rear bumper of the Dodge breached first, for the engine end was pointing down. As the spindly arm of the crane swung the car around onto the dock, water gushed out the windows. Riding down one of those foaming streams was Aranov's fedora. John Kost glanced away.

When he looked back, Delbert from ID was walking up to the Dodge, which was leaking from its door and trunk cracks. Standing on his tiptoes to inspect the interior, he warned everyone to stay clear until he had a chance to go over it. But then Ragnetti passed in front of John Kost and made for the car, ignoring Delbert's protests as he relieved the technician of his black bag and began rummaging through it.

"What the hell you doing, Sarge?"

"Keys in the ignition?"

"No, I don't see them, but—"

"Then shut the fuck up." Ragnetti took a hammer and a punch from the bag.

John Kost kept expecting Coffey to step in, but he stood by as grim and speechless as the other cops while Ragnetti, with two ringing blows, drove the lock back into the trunk. Then, using the claw of the hammer, he wrenched open the lid. A green tide poured out, drenching his trousers to the knees—but no Aranov.

The wait would go on. John Kost wrapped himself in his arms.

"Satisfied?" Delbert asked Ragnetti. "Mind if I get to work now? What if there's any work that hasn't been spoilt!"

The sergeant seemed in a daze, but then jumped up onto the crane platform and began running one of the spotlights back and forth across the dim bottom of the slip.

"Excuse me, Pat," John Kost said. "I need some air."

"Sure."

He strolled over to the Hyde Street Pier and followed the worn planks out into darkness. He'd prayed for Sylvia's sake, as well as his own, that this would have been the end to it. But were they all being tested like this because Nathan was still alive some-where?

Leaning against a piling, he began tracking the progress of a freighter that had just materialized out of the Golden Gate. A cop took nothing on faith, but is that what he was being asked to do? To trust against all evidence that Nathan was well?

Sooner than expected, the rust-streaked hull and peopleless decks of the ship were gliding past his eyes. Even the bridge windows showed no sign of life. A tug, churning out from the Embarcadero to meet it, suddenly slowed as if the skipper had just caught sight of the hammer and sickle flying redly through a thicket of radio antennae.

"His mike cord was cut," Ragnetti said from behind. "And the distributor cap's gone."

John Kost accepted this report in silence. He'd never believed in anything but the worst possible news, so how could he be genuinely disappointed?

"We going after them now, John?"

"After whom?"

Ragnetti apparently had no answer, for he kept quiet.

He knew that he had none either.

After several moments of no sound but the wake of the Soviet ship playing itself out among the pilings, he said, "Good God, Vincent, how can a man who knows the entire libretto to *Tosca* be dead?"

But turning, he saw that Ragnetti was no longer behind him.

22

L YDIA THRIPP SWEPT open her door only to be shocked by John Kost's appearance. He looked positively haggard. His lower eyelids were dark with sleeplessness, and an air of weary abstraction hung around him. They embraced, kissed, and he muttered something about how nice she looked this evening. She smiled, but it was squeezed out of her more by convention than any sudden feeling of happiness: she'd been anything but happy of late. "I hope you don't mind a Lenten menu. Fresh turbot."

"No, fine. Turbot's fine."

"We're running behind. Will you see to the martinis? Charles likes his absolutely dusty."

He frowned at mention of the admiral, which slightly bemused her in that they'd never met, and dragged himself off toward the cocktail cart. "The Kropotniks said you were out of town."

"Yes, that's right." She swept open the two leaves of the dining room door, revealing a Louis-Napoléon Bonaparte table scintillant with candles and silver. "Just got back this morning."

"Where'd you go?" He tilted a bottle into the light so he could read the label. "Gin or vodka for your friends?"

"Gin, I'm afraid. Los Angeles—shopping."

"Did you have a pleasant trip?"

"Not particularly. And what's my Vanya been up to?"

She didn't care for the way his eyes grazed past her own as he said, "Just work." He poured a dash of dry vermouth into the martini pitcher.

"That's it—*trés brut*. Any progress with your investigations?"

His expression turned so sharp she wondered if she'd asked something wrong. But then he bent his head into his task and said quietly, "A little."

"Good."

"Yes. Can you do something about the heat, Lydia Dmitrievna?"

"Too warm?"

He rolled his eyes.

"We'll have our cocktails on the patio then," she compromised.

The chimes sounded, and he asked, "D'you want me—?"

But she motioned for him to stay at the cocktail cart while she herself answered the door. She didn't want the admiral to realize that John Kost was as familiar with the flat as he was—jealousy doesn't always wane in equal proportion to desire. "Charles . . ." As usual, his paranoia had dictated that a Marine guard be posted in the corridor; but she was careful not to let her eyes comment on this as she accepted his kiss and smiled at the lieutenant commander standing to the left and slightly behind him. "How lovely you could make it."

"Mrs. Thripp," Charles said, removing his hat and stepping inside, "this is Mr. Jennaway. He keeps all my spies in line."

She found Jennaway to be sweetly boyish, although well past thirty. He winked as he took her hand in his; he had a gentle touch. "It's a good deal less romantic than it sounds, Mrs. Thripp."

"Call me Lydia, please."

John Kost had come out into the living room, and she was struck once again by what a commanding first impression he made. Although standing between two officers in glittering dress blue uniforms, he seemed far more dignified than they, almost princely so—what a shame he'd decided on police work instead of politics. "And you must be John Kost," Charles said as if immensely satisfied with something or other. He probably believed that he was being charming.

Trust John Kost to mask his exhaustion and say as if he meant it, "Admiral, Commander—a pleasure."

Handshakes were exchanged, and she kept the silence that followed from stiffening by announcing that cocktails would be served on the patio. Yet, she was disappointed to find the balcony cooler than expected and was ready to lead the three men back inside—when she realized that the sunset was magnificent, striped by fuchsine cloud bars, and the westerly breeze was as fresh as the sea itself. Her servant had already arrayed the cocktail service on the table and withdrawn, so she said, "Excuse me while I get a wrap. Unless it's too cold for you gentlemen out here?"

All but John Kost came to their feet and protested that they were fine. He was staring out over the city, his eyes vacant.

When she returned to the patio snug in her ermine stole, Charles was already zeroing in on the inspector's Russian background, asking him about his father's part in the Civil War. Ordinarily, she'd never permit such a callous grilling of a guest, not to mention her present lover. But these were not ordinary circumstances, and she gestured for the three men to remain seated while she took her customary place in a thronelike rattan chair, then quietly began nursing her martini, watching them.

". . . General Deniken sent my father and a troop of Don Cossacks. A token of goodwill to Admiral Kolchak in Siberia," John Kost was calmly saying, so far betraying no irritation but sounding cautious—undoubtedly he already sensed that the admiral's purposes this evening weren't entirely social. "But the two White fronts became so cut off from each other my father became less Kolchak's liaison to Deniken and more the admiral's executive officer." He took a sip of vodka neat, a carafe of which he'd set aside for himself—he detested gin.

"This Kolchak," Charles asked, "he was shot by the Reds, wasn't he?"

John Kost looked him straight in the eye. "Yes, and his body dumped in a nearby river. But my father and I were gone to Manchuria before then."

"They must've been exciting times, Inspector." Jennaway found his own remark insipid, for he suddenly smiled.

John Kost nodded without comment.

"Too damn bad we didn't throw more support than what we did to your father's people," Charles said.

"Do you really think so?"

"Don't you, Inspector?"

"No, actually. It would've just made for a longer and bloodier Civil War."

This clearly disturbed Charles—he probably wasn't used to the company of frank and reasonable men, but then he nodded as if he appreciated John Kost's opinion and shifted strategies. "Have you had a chance to visit our district intelligence office down on Market Street?"

"No, I haven't."

"Well, it's high time we did something about that." Charles turned to Jennaway. "How about giving our friend here the grand tour tomorrow?"

"Aye-aye, sir," he said cheerfully. "What time would be convenient, Inspector?"

"I'm sorry, it's out of the question. . . ."

She realized that John Kost seemed to be staring at the left shoulder of her stole. Most likely, it was just one more symptom of his distracted state and she resisted looking down at herself.

"You see," he went on, "one of my men has disappeared."

"Disappeared?" She was disconcerted that he'd said nothing about this until now. "Who?"

"Aranov." John Kost studied her wrap a second longer, then shifted toward the two officers as he recrossed his legs. "We found his Dodge last night. In a berth off the Hyde Street Pier."

"Oh, yes, I saw the missing bulletin your department sent us."

Jennaway set down his martini as if suddenly it were in poor taste to be drinking. A sensitive fellow: she liked that. "Was he inside the car?"

"No."

"Any signs of foul play?"

"The microphone cord had been cut and the distributor cap removed."

Charles was shaking his head. "Good Lord, do you have any idea who'd do such a thing?"

"We don't, Admiral," John Kost said.

Lydia sensed that he wasn't telling the truth, just as he had lied earlier this evening when he said that he'd just been working since they'd last seen each other. At last, she glanced down at her shoulder: tangled in the white-speckled fur was a sprig of mountain cedar, brown and dried. At that instant, her servant tinkled a china bell at the patio door, and Lydia urged the men inside for dinner.

During the amble to the dining room, she brushed away the sprig.

Over the first three courses Charles was largely silent, leaving the talk to the other two men. Perhaps he realized, as much as he could ever admit his own misjudgments, that his blunt maneuvering was getting him nowhere with someone as perceptive as John Kost, who at the moment was turning the tables and asking the lieutenant commander about his own past. "Then you began your naval career in intelligence?"

"Oh, no, I was in bomb and mine disposal."

"Sounds terribly important," she said. Then, although already aware of the answer, she asked, "What is it?"

Jennaway picked at his portion of jellied sturgeon with his fork. "Well, it was my job to see that a malfunctioning piece of ordnance was safely gotten rid of. Once again, it sounds more exciting than it really was."

"Then you never had one go off on you," John Kost said.

There was laughter around the table, and either this burst of gaiety or the arrival of the borsch somehow signaled Charles to ask, "Tell me, Inspector, what do you make of the Soviets in town for the Conference?"

"I don't understand your question."

"Are they playing their usual games?"

John Kost glanced accusatively at her before answering, "I have no idea what games they play."

She realized that she had no choice but to intervene. "Charles is concerned about Molotov's presence here."

"He's not here yet."

"When he arrives, I mean."

"There's not a more dangerous man in the world, except Joseph Stalin of course," Charles said, turning to Jennaway for support, although—to his credit—the lieutenant commander offered him no more than a wan smile.

"What about Adolph Hitler?" John Kost asked.

"*Kaputt,*" Charles said. "No, this last year we've rounded the bend as far as strategic threats go, and the man we've got to stop now is Vyacheslav Mikhailovich Molotov"—she saw a corner of John Kost's mouth twitch at the admiral's butchered pronunciation of the commissar's forenames—"before it's too late."

"Stop him?"

"You bet. Any damned way we can. You disagree?"

"In my view Molotov's the least threatening fellow in the Politburo. What you just said might make sense if applied to Beria, even though he's only a candidate. But Molotov's on shaky ground, I hear. He has a Jewish wife—and has refused to distance himself from her as Stalin would like. I rather admire him for that."

Charles was grinning, although a slight floridity had come to his jowls. "You seem to know a bunch about the Politburo."

"This and that." John Kost refilled his glass with vodka. "All of it heard through a very long keyhole."

"How about listening through that keyhole for the sake of your adopted country?"

The glass stopped halfway to John Kost's lips. "Are you suggesting I haven't been?"

Unwisely, Charles shrugged.

"Excuse me, Lydia Dmitrievna. . . ." John Kost had set down his glass with a splashing knock and come to his feet. "But with my best man missing I have no time to waste justifying phobias about the Red Menace."

He left, and the table fell silent.

"Forgive me, my dear," Charles said at last. "The fellow's obviously under a good deal of pressure."

She sensed that a few tears were in order, so she refused to blink until her eyes began to smart. "Yes, I've never seen him like this before. Will you pardon me a moment?"

"Of course," Charles said.

"Certainly," Jennaway said, tossing down his napkin and rising.

But once inside her bedroom she checked her eyes only to make sure this attempt at weeping hadn't made her mascara run. Then she took a drink from the flask she kept in her nightstand drawer to ward off insomnia. Her little dinner party had gone much better than expected. . . . *The man we've got to stop now is Vyacheslav Mikhailovich Molotov . . . before it's too late.* John Kost had a policeman's memory for words and would make an impeccable witness.

For the past several days, if in their nebulous and erratic passage they could be called *days*, the prisoner had experienced a shearing of body and soul that had left him with the sensation he was floating a meter above his prison clogs. He felt both invincible and completely vulnerable, famished but unable to swallow the buckwheat gruel given to him at intervals he suspected to be grossly irregular in order to further addle his sense of time.

But now at last things were coming to a head. Absolutely. Undeniably.

After being frisked for weapons, an absurd proposition in itself for one who has been locked away in the Lubyanka for at least a fortnight, he was escorted upstairs into a large office that was dark but for a green-shaded electric lamp on the desk at its midst. Behind the desk sat a man younger than himself by at least ten years, a studious-looking fellow with a round head and stubby hands that were clasping a sheaf of papers. He didn't glance up as the prisoner was deposited into the chair set squarely in front of his desk. His pince-nez were glinting, so it was impossible to make out his eyes.

The drapes along one wall of the office were drawn, but the prisoner sensed that it was night.

He had been seated for some minutes, a guard standing at parade rest on either side of him, when the man tugged at his fat underlip with his fingers and sighed. "Your name please," he said with a Georgian accent, his voice not unkind.

The prisoner gave him the name he had gone by in Teheran for more than a quarter of a century.

"Your real name, if you will."

To share that might mean death. Or did the man already have it in his possession like everything else? Still, the prisoner stuck to the alias, which, in truth, now seemed more like his own name than the one he'd been baptized with.

"Very well," the man said without ire, "we'll come back to this question later. Your age please."

"Fifty-six."

The tip of the man's fountain pen scratched across the form he'd taken from one of his desk drawers. "Your marital status."

"Single."

The little circular lenses jerked upward, but still the eyes behind them were obscured by reflection. "Have you ever been married?"

"No, never."

"Any education?"

"Well, at the music conservatory I—"

"Thank you." The pen continued to scratch across the paper. "Your vocation."

"Musician. All my family have been musicians."

"Including your paternal uncle?" the man asked.

The prisoner hesitated, wondering where this question might lead, but then said, "All my family, Your High Excellency."

A breathy chuckle. "In your absence from the country, we've

255

dispensed with that mumbo jumbo. I'm a simple policeman. You may call me comrade commissar."

"Thank you, Comrade Commissar."

The man folded his hands over the form. "Do you have any idea why you were arrested in Persia by our occupation forces?"

"This has been an absolute mystery to me from the beginning, Comrade Commissar."

The man nodded as if he understood, perhaps even sympathized. But when he spoke again the prisoner froze, for during that brief pause the voice had hardened immeasurably. "You are accused according to Article Fifty-eight, Paragraphs A, B, and W of the Soviet Penal Code. You are an enemy of the people, a traitor of the motherland and a parasite. You are not a musician, although you may have been trained as one. You are a black marketeer and an agent of British intelligence in Teheran. How do you respond to this bill of indictment?"

"Comrade Commissar," he stammered, his head spinning although an inner voice told him not to be surprised—he had not been brought to the Lubyanka in irons to be given a medal, "I'm flabbergasted at such charges. Although I've spent years out of the motherland, I've always remained faithful to her . . . and . . . and the aspirations of the Soviet Revolution."

"Quite possibly."

The prisoner seized this flicker of hope: "I assure you, Comrade Commissar."

"But that's only your assurance. Who can corroborate it for you?"

"Colonel Alalykin—he searched my flat in Teheran and took me into custody—said my constructive attitude would be duly noted."

"Your behavior as a prisoner and your loyalty to the Revolution are two different things altogether. Alalykin's in no position to affirm the latter. Might there be someone else who can?"

The prisoner closed his eyes. Truly, the entire world had been reduced to this prison, and it would be foolish for him to take into consideration anything beyond its walls. "My cousin."

"Speak up please."

"My cousin, who works for you, Comrade Commissar."

"Works for me?"

"I believe him to be one of your officers."

"His name?"

The prisoner gave it.

"And this is your surname as well?"

The prisoner dipped his head once.

"I see," the man said, unlocking his pencil drawer with a skeleton key and bringing out a ledger. He opened it to two yellowed pages that had been bookmarked; they were dark with inked-in transactions. "Do you know what this is?"

"No, not really," the prisoner said, although he could clearly see the heading *Beria, L.*

"Did your cousin give you this book for safekeeping?"

No longer did the prisoner hesitate in answering. He had stopped agonizing, and a weary, almost soothing acquiescence had come over him. "Yes, a long time ago." At first he'd imagined that Alalykin had burst into his flat specifically searching for the Okhrana's master pay voucher, which his goons had found in due course—along with a small fortune in jewels and gold—by ripping up the floorboards with pry bars. But then the colonel had looked so astonished upon scanning the pages of the ledger the prisoner had realized that his purpose in coming had simply been exploratory. "My cousin just said this document might one day have historical value."

"Did he also happen to mention that it's a forgery that was intended to discredit the most worthy heroes of the Revolution, that it's libelous down to the last entry!"

"No."

Suddenly, the man ripped out the two pages he had marked, noisily crumpled them into a wad, and lit it with his cigarette lighter. After a moment he dropped this flaming ball into the metal wastebasket beside his desk. The room had filled with smoke, through which he smiled. "That excises the most defamatory part. And as your good cousin suggested, the rest might one day have a certain historical interest. You may prepare yourself for release."

"Comrade Commissar?" the prisoner asked, not having believed his ears.

"Go back to your cell and gather your necessities. I'm finished with you."

Speechless, again feeling disembodied, the prisoner was led by the guards out of the office and downstairs once more. Yet, it seemed to him that they descended one level more than necessary, to the basement of the prison perhaps. This was confirmed when he was shoved into a strange cell. Its outer wall had been mottled white with salts left by the seepage of water.

"Stand with your forehead against the wall," one of the guards commanded.

As he did so, he saw from the corner of his eye that another prisoner was already leaning in this position against the wall—and the flabbergasted words rushed out of him: "Good God, is that you, Alalykin!"

The voice that answered was a dispirited croak. "It is I."

"What has happened?"

"The inevitable, I suppose."

"But I'm to be released, Comrade Colonel."

"Yes . . . released."

"Quiet and face the wall!" the same guard barked.

A scuffling of hobnailed boots on the cement floor behind him told him that more men were entering the cell. And then it came to him, the same sense of inevitability that had taken the spirit out of the colonel who had arrested him. However, instead of feeling outraged and betrayed, he too became curiously indifferent to all this. It was as if he were too tired to be afraid. He suddenly realized that the whiteness on the walls was not a residue of salts but rather quicklime, which had been splashed there to eat away the old evidences of blood and tissue; even this ghastly attempt at tidying up the cell had no power to terrify him. Release. Yes. Absolutely.

Something metallic tapped against the base of his skull.

He could hear a man breathing heavily behind him. He felt the urgent need to ask, "Is my cousin dead then?"

"Oh, yes," the fellow said, "he's as good as dead. But aren't we

258

all? He himself would appreciate that. And he's lasted longer than anybody. He'd appreciate that too."

"You know him then?"

"Quite well. There's always been a certain affection between us."

"Affection?"

"Well, an understanding."

"And what's your name? I'd like to know your name."

The man laughed softly as if he'd heard this request oftentimes before. "I'm Funikov."

Then came a deafening reverberation in the cell. The prisoner never knew if it was his or Alalykin's.

23

For the second time in three days tule fog had come down the rivers onto the bay, stinking of dead rushes. Now, with first light, it was giving up its hold on the city, and by craning his neck Ragnetti could begin to make out the underside of the Bay Bridge even though visibility across the water was still no more than a couple of yards. When trucks weren't rumbling overhead, he could hear as well as feel the condensed fog dripping off the trestlework—Pier 24, on which he waited with a cigar going, lay at an angle under the span.

His breath suddenly caught in his throat, then became fast and shallow. He pitched the cigar over the side. Since seeing the Dodge winched to the surface, he would start suffocating the instant he stopped moving or doing something. As long as he kept in motion, kept busy, he could breathe okay and wouldn't get half sick.

Shutting himself up in the phone booth next to the dock foreman's office, using his handkerchief to wipe the clamminess off the handset, he then dialed the on-duty Communications sergeant: "Yeah, this is Vince Ragnetti. How about doing me a big favor . . . ?" He asked to have the watch commander at

Vallejo PD call him at the number he then read off the pay phone. Vallejo was a jerkwater town on the east side of San Pablo Bay, but it was separated only by the Napa River from the Mare Island Naval Depot.

He stared down at his spats. He had put them on this morning when it was still black outside the bull pen windows.

Five minutes later the phone rang.

He was away from the booth, pacing the dock, and had to run. It was the Vallejo PD watch commander. "Yeah, Lieutenant, thanks for calling back."

"What can I help you with?"

"Tell me, d'your coloreds up there got themselves a honky-tonk?"

"We don't have many, other than those in the service."

"That's what I meant. Navy coloreds."

"Well, then, there's the Lounge. But that's out in the county."

"Where'bouts?" Ragnetti asked.

"On Highway Thirty-seven down from the main gate. But even the deputies won't go near it. Shore Patrol's got to handle that dive."

"So it's strictly a jigaboo joint?"

"Nothing but eyeballs and grins from opening to close." The lieutenant laughed at his own joke—Ragnetti couldn't find it in himself to laugh even though he supposed it was worth one. "You working something up this way, Sergeant?" the lieutenant asked as if he smelled a SFPD invasion coming to his little burg.

"Naw, just trying to verify an alibi. I don't even think it's worth a trip. I'll call the bartender. Thanks for your help."

"Anytime."

Stretching as he came out of the booth, Ragnetti strolled to the pier's end to make sure nothing was steaming out of the channel that lay between him and Yerba Buena Island. A gull shot down out of the fog, and he flinched before realizing what it was. "Jesus." He looked bayward again. "Come on, come on. . . ."

Late last night, Coffey, John Kost, and he had gotten into it. The captain and the inspector had obviously agreed beforehand that only "discreet information" was to be shared with those parties already advised of the situation by the FBI, meaning the other intelligence services in town, period. Ragnetti had cried politics, and Coffey had surprised him by saying, "True"—the chief didn't want any fingers pointed at the Russians, what with the Conference only a week away. After this was said, Ragnetti's argument that the beat cops had the best chance of collaring Pugachev and Tikhov fell on deaf ears. John's included. He even threw off his moony look long enough to say, "An APB and a manhunt will only drive Pugachev deeper underground, Vincent."

Funny, Ragnetti now thought, but John hadn't included Tikhov. Coffey and he had probably been withholding something on this Russian too.

Then the rapid breathing and the nausea hit him again.

He'd stopped moving. Stopped doing things.

And for a minute he'd forgotten why he was there.

Hurrying back to the booth, he slammed the folding glass door against the rank chill and had the operator connect him with the Lounge in Solano County. "Bill it to this number, babe," he said, giving his home phone—a first in over fourteen years as an investigator. He didn't want the department to have anything linking him to the honky-tonk. From now on, for as long as he decided to remain a cop, he'd do everything on his own, leaving Coffey and John Kost in the dark as much as possible. He'd rely on nobody else to back him up, no matter how much the call raised the hair on his neck. That's how he would atone for what in a moment of aggravation he'd said to Aranov. Atonement would eventually make him feel better. That is why when at four this morning the call from Twelfth Naval District had come in to his desk, where he was fitfully sleeping, he'd decided to meet the minesweeper on his own and not wake John with the news that a floater had been found by the Navy. He would do what had to be done on his own, just as he'd made Natty do.

"The Lounge," a soft Negro voice said with a lot of hubbub in the background—a typical wartime beer bar, going like Saturday night on a Wednesday dawn.

Ragnetti said, "Yeah, is Tillie there?"

"Hang on. . . ." The bartender could be heard asking if anybody knew when Tillman would be in, and finally somebody hollered, "Sixteen hundred."

"Thanks," Ragnetti said, "I got it."

"Any message?"

"No, I'll catch him myself." He hung up, stared vacantly through the misty glass for a moment before bolting from the booth: the bridge of a ship was inching above the thickest layer of fog toward the pier. Its horn boomed twice, and the sound echoed back into the warehouses along the Embarcadero.

He wiped his nose with his fingers and told himself he wasn't going to do anything stupid in front of a whole shipload of sailors. Regardless of what his eyes would see in the coming minutes, he would keep a poker face by pretending it was a total stranger. Regardless of his old and secret fear that seeing just one more horrible thing would make him go crazy forever, he'd show nothing.

It seemed to take an eternity for the little gray ship to pull alongside the pier, but as soon as he started up the accommodation ladder, he found himself wishing that it had taken longer. Reaching the top and shaking hands with an Ivy League–type kid who claimed to be the skipper, he was overcome by a queer sensation that none of this was happening, that the fog meant it was all a lousy dream. "We found him last evening just before nightfall," the young captain said, leading him aftward along a coldly sweating rail, "but we couldn't return to port until we finished clearing the channel."

"You got Jap mines out there?" he asked, proud that he could backchat despite the pounding of his heart.

"You never know."

"How's that?"

"One of their long-range submarines might lay a few."

"Oh, sure. Any ID on the body?"

"Not even any clothes, except for the damnedest thing—a sock on the left foot. Only a sock."

"You save it?"

"Yes."

263

"Good."

"What kind of shape's the body itself in?"

The captain just bit his lip, and Ragnetti felt his own outward calm crack. He wished the kid had said something instead of doing only that. Words prepare you.

A Stokes stretcher awaited him on the wet afterdeck. It cradled a white canvas bag. Because of the fog, or maybe his light-headedness, he felt as if he were beholding it through a gauze.

A seaman loosened some lacing but looked to the captain before parting the canvas. "Go ahead, sailor," he said.

Ragnetti inhaled and glanced down.

Swollen to twice its normal size, the face didn't look human. Fishlike, maybe. Through the puffed-up lips, the tongue was protruding. One eye was open, but it seemed as if the sea had dissolved the pupil.

Yet, he had no doubt who the floater was. The hair was light brown, thin.

All at once, he realized that he was on his knees with his fists jammed against the deck, grunting for breath. "Close it up, for Chrissake close up that goddamn thing!" some idiot kept shouting as if he'd gone out of his mind. After a moment it came to him that he was the idiot who was shouting.

Quietly excusing herself, Mrs. Friedman—Sylvia Aranov's mother—got up from the sofa and crept off to the kitchen in her stockinged feet to make tea. The room filled up with a silence that accentuated the ticking of the mantel clock. Early-afternoon sunlight slanted in through the bay window and fell warmly across John Kost's fisted hands. He relaxed them, but when he looked down at them a few moments later, they had curled into fists again.

A Hebrew prayer book lay on the cocktail table atop a copy of the *Saturday Evening Post*.

Coffey stirred in the overstuffed chair Mrs. Friedman had insisted he take. He cleared his throat. "Sylvia—" Her head snapped toward him, birdlike, the skin at her temples and along

264

her brow so colorless the veins stood out like tiny blue branches. "My dear, we've got to talk about the service."

She, who had said nothing since their arrival, who had listened dry-eyed and without protest to the uncontestable finding by fingerprint and dental X-ray comparison that the remains were those of her husband, now spoke so sharply the captain jumped a little: "What do you mean?"

"Well," he went on as if explaining to a sick child who mustn't be agitated, "the department must honor his memory."

Her face went perfectly still for a split second, then she burst out with a husky laugh that astonished Coffey and brought Mrs. Friedman running from the kitchen. "Sylvia . . . honey?"

John Kost realized that he'd been expecting something like this: it was as if huge black doors were swinging inward.

She ignored her mother and glared at the captain. "There's not going to be a service."

"But there has to be."

"*Has* to be?"

Mrs. Friedman sat beside her daughter on the sofa and began rubbing the young woman's hands and arms as if she were freezing to death. "Of course there's going to be a service. What nonsense—no service. I'll get ten men from my synagogue and we'll—"

She jerked out of her mother's kneading grasp, then leveled her eyes on John Kost, although little spasms kept rocking her head. "Was Nathan a hypocrite, John?"

"Of course not."

"Then I doubt very much if he'd appreciate us making him one now. You knew him more intimately than anyone, John. Far more intimately than I. What d'you say?" The grin that followed was eerie if only because her unrouged lips seemed to fade into her pale face.

"I already answered you, Sylvia," he gently said.

"Would he want a fuss then?" she went on.

"She's upset," Mrs. Friedman said with a pathetic smile. "You gentlemen understand."

"Answer me, John—would Nathan want a fuss?"

265

"What do you want me to say, Sylvia?"

"Something perfectly appropriate, charming. That's your forte, isn't it?"

"Sylvia," Mrs. Friedman said more sternly.

"I'm talking to John, Mother. And please don't touch me again."

He took a breath and said, "Nathan would expect us to remember that he died doing his life's work. And that he did this work well."

"Oh, no!" She fended off her mother with her forearms. "He died trying to please you!" Mrs. Friedman was finally able to clasp her shoulders and keep her from rising. "Did you really think he was suited to be a cop like you! Suited to the filth like you and Ragnetti!"

"Sylvia, Sylvia—don't do this, honey. These gentlemen were Nathan's friends."

"They are his murderers!" Her eyes gleamed from the satisfaction of having said it. The thing at the core of her silence these past five days had finally been ripped free. "He stayed at it because he adored you, John Kost! Hungered for your praise! You want a service?" She again broke her mother's grasp. "Then here's the manual! You officiate!" She grabbed the prayer book off the table and hurled it at him, striking him flat in the chest.

He ignored the blow, then folded his hands in his lap and stared at them until Coffey said, "I think we oughta go, Johnny."

At curbside, he decided he wasn't in any shape to drive and offered the captain his keys. Taking them, Coffey patted his back. "It's all right, Johnny—she'll snap out of it. She's a tough cookie."

John Kost nodded. He leaned back in the front seat and covered his eyes with a hand just in time.

"Ain't nothing to hold back," Coffey said, starting the engine. "Go ahead now. Out with it all, son."

"Let this cup pass from me, Pat," he said, trying to make it sound like a joke if only because he was ashamed of having broken down. But he was also perilously close to confessing what had happened at Yosemite; telling how this morning, while

266

Elena and he lay in his bed, she had so bungled her original story of assassinating Anthony Eden he'd suddenly realized that he was concealing a homicide for the sake of a clumsy lie. Yet, instead of telling Coffey all this, he only repeated, "Let it pass from me."

"The postmortem, you mean?" Coffey asked, pulling away from the house. "Hell, let me cover that base for you. You go home and—"

"No, I didn't mean the autopsy. That's my responsibility, not yours."

"Then have Ragnetti go. You're beat."

"Vincent drew Elliot's. Nathan had Fenby's and the Laskas'. No, it's my turn on the rotation." John Kost stared out the windshield. Under the high sun the neighborhoods looked overexposed, unfamiliar. "It's not the same city."

"Sure it is. It's always the same." Coffey got in the right lane so he could park in front of the coroner's building.

"You know, Pat," he blurted, wiping his eyes, "I'd never do anything to shame you or the department. Never."

Coffey looked uncertain, and for an instant John Kost was sure he was going to ask what was going on, and he was prepared to tell him everything, to cleanse himself of Elena's lie before it was too late. But then the captain only offered his hand. "A deal, Johnny. Let me go in with you. We'll do this one together."

"No, this one's mine."

Ragnetti took a swig of Chianti before pushing open the car door with his elbow and lumbering outside. He squinted a moment into the dusky golden sunlight, then began crunching over the pea-gravel parking lot. His eyes settled on where the telephone line looped down from the pole to the metal box on the side of the Lounge. Taking a butterfly knife from his trouser pocket, he snapped it open, then gathered a length of line into a loop and severed it. He clicked shut the blade and turned heavily toward the garbage cans at the back of the beer bar. Picking up two of them, he carried them around to the front of the place, depositing them on the shoulder of Highway 37.

A Navy truck rumbled past, raising the dust, but the driver

paid him no mind. "Fuck you," he said anyway, then plodded back to his Dodge, which he'd left idling, and got in. He had another drink before driving away. He headed west, pulling the visor down against a big red sun. It seemed to bob against the horizon.

He made his U-turn a mile later, then jammed the gas pedal to the firewall. The engine began howling. A tenor howl. All the recent Dodges were six cylinders, that's why they had been fobbed off on Homicide instead of Patrol or Traffic; whenever he got outside the city he missed the throaty eights of the early thirties, the sensation of being pushed back in the seat as the speedometer needle climbed the glowing green numbers, the wind sucking his hat into the backseat. "Hah!"

He was doing seventy when his front bumper bashed the garbage cans, sending them end over end halfway to Vallejo. The crash was loud even with the windows rolled up, but just for good measure he laid on his brakes and let them scream as he spun around to a smoky stop. Then he jumped out of the car, turning his ankle but recovering his balance within a couple steps, and lay over the hood with his revolver in both hands.

Colored sailors started tumbling out of the joint, rubbernecking for the car wreck they had just heard.

"Police!" Ragnetti hollered. "Nobody moves till I say!" Hands started going up, but he told them there was no need. "Tillman." He looked straight at the sailor in horn-rims. "Yeah, you—step over here. The rest of you get your butts back inside. And stay inside!"

Tillman slowly came around the front of the car, glancing at the dent in the bumper. His face was defiant, but his voice shook a little as he asked, "What's this all about?"

"You. It's about you. Get in the car."

"I'm not going anywheres without my friends knowing where I'm headed."

Ragnetti smiled as he holstered his revolver. Despite the Deep South accent, this was no backwoods nigger. "We're driving round to the back so we don't draw a crowd, okay? That's all there is to it, unless you want me to get out and slap you some."

Tillman eased inside as if anything but the seat would burn him. "What was all the racket for?" he asked as Ragnetti drove forward.

"So I didn't have to go inside. I can't think of a better way to get a shiv between the ribs." He killed the engine. "You want a drink?"

"No, thank you. What PD you from?"

"Let me ask the questions." Ragnetti took another swallow of wine. He told himself to slow down; this was his second fifth since midmorning. "You work that ack-ack boat?"

"Sometimes."

"Was one of those times the night you linked up with the *Lorelei* down in China Basin?"

Tillman couldn't keep the shock off his face. "I don't know what you're talking about."

Ragnetti chuckled and reached for the ignition. "Then let's see if the booking tank downtown jogs your memory. By the way, I'm with Homicide."

"Wait, really—I don't know what you mean, Officer."

He could smell Tillman's fear, and it made him seethe instead of feel sorry for him. "You fucked with my family!"

"I don't know your family, man."

Ragnetti blinked at him, then rubbed his face in confusion from his own outburst and tried to remember what he'd been asking. "So . . . so you didn't tie your launch up to the *Lorelei?*"

"No, nothing like that happened. Who said so? If he did, I don't know him."

"A cop said so. In his notebook. And now he's dead." Movement across his side mirror told Ragnetti somebody was at the back of the Dodge. Twisting around in the seat, he saw that a half dozen sailors had come out the back door of the Lounge and were standing in a horseshoe a few feet off his rear bumper. He cranked down his window. "I told you to get your asses back inside—and keep them there!" Nobody budged. A couple of them even crossed their arms over their blue jumpers. One bad thing, Ragnetti thought, had to be said about the war effort: it was

269

making for a different kind of nigger. Drawing his Colt again, he got out.

But his shoes had no sooner touched the gravel than he heard the opposite door spring open. Tillman was rabbiting toward the fence at the far end of the lot.

"Stop, you son of a bitch!"

The sailor kept running, although he'd lost his glasses. Ragnetti could see the lenses sparkling in the gravel.

He raised his revolver to eye level and centered the sights on Tillman's back just as he bounded over the fence. He was squeezing the trigger when his legs went out from under him. It was all he could do to hang on to his Colt as he fell on his side.

One of Tillman's buddies had tackled him. The black face was inches from his. Gasping, he swung around his revolver until the muzzle was resting against the tip of the sailor's nose. "You're dead." He could see it in his eyes: the man knew he was going to die. "You had to go and fuck with my family. So you're gone. Bye-bye."

Then somebody shouted, "Shore Patrol!"

He thought it was a bluff until he heard the siren. It was close by. "Shit." After a few seconds more, he lowered his Colt and said to the sailor, "Get the fuck outta here."

He and the others were gone in the time it took Ragnetti to stagger to his feet. "Scram!" he bellowed after them, reeling. "Piss your pants and get out!"

As he sped westward on Highway 37, into the red wafer of a sun, it gradually came to him that he'd screwed up bad, that he'd nearly shot somebody while drunk. Hunching over the steering wheel, he made up his mind to check into a hotel in San Rafael and sleep off the wine before returning to town. He'd sleep off the whole lousy world.

24

JOHN KOST STOOD on the front steps of St. Basil's. Out of the sun, which was squeezing down between the two opposing facades along the street, he kept expecting Elena to appear. This afternoon, behind the rarely locked door of his office, he had just matched Tikhov's arrest card to the fingerprints he'd taken off the corpse in Yosemite—when she rang to tell him that she wanted to walk to vespers, that it was a lovely city for evening walks, and would he mind? Wondering if her real purpose was to make sure he didn't show up at the consulate, he still said yes. Did she care more about Martov's feelings than she was admitting? He now looked eastward: a broad shadow was inching up Russian Hill. In this direction he'd been watching for his father, who at last rounded the corner from Polk Street, his burka spreading on the breeze. He stopped to check a telephone-booth coin return before hobbling across Van Ness against the signal.

"Papa!" John Kost shouted, thinking of the traffic. But the old man ignored him as he continued across the street and huffed up the church steps, his face pink from his Saturday-afternoon steam bath. Without a word he held out his hand, and John Kost

271

slipped him the brown-bagged half-pint. Concealing it inside his burka, he went on into the church.

The old man was no sooner through the door than a taxi let Lydia off. John Kost gave an inward groan at the futility of trying to avoid her further, as he had ever since her dinner party on Tuesday evening, and went down to the curb to greet her. *Why must all my relationships deteriorate into a gentle but tedious process of extrication?*

"Have you been waiting for me long?" She canted her powdered cheek toward him so he could kiss it. "Thank you," she added as he picked up the Thripp Shipyards envelope that had tumbled out of her black sable muff. In it was her weekly donative, which was invariably more than his monthly salary.

"I want to apologize for my behavior the other night," he said, shading his eyes for a glance westward.

"Nonsense. Charles was a complete boor—and I told him so after you left."

"Really?"

"Oh, we had quite a scene. Poor Jennaway was absolutely scarlet-faced."

He could tell she was lying, but pretended to be pleased. "Thanks for understanding, Lydia Dmitrievna."

She took his arm. "Shall we go inside?"

"I'm afraid I'm waiting for someone."

She searched his face, then let go of him. "As you wish," she snapped, moving so quickly up the steps he didn't have time to open the door for her.

So she too knew about Elena and him.

Who, then, in the entire city *didn't* know about the affair and insinuate an opinion on it? Only Pyotr Martov, the injured party, did a convincing job of feigning ignorance. Twice since Thursday afternoon, when John Kost had gone back to work after eighteen hours of vodka-blanked sleep, Martov had summoned him to the consulate to discuss Molotov's arrival, and on both occasions—as at Mrs. Testa's—he'd given no sign that he resented being betrayed by his wife. His complaisance was beginning to grate on John Kost if only because he couldn't fathom it. But why would Martov say such an absurd thing as "I'll have a surprise for you at the end of the week, Ivan Mikhailovich!"—unless that surprise was a showdown.

He peered into the sun for her again. Soon it would be gone.

At least two unpleasant chores were out of the way: the delivery of his father's vodka ration and the widening of his breach with Lydia. Now only one more remained undone, although it was immeasurably more troubling than the other two. He had to let Elena know that he intended to tell the department about Tikhov. Nothing could be solved until he revealed what had happened in Yosemite, and she had to understand. His decision had been made in degrees, beginning with a drive out to Sylvia Aranov's house on Thursday night. As he later learned, she'd gone east with her mother to be with relatives, but the blacked-out windows had suggested something more final than that. Idling out front as if waiting to pick up Nathan on the rush to a Homicide call, he had realized with anger stronger than grief that the man who'd brought down all this darkness, who'd inflicted a vicious chopping wound on Nathan as he had on young Fenby, was still somewhere on the peninsula. He was getting ready to slash again, and John Kost was no closer to finding him.

He'd even begun to suspect that Elena didn't want him to find Pugachev.

She came to his apartment day or night at will, contemptuous of the very idea of making excuses to Martov, and he was utterly powerless to turn her away, to believe that her misery was anything but genuine, even though he knew she was sprinkling lies over his bed as his father sprinkled insect powder over hotel sheets whenever they traveled. The only lie she shrank from was to say that she loved him.

He stood taller. A woman was walking toward him. *How simple this would be if I had no feelings for her!*

But she wasn't Elena.

Yesterday morning, he'd taken another step toward the decision to tell Coffey about Tikhov when Jennaway dropped by the Hall of Justice and apologized, as best he could without seeming insubordinate, for his admiral's "head-hunting tactics."

273

"And how do you yourself recruit agents?" John Kost asked.

"Well, I usually try to establish a bit of trust and mutual interest before popping the big question, Inspector. But I don't count fellow professionals among my prospects. All I'm saying is—if you people need any help, don't hesitate to give us a holler." This apparently sincere attempt at fence-mending had only convinced John Kost that Naval Intelligence, as well as the FBI, Secret Service, and State Department Security, had to be made aware of Tikhov's death in order to start a concerted hunt for Pugachev. If they could learn why the resident had attacked him along the Merced River, they'd be closer to understanding what Pugachev was up to. But Elena would have none of it. If the U.S. authorities found out about Tikhov, her daughter would die. Each time he suggested that she seek asylum until all of this could be sorted out between the two governments, she became hysterical. "Don't you see!" she'd cry, lacing her fingers through his as if to tie his hands. "If I even appear to be thinking that, my baby's dead!"

The choir had begun.

He checked his wristwatch, then strode around the corner for his car.

Five minutes later he pulled into the loading zone in front of the Soviet mission without having seen her along the way.

Grigor Pervukhin answered the door. "Ah, Inspector Kost."

"Is Madame Martova here by chance?" He had resolved not to explain why he was asking.

"I'm not sure. Please come in and have something to drink while I find out."

Left alone in the sitting room to quench his unease with a glass of excellent vodka, he hoped that something unexpected but perfectly innocent had prevented her from going to vespers.

Soon, Pyotr Martov strolled into the room, smiling and tapping a large envelope against the side of his leg. "Ivan Mikhailovich, I'm so very glad you came by. This was in today's diplomatic pouch."

"What is it?"

"Just open it, please."

He undid the twine bow and brought out an old photograph. He started to say something about Elena, but then fell silent. Even after nearly thirty years, he knew at once it was she, and in that moment it seemed as if she'd just swept through the door of their Moscow flat, safely returned from shopping, her arms loaded with bread. Everything about her, even the music of her voice, came back to him with a jumble of emotion that included resentment that she'd ever left him alone. "Thank you, Pyotr Aleksandrovich," he finally said. "May I keep it?"

"Of course." Martov frowned in the midst of his expansive good mood. "I'm afraid the information you got about her death was colored by anti-Bolshevik sentiment."

"Meaning?"

"She wasn't shot. She was struck by a trolley and died in hospital. I was sent a Photostat of the death certificate. Yes, that's it there."

Studying the document, he suspected a forgery, but put aside his doubts long enough to nod his appreciation. Then he forced himself back to the present. "Elena Valentinovna was expected at church."

"Quite. She left a half hour ago."

"She never arrived."

"Well, she comes and goes as she pleases."

"I'm concerned, Pyotr Aleksandrovich."

Martov caught John Kost's look, and his fastidious smile collapsed. "Let's take your car. I've given Ruml the night off."

It had begun with a white woman, a divorcée. She waited on the soda fountain at the Mare Island exchange and always came over to his booth, even when she had nothing to serve him, and asked him what book he was reading, whether it was any good or not. She said she liked books too, and one thing led to another. But they were careful and nothing bad would've come of it had Port Chicago not blown up last July. He now clearly saw this: how the explosion had been the start of everything bad for him.

After nightfall he'd been steering his launch back into the

floating dock on the Napa River when the whole sky lit up. The shock wave almost knocked him overboard. He would've sworn he was sitting right on top of the blast, and it surprised him to learn later that it had been centered fifteen miles up Suisun Bay at the Port Chicago Naval Magazine. Nearly four hundred ammo handlers had gone up in smoke, most of them Negroes.

"Poof," Woodrow Tillman said, watching the snowy mountains creep past the crack in the boxcar door. The quarter moon was a smudge. He had lost his eyeglasses running away from the crazy detective outside the Lounge, the same one he'd seen on Pier 46 the week before. But glasses or not, he was headed home to Mississippi. He'd swapped clothes with a bum in the switchyard at Fairfield and was done with the Navy.

Three weeks after the Port Chicago disaster, the colored stevedores who'd survived were bussed over to Mare Island and ordered to start loading again. Well, the big blow had happened while two ammo ships were being loaded, and the Navy could give no answer why they'd gone up, so over three hundred Negro sailors respectfully refused to work, saying they deserved an answer before somebody tripped off another explosion. The brass started leaning on them, bad-mouthing them for being lazy cowards, but when they were done ranting, fifty men still wouldn't load. They were slapped in the brig and eventually court-martialed.

Woodrow Tillman had not been among them.

Two of these handlers, before they were jailed, had come to him and the other coxswains and said, "Don't go on working for the white man. Stick together and we got the motherfuckers by the balls, see? What they gonna do—V-mail this shit out to the war? Don't you see?" Tillman had seen, but he'd also been afraid. The commandant of the Twelfth Naval District said that anybody who refused to load would be tried for mutiny and shot. As things turned out, the ringleaders got fifteen-year sentences, but nobody could've said beforehand that they weren't going to get death.

Yet, months after the court-martial, Tillman had found himself wishing he'd been among those convicted. It was the damnedest feeling, this need to bring trouble on himself just to have peace of mind. Mabelline Shipley, the woman at the exchange, said she understood why he felt guilty. Here she was white as sugar, but she admired him for feeling the way he did. He'd known from early on in the relationship that she was political; she was a progressive thinker, especially when it came to race, and even admitted that she'd toyed with the idea of joining the Party for a while. Her sister Emma had been a member but quit when she and her husband, a longshoreman, got fed up with what Stalin was doing to the Revolution.

Now, listening to the wheels clack over the rail joints, he looked back and saw how the three of them—Mabelline and the Laskas—had primed him until it seemed the most reasonable way in the world to get back at the admiral by transferring a few crates of cast explosives and chemical detonators to a fishing boat in China Basin. And he had fancied that he'd gotten away with it, despite the cop in the cruiser shining his spotlight on the ack-ack boat and the *Lorelei*, until the detective had shown up at the Lounge.

The train was slowing. He stepped away from the door and deeper into the shadows. Another long grade? No, it was most definitely coming to a stop. He went to a corner, stooped, and tried to make himself small.

The brakes locked with a lurch.

He waited as all motion ceased, wondering if this was the end of the line.

After a long while, twenty minutes maybe, he heard boots stubbing against the hard spring snow. He would've run right then, but the footfalls seemed to be coming toward him on both sides of the car. It might be railroad police, but he doubted it—not way up here in the mountains. More likely it was the crew doing this or that. If they caught him, he'd be real Jim Crow and they'd probably let him go his way.

As the footfalls drew ever closer, he buried his face in his arms so his eyes wouldn't flash if they shined their lanterns inside the car.

And shine their lights they did—forever it seemed.

"Well, lookee what we got here," a white voice said.

Tillman finally looked up, grinning.

"Military haircut, Sheriff. Sure as day, this one won't get to work on our county farm."

The confidence that Vanechka would think of a way to save her daughter had come to resemble her faith in its willing abandonment of reason. No longer did Elena dwell on how he might possibly do this. Speculation was an invitation to doubt and despair, her constant companions for years now. *Vanechka would think of a way.* Only by this conviction could she go on; without it, she was lost, separated from God. If she'd eternally forfeited her own soul, which she often believed, the forfeiture had been through sin, wanton and licentious sin. Yet, in all those years had the choice been anything except between sin and death, she would not have sinned. And this was the basis of her appeal for mercy: she had not been strong enough to choose death.

An automobile horn startled her.

She stepped back onto the curb, offering the driver a shy wave in apology. The American smiled and waved back, and she laughed if only because it was within the perverse nature of sorrow for it to be studded with little moments of happiness like this. Strolling on toward vespers, surrounded by a pale green sky and rectilinear buildings, she was reminded of other walks long ago. It had been her habit before Leningrad performances to take the air down Nevsky Prospect, past the old Admiralty—

Another automobile had turned into the intersection she was preparing to cross. It stopped, blocking her way. She thought that she'd somehow transgressed against the traffic regulations once again, but then she caught the driver's gesture for her to approach. She didn't.

He opened his door and got out, leaving the motor running. She backstepped.

He said something in English, but the only thing she made of it was that she shouldn't be frightened. Parting his coat, he revealed a gold star attached to his belt. Vanechka had one just like it, and at last she understood that this was one of his men sent to pick her up for vespers. Was she that late? Darkness had fallen. He opened the passenger door for her. He stank of perspiration and wine, which surprised her: all the Americans she'd met had been so well scrubbed. She set her purse close beside her on the seat. "John Kost send?" she asked.

"Yeah, John send," he said, keeping his smallish eyes on the street as he drove away from the street she'd intended to follow.

"St. Basil's?"

"Yeah, sure."

Afraid that he might assume she understood more English than she did and try to engage her in a fuller conversation, she sat back and said nothing more, expecting him to turn east again. But he didn't. She knew that the church was east from the consulate, yet upon reaching the next main thoroughfare he veered west.

He said something, his voice low.

Smiling, she shook her head that she didn't understand, and he repeated himself more slowly. Something about Aranov. She knew of his death and how much Vanechka had cared for him, so perhaps he'd sent one of his underlings to take her to a memorial service for Aranov. That made more sense than anything, even though she believed the man had just asked her if she liked salt water. An idiom? "I do not understand," she said, blushing at her textbook English. There had been an opportunity to learn it at the state ballet school, but she'd devoted all of her energies to dance, to trying to outdo Galina Ulanova. Besides, she had no ear for languages.

He hiked his shoulders as if to say that he didn't care.

Eventually, the boulevard ended at the ocean.

Off to the right a white building was perched atop some shoreline rocks, its windows blacked out. She didn't take the time to transliterate the Roman letters along its roofline, but believed the place to be a restaurant. In the opposite direction a deserted beach curved south into the night, and behind the sand a pair of enormous windmills stood dark against the glow of the crescent moon.

The man parked in a lot next to the beach and stilled the

motor. He turned to her and said just one word: "Pugachev."
Then he lit a cigarette and waited for her reply.

In the midst of her rising panic she also felt betrayal.
Vanechka, to spare his own tender feelings, had ordered this crass
man to find out about Pugachev. "I do not understand," she said.

He backhanded her.

When she touched her lips with her fingers, they were wet
with warmth, and she could taste blood on her tongue.

"Pugachev," he said with the same inflection as if to tell her
that his brutality was tireless.

"I don't know anyone of that name," she said in Russian. "Ivan
Mikhailovich already asked me. Is he asking again now?"

He rolled down his side window and flicked out his cigarette.
"Where's Boris Pugachev?"

"I do not know. Please." She hated to add this begging word,
but she was thinking of her daughter.

Sighing, he reached for the keys in the ignition, and she
believed that he'd given up and was going to restart the motor
when he pocketed them instead. Then, quite peculiarly, he
rested his chin on his chest and stared down at his hands, which
he'd steepled together. His eyes were glinting, and she thought it
was from sudden moisture. "Pugachev killed Natty," he said in a
hush. And then he sobbed once, giving her the clearest idea yet
what this was all about—the man had been Aranov's comrade
and was somehow blaming her for his death.

She was trying to touch his face when he spun around and
pinioned her by the wrist. "Pugachev! Pugachev!" he cried.

"I do not know!"

With his knee, he sprung the latch, then kicked open the door.
Growling, he dragged her out his way, letting her drop to the
pavement before picking her up again and flinging her over a
concrete parapet onto the beach. Although it took several seconds
for him to plod up to her, she didn't try to run. She had only a
hazy notion of where she was, and seeing him weep had made
her hope his rage would soon collapse into tears again. "I do not
know Pugachev," she gasped, then spat—sand was clinging to her

bloody lips. She started to crawl toward an unlit lamppost, intending to wrap herself to it until he tired of beating her and left.

She thought of the pistol in her purse, but knew that she would never use it. It was the last good thing she believed of herself: she would never take another life to save her own.

She was almost to the lamppost when he seized her by the arm and the hair and began driving her before him toward the ocean.

All the way down to the surf he said nothing, although his breath was roaring out of him.

The first ripple of water was like ice around her ankles, but he kept pushing her out until a big swell rose up around their waists, almost knocking them over. He slapped her once more, then gripped her shoulders and muscled her under the surface. The strength of her legs was no match for his arms, and the breath she was holding began to ring in her ears as it went stale.

Suddenly, he yanked her up into the sweet night air. "Pugachev!" he bellowed.

"No . . . please!"

Under she went again. Clawing at him, her hands found his gold star and tore it away from his belt. She began jabbing his thigh with its points, but it had no effect on him.

Then she quit thrashing. Everything had turned lucid at the eye of the storm. Only one thing mattered: if she died on this beach, her daughter would die as well. She had to make him stop trying to drown her. After that, *Vanechka would think of a way*—for she'd come to trust him again if only because he would never allow something like this. The man was acting on his own.

When she was pulled to the surface again, she cried, "Yes! Pugachev!"

He shook her so hard she bit her tongue. "Where?"

"Purse."

She could feel his confusion as increased pressure in his grip. "*Where!*"

"Purse. Auto."

He started shoving her back toward the parking lot, roughly grabbing the back of her dress whenever she stumbled. He was muttering something she didn't understand—other than the fact that it was a threat.

At the car, he took his electric torch from the glove compartment and shined it into her purse. He began scattering her articles across the seat, grunting at the discovery of the pistol before hurling it out onto the beach. "Where!"

"Here," she said in Russian, handing her facial-powder compact to him. He tore open the case, damaging the clasp, but found nothing inside except the puff. "Where!"

With a quivering fingernail she pried the mirror out of the lid and shook the slip of paper jammed beneath into his open palm.

He glanced at the telephone number, then up at her. "Pugachev?" he needlessly asked.

Nodding, she staggered over to the lamppost and leaned against it, shivering. Then she ground the heels of her hands into her eyes—it struck her what she'd just done. Perhaps it would have been better to die in the surf.

He was coming for her again.

"Please," she moaned, "please . . . for John Kost. Go."

She froze as she felt his hand reach under her dress. The sensation gnawing at her stomach was the same as it had been on that other night. "No . . . I beg you." That too had been out-of-doors: in the dewy grass behind the dacha, her reeling head lifted slightly toward the remote stars.

He yanked one of her silk stockings off the garters and slid it down her leg, upending her as he whipped it off her foot.

Nothing happened for a moment.

She looked up at him. He twisted one stocking into a cord, then slid it between her teeth and tied it off behind her head with a knot so tight her scalp began hurting. Next, he forced her arms around the lamppost and bound her wrists with the second stocking.

Then he walked back to the car.

From the Dodge, Pyotr Martov watched John Kost conferring with the uniformed policeman on the corner two blocks down from the church. He looked as if he wanted to latch onto the fellow and shake the information out of him. But then, patting the patrolman's shoulder as if in defeat, he trotted back to the car. "How love makes for a poignant haste," Martov whispered.

John Kost got in. "He hasn't seen her, but he'll start looking."

"Excellent." He realized that the inspector had paused with his hand on the shift knob to stare at him.

"Do you honestly mean that?"

"I'm sorry?" Martov asked.

"How do you really feel about this?"

"What's the good of such talk, Ivan Mikhailovich? I've come along to search for her, haven't I?" Then Martov broke out a cigarette and lit it. He sensed in the ensuing silence that John Kost was on the verge of bringing up something disruptive, but after a few seconds the inspector shifted into gear and drove on. Somewhere under the dashboard a police radio was squawking, but Martov couldn't see it. "It's her habit to take walks without telling me, you know," he went on, smiling behind his cigarette. He asked himself why he was smiling, and the answer had less to do with Elena, who was really a foregone conclusion between them, and more to do with the expectation that now, at long last, they might set aside the subterfuge that had so far soured their relationship. But first some unavoidable disagreeableness had to be weathered. "Until you showed up at the consulate, I would've guessed that she'd snuck off to your flat again."

John Kost braked in the middle of street, forcing the cars following to go around. "She's missing right now. My man, Aranov, was missing too. And now he's dead." He shook his head, his fine teeth showing clenched between his lips. "Have you ever loved that woman, honestly?"

"Oh, yes," Martov said with such conviction he surprised himself. The inspector could have the present, but the past was inviolate—and completely his.

"But what about now?"

Martov didn't reply.

"Maybe I understand your indifference," John Kost said. "Most loves don't last. I was married once, and I doubt it would've lasted. She didn't love me, and with time that might

283

have poisoned my love for her. I don't know. But what of your feelings for your own daughter?"

"My daughter?" Martov found himself at a loss for words.

"I know what they've done with her."

He told himself to calm down, to take this slowly. In the next few minutes he might learn more than he had in twelve days of indirect inquiry as to why his estranged wife had come to San Francisco. Instinct told him to look concerned. "What's happened to Anya?"

"You don't *know?*"

"Know what?"

John Kost hesitated, then accelerated down the street again.

Martov was alarmed he might say nothing more, that this precious opportunity would pass and he'd learn nothing of Elena's intentions. He had to gamble. "She's not my daughter," he said.

"What d'you mean?"

"Just what I said."

"Explain, dammit!"

"As far as I know—Anna's patronymic is Lavrentievna. . . ." Then Martov sat back and watched John Kost's face tighten as the words sank in. He looked devastated, sickened, and Martov found himself feeling sorry for him. The man really did love her, and he refused to fault him for that. "You mustn't think unkindly of her. Beria raped her the first time. After a performance he invited her out to his dacha and forced himself on her. She came back and begged me to kill him." He chuckled unhappily. "She asked me to shoot the head of the secret police."

"I would've done it," John Kost said with just the right intonation to make Martov smile in admiration.

"Yes, I rather think you would've. But I'm not you, Ivan Mikhailovich. And when I did nothing but counsel caution, she in turn did nothing to put off Beria's further overtures. She became one of his mistresses for a while. It's quite possible she still is. I really don't know."

John Kost drove blindly against a stop signal, and Martov was on the verge of telling him until he saw that there was no

284

cross-traffic. "I'm going to be honest with you about something—"

"Yes?" the inspector interrupted, visibly dragging himself back to the moment.

"—with the hope you'll be just as considerate of me. . . ."

John Kost nodded from him to go on.

"What happened between Beria and her only persuaded me to resolve a longstanding ambivalence in my own life." Martov added with a smile, "Not that she and I didn't have our season of passion." Although he saw how John Kost understood at once, he was then taken aback by the degree of his perceptiveness.

"Pervukhin and you?"

"Why, yes . . . Grisha and I."

They had come to the Embarcadero. A sliver of moon was wedged between the decks of the Bay Bridge. "Why is Elena here?"

"Precisely the question I've been waiting to ask you," Martov said. "We must assume Beria sent her. And if something's indeed happened to her Anya, Lena has come under duress."

"And what about your own duress?" John Kost asked.

"I don't understand."

"Didn't you volunteer to assassinate Anthony Eden?"

Martov was ready to laugh when he realized that the question was in earnest. *What?*"

"By holding the girl, Molotov is forcing you and Elena to kill Eden at a reception next week."

"Who told you such a preposterous thing?"

"She did."

"It's nonsense."

"Then prove it to me," John Kost said with menace in his voice.

"How?"

"Tell me where Boris Pugachev is."

"In Moscow, I presume." Martov put out his cigarette. "He was taken off the flight to San Francisco at the last minute—by the secret police, I'm sure."

"Why them?"

"Well, poor Boris has dropped out of sight since. That means only one thing."

"You knew him?"

"We served together in Belgrade before the war."

John Kost's breathing had grown uneven. "Then who arrived at Hamilton Field in his name?"

"I think you should ask Lena. I'm not being impudent when I say this, Ivan Mikhailovich. She'd never tell me. Our past. But she might tell you. The other night at Mrs. Testa's, this is what I wanted to talk over with you. But you were called away. I wanted us to start working together." Martov took his vodka flask from his jacket pocket and offered it to John Kost, who declined.

"Why're you being so forthright with me?"

"It's a question of choice." Martov said after a nip. "I have none. I've got to find out what Beria's up to. You see, in my business the fellow who's left out of the know usually winds up the sacrificial lamb. I've never aspired to be a lamb. Oh, I'm not promising that when I find out I'll go on helping you. But until that time—"

A string of numbers trickled from the hidden radio, and John Kost grabbed a microphone from under the dashboard. "Go ahead with your traffic, Central One."

"See the WC at Richmond Station ASAP reference your BOL this date."

He acknowledged the female dispatcher, and Martov asked, "What is it?"

"Lenochka," John Kost said, spinning the steering wheel so sharply the tires chittered.

25

THE TELEPHONE COMPANY SUPERVISOR was staring at the trail of splatters his trouser cuffs had left on the floor of the exchange lobby. "I should've asked before, Sergeant," she said, meeting his eyes again. "May I see your identification? It's policy." Ragnetti parted his jacket. A gander at his gold star usually did the trick, but the woman was looking at his midriff as if she had no idea what he was doing. Only then did he see that his badge was missing. He must've lost it in the surf. Taking out his sopping wallet, he held his plasticized ID card up to her face. A nun's sour face. "Very good, Sergeant Ragnetti." She handed him an index card. On it was an address in Mission District.

He started for the parking lot entrance, but then turned at the revolving door and asked, "You sure this is for the number I gave you?"

"Yes, Sergeant."

Revving his Dodge's engine, he suddenly turned off the ignition and sat back. A hankie, ivory-handled brush, lipstick dispenser, and cigarettes with funny-looking cardboard mouth-pieces were strewn across the passenger side of the seat. He raked them together with his fingers, rolled down the window, and chucked them outside. Then he propped his knees on the dashboard and filled his mouth with Chianti.

It was only ten past eight o'clock, a bad time to hit the address the way he wanted to. He had no intention of making an arrest, although he'd swear at the shooting inquest that a lawful collar had been his plan from the word go and that Pugachev had bitched it up. Justification would hinge on the small nickel-plated pistol that would be found within an arm's reach of the body. Presently, that pistol was in Ragnetti's jacket pocket.

But at this hour plenty of pedestrians would be on the sidewalk out front, churchgoers to and from the Mission Dolores down the street, and the neighbors would be awake. Not to mention the bastard himself. He wanted to catch him dopey and unaware, the same way the guy had probably caught Aranov. But he also wanted him to wake up just enough to know what was about to happen to him.

What about the woman on the beach then? he asked himself, figuring she was bound and gagged well enough for him to risk waiting awhile before heading down to Mission District.

Restarting the engine, he promised himself he wouldn't queer this job like he had the Mare Island interrogation. He'd go into the hole for a couple of hours and calm down. Then he'd hit the address.

Bursting through the doors of Richmond Station with Martov two steps behind, John Kost made headlong for the utility room where bodies were stored until transfer to the morgue could be arranged. "Inspector!" the watch commander hailed him from the far end of the corridor. "Not in there—my office."

He ran the rest of the way. She was alive, then.

Wrapped in a woolen blanket, her hair wet and stringy, she sat with her bare legs folded beneath her on the WC's sofa. Sand was flaking off her shins and feet. She was shuddering. Her face had been beaten. Pummeled. He hid the rage that swept over him, afraid she might mistake it for disgust. Her dull eyes shifted from the floor to him, then to Martov, and finally back to the floor again—all without apparently recognizing either of them. Yet, when he touched her shoulder, she seized his hand and wouldn't let go.

"Patrol found her tied to a lamppost on the beach," the WC, said, joining them. "She wouldn't get inside the ambulance we dispatched, and all the boys could make of what she said was that she wanted to see you, Inspector."

John Kost saw it in the WC's smile: the same comment everyone seemed to be making about them. "Her name's Elena Martova," he said coldly. "This is her husband."

Martov offered to shake, but the WC simply touched two fingers to the bill of his service cap and went on looking at the way Elena was clinging to John Kost. "Leastways, that face can use some iodine."

"We'll see to it. If you'll excuse us now. . . ."

"Sure."

As soon as the WC had shut the door behind him, Martov knelt beside her and asked in Russian, "Who did this, Lena?"

For the first time she seemed to realize who he was, but instead of answering she reached inside the blanket and came out with a gold five-pointed star. It was mounted on a belt-clip attachment. John Kost gently took it from her, read the number, then shut his eyes.

"What is it?" Martov asked.

"Good God."

"What's wrong, man?"

"My sergeant did this."

"*What?*"

"It's my fault."

"How is this possible?" Martov demanded. "Isn't he under orders?"

"I should've seen the signs. He hasn't been himself since Nathan. . . ." He didn't finish, for Elena was now squeezing his hand so tightly his fingers were going numb.

"We must talk alone, Vanechka." Her voice was an old woman's. "Just us."

Martov turned away in protest.

"Not here," John Kost said, stunned to think that his own

people were now a threat to her as well. "We've got to hide you first. Somewhere safe."

"The consulate?" Martov asked.

"The last place I'd let her go."

"But your flat's no good."

"Agreed. No, I was thinking of my father's."

"Will he take her in?" Martov asked.

"He's a Don Cossack."

"So?"

"He'll turn away no one asking for refuge."

"Do you expect us to rely on some worn-out frontier tradition?"

"It's my father who is worn-out," John Kost said, taking her up in his arms, "not his traditions. The door, please."

As they were speeding down Geary Boulevard toward the heart of the city, she began to weep. A good sign, John Kost thought. Martov reached over from the backseat to console her, but she twisted away from him. "I mean you no harm," he said with surprising tenderness, "and I hope nothing unfortunate happens to Anna Lavrentievna."

She squirmed up against her door and shouted across the front seat at John Kost, "What have you done! What have you told him!"

"Most everything he knows," Martov answered for him. "As I've confided a great deal in him. . . ." He took a moment to light a Pushkin.

"No, no," she moaned.

"Oh, have no fear, Lena, he's a gentleman and reacted with admirable bourgeois outrage. He said he would've shot Beria."

She lowered her head, and John Kost could almost feel her anger deteriorating into shame. "We're going to save your child," he said. "You, I, and Pyotr Aleksandrovich."

"You can't rely on anything this man says!"

"Who then can I rely on?" he asked, yet without reproach; quite simply, she had to realize how isolated his own situation now was. His circle of trust had shrunk to those in this car, and even it was a nest of doubts.

She said nothing more until after she had gotten out of her wet clothes and into his father's bed. "Vanechka," she weakly called to him, "will you light the icon in here?"

Doing so, he said, "Pyotr will bring some of your things to the Hall of Justice in the morning. He'll say you've taken to your bed ill at the consulate." Shaking out the match, he suddenly leaned down and kissed her bare shoulder.

She winced as if his touch had hurt her. "We must talk—"

Mikhail Kostoff had shuffled into the room, bearing tea, iodine, and cotton swabs on a tin tray. He had caught the intimacy between them and glanced behind to check if Martov might have seen. Then he grinned salaciously.

"Papa, leave the tray and shut the door, if you will."

"Does the Bolshevik require tea?"

"You'll have to ask him."

Scowling, the old man turned back for the living room.

John Kost saturated a swab with iodine and dabbed her swollen lips. Her own teeth had cut them in several places. She didn't cringe, as if corporeal pain were nothing in comparison to what was gripping her spirit. She suddenly brushed aside his ministering hand. "You once asked me about Pugachev. . . ."

"Yes?" he said when she didn't go on.

"Your man . . . he wanted to know where Pugachev is."

"Did you tell him?"

"In a way. I had a telephone number hidden in my compact," she said miserably, on the verge of tears once again. "I never told you because I couldn't . . . for my Annushka. . . ."

"I know." He kissed her forehead. "Can you recall the number?"

"No. I'm sorry. But you've got to stop your man from finding Pugachev. If anything happens to him, my daughter . . . they'll. . . ." She couldn't finish. "I'll tell you everything about Pugachev. About Beria. Everything. But first you must stop your man."

"I'll try. Rest now."

He was at the door when she asked, "Will you send in your father? I don't want to be alone."

"Of course."

He found his father and Martov sizing up each other across the kitchen table. Apparently some words had finally been exchanged, for the old man snarled, "Why didn't you tell me he's second-in-command of those vipers on Divisadero Street?"

"You didn't ask, Papa."

Martov gave a brittle chuckle, then took a sip of tea from his glass.

"Well, get him out of here before I get my saber and do it myself."

"We're both leaving in a minute. And indeed—I'd like you to keep your saber handy while I'm gone. Let no one in but me." He took a gulp from his own glass of tea, which had gone lukewarm. "Elena Valentinovna asks for your company."

The old man's face softened. "At once." As he shuffled past, John Kost delayed him by the arm.

"Papa, I believe we're in Pyotr Aleksandrovich's debt for something."

"His debt?"

John Kost took the envelope from his overcoat pocket and handed it to him.

The arthritic fingers struggled with the twine for several seconds, during which John Kost realized that he'd been waiting most of his life to see the look that was imminent in his father's eyes, that it would tell him how the tsarist colonel had truly felt about his *tziganka* lover. "Some help with that?"

"No, no." Mikhail Kostoff slowly slid out the photograph. His face went to stone and he stared fixedly at the sepia print until an eyelid twitched. Then he stuffed it back into the envelope and rushed for the bedroom.

"Papa—?" But the door had slammed shut against him.

The Chekist snapped awake. Once again, he'd been dreaming of that fortresslike house near Mexico City, the crunch of his alpine ax as it came down upon that bowed head, the amazed look on the face of Trotsky's Judas of an aide, Ramón—

The Chekist sat up.

292

Like any other creature of the taiga, no drowsiness dulled the knife edge between his sleep and wakefulness. He listened for a few seconds, listened with his nerves as well as his ears, then quietly left the bed and crept into the darkest corner of the room. Moonlight was penetrating the drawn shades, falling brightly across the rumpled sheets.

He listened again.

There was a sighing from the adjoining flat, a toilet tank refilling.

But that was not what had awakened him.

Ragnetti kicked open the door and hurtled through it. His flashlight beam flitted across an empty bed, then swept clockwise around the room.

No one.

He thumbed off the flashlight and felt the pillowcase with the back of his gun hand. It was still warm.

Then his breathing slowed enough for him to hear that the bathtub taps were running. The bastard was taking a soak and probably hadn't even heard the hinges splintering out of the jamb.

The closed lavatory door stood at the end of a ten-foot hallway. The hall was lined on one side with closet doors and on the other with paned windows that looked down on the street three stories below. Up the block, the moon was shining on the towers of the basilica at the Mission Dolores.

Starting toward the lavatory, he swept his Colt up to eye level.

He was almost there when a closet door sprang open, shoving him against a window. He wheeled as he fell, firing once. The boom was mixed with the tinkle of breaking glass, which was now showering past his eyes. He squeezed the trigger again but knew right away that the bullet had gone into the ceiling—for he'd come to rest with the small of his back against the sill and the upper half of his body tottering outside. He could see the moon and a couple faint stars. He had to let go of his revolver to grasp the sides of the window frame, and after a surprisingly long moment it clattered against the sidewalk.

Grunting, he was getting ready to pull himself back inside

when he felt hands grab his outstretched legs and begin to push them upward.

"No!" he begged.

But by then it was too late. He was already falling.

"*Sooken-sen!*" the Chekist hissed. Son of a bitch!

Clasping his right forearm, his thumb pressed into the deep gouge of the exit wound, he looked out the shattered window at the figure sprawled below. "Fucking police!" He turned for the closet, his bare feet slipping in a pool of his own blood.

You've been shot before, he reminded himself, *and came through all right*. The important thing was to leave without delay. Other policemen were on the way—if not already outside in the corridor. Resisting the onset of nausea with voluminous breaths, he set his Nagan on the floor and wrestled into his overcoat. Then picking up the revolver again with his left hand, he tried to grasp the topmost of two pasteboard boxes with his wounded arm. But it was no good. He couldn't, and transferring the box to his left arm would only deny him use of his Nagan as he burst from the room. "Son of a bitch!"

He tried to think of another way, but finally shut the closet door. If they knew how to find him, they knew everything else. Had the woman done the unexpected and talked?

No police awaited him along the corridor, but he took the fire escape instead of the staircase—and nearly fainted when he had to hang by his arms to drop into the alley.

Elena's eyes opened on an old man's candlelit face.

It took a moment for her to recall who he was and why she lay in this strange bed that was gritty with sand. Then relief washed over her anxiety. "Has Vanechka come back?"

"No, my dear," Mikhail Kostoff said. "Sleep."

"I can't. The aching in my face."

"Would you like some vodka?"

"No thank you."

"More aspirin?"

"No."

He was still gazing at the photograph he'd been clutching all night. Earlier he'd explained that Martov had given it to him, an act of generosity she somehow mistrusted. What did he hope to gain from the Kostoffs? "They say she was killed by a trolley car. . . ." A corner of his mouth curled downward. "The lying swine."

"May I see?" she asked, holding the covers against her breasts as she rose to take the photograph. With a possessive reluctance, he handed it over. "Oh, yes," she said—there was no mistaking the woman in the picture to be anyone but Vanechka's mother: the black hair and warm brown eyes were the same. "She was lovely."

Mikhail Kostoff swallowed the last of the vodka in his glass. The little bottle on the nightstand was nearly empty as well, but he seemed only moderately drunk. "She was," he said at last. "But more than lovely she was willful. She had her own means, you know. There'd been other patrons before me. And it showed. Dear God, how it showed. What a frank laugh she had!" Accepting back the photograph, he himself then laughed, and happily enough to make her smile despite her throbbing face. "She was everything a forty-year-old boy could want." In a blink, he turned somber again. "But I was done in by my own desire. I fell in love with her, you see. And early on I gave her the hope I'd one day marry her. Desire's a craven thing, you know."

"Yes, oh yes!" she said, but then glanced away when she realized she could never share how this truth had been revealed to her. Yet, it was a consolation to believe that the old man would understand, just as his son had apparently understood and already forgiven her. These were rare men, this father and son, and not merely quaint relics of a detestable era, as Martov intimated. At length, she asked, "Why didn't you marry her if you loved her so?"

"An officer of the Imperial Guard?" Again he laughed, but morosely now. "An officer who married an actress, let alone a Gypsy singer, was obligated by his honor to leave Petersburg, to rejoin some ordinary regiment. So each month I made the twelve-hour train trip to Moscow—and perpetuated the lie. Of all the things I've done in my days, I fear God will find that to be the most loathsome. It's unforgivable, to lie to your lover."

Once more she looked away, only to reach blindly for his hand.

"No, no, daughter, don't try to comfort me. I can't be forgiven this. Nor can I forget her look each time I arrived at her apartment near the Nikitskaya Gate. It's impossible. And why can't I? Because her son has that same look!" His expression turned cunning. "But I have my pride too, and I won't tell him the very thing that'll slap that insufferable look off his face. . . ." His hand unsteady now, he drained the bottle into his glass—over these past few minutes he'd visibly crossed over into a deeper, more melancholy drunkenness.

"What is that thing, Mikhail Mikhailovich?"

He stared into his glass. "I resigned my command."

"Of the Tsar's Own Convoy?"

"Yes."

"To marry his mother?"

"Yes, for my Alla. Oh, the decision was made easier because a war was coming and I more properly belonged in a line rather than a ceremonial regiment. But nevertheless I resigned in the spring of 1913. I did indeed resign!" he cried, but then fell silent with the faraway softness gradually flooding back into his eyes. "I was allowed to personally tell His Imperial Majesty of my decision. And you know, my dear, he was truly a tenderhearted fellow. Somehow this has been forgotten in all the vituperation that's been heaped upon his memory. But he said that he understood and that he'd miss my service. He told me it was the greatest fortune in his life that he'd found genuine love in his marriage. . . ." He reached for the bottle again, but then grumbled when he saw that it was empty. Rummaging in the nightstand drawer for another, he found only a dagger and what was probably his baptismal cross.

"Did you propose to Alla?"

"Of course."

"And what'd she say?"

"She refused me. She was heavy with our child, but she said

296

she no longer wanted to be my wife. So I joined my new regiment. The war started the next summer, and I saw neither her nor Moscow ever again." He came to his feet on a teetering lurch, tossed his arms wide to steady himself, then snuffed the icon taper with a wave of the photograph, casting the room into darkness. "Sleep now, my dear."

"You should tell Vanechka," she said. "He needs to know this."

The old man said nothing, and a moment later she heard him stumble against the kitchen table and curse, which reminded her of her own father, trying to make his way through their darkened house in Leningrad, reproachfully mumbling his own name of Valentin.

As John Kost watched the ambulance's tail lamps pinch out at the far end of Eighteenth Street, someone approached him from behind and coughed as if not to startle him. "What d'you want done with Ragnetti's wheelgun, Inspector?" Delbert from ID asked. "I already bagged the two spent casings and four cartridges. He was using approved ammunition."

"I'll keep the revolver."

"Then I'm about done."

"Fine, thank you." But when a few seconds later he turned, Delbert was still standing there.

"What's going on, John?"

"Who the Devil knows?"

"All right, forget I asked."

"Wait—I'm sorry. I'm not trying to keep you in the dark. It's just that I don't know myself."

The streetlamp caught Delbert's unsettled grin. "You sound kinda scared."

"I am, old fellow. The world's come calling, and suddenly it's like we don't have two nice big oceans on either side of us. Now go home and get some rest."

"Will do." But then he slipped something into one of John Kost's pockets before saying over his shoulder on the way to his car, "You may want to hang on to this too, John. I didn't have time to put it on the evidence list. Good night."

It was a small nickel-plated pistol. The serial number had been ground and buffed off the frame. A throwaway. So Ragnetti had come here to kill Pugachev and then justify it by planting this cheap handgun on the corpse. A stupid thing to do that would never stand up to a careful investigation. Had he wanted to be punished for it, then? Whatever—Delbert had just saved his job for him.

John Kost strolled back to the browning bloodstain on the sidewalk, his shoes crackling over the shards of glass, and peered up at the busted-out third-story window. Had the telephone-company supervisor not been made unduly suspicious by his asking for the same address Ragnetti had requested, he might have gotten here before. . . . Then he reminded himself that it was dangerous to start second-guessing all this: it was like loosing a homing pigeon that would wing directly back to self-recrimination about Aranov. He was finished with being in a funk. There were things to be done.

The squeal of car brakes spun him around: Jennaway had shown up. The lieutenant commander stepped out of his Plymouth in a civilian suit with a bulge under his jacket. "Inspector." He offered his hand, although his eyes were on the big bloodstain.

"Thanks for coming, Mr. Jennaway."

"It's Dennis—and thanks for calling. How's your man?"

John Kost pointed up at the window. "Broken jaw and left leg, his skull's cracked most likely. The attendants took their time, fearing a broken back. That's why we just got him off to the hospital a minute ago."

"He fell *thirty* feet onto concrete?"

"Yeah."

"Was he conscious?"

"No, so forgive me, if I don't have a clue what he was trying to do here," John Kost lied. He wanted to see how well the ONI man could be trusted before he revealed how Ragnetti had latched onto Pugachev's trail. He couldn't bring himself to drag Elena's name into this. "Let's go inside."

"Sure."

In the hallway between the bedroom and the bathroom, John Kost directed his flashlight first at the pool of blood on the linoleum and then at the .38-caliber hole angling shallowly into one of the three closet doors.

"Seems your guy got off a shot," Jennaway noted.

"Two of them." John Kost's beam swept up to the ceiling and froze on the neat boring there. "The blood begins inside the closet—"

"So your guy got the bastard!" Jennaway said brightly.

"Yes, but not bad enough to keep him from making it down the fire escape." John Kost pulled open the last closet door before the bathroom. Stacked within were two Ivory-soap cardboard boxes, and he offered Jennaway his flashlight to inspect their contents. "Is this stuff yours?"

Jennaway brought out a dark-brown brick and sniffed it. "Cast explosives—definitely military." Laying the topmost box on the floor, he winced when he saw that one side was smeared with blood. "Looks like he tried to pick up this one and couldn't." He started through the bottom one. "Chemical detonators. You find the wooden crates and original cardboard boxes these came in?"

"No."

"Too bad. The shipping labels would tell me in a glance. Still, my hunch is that it's Navy ordnance. But we won't know that until we run an inventory at all the magazines in our district. We can start at the most obvious one—Mare Island."

"When?"

"As soon as I get back to my office."

"Good." John Kost continued to stare at the boxes. "How much damage could this do?"

"Depends. See, blast overpressure is what we call the pressure of an explosion in a specific area—"

"Could it bring down a hotel?" John Kost interrupted. "Like the St. Francis, say?"

"Oh, no. It'd make a mess of the lobby though."

"What about a house?"

"Yeah, maybe, if this guy knew what he was doing. You got any idea what he had in mind?" Jennaway was looking at him in a way that made him wonder if any ONI agents had seen him tonight taking Elena to his father's apartment, or later dropping Martov off at the consulate.

"No, Dennis. That's why I'm asking."

"Who's this dump rented to?"

"We're almost positive it's an alias. But before you go, I'll give you the description we took from the landlady."

"Well, at any rate," Jennaway said, his toothy grin underlit by the flashlight, "his plan got torpedoed by your sergeant, wouldn't you say?"

"What if he finds other explosives?"

"They sure as hell won't come from the Navy or Army. In about ten minutes the shit's going to hit the fan at every depot within the boundaries of Twelfth Naval District. You won't be able to sneak a firecracker out of these installations."

"How about dynamite? What if he got hold of some sticks of dynamite?"

Jennaway chuckled. "Then he'd need a steamer trunk to lug it to his target—if he needs the equivalent blast overpressure to do the job. No, this guy's game is up, John."

26

MOLOTOV HAD ASKED the State Department for a bulletproof limousine and an armed escort to meet him upon arrival at San Francisco Municipal Airport. And so on Monday afternoon John Kost found himself in Ragnetti's Dodge, Homicide's most presentable car, waiting to lead a black Packard with windows like Coke-bottle glass out onto the flight line as soon as Molotov's U.S. Army transport touched down. The head of the local Secret Service office was behind the wheel of the limo, and lounging beside him was Robert Cade in his straw boater, looking bored. Four of his agents were in yet a third car, a Ford convertible with the soft top retracted so they could stand to fire their Thompson submachine guns. It'd be their job to bring up the rear of the convoy.

Earlier, Cade had sauntered across the tarmac to John Kost's Dodge and asked him about the "rattlesnake" Ragnetti had stumbled on. Did he think it'd been Pugachev? Did the PD have a physical on the joker who'd rented the apartment? Fortunately, word had then come from the control tower that Molotov's plane was approaching the bay, and Cade trotted heavily back to the Packard, sparing John Kost some tiresome sidestepping: he was working closer with the Office of Naval Intelligence than he wanted the FBI to realize, at least for the time being. Jennaway had let it slip that he thought Cade lacked finesse, and John Kost hadn't argued.

Yesterday morning, Ragnetti had come around enough for the hospital to send for John Kost. Ragnetti hadn't suffered a broken spine or skull fracture after all, but a severe blow to the back of the head had given him a concussion and black eyes, as if he'd been on the losing end of a slugfest. John Kost thought that there were tears on his face until the nurse explained that his mother had just been by to treat the shiners with warm olive oil. John Kost then ribbed him about looking like he'd gone fifteen rounds with Joe Louis,‐ but instead of rising to the joke Ragnetti hissed through his wired jaws: "Listen, dammit . . . get her outta here. . . ." Then, straining against the impediment, he repeated what an informant he refused to name had told him over the phone—how an ammunition launch from Mare Island had tied up to a fishing boat called the *Lorelei* in China Basin, how Wallace Elliot had seen it all, and finally how Ragnetti had tried to lean on the launch's coxswain, a colored kid named Tillman, at a tavern in Solano County, but had only "bitched it up" instead. He had said nothing about his encounter with Elena, which disappointed John Kost.

Less than fifteen minutes after telephoning Jennaway from the Hall of Justice with this information, he was surprised to get a call back from him: Woodrow Wilson Tillman was in Navy custody.

"Fast work, Dennis," he said, absently scribbling the name Anna Lavrentievna in Cyrillic letters on his ruled yellow pad.

"Thanks for the compliment, but we already had him in the brig at Mare Island."

"What for? Surely not this *Lorelei* business."

"No, for AWOL. He was picked up near some flyspeck in the Sierra called Truckee Saturday night. We're set to question him at fifteen hundred. You want to take the water taxi up with me?"

"If you don't mind."

"Of course not. And consider it confirmed—the explosives and detonators are ours. We came across a forged requisition from a nonexistent supply officer to the distribution control officer up at Mare Depot. I don't know what this kid was thinking. We would've nailed him sooner or later."

By six that evening Tillman, a frightened and studentlike young Negro, had confessed his part in William and Emma Laska's acquisition of explosives. The couple had insisted on *Navy* explosives, according to the coxswain, although he had no idea why. An unexpected bonus from the interrogation came with his claim that a civilian employee of the Mare Island exchange named Mabelline Shipley had introduced him to the Laskas—Mrs. Shipley was Emma's sister. While Jennaway and the Navy criminal investigator continued the grilling, John Kost slipped out of the room and called the bull pen, ordering Mulrenan to go through Aranov's supplemental reports for any reference to Mabelline Shipley. He would hold for as long as it took. "Got it," Mulrenan said after only a few minutes. "Aranov says here he interviewed her on the tenth because she was one of the callers during the time Elliot got plugged."

"Did Nathan note the address?"

"Yeah."

Of course he had—John Kost bowed his head for an instant. "This is her day off. Arrange for a Potrero Station backup and arrest her for investigation."

"You got it, Inspector."

By ten that evening Jennaway and he were sitting at another table, this one in the Hall of Justice and this time across from a tall, rawboned woman. She refused to talk, even when Jennaway tried to frighten her with the seriousness of the federal charge of treason that would be added to the forthcoming California murder complaint against her. When she finally said something, it was to demand her lawyer. Before the attorney, a notorious obstructionist, could arrive, John Kost hoped to find a chink in her armor. "She was used, you know." He then paused.

"Who?" Mabelline asked warily.

"Emma. They used her, then had Laska get rid of her."

"Go to hell. You didn't know her. Will either."

So she knew Laska was dead. "What don't I know about them, Mrs. Shipley?"

"Just go to hell." But she was watching him more intently.

"I think Laska was always willing to die for the Party. Kill for it too. That goes without saying. But the choices were all his that night."

"What're you saying? What's this all about?"

"You tell me, Mrs. Shipley—what choice did your sister have? Did Emma even get to say good-bye to you? Or was she left completely in the dark until Laska blew her brains all over the sofa?"

Her long, homely face twisted into a scowl, but he could tell that her eyes were visualizing her sister's death.

"You know," he went on, quickly now, "if you hadn't made that bogus prowler call your sister might still be alive. With two cops there Laska might never have dared to murder her in cold blood." Then he threw her off-balance with: "What kind of car does your attorney drive?"

She gave a baffled shrug. "Why?"

"I want our garage attendant to wave him right through."

"A big silver Olds."

"Excuse me. . . ." From the bull pen, John Kost anonymously called the Traffic Bureau, reporting a drunk driver in a silver Oldsmobile circling the Hall of Justice. By the time he had returned to the interrogation room, Mabelline Shipley's mascara was trickling down her cheeks and she was pouring out her heart to Jennaway. John Kost had half-expected her to crack during his brief absence: the lieutenant commander had a naturally commiserative face, and she was not the tough customer she'd imagined herself to be during the first few minutes of questioning.

The Laskas had indeed gone underground for the Party in 1935. She herself had never joined, explaining with a tearful sigh that she wasn't much of a joiner, that she liked books more than meetings. The evening Patrolman Elliot was lured to 233 Carbon Street, Laska had phoned her with an order to report a prowler to the PD, although Laska didn't tell her why this was necessary.

"Then I heard the news on the radio that night, and I was just sick. I never thought anything like that would happen. And the worst thing is"—she began sobbing—"I was too scared to go to her funeral."

Before her attorney finally pounded on the door and called the interrogation to a halt, Mabelline Shipley told them everything except the one thing John Kost was desperate to know: the current whereabouts of Boris Pugachev. He believed her when she said she didn't know who he was; in recent months the Laskas had dealt only with a hulking Ukranian émigré named Zyla—the name on Tikhov's fake driver's license.

Regardless of the usual doubts that fluttered around that grimy little room, he had trusted that Tillman and she had confessed so readily because they were the most insignificant—and ignorant—players on the board. It had been their part to stay in the wings of the mission, attending to a logistical need that so far made little sense to him. Why the insistence on Navy ordnance? Wouldn't commercial explosives have done just as well? And been less dicey to procure?

Suddenly, the Secret Service driver laid on the Packard's horn.

He glanced up: to the east an olive-drab dot was standing out against the spring cumuli over Walpert Ridge. Molotov's plane. With a grinding noise, he found first gear and began inching through the small crowd, tapping on his own horn to clear the way.

Without warning, a man stepped out of the throng, opened the passenger door, and got in. John Kost's hand was inside his jacket and closing around the grips of his revolver when he saw that it was Martov.

The vice-consul didn't sit back. He kept looking straight ahead. "I have but a moment. The consul general expects me at his side. Nod as if I'm giving you instructions."

John Kost did so.

"I have the information you asked for." Martov blew on his hands as if they were cold. It was a warm afternoon. "The hospitality ship is a special communications vessel. . . ." He didn't go on.

"That's it?"

"Yes."

"What use is that to me?" John Kost asked, exasperated. "I could've guessed it was a link to the Kremlin. It's top-heavy with antennae, for God's sake!"

"Keep your voice down. You're missing my point. I said *special*. That means secret police. It provides encoded shortwave service to Vladivostok, and then secure telephone circuits take over the rest of the distance to the Lubyanka."

"The Moscow prison?" John Kost parked on the flight line: the Army C-47 was taxiing toward them, backdropped by the milky-green waters of the South Bay.

"Yes, where Beria has his office."

"Good, thank you. That could be useful."

"Do with it what you will, but I'll have no chance to meet with you again until after the Conference begins. Tell Lena my apologies for her illness are beginning to wear thin. She may have to make an appearance in a few days. Otherwise, they'll think I'm covering up a defection. And I won't do that." He got out and walked briskly toward the rest of the Soviet welcomers.

"Sorry, old fellow," John Kost said to himself, "she's not setting foot in your consulate again."

Six beefy men alighted from the plane and formed a protective gauntlet at the base of the airstairs. A minute later they were followed by a bespectacled man with a bourgeois air of self-satisfaction. Yet, Vyacheslav Molotov took careful stock of his new surroundings, assessing the disposition of the crowd and the readiness of American security, before approaching the Soviet delegation through an electrical storm of flashbulbs.

During some rather restrained kissing and handshaking, a dapper man in his midthirties detached himself from Molotov and made directly for John Kost's Dodge. He jerked open the passenger door and demanded in English, "Is this our car?"

"Who're you?" John Kost asked just as tersely as he'd been spoken to.

"Ambassador Gromyko. Is this the car now?"

"No, the one behind."

Gromyko caught Molotov's eye with a wave, and together they converged on the Packard, appearing to relax only when they were seated behind Cade and the Secret Service agent. Shrugging at what to do next, their holsters flouncing under their double-breasted coats, two of the Soviet bodyguards jogged up to the limousine, but Gromyko crooked a finger and pointed for them to ride in John Kost's car. Curious: they preferred the American escort to their own.

He smiled to himself as all six of the thugs piled into the Dodge, rocking it as they jockeyed for space and advised one another to fuck their mothers.

He welcomed them to America in Russian, and they fell silent for the whole of the drive into town.

Mikhail Kostoff's bedroom was too small to hold the armoire, so it stood just outside the door. From it she now took a burgundy-colored babushka, her knee-high boots, and overcoat, which Vanechka had gotten with a suitcase of her other things from Martov, and put them on.

"It's time, Mikhail Mikhailovich."

Rising from the table, the old man made the sign of the cross and said, "God be with you, child."

These two days had convinced her that she could never stand a long confinement. She was ready to scream and scratch the walls. Yet, she was halfway down the unlit corridor that stank even more than the flat had of cooked cabbage—when her heart began palpitating and she couldn't get enough air. But she hurriedly limped down the stairs, clutching the kerchief knot at her throat, and looking neither right nor left at the doors closed against her for fear one would suddenly spring open. And then *he* would be looming there in his long summer overcoat, his smile couched in sadness.

Fortunately, Vanechka was coming through the entryway as she reached the ground floor. Seeing her, he stopped short, and his expression turned severe. Once again she was sure that he hadn't forgiven her, that what she'd mistaken for forgiveness was only pity. "I'm sorry for this," she whispered.

His gaze lingered on her mottled face, which made her feel wretched, and then wordlessly he undid the babushka and let her hair fall free.

"What's wrong, Vanechka?"

"Let's go."

"No, what is it?"

"Nothing."

"Please."

"I told you to dress inconspicuously," he said, helping her into his automobile.

She had to wait for him to go around and get in his side before she could say, "I did."

"For Moscow, not San Francisco." Keeping an eye on the rearview mirror, he started down the steep hill, driving much faster than usual. "And if I had my way—"

"Please don't," she interrupted. Was he punishing her for the past? She prayed to God he wasn't, for she'd begun to love him and didn't want to imagine that he was capable of anything small. "I've got to do this."

"What does it matter? He refuses to talk about you, so he'll refuse to see you."

"It matters, Ivan Mikhailovich."

"For his sake?"

"No, for mine."

He was quiet for a while, and the storefront lights burst out of the shadows like distractions that kept her from thinking of something that would make her feel close to him again.

"My father's phone is listed, so I'm going to move you," he said. "By Wednesday at the latest." Then he looked at her. "In a way I wish you still had that pistol."

Was this what it was about then? He didn't believe her when she'd said his man had thrown the Tokarev out onto the beach? Or was it that he was still reeling from what she'd told him Sunday—the purpose of her coming to San Francisco with a pistol stashed in her luggage?

Strange, but she herself couldn't recall it without seeing the words tumble off Beria's thick underlip: "You are to assist the colonel with whatever he requires. . . ." No, she'd told Vanechka in a whisper so his father wouldn't overhear, she didn't know the colonel's name, only that he was an experienced assassin. "You are to rent a house somewhere in the city for a reception to be held on the first night of the Conference. The main room must be no larger than one hundred and fifty square meters. The affair is to begin at nine. You are to leave at a quarter after—no excuse will be necessary—and walk back toward the consulate. . . ." Vanechka had asked if Anthony Eden would be attending, then. No, she had tearfully confessed, that had been a lie. Molotov had not charged Martov and her with helping to murder the British foreign minister; she had never even met the commissar. The reception would be exclusively for the Soviet delegation, with Molotov and Gromyko the guests of honor. "On your walk back toward the consulate, the colonel will meet you. He expects to receive a new passport and an airplane ticket to Rio de Janeiro. He is to get a bullet instead. Afterward, drop the pistol beside the body and walk away. Believe me, the police will be too busy at this point to respond with any promptness. Take a taxi to the airport and use the ticket yourself. You will be met in Rio. Oh," Beria had added with the stark smile she sometimes feared Anna had inherited, "right before you pull the trigger, I'd appreciate it if you told him, 'Your little bluff is up, old fellow.'"

That Vanechka had been mulling over these things while he drove south through the city was confirmed when he suddenly asked, "The airline ticket—where is it now?"

"The suitcase Martov sent me. Sewn in the lining."

"I want it."

"Because you don't trust me? Because I was ordered here to kill a man?"

"Could you have?"

"Yes, anything for my child!" Then she had to struggle not to weep. "But never for myself. Not even to save you . . . and I love you."

Her admission seemed to have no effect on him. Was he stepping back from the passionate words he'd whispered again and again that night in the Yosemite? She studied his immobile face for a few seconds, then said, "What are you keeping from me? Tell me. You're holding something back."

But they had arrived at the hospital, and he turned off the motor.

He had phoned ahead for an orderly to be waiting at the rear entrance for them, and now as the door swung open, he motioned for Elena not to leave the car too soon. Getting out, his hand thrust through the parting of his jacket, he scanned the lot before saying, "Quickly now—inside." He nodded at the Mexican orderly, who seemed morbidly fascinated with her battered face.

"Elevator's straight ahead, sir."

"Thank you," he said, although he'd already made up his mind not to use it. Despite her limp, she took the stairs as quickly as he did. When they paused for breath on the fourth landing, he looked at her, wanting to confide in her that Ragnetti had wounded the colonel during their confrontation in the Mission District apartment. She deserved the truth. She'd just said that she loved him, and the survival of their love depended on the truth. But no, he realized as he saw the terror in her eyes, she would stop functioning if she believed Anna Lavrentievna to be dead. And a wounded Pugachev, figuring that the game was up, would undoubtedly have informed Beria that he had been betrayed.

On his orders, a patrolman—a veteran with two shootings under his belt—had been posted outside Ragnetti's door. The cop tossed down a dog-eared copy of *Collier's* and gave him a nod. "Hi, Inspector." He too stared at Elena, who turned her face.

"Anyone else to see him?" John Kost asked.

"His mother all afternoon. But nobody other than her."

"Keep a sharp watch while we're inside."

"You bet."

John Kost ushered her through the door. Yesterday, he'd brought from St. Basil's an ancient icon of the Virgin that was loaned out to the families of the sick or dying, and he was now gratified to see that the taper was still lit before it on the nightstand. This was the only illumination in the room, although it seemed bright on Ragnetti's head bandages and leg cast. His eyelids parted slightly, but John Kost wasn't sure if he could focus on anything. "Vincent?"

Ragnetti groaned, then shut his eyes again. Had he caught sight of Elena?

"Vincent, I've brought someone."

"Go away," he said through his clenched jaws.

Kneeling, she seized his right hand in both hers. She began weeping as she whispered, "Vanechka, tell him I forgive him. . . ."

"She says she forgives you. Forgives you as she herself hopes to be forgiven by God for her own transgressions which—"

"Come on for Chrissake!" Ragnetti hissed. "Get the fuck outta here—*out!*"

"She says she understands why you did what you did to her. She understands about Nathan—"

"No, she don't!"

His worst expectations for this meeting were being realized: Ragnetti was up on his elbows, his head rocked by spasms and his eyes wild. "Easy, Vincent—we'll go."

"Nobody knows!" His fingers raked at his bared teeth as if trying to rip away the wires. "Nobody!"

"Lie still," John Kost said, pulling Elena away from the bed. The strange rackings coming up Ragnetti's throat were sobs. "We're leaving. I'll come see you again in the morning. Rest."

Ragnetti flopped back down, crying out in pain as his head hit the pillow. His eyes were overflowing. "I killed Natty, John—oh, fuck me."

"You killed no one. Bad luck took Nathan. The same bad luck that just as easily could've taken you or me instead."

"I sent him alone that night. I was sore because you left him in charge. So I let him take on Pugachev alone. I murdered him."

"Oh, dear God, is that what you believe?"

The nurse then came through the door, but John Kost

vehemently waved her out again. He withdrew to the window and lowered his head. Silence gradually filled the room. He watched his candle shadow tremble against the blackout shade; it grew and shrank on the sputterings. When he finally turned, Ragnetti had rested his hand on her hair, and she was clasping it to her so he couldn't let go. The triumph in her face frightened him with its intensity, its doggedness, and reminded him that she was still a stranger to him.

27

Department of fish and game," the receptionist in Sacramento finally answered.

"Commercial registration, please," John Kost said, gulping hot tea from a paper cup—he was now chronically drowsy in an aching, prickly way. It was almost three, and the clerk had promised a call back before noon with information from the *Lorelei*'s registration forms, which evidently had vanished as mysteriously as the purse seiner itself.

"Commercial," the selfsame harried fellow said.

"John Kost again."

The clerk let out a breath. "Yeah, Inspector, I'm still hunting for the paperwork. I don't know what the hell happened to it. Have you tried our San Francisco office?"

"They referred me to you," he said frostily.

"Oh, yeah, well, I guess—"

"Enough guesses. This involves national security. Either you find the *Lorelei*'s documentation by nine tomorrow morning or I have the FBI seal off your office until it's found. Good afternoon." He replaced the handset in the cradle, then got up from his desk, which was piled six inches deep around the blotter with interdepartmental memoranda, wanted flyers, Teletypes, and all the other accumulation of two and a half weeks of neglect. He lingered at his door, leaning his shoulder against the jamb, staring out into the bull pen. The tops of the desks, the window glass, even the air itself looked dusty; the room suggested some Egyptian tomb just recently cracked to the light after centuries of black silence. A trap for old echoes.

He was relieved when his telephone rang: he hadn't really wanted to wander out among the vacant desks again. "Inspector Kost, Homicide."

Nothing but static came over the line for a few seconds, then: "Vanka?"

He sat up. "Who's this?" he asked in Russian—something within him, his caution maybe, already knew what the call was about.

The voice was deep, sad, melodic. "The last morning we had together near Irkutsk I dressed you in your white *roobashka*. You looked such a perfect little Cossack in that tunic."

John Kost's shock came as a burst of light behind his eyes. For a few seconds he was blind to everything except a tattered Baltic Fleet uniform out of the past. "Who is this . . . ?" he needlessly repeated, for he knew perfectly well who was on the other end of the line. He told himself to forget the sailor who'd played Mussorgsky on the gramophone, who'd taken him out into the taiga to make star-whispers, and to remember only that he was dealing with Nathan's murderer. "Never mind. I doubt I'll ever learn your real name."

"That's true, Vanka."

"For convenience sake, may I call you Pugachev?"

"If you please."

He was determined to take control of the conversation from the outset. Other murderers had phoned him to gloat, to tantalize without revealing genuine leads, and he wasn't going to allow that. Not when it was Aranov's killer. "Did you know of me, my job here, before you left Moscow?"

"No, it was a happy surprise. And it gladdened me to find out

314

you're something of a Chekist as well. I'd like to believe I played a part in your choice of vocation."

"I doubt it. Our jobs are nothing alike." He was trying to come up with a way to summon someone down the hall to initiate a phone tap; but then, eerily, Pugachev revealed that he was thinking along the same vein.

"I'll phone back later. An even briefer call to arrange a meeting. Is that possible—what if we remember the love we once had for each other? If we can trust each other for an hour or so? What d'you say? Will you stay at your desk until I call again, old fellow?"

Given such a promise, the man would have his location pinpointed until the next call, which might never come. John Kost asked himself if he was about to be attacked here in the Hall of Justice. Yet, he said, "All right, I'll wait. But I want you to be aware of something, Colonel. . . ."

"Yes?"

"Beria sent Elena Martova here to eliminate you after you do what you must do at that house in Pacific Heights. He told her to tell you your bluff is up, before she shot you. Now I have no idea what that means, but I'd be willing to bet you're a dead man—unless you surrender to me at once."

Pugachev chuckled. "Clever, my dear Vanka."

"If it's only cleverness, tell me where Tikhov is."

The silence went on so long he thought Pugachev had disconnected, but then the colonel said, "Stay at your desk." And with that he hung up.

The Chekist shambled from the telephone booth outside the main gate to Thripp Shipyards and started across the Islais Creek Bridge. His face was drawn. He halted midspan as if to survey the ruffled waters of the channel. But his eyes were blank, his vision sucked into the vortex of the past: Kronstadt, Irkutsk, Mexico City—the bloody ball of wax that passed itself off as the world. *Always remember that in the whole of the universe there is precious little morality except for the small number of iron-willed, high-principled natures that have crawled up from filthy oppres-*

315

sion and untold poverty in accordance with Darwin's theory! Whose words were these? And why were they ringing inside his feverish brain? Shaking his head, he patted the blue pea jacket he'd bought to replace his overcoat, then went on his way. The trenching tool was still there, secure within the elastic loop he'd safety-pinned onto the lining, and the left pocket was weighted down with his revolver.

As long as he had these, he wasn't finished.

Or was he?

Think! he cried inwardly.

Under whose sway was the Martova woman at present? Had the big plainclothesman found him Saturday night due to her? He was not convinced of this, for she had known nothing about the boathouse and yet a detective had shown up there too; otherwise he would have started a message on its way to the Lubyanka saying that the hostage at Lake Lagoda was no longer needed. In Madame Martova's defense, it had to be noted that the big policeman had burst into the Mission District flat alone, which suggested that he'd acted on some unexpected lead, a complaint from the overly suspicious landlady perhaps. But why then Vanka Kostoff's claim that Elena Martova had been sent by Beria to eliminate him? No, he told himself that had been a ruse, she was a smart woman who knew what "strict punishment" meant. She'd never talk to the Americans. Maybe she was working on Kostoff's investigation from the inside in order to derail it, in obedience to her own special orders.

But what of Kostoff's saying that his bluff was up?

That had been a thunderclap on a cloudless afternoon, and now he had to resign himself to what he'd always known would come: the pay voucher proving Beria's work for the Okhrana was in the Little Boss's hands. His cousin was most likely dead, and he himself could neither go back to the Soviet Union nor seek political asylum from the American authorities, who'd only gas him for murder. "That's it then," he said with a quiet laugh. As Vanka Kostoff had so accurately reflected, he was now a dead man.

Wherever he went, Beria would send assassin after assassin

after him until the job was done. It had happened to the defector Krivitsky, the Paris resident before the war. Mobile Group had stalked him from France to New York and finally gotten him in a hotel room within blocks of FBI headquarters in Washington. So much for federal protection. The Latin American intelligence services were even less reliable, as he knew from his experience with the Mexicans.

"But do I want to run?" he said, plodding along the north side of the channel, watching the sea gulls skim across a gray backdrop of corrugated-tin machine shops. Every man wants his life to go on for as long as possible; but if this were absolutely true, why was he feeling such relief, such liberation at the prospect of his death?

What then must we do? he asked himself for the second time in his life. Originally the question had been Tolstoy's, but in the third winter of that pointless European war, with the monarchy showing ever-greater ineptitude, it seemed as if the good Count Leo had bequeathed it to the sailors of the Baltic Fleet. *What then must we do?* was whispered time and again in the passageways of the *Aurora*—asked in behalf of the masses, the oppressed, the hopeless. He'd begun his political awareness in sympathy with his petty officer, Zakusov, the same devoted anarchist he gunned down six years later among the ruins of Kronstadt. In any event, poor Zakusov would have been shot sooner or later, for in time the Bolsheviks liquidated all the adherents of Mikhail Bakunin, who'd proclaimed that men are basically good and deserve complete freedom but are corrupted by the institutions thrust upon them. A worthy proposition, or so it'd seemed to a naval conscript fresh off the man-empty taiga. *Death to statism! Even ultrarevolutionary statism!*

And now, thirty years later, he had come full circle: *What then must we do!* Bakunin had called for the violent overthrow of government—not just the pathetic Romanov sort, but all governments everywhere. He'd said there are times when revolution is impossible, and times when it's inevitable. Had the Chekist stumbled into one such time of the latter kind? Bakunin had also predicted that a dishonest revolution would bring new forms of slavery and poverty to Russia. Oh, yes! His hand flew to his brow: his infected gunshot wound was burning him up again.

Letting himself in his last refuge, a two-room bungalow overlooking the channel, he rushed for the kitchen and lit the stove under a large pot of distilled water. Then he broke the seal on a bottle of vodka and poured himself a bumper. "To spontaneity," he toasted.

No longer would he be satisfied to blast Molotov and his cronies into pieces. If Beria didn't have the guts to kill his rival on Russian soil, the Devil could take them both. Besides, Kostoff knew now what had been planned for the reception. Yes, fate had made this plan fall apart, but it had also landed him in San Francisco at a pivotal moment in history. Had poor Zakusov, standing on the brink of death at Kronstadt, glimpsed the coming of this hour when he cried: *Your beauty is dear to me . . . !*

The water had begun to boil.

He reached down into a innocent-looking shopping bag for a handful of dynamite sticks and dropped them into the pot.

The steam felt good against his wound, and he began passing his right forearm back and forth through it. But then, remembering the ferocious headache these fumes had given him earlier, he soaked his handkerchief at the faucet before tying it around his face.

The dynamite had come from a shipyard magazine; marine divers used it to loosen propellers frozen by corrosion onto their shafts. Fifteen sticks. He would need twice that. And so he'd telephone for more, no matter how loudly his source complained that the police were keen on missing explosives right now. "No wonder!" he chuckled to himself.

A pale-yellow liquid had begun to float atop the water. Nitroglycerin.

Suddenly a lick of flame wormed up the side of the pot and nearly flitted inside before he could turn off the gas.

For a moment he stared down into the simmering water, then threw back his head and laughed uproariously. Even this little bit of nitro would have left him dripping off the ceiling.

Spontaneity had indeed returned to his life.

He lit the stove again, but adjusted the burner lower.

After five minutes more of boiling, he set the pot in the sink and waited for the water to stop bubbling before skimming the yellowish scum off with a cheesecloth and gently wringing it into a measuring cup. He opened the icebox door, and a theatrical-looking fog gushed out and slunk along the floor like a wraith. From a crevice in the blocks of dry ice crammed inside he removed a tubular glass vial. At the sink he poured what he'd just cooked off the dynamite into it. He figured he needed about two liters. He had one so far, with a second vial waiting to be filled.

But first, sadly, he had to attend to Vanka Kostoff. Two of the inspector's men had nearly gotten him over this past fortnight, and he could no longer trust his luck to escape another try by the police to nab him.

He locked the flat behind him.

Hailing a taxi on Third Street, he had the driver take him downtown, where he stepped into a telephone booth miles from the one he'd used earlier. It was an effort to dissemble his high spirits, the excitement of believing—even if it might well be delusion—that something momentous was going on inside his soul.

John Kost let his telephone ring three times, then grabbed the receiver. "Kost, Homicide."

"I'll be brief, Vanka—don't interrupt. Leave the Hall of Justice now. Alone. If you're not seen walking north along Columbus Avenue within four minutes, the meeting's off. Stop in Washington Square and use your eyes. Will you be armed?"

"Yes."

Pugachev chuckled. "I too, Vanka. Until Washington Square then." He hung up.

Crossing his office to the door, he checked the bull pen windows. They were dark. Pugachev had waited for nightfall.

Let off by the elevator, he hesitated in the lobby, rubbing his palms together, and the on-duty desk sergeant asked, "You need something, Inspector?"

"No." He looked at his wristwatch: one minute was spent.

If he vacillated and missed the four-minute deadline to show himself on Columbus Avenue, he might never have another chance to find out about Elena's daughter. He told himself this is why he was taking such an outrageous risk: to ask Pugachev how Anna Lavrentievna might possibly be spared. If she was still alive.

He pushed through a door and started up Kearny Street at twice his normal stride, checking the alleys and high windows as he went. Pedestrians were few, for which he was thankful.

He reached Columbus with thirty seconds to spare, staying close to the curb so he could clearly be seen. He intended to keep to the west side of the boulevard until Washington Square so any car trying to approach him from behind would have to cross the opposing lanes of traffic. That would incite horns, giving him a few seconds more to react to the attack.

A tall man in dark clothing suddenly rounded the corner from Stockton Street. John Kost's gun hand slid inside his coat, but then fell to his side again. "Good evening, Father." The Roman Catholic priest touched a finger to the brim of his homburg and went on his way. He knew him from nearby St. Mary's Cathedral.

He was starting to face forward again when he glimpsed a Hudson sedan two blocks behind. It was angling into a parking space, its headlamps off. He frowned, but kept walking.

From across the street, Washington Square looked deserted. Still, he approached it with a darkened storefront to his back, scanning the trunks of the shrubbery for shoes. He saw no one until a bench under a lamppost rounded into view. Sleeping on it was a drunk Marine, his knees cocked and his arms thrown over his eyes.

He shifted his revolver from his shoulder holster to his jacket pocket, then kept his forefinger on the trigger as he flashed his badge and rousted the youth. "Move along, son, before the Shore Patrol scoops you up." The boy rose groggily but without protest, leaving behind a makeshift pillow of Sunday's comics-wrapped *Examiner*, which John Kost assumed to have been the Marine's until he saw the Cyrillic letters VANKA written in black crayon on it.

Unfolding the newspaper, he read what had been neatly printed over a portrait of President Truman: TURN TOWARD THE BAY ON JONES.

Six and a half minutes later, he paused at the intersection with Jones Street, which sloped down to the restaurant lights on Fisherman's Wharf. "Of course," he muttered. This is where it would happen. Pugachev wanted to use the tourist crowd, mostly servicemen and their dates these days, to put him at a disadvantage.

The bay glistened more blackly as he descended toward it.

He thought of putting his revolver back in his shoulder holster, but then made up his mind against it. Pugachev probably knew how he ordinarily carried his weapon and might be counting on it.

At the waterfront the air turned noticeably damper. It smelled of fish and salt. Passing through the steam off a crab caldron, ignoring the vendor's pitch, he eyeballed the crush of out-of-towners: teenage GIs in olive-drab, spending their last night on the town before being restricted to Fort Mason for forty-eight hours and then shipped overseas. They were noisy, particularly those lucky enough to have found girls, and he kept starting at their shrill, quarrelsome laughter. Glenn Miller's "Moonlight Cocktail" was coming tinnily from a loudspeaker on the roof of the Exposition Fish Grotto.

Slowly, he moved down the breezeway between Joe DiMaggio's restaurant and a souvenir shop. Popcorn pinged and piled up behind the glass window of a snack booth. The swarming preponderance of olive-drab uniforms was a blessing: he could concentrate on the few figures in civilian dress.

Emerging onto the centermost of three wharves, he stopped and gazed around the lagoon. It was crammed with trawl boats, their masts and rigging like a burned forest against the livid western sky—then, as if of its own accord, his gaze shot past the boats and back to the far end of the wharf on which he stood.

A man in a pea jacket was waiting there, his hands in his pockets. Then he slid out a hand and gave an inhibited wave.

John Kost didn't respond.

Pugachev had chosen a location where no one could steal up on his flanks. But why had he purposely trapped himself on the end of a narrow dock, unless he was sure he could deal with anyone trying to corner him?

He glanced down the twin lines of boats bobbing alongside the wharf, thinking that Pugachev had planted a backup aboard one of the craft. But a murmur of Italian, soft with unconcern, convinced him that nothing had happened to alarm the fishermen prior to his arrival. They were calmly coiling their lines and stacking their empty fish boxes for the night.

He started for Pugachev.

With each step, he asked himself if the angular face and piercing eyes were familiar. But no—he couldn't recall what the sailor had looked like.

It was the timbre of the voice, richer and mellower than it had seemed over the phone, that convinced him this was the same man. "Hello, Vanka."

John Kost halted ten feet away from him. For a moment he could think of nothing to say. He was clenching his pocketed revolver so tightly his hand was trembling; the strange tenderness in Pugachev's face disgusted him. "Have you made up your mind what you're going to do, Colonel?"

Pugachev shrugged—a consummate Russian shrug, wry, fatalistic. "I'm going to have a little talk with you. Is that good enough for now?"

"It depends on what we discuss."

"Then you choose, my dear Vanka—business or pleasure."

"Business. It's all we have left in common."

"Very well. Permit me to begin then. . . ."

John Kost nodded.

"What happened to Tikhov?"

"I killed him."

Pugachev's eyes widened, but he kept smiling. "Why?"

"Because you sent him to Yosemite to kill me."

"And how did I know you'd be going there?"

"Elena told you." Carefully so as not to alert Pugachev, who was no doubt grasping his own handgun, he shifted over to a

322

chest-high piling and rested his back against it. "But when Tikhov came at us, she thought she was the mark. She still does."

"What'd you think, my dear Vanka?"

"Oh, I quickly realized it was me you wanted. My men and I were getting too close to the truth about Laska. . . ." He paused. "About Officer Elliot's notebook and the *Lorelei*."

Pugachev nodded as if to admit that all of this was fundamentally correct. "You've fallen in love with her, haven't you?"

"Yes."

"You're not the first, you know."

"I don't need to be."

"Well said. Where's she now?"

"Under my protection."

"As were the two plainclothesmen you ordered to apprehend me?"

John Kost ignored the implied threat. "Now you tell me about Laska."

Again the Russian shrug. "What's there to tell? The world is filled with Laskas, fellows aching to bare their breasts on an altar. Any altar will do."

"How'd Tikhov get him to shoot his wife and then himself? Tikhov was there. I've got proof."

"Yes, he was." Pugachev stared off across the lagoon, which was being spangled by the bright lights of the restaurants, although John Kost knew that he was still locked in the man's peripheral vision. "I myself was present for none of this. What I know came from Tikhov—a rather inept fellow, I'm afraid." He looked back at John Kost. "You must never give Iosif Stalin a way to both use and destroy you at the same time. He finds such an offer irresistible. And that's precisely what Laska did—without his wife's knowledge, of course."

"But whose idea was it to murder Elliot for his notebook?" John Kost asked.

"Laska's, I'm telling you. But when he brought up the notion, he was sure Tikhov would dismiss it on the spot. Really, who would expect a fellow to shoot his wife, a policeman, and then himself just to make certain no one would find out about the

Lorelei? Still, such an offer was guaranteed to make a dramatic impression on the Big Boss? Yes?"

"And it was accepted?"

Pugachev laughed under his breath. "Within twenty-four hours the proposal was sealed with the Big Boss's blessing. Tikhov said the look on Laska's face was something to behold."

"But did he actually expect Laska to go through with it?"

"Of course not," Pugachev said. "Approval came forty-eight hours before that Sunday evening. That's too long for a fellow to sit alone with his second thoughts. . . ." In his sonorous voice he went on to explain how Tikhov had been instructed to tell Laska on Saturday morning that the Big Boss had changed his mind. The resident would shoot the policeman in the Laskas' flat, and then the couple would be whisked out of the country. But a few minutes before Wallace Elliot was lured to 233 Carbon Street, Tikhov broke some rather distressing news to Laska: it had been decided at the highest levels that the original plan was best—the longshoreman would have to pull the trigger on Elliot, his wife, and himself in order to give the encounter the look of a tragic domestic dispute. No other way was possible. "But then," Pugachev went on, "when the grand moment came, poor Laska couldn't shoot himself. Not even for the Big Boss. Tikhov had to grab his hand and pull the trigger for him. An unfortunate turn, for it left Laska only wounded, and I believe this is where your Homicide directorate came in. 'The best-laid plans'—yes?"

John Kost fought the urge to ask how Aranov had died. He couldn't bear to hear that. "What're your own plans now?"

Despite the bayside chill, Pugachev was sweating. He let it trickle down his neck unwiped. "In light of what Elena Martova has told you about her true assignment?"

"Yes. My sergeant got you pretty bad, didn't he?"

"An insignificant wound. I have a fever, but it's breaking." Pugachev sighed. "Well, at the very least I know who betrayed me now."

"You mean to say there are others here who know what you're up to?"

Watching him closely, Pugachev grinned, then changed the

subject. "Poor Laska. He went out thinking the Big Boss had approved his selfless plan—when Stalin didn't know a thing about it."

"Beria sent the go-ahead?"

Pugachev nodded. He was looking across the lagoon again, seemingly at the strollers on the far wharf.

"You haven't answered me," John Kost said.

"About what?"

"Are there others here helping you?"

"That no longer matters."

"Then what does? What comes now?"

An exalted look came into Pugachev's face. "What follows now will be perceived as sickness on a grand scale. But it is actually health, my dear Vanka. The health of the world."

"I don't understand."

The look dimmed. "What more is there to say? I have no place to go."

"You can give yourself up to me."

"Isn't it the practice in this state to stuff a fellow inside a contraption something like a diving bell—and then fill it with poisonous gas?"

John Kost didn't answer.

"Forgive me if I insist on choosing the manner of my own death."

"What can you hope to accomplish here?"

"You think very clearly, Vanka. You also have extraordinary self-control. Not once have you asked me about your man who was waiting for me in the boathouse. And I admire that. . . ." Pugachev sidestepped twice, his hands still thrust inside his pea jacket pockets. John Kost quit leaning against the piling. "But you're still making the same mistake you made so long ago at Irkutsk. . . ."

"And what was that?" John Kost thumb-cocked his Smith & Wesson's hammer for faster single-action fire.

"You asked if we might hunt sable together. But you see, old fellow, one doesn't hunt sable. He traps them."

Then Pugachev's left hand came out clutching a revolver.

325

While using his free arm to swing around to the backside of the piling, John Kost fired from his pocket without drawing—but knew at once that his shot had missed. The bore of Pugachev's revolver leveled on him, and he let go of the timber and fell into the water between the hulls of two boats.

Three bullets sizzled down around him as he stroked under the wharf, still fisting his Smith & Wesson.

Bursting to the surface, painfully bashing the crown of his head on the undersides of the planks, he heard the distinctive bark of a Thompson submachine gun. The firing seemed to be coming from across the lagoon. Was it meant for Pugachev or him?

Footfalls started thundering down the dock—Pugachev was fleeing.

He threw the crook of his left arm over the lip of the planking but was too breathless and weighted down by his clothes for the moment to pull himself up. Lifting his head, he was able to catch sight of Pugachev again just as he lunged over the gunwale of a boat. An instant later the side of the wheelhouse exploded into splinters from a volley of Thompson bullets. The sound of shattering glass followed: Pugachev had crawled inside the enclosure and smashed out a window to return fire across the lagoon. His muzzle flashes flamed bluely out of the wheelhouse.

Twisting around, John Kost tried to see whom he was shooting at—but had only a glimpse of a straw boater before the tommy gun started rattling from a new position.

Screams, both male and female, were now filling the brief lapses between the shots.

Finally muscling himself up onto the wharf, rolling away from its edge with both hands clasping his revolver, John Kost saw that he had a perfect sight picture on Pugachev's retreating silhouette.

"Stop!" he shouted in Russian. He began nudging back the trigger—but then let up the pressure.

Pugachev was backdropped by a shifting mass of GIs and fishermen in yellow slickers. His right arm was hanging limply at his side as he ran into the crowd and vanished.

John Kost struggled to his knees but could rise no higher. His chilled leg muscles wouldn't let him give chase. Gasping, he fell back down against the planking.

A minute later, Robert Cade came trudging along the wharf toward him, his Thompson tucked under his arm and his boater pushed up off his beaded forehead. He looked down at John Kost, but said nothing. Sirens were mingling their wails as the northside cruisers converged on the waterfront.

"Get him?"

"Nope," Cade said, "but the son of a bitch damn near got me!" He showed the submachine gun's wooden stock: one of Pugachev's bullets had chewed a long gash in it.

"How . . . how long you been tailing me?"

"Since this morning."

"Why?"

"Get up"—Cade offered him no help—"and let's get outta here. You're the miserable prick who's got all the explaining to do."

"I resent being shadowed," John Kost said, although he had no problem keeping his outrage under control. He had realized the FBI was keeping tabs on him ever since this morning when he'd glimpsed Cade's Hudson falling in behind his Dodge a few blocks away from his apartment. Knowing this had made it easier for him to do what Pugachev had asked; but he had no intention of admitting it to the agent now. "You could've gotten me killed."

"Killed!" Cade's fat neck was glowing pink. "In case you don't know it, I pulled your chestnuts out of the fire! And what about you going to a chitchat with Pugachev without telling me— remember the agreement we had, *Ivan!*"

"Bob, Bob," Coffey said wearily, handing the agent and John Kost each a generous slug of Irish. "I think all Johnny's saying is that he was counting on a tad more trust from you boys."

"Trust, for crapsake!" Cade stopped ranting long enough to down a swallow. "Kost is quiet as a mouse for days—and then somehow links up with the joker we're turning the city upside down for! A guy who was sitting on enough high explosives to

327

make San Francisco look like 1906 again! And I'm supposed to trust him!"

"I've already told you how Pugachev called the shots for this meeting," John Kost said, unruffled. His explanation was paper-thin, so he had to unroll it in measured responses—and without flashes of temper. "It was sudden. Even had Pugachev not said for me to come alone, there would've been no time to contact you." He had also made up his mind to say nothing about his relationship in Irkutsk with the man. Cade was already rabidly suspicious simply because Pugachev and he were both Russian. But he also knew that he could no longer put off the matter of Tikhov. "And there are other complications to this thing as well. Complications you both should be made aware of—"

He was interrupted by a knock on the door, and at Coffey's command Jennaway stepped inside, his appearance convincingly civilian but for his spit-shined shoes.

"Hey, there, Dennis. . . ." Cade marshaled enough courtesy to shake the ONI officer's hand.

Coffey introduced himself and thanked him for coming. "Inspector Kost here asked for you to be in on this."

"I appreciate it." But Jennaway gave John Kost an odd look: the inspector was in starched denims borrowed from the jail next door.

"John went swimming tonight," the captain explained.

"And bitched up collaring Pugachev," Cade added.

"Oh?" Jennaway accepted a glass from the chief with a nod. "How'd you find him, John?"

"It's a long story," he said evenly, "and it begins with me killing his right-hand man in Yosemite on the thirteenth."

The office had gone silent.

Coffey was first to stir. He had a faint smile as if he thought they were being joshed. "What're you talking about?"

Careful to meet each man's bewildered gaze, John Kost told them how, in prosecuting the Elliot investigation with a full head of steam, Aranov, Ragnetti, and he had unknowingly forced Pugachev, the colonel of a special assassination unit, to send the resident in San Francisco to Yosemite to kill him. "His name was

Tikhov. He went by the alias of Zyla. And without warning he opened fire on Madame Martova and me." At last he looked at the floor. "We fought out in the river. I broke his neck. Hid his body in a snowbank."

"Broke his neck?" Coffey grimaced.

"I had to. I'd only wounded him with my handgun." He neglected to mention that it'd been with his hideaway derringer and not his service revolver, which had been locked up in the hotel safe with Ruml's and Elena's pistols. Telling them why she had come with a Tokarev to San Francisco would've opened a whole new can of worms. One mess at a time.

"Christ, Johnny, was it a justifiable homicide?"

"I swear to God, Pat."

"Then why'd you say nothing about it?"

He saw that Cade was grinning at him. He had to look away to keep his temper. "Madame Martova begged me not to report it."

"Whoa, Ivan," the agent said with bald glee, "you mean you kicked sand over a homicide because a foreign national—and most assuredly an intelligence operator—batted her eyelashes and said *mum's the word?*"

Unexpectedly, Jennaway came to his rescue. "I doubt it was that simple, Bob."

"No, it wasn't simple," John Kost said. "Not in the least. She convinced me that if the wrong people in the Soviet Union learned of Tikhov's death, her daughter—she's being held hostage near Leningrad—would be murdered. Also, she told me that if I held off notification about the homicide, she'd help me break the Elliot and Fenby cases."

"Oh, for crapsake!" Cade said. "And you believed her!"

"Yes, and I still do—with good reason."

"Name one."

John Kost hesitated, waiting for Cade to grin again before he said, "Last Saturday night she told Ragnetti where Pugachev was hiding. She did this at risk to her own child. Not to mention herself." He savored the agent's inability to come up with a retort, then turned to Coffey. "Vincent felt much about arresting

329

Pugachev as I did tonight—with three brother officers already dead, he wanted to take all the risk himself. Not terribly smart, I suppose. But I think you can understand how we felt. Especially after Nathan."

Coffey nodded.

"And I'll understand if you have to relieve me of my duties pending a disciplinary investigation."

A momentary hush followed. Coffey slowly ran the tip of his tongue around the inside of his lips. Then he sat straighter. "I'm going to need Lucifer's help to come up with some cock-and-bull to explain away tonight's shoot-out on the wharf. Jesus, are we lucky none of you cowboys can hit anything!" He looked to Cade. "Can you run interference with Mariposa County over a certain DB we're gonna help them find in a snowbank?"

Cade threw up his hands, but then sighed and said, "What's to lose at this point? Kost has the bunch of us up to our necks in this crap. I'll have two of my men in Yosemite tomorrow."

"And you'd agree this is a matter of national security?"

"That's been my goddamn point from the start!"

"How about you, Mr. Jennaway? What d'you say?"

"Definitely national security."

"Good then," Coffey said, "because that's the picture I'm going to paint for my boss—to keep the dogs off John here until this is sorted out." He finished the last of his drink. "Now, enough potation and I'll order up some coffee. We got a long night ahead of us."

John Kost tried to thank him with a smile, but couldn't catch his eye.

28

Lᴏᴅɪᴀ ᴀɴsᴡᴇʀᴇᴅ the door in her magenta silk robe. "Why, Ivan Mikhailovich," she said distantly. But then tiny lines formed at the corners of her mouth, the inkling of a smile. She was pleased to see him, then, at this telling hour. When he'd come here very late or very early, it had always been for one reason. "Come in."

The dawn sun was flooding the living room. For the first time he saw that in the midst of all this genteel immaculateness a few vague stains dappled the carpet. "I wanted to see you before things got too hectic today." He draped his jacket over the back of the sofa, which was his habit, and she in keeping with her own part in this little rite of conciliation carried it to the entryway closet. "The Conference begins at four-thirty, but I'll be chasing my own tail long before that."

"Poor darling." The metal hangers chimed as she made room for his jacket. "Have they announced the order of speakers yet?"

He was staring at the back of her head. "I really don't know. I hear Truman's supposed to go first—by wire from Washington."

She turned, smiling. "I'll make some tea. Then why don't you bring it into the bathroom with you?" Another ritual, one suggesting a sense of domesticity they'd never really been able to cultivate between them. A few minutes later he was perched on a wicker stool, engulfed by the dense steam of her shower bath. Through the tub enclosure he saw her as a misshapen blur rippling in flesh tones back and forth across the pebbled glass. "Are you hungry?" she asked.

"No." He slipped a white envelope from his shirt pocket and lodged it in the bristles of her brush on the vanity.

Then, quietly, he got up and left the bathroom.

In the dining room, he ran his hands over the back of one of the Second Empire chairs and foresaw—with regret stronger than he'd anticipated on his drive from the Hall of Justice—how all of this would soon be crated and stored by the U.S. marshal. He would miss this room. He'd miss her.

"Ivan Mikhailovich?" She was standing framed by the open double doors, toweling her hair with one hand and holding the envelope with the other. "What's this?"

"An airline ticket." He slipped past her and on into the living room. At the cocktail cart he poured them each a vodka.

She followed him out, her expression quizzical but not yet alarmed, and took the drink from him. "I know it's a ticket. To Rio. But why?"

He sat on the sofa. "I trust you keep a valid passport. I have yet to know an émigré who doesn't."

"What does my passport have to do with this ticket?"

"If all goes well between us this morning, they and my goodwill will get you out of the country."

She sank into the love seat opposite him, her drink untouched. "You're frightening me."

"Then we're even—because five hours ago you gave me one of the worst shocks of my life."

Naturally, she appeared less mystified than she should have: her genuine bafflement was usually colored by indignation. "What are you talking about?"

"I got back to my desk after a late meeting at one last night," he began calmly, although he could do nothing about the overtone of resentment to his voice. "A packet from the Department of Fish and Game was in my in-basket. . . ." She turned her face away from him, fidgeting the glass in her hands. But he went on with the same enforced calm, explaining how a note attached to the packet, which contained the owner registration forms for the purse seiner *Lorelei*, invited him to phone at any hour he saw fit the clerk from the San Francisco office who'd taken the application. "So I awakened the fellow, apologized for the hour, and asked him what he recalled of Irene Straus, the owner of the *Lorelei* as of the twenty-first of this January. He said it was funny, but the woman—a handsome woman, incidentally—had a faint accent much like my own. This led me to take a hard look at the handwriting on the application before me—and then to compare it to that of a dinner-party invitation I still happened to have on my desk."

At last she met his gaze head-on. "I thought at very least we were friends."

"Oh, this is an extraordinary show of friendship. You'll come to appreciate that when you're sunning yourself in Rio instead of stagnating in a federal prison. I doubt stagnation would become a vigorous woman like you." He didn't want to be ironical toward her, but it was preferable to the raw anger he was feeling. "I wish the *Lorelei* had been all, Lydia Dmitrievna."

"What do you mean?"

"About the same time in January a fellow with the Soviet consulate named Tikhov—heard of him?"

She kept silent.

"Well, anyway, he was picked up by Traffic for using all four lanes on Market. Hearing about this, I assumed he'd been driving a consular car. But then again that didn't make sense—the blue-suiter would've seen that diplomatic immunity was at issue right away and not hauled Tikhov in. Unfortunately, the arrest report was ripped up. But about two hours ago it hit me that the Traffic cop would've radioed in the stop, giving dispatch the license plate for the log." His eyes bored into hers. "The car is registered to a local who lives out in Sunset District. He also happens to be the head timekeeper at the Islais Creek facility of Thripp Shipyards."

He hadn't expected her to cry, nor did she now. Instead, her head slowly sank as if she understood how the rules to her world had just changed. She coiled a strand of wet hair around her forefinger. She was no stranger to such cataclysmic shifts; the first had devastated her girlhood in Petrograd. He wanted to feel sorry for her. But couldn't. "What do you require of me?" she asked, her voice flat.

"Everything you know about the colonel calling himself Pugachev. And then your cooperation in regards to Elena Martova's daughter."

"Is this all for that woman then!"

"That's not your concern. Your concern is your freedom." An argument over Elena would accomplish nothing; he refused to be drawn into one. "Where's Pugachev?"

"I don't know," she said flippantly. But she must have remembered the threat hanging over her, for then she added more earnestly, "Truly, I don't. He was staying at a small house the corporation owns down along Islais Creek. But he's gone now."

"How do you know that?"

"From the landlord."

"The address?"

She gave it to him.

"We know he's moved several times," he went on. "Did you arrange for him to stay at Thripp properties?"

"Yes."

He realized that, with adequate manpower devoted to the investigation, this common thread running through Pugachev's movements would have been detected. "Did he ever stay here?"

She frowned. "Of course not."

"What was Pugachev's assignment?"

She started to say something, then balked and took a gulp of vodka.

"He had to leave behind his explosives in your Mission District flat," he said. "Whatever role you played, I assure you the last act's over. Now the Navy, FBI, and my own department are closing in on those who had anything to do with the theft from Mare Island Depot. There's also the matter of three dead cops."

She stared through him for a moment, then said tonelessly, "Beria needs Molotov out of the way. Such things are never discussed, as you might well imagine, but that's what it's all about."

"Why?"

"Molotov's a threat to Beria. He has to go. Also, that would make a vacancy in the Politburo. Molotov's a full member while Beria's only a candidate. And the plan, had all gone well instead of as it did, wouldn't have involved Americans. I had nothing to do with these terrible killings. You've got to believe that. But your officer, Elliot, he spoiled everything by being at the wrong place at the wrong time."

"Where would the explosives have been used?" he asked, if only to confirm what Elena had told him and Pugachev had failed to deny.

"At a house in Pacific Heights. The bomb would've gone off at a party just for Soviets. As I said, only Russians would've been affected."

"Except for one American."

Her eyes darted back and forth. "Who?"

"Your admiral friend."

"What? I don't—?"

"Oh, he wouldn't have been murdered. But I'm sure the old boy would've found being framed for Molotov's and only God knows how many other deaths just as odious—despite his rantings about the Bolshevik menace. Was this little twist to the plot your inspiration?"

She tossed her hand in front of her face in a gesture of dismissal. "Oh, yes and no—Charles actually inspired it with all his idiotic blathering about Molotov. How necessary it was to stop him, whatever the cost."

"And that's why the explosives had to come from the U.S. Navy?"

"Yes."

"Then explain something. Navy explosives and detonators aren't numbered or marked in any way. Other than on their

335

crates and cardboard linings. And they were found in soap boxes at the Mission District flat."

"I had nothing to do with that end of it."

She was reaching across the cocktail table for the ceramic dish in which she kept her cigarettes—when he caught her by the wrist. *"Please*, woman."

She shut her eyes, briefly, then leaned back out of his grasp. "The marked crates were stored separately at another location. In case the explosives were discovered by the police before tonight— not that it did any good. You still traced them back to Mare Island. This afternoon, my timekeeper would've put them in the garbage cans behind the house in Pacific Heights. That and Charles's public remarks would have shifted the blame away from Beria." Her voice softened. "Has my poor man been arrested?"

"No."

"Will he be?"

"That depends on you."

"You must understand—as I got caught up in this, those around me did too. But not of their own choosing. He has a family. Please take that into consideration, Vanya. Please."

"I'll try. How do you communicate with Moscow?"

"The consulate's diplomatic pouch."

"That won't do. I haven't time." He came to his feet. "Get dressed. And warmly. There's a chill this morning."

"Why? Where are you taking me?"

"Do exactly as I say, Lydia Dmitrievna."

"You didn't go to Los Angeles last week, did you?" John Kost asked, driving north along Montgomery Street toward the Embarcadero.

"What makes you say?" Lydia had turned sardonic since they'd left the Clift Hotel. She took a long pull off her cigarette holder and flushed the smoke down her nose. "If I said I went to Los Angeles, I went."

"Very well then, that settles it." But then he brushed her ermine stole with his fingers: "It's just that last Tuesday night I noticed a sprig of cedar right here. Yosemite seems to have a good

336

deal of cedar, wouldn't you say?" She looked straight ahead and adjusted the white scarf she'd wrapped around her yet damp hair into a turban. "By chance," he persisted, "Pugachev didn't order you up there to inquire about Tikhov, did he? I can always check with the rail company to see if Mrs. Straus—"

"Tell me where we're going," she interrupted, "I don't like this!"

"Nor I." He turned off the boulevard and parked in the lot for Pier 35. The slips on either side of it were empty, the waters agitated by a morning breeze.

"What's here?" she demanded.

"Nothing. But a short walk up the Embarcadero you'll come to Pier Thirty-nine. Anchored off it is a communications ship, which I've been told allows prompt linkage to Eleven Dzerzhinsky Street." The address of the Lubyanka Prison. "Forgive me if I don't drive you all the way, my dear, but an FBI agent's keeping an eye on the ship, and I wouldn't care for him to see me in the neighborhood. It smacks of collaboration, and I'm already under suspicion."

Her hand closed the stole around her neck. "What am I supposed to do?"

"Board the ship. . . ." He took out one of his business cards and began scribbling with his fountain pen on its back.

"And?"

"Inform Beria that the assassin Pugachev is beyond his control. The colonel knows he's been double-crossed but refuses to deliver himself into the hands of the authorities, be they Soviet or American." Then he added just for her benefit, "He tried to kill me last night. But don't bore Beria with the inconsequentials. Just tell him that Elena Martova is under my protection"—the pain in Lydia's eyes at her mention made him pause—"and that I'll use her testimony before the judiciary of the new United Nations to prove his part in any misfortune that arises from Pugachev's being in my city—unless, without delay, he flies Anna Lavrentievna from Leningrad to the American embassy in Stockholm. Now, I realize Leningrad's six hundred miles from the Swedish capital and the child's being kept on Lagoda—so I'm giving him until seven this evening, Pacific War Time, to do all this." He had expected many things from her at the end of his carefully prepared speech, but not a cunning laugh. "You think the commissar will refuse, my dear?"

"Not at all. He'll give up the girl without batting an eye—then make a mental note to have you, Martova, and her little she-bastard murdered. You've thought of everything, Ivan Mikhailovich, except the one thing that matters—how to survive after you've crossed Lavrenty Beria. He leaves the date open, but he never forgets. Did you somehow fancy the three of you would live happily ever after?"

"Just send the message," he said, itching to slap the haughty look off her face. "When you have his reply, take a taxi to the Hall of Justice." He handed her the business card. "Give this to the desk sergeant and wait in my office if I'm not there. That's all for now." Yet, as she began to get out of the Dodge, he seized her by the coat sleeve and asked, "Why, Lydia Dmitrievna? Why'd you throw lots in with such men?"

And for the first time she began to weep. She looked off toward the bay, taking a moment to gather herself before saying, "Early on, when I still had choices, I suppose it was just my way of trying to go home. Being married to a man like Mallory Thripp makes you think of going home. I imagined that if I could only destroy him and all those like him. . . ." She bit her lip. "But at the very start I was just trying to make sure Hitler didn't gobble up Russia. Was that so awful? Oh," she said with a dispirited smile, "there's no good answer, Ivan Mikhailovich. Not to anything anymore. And that's why I've been such a fool with you. You were supposed to be the answer to everything. But you should know this—when Elena Martova disappeared Saturday night, I didn't send a message. I should have and I wanted to. But I didn't."

"Why not?"

"I couldn't bear the thought of you hating me." She yanked her sleeve free of him, then slammed the car door and hurried as best she could in her high heels toward Pier 39.

. . . It wasn't you I tried to kill, my dearest Vanka, but rather the Chekist within you, the Chekist within myself, all future Chekists everywhere. . . . With glazed eyes, he bit the cap of the pen and regarded the sienna glow at the end of the drainage pipe in which he sat, hunched and feverish again. He'd been impatient all night to put down his thoughts, but enough light had come only in the last fifteen minutes. *By the time you receive this letter, I shall have reduced to carrion the men, or at least the same species of men, who either necessitated the Revolution with their greed or betrayed it with their self-aggrandizement—*

Suddenly, he clenched his teeth to hold in a groan: the slightest sound echoed down the pipe like a shot.

Red strings of blood poisoning now ran up his arm from the wound. Before abandoning the bungalow on Islais Creek Channel last night, he'd boiled off the last of the nitroglycerin from the dynamite left on the back stoop in his absence, then lashed his right forearm to the crook of the kitchen faucet and scrubbed out the pus-white hole with Epsom salts, lanced the numerous abscesses with his folding knife, then finished the torture with an irrigation of hydrogen peroxide. Twice he had passed out from the exquisite interplay of pain and his refusal to cry out, regaining consciousness only to find himself dangling at the end of his arm. He suspected he might lose it, although seeing a doctor or a chemist was out of the question. Certainly the police had notified them all to be watchful for a wounded Russian.

No, he'd show himself in the city only one more time.

This will be a blow for goodness, which is more effortless to mankind than evil; a sacrifice made in elemental sympathy with you, Vanka Kostoff, who is helpless but to love those who would betray you, and with your Elena, who has been forced to surrender her natural dignity to preserve the life of her child; and with the child herself, who with luck might well live long enough to see a world unspoiled by government! Glancing down, he realized with mild surprise that he'd penned these thoughts. His fever, which had been gaining ferocity after each remission, was now jangling his grasp of time and place. His pulse was incessantly rapid, his tongue dry and coated with something distasteful. He didn't have long before his body would fail him.

Setting aside the attaché case he'd been using as a writing desk, he rose gingerly to a crouch and staggered down the pipe. Parting the willows that masked its outlet, he gazed into the dense stand of eucalyptus. Sutro Forest, it was called, an idyll of knifelike leaves spreading over a hill in the midst of the city. It smelled like cough medicine, a warm and sensuous woodland with none of the predaceous alertness of the taiga.

God, but how my thoughts race. They're burning me up! However, one thing remains brighter than flame: there must be no universal government, and it has fallen upon me to remind the world of this truth!

With amazement, he realized that he was squatting on his heels once again deep within the pipe and had recorded this very thought!

So be it, then.

He would take the day as it came and not argue with how his senses perceived it. He was done with self-argument.

So act I must, Vanka, for to do nothing when betrayed on all sides is to cease being an instinctual man. I have not found it possible to be such a fellow in a long while. This afternoon I shall reinvent myself, as I have so often before, but this time the invention shall endure though the mold breaks—for it is now more than my pride demanding that the impossible be done brilliantly. It is the predisposition of mankind itself, and once more the Baltic Fleet stands ready to inaugurate the thwarted inclination of all humanity. . . .

Lydia was sitting stone faced in his office, her stole draped across her knees. She failed to greet him, which led him to believe that she'd been waiting for some time. His watch told him that it was three o'clock. Where had the day gone? "Well?" He began sorting through his telephone messages, hoping one of them might be from the State Department security man he'd hounded for news at the Federal Building not twenty minutes before.

"The transmission was acknowledged at highest levels."

He glanced up at her. "What's that mean?"

"Just what I said."

"Will *highest levels* comply?"

"Perhaps." Pursing her lips, she shrugged. "Perhaps not."

He suspected that this sudden ambivalence over Anna's release—after saying Beria would give up the child without batting an eye—had more to do with her own bitterness than anything the commissar might have conveyed to her. Yet, since seven this morning, when she'd transmitted the demand from the communications ship, Beria had had eight hours in which to transfer Anna from captivity at Lake Lagoda to Stockholm. More than enough time. Something had gone wrong. "If you know more than you're saying, now's the time to tell me, Lydia Dmitrievna—while I'm still of a mind to let you use that ticket."

"The transmission was received. That's all I know." Her eyes were fixed stubbornly on his, making him believe that she was telling the truth. At any rate, she had done what he'd asked, and keeping her any longer would be punishing her for Beria's intransigence.

"I'll drive you home," he said.

"No, I'd like a taxi instead—to the airport."

"Your flight isn't until eleven tonight."

"I was able to get on an earlier one to Mexico City. There I'll catch my original plane and go on to Rio." She obviously had been spooked by something.

"What happened today?"

"Please, I find your innocent look insulting."

"I'm beyond the point of pretending anything with you," he said. "What happened?"

A wounded pause. "Your FBI man followed me when I left the ship. I got out of my taxi in Chinatown and lost him. But I'm sure others are waiting for me at the Clift. I've seen my attorney and been to my bank. I took my passport from my safety deposit box. I'm as ready as I can be. Please call a cab."

He nodded, then began dialing. He heard a click from across

the room: she had gotten up and left, shutting the door behind her.

He completed the call, then hung up and whispered sadly, "*Au revoir*, Lydia Dmitrievna."

After dropping her off at the Embarcadero this morning, he'd driven directly to the Federal Building, hoping to find Cade at his desk early on this, the first day of the Conference. He wasn't disappointed. Leaving out any mention of Lydia Thripp, he told him of his maneuvering with the Soviets for Anna's release. Cade blew up, hollering that a flatfoot had no business meddling in an international affair—until John Kost got a word in edgeways: Elena might be persuaded to inform on Beria's operations once her child was safely in American hands. Cade took the bait, but said out of the side of his mouth as they hurried down the hall toward the State Department cubicle, "One thing, Kost—don't try to fuck me again."

"I don't recall doing it in the first instance, Robert."

"Level with me, for crapsake—you got another lead on Pugachev's whereabouts, right?"

"Wrong."

"Then you figure he's finished? Laying low until he can get outta the country?"

"I don't think so," John Kost said, amused that for once the agent was soliciting an opinion. "He's up to something, otherwise he'd never have tried to kill me."

"I don't follow."

"He needs me dead."

"So?"

"He still has plans I could ruin."

"You're saying he'll go ahead with bumping off Molotov? Even with no explosives?"

"Maybe. But whatever he has up his sleeve, his motives are now personal, I assure you."

Cade mulled this over for a moment. "Okay, why not? I'll start working that angle—old Vyacheslav did some dirt to Pugachev he's never forgotten. By the way, as of this morning Molotov can't step from his hotel room without a half dozen of my boys flocking around him."

"Did you tell them about the problem with the blowup?"

"Yeah, yeah," Cade said, annoyed.

After seeing the colonel at close range on Fisherman's Wharf, John Kost felt that the enlargement of the photograph Cade had snapped at Hamilton Field didn't define Pugachev's angular features well enough for a spot-check identification. Also, it accentuated his ankle-length overcoat, which he'd shed since in favor of a pea jacket, and subconsciously the cops who'd seen the blowup would be looking for that coat.

From the Federal Building he had sped to the bungalow owned by Thripp Shipyards along Islais Creek Channel. The place had been stripped and cleansed of any evidence that Pugachev had been there, although an unusual odor lingered in the kitchen. It had given him a vague headache. He'd only been able to liken it to ether. Had Pugachev been anesthetized and treated by a doctor on the table? Without success, he tried to identify the smell all the way to his father's flat, where he hurriedly told Elena that he'd prepared a new hiding place for her: a houseboat in Sausalito belonging to a retired plainclothesman he trusted to guard her. But while only yesterday she'd complained of cabin fever, she now refused to go, insisting that she was comfortable with his father and saw no reason for the move. He would've argued except that within minutes he had to be at the Soviet consulate to finalize motorcade arrangements with Pyotr Martov—and had already made up his mind to return from the Opera House after the opening session and forcibly remove her to Sausalito, if need be. Afraid to raise her hopes only to see them dashed later in the day, he had said nothing about the message he'd sent to Beria.

Now, alone, his eyes kept gravitating toward his silent telephone. The State Department Security man had a Teletype link to Washington, but so far no word had clattered over it from the embassy in Stockholm that a small Russian girl had arrived in Sweden. He couldn't understand the delay.

The Chekist waited until fifteen minutes after four before approaching the Opera House through the light rainfall. Prior to that, the arriving delegates had been too few for him to test the alertness of the two FBI men posted at opposite ends of the arcaded portico, let alone those agents most assuredly within. Any one of them might look past his gold-wire-rimmed glasses, pin-striped, double-breasted coat off a thrift-shop rack, and meek stoop from the shoulders—all affectations to suggest the chronically penitent aspect of an apparatchik—and recognize Boris Pugachev. Yet, if that happened, he would simply draw his revolver from the ankle holster he'd fashioned, sprint for the first nine rows—those reserved for the delegates—gunning down anyone who tried to stop him, and detonate his attaché case by giving it a good hard shake.

His vials of nitroglycerin had thawed completely by now, making it even more unstable than when he'd frozen it.

Anthony Eden, Smuts of South Africa, Soong of China—most of the principals had already been dropped off by limousines. All but the Soviet VIPs had been ushered inside, and he counted on them to show up at the last minute. At any rate, this self-appointed mission didn't specifically call for Molotov's death, did it now? How was the commissar any more important than the others of his universal ilk?

"Your credentials please." The military policeman at the door extended his white-gloved hand.

The Chekist gave him an awkward smile.

"Do you speak English, sir?" The young soldier began looking for one of several translators posted in the foyer to assist with the processing.

"Is this what you require?" The Chekist had taken out his credentials. They identified him as Yakov Sedin, security specialist, and had been prepared for him by the Lubyanka's forgery shop in the event his Pugachev incognito was compromised. The MP compared the name to a master list and as expected, failed to find Yakov Sedin. His forefinger trailed down the S page once again. "A problem?" the Chekist asked, no longer smiling.

"You mind standing to the side for a moment, sir?"

"Not at all." He thought of his revolver, but decided to wait. It would be nice to have Molotov too.

At the MP's wave, a lieutenant approached from the center of the foyer, where he'd serenely been reviewing the flow of delegates inside. "What is it, soldier?"

"Sir, this gentleman's name isn't on the list"—the soldier checked an African delegate's credentials and let him pass—"but his papers look okay."

The lieutenant borrowed the manifest and came to the same conclusion—the name Sedin was nowhere to be found, not even after he checked the Y's in the hope it had mistakenly been alphabetized under Yakov.

"I demand to speak to your superior," the Chekist said.

"I don't think that'll be necessary, Mr. Sedin. Let me get your delegation's security liaison. He's been here since noon. I'll have no objection if he clears you."

He glared, but then said, "As you like."

Waiting with his back to the incoming delegates, he glanced at his pocket watch. Molotov and his people would arrive any moment. He needed only a few minutes before that, but precious seconds were wasting away. His timing device was an American travel alarm clock, removed from its case to make it thinner, connected by tiny insulated wires to two electrical blasting caps he'd taped to one of his two vials of nitroglycerin. Knowing how the first sessions of conferences are invariably delayed for this reason or that, he had attached a clothespin to the winding knob of the clock; that way, simply by tugging on a string that he'd left dangling an inch outside the case, he could activate the bomb.

Emotionally, it would be easier to make a pell-mell dash inside, slam the attaché case against his knee, and vanish in the dazzle. But if he did that, he wouldn't be able to savor the salty fumes hanging over the tattered seats, to assess the carnage that would tell him if he'd succeeded; even though the alternative involved an excruciating wait. But in the smoky aftermath he had a statement to make—before the MPs and FBI agents raced from the foyer and shot him dead: *Brothers, I have done this to ignite the absolute liquidation of the political, judicial, financial, and administrative state—!*

The lieutenant came back with a Soviet official and a female interpreter in tow. The Chekist had ridden into the city from Hamilton Field with the fellow. Govorov or something like that. Detached from a militia desk job to the Commissariat of Foreign Affairs for the Conference—one of Beria's people.

"Is Mr. Sedin part of your security team?" the lieutenant asked him through the interpreter.

The official's eyes were riveted on the Chekist's face, which slowly broke into a hectoring smile. "Of course you know me," he said in Russian. "What's this fuss all about? I'm here to check for explosive devices. Tell this nice lad you know me so I can get on with it."

Govorov continued to stare, but finally he managed to mutter, "*Da.*"

"Very well then," the lieutenant said. "Thank you for your patience, Mr. Sedin."

"You're welcome."

But the Chekist had taken only three steps toward the auditorium when the young officer delayed him once again. "Oh, I'm sorry, sir—I'll have to examine that briefcase."

The Chekist turned. "What?"

"Conference rules, Mr. Sedin." The lieutenant wore a white leather holster on his waist belt. "Kindly open it."

He studied the American's expression and saw that there'd be no changing his mind. Stooping, he rested the attaché case on the carpet. His left hand was within inches of reaching under his trouser cuff for his Nagan, but instead he snapped open the clasps and raised the lid.

The lieutenant knelt opposite him. He leaned directly over the case. Good. From that angle he was less likely to detect the false bottom, or notice the string that was tied to the hidden clothespin.

First he took out the electric torch, unscrewed its base, and inspected the batteries. Satisfied there was nothing untoward about it, he moved on to the tools: a pair of needlenose pliers, some wirecutters, a machinist's hammer, and small mirror; all innocuous-enough looking for him to turn his attention promptly to the stethoscope, which he felt moved to try on before he realized that he had nothing to listen to. He grinned—he was slightly buck-toothed—and at last came to his feet. "Thanks again, Mr. Sedin."

The Chekist shut the case, rose smiling, and started for the auditorium once more.

29

Rain was speckling the windshield as John Kost waited in front of the Soviet consulate. He'd already jacked open his shotgun to make sure there were live shells in the magazine, then wedged the piece back under the seat. He turned off the wipers. Their screaking over the glass was setting his teeth on edge.

Maybe Cade was right. It would happen somewhere between the St. Francis Hotel and the Opera House. This morning at the Federal Building, he had shared the gist of Lydia's confession with the FBI agent and the State Department man, although he'd been less than truthful about the source of his information by hinting that it came from Elena Martova. Cade had grafted on to it an unshakable belief that Pugachev would still strike at Molotov, probably before the commissar reached the full security at the Conference site itself.

John Kost wasn't so sure.

For one thing, Pugachev's only apparent reason for assassinating Molotov and his clique—unless he harbored some personal grudge against the commissar, which John Kost doubted—had been Beria's orders. And now that his boss had betrayed him, what purpose was there in murdering Beria's rival? None. Nor was he convinced that the man killed to satisfy some perverse inclination. He took a life only when he had to for the sake of the job. Young Fenby had been guarding Laska, who might have talked. Aranov had come close to finding something inside the boathouse. And Ragnetti had discovered Pugachev's lair. All logical reasons to use deadly force, as any one of them could've botched his mission.

But what was Pugachev's new imperative now that the secret police had cast him adrift? What would that sailor at Irkutsk have done if denied all hope?

Martov swept out the front door of the consulate flanked by Ruml and Pervukhin. Over the telephone he'd asked for John Kost to take them in his Dodge, which was less conspicuous than the Cadillac. He took the front seat beside the inspector, leaving the back for his men.

"Good afternoon, gentlemen," John Kost said.

"Yes, Ivan Mikhailovich, a good afternoon," Martov muttered, the smell of his fear penetrating his cologne. The other two Soviets failed to respond. Pervukhin's eyes were preoccupied, and Ruml had rolled down his window to scan the street.

Martov reached up and tilted the rearview mirror so he could have a glance behind the Dodge. "Where's your FBI friend?"

"Waiting at the St. Francis."

"How many of his men are with him?"

"Six." John Kost crept away from the consulate. The air gushing in through Ruml's window was cold on the back of his neck. "You'll catch pneumonia that way, Viktor Fyodorovich."

"Ekh," Ruml said, "what's health to the Russian is death to the foreigner."

Martov turned his head and snapped, "The inspector's asking you to roll up the window."

"But how can I shoot through the glass if it's closed?"

"You shan't. Lower it again if the need arises." Martov sat around and shook his head.

John Kost stopped for a swing-arm traffic signal. Over the engine noise the rain pattered on the sheet-metal roof. He was a hairbreadth away from making some elusive connection when Ruml tapped him on the shoulder. "Ivan Mikhailovich—"

"What'd you just say, Viktor Fyodorovich?"

"I said nothing. Didn't you hear the signal change?"

He hadn't, and still his right foot remained on the brake pedal. "You said something about health."

"Just an old saying of my father's—what is health to us is death to the foreigner. Except he used to say *German* instead of foreigner."

And what had Pugachev said on Fisherman's Wharf last night? *What follows now will be perceived as sickness on a grand scale. But it is actually health, my dear Vanka. The health of the world.*

A car horn startled him, but he failed to accelerate across the intersection. He was wondering what flaw within himself had blinded him to Pugachev's meaning—for now its simplicity, its symmetry, blazed before him. Long ago in parting at Irkutsk the sailor had whispered to him: *You are the last goodness left, old fellow. Not a single day shall pass without my remembering you as the goodness that has gone out of my life.* This afternoon, after decades of blood, Pugachev would try to restore that goodness, not as John Kost understood goodness, but as an exhausted veteran of the Cheka might.

"What're you doing?" Martov asked as the horns from behind went on braying. "What's wrong?"

John Kost reached for his microphone. Raising the dispatcher, he ordered her to phone Jennaway at the Naval Intelligence headquarters. "Have him meet me in the foyer of the Opera House ASAP. Advise of his acknowledgment."

"What's going on here!" Martov demanded.

The Chekist emerged from the shadowy wing onto the stage. He could feel the warmth of the klieg lights on the right side of his face; they were strung beneath the opera boxes foliating above the general seating in a horseshoe of gold leaf. To his left on a riser a meter and a half above the one on which he stood, the forty-six flags of the United Nations were arrayed in a semicircle. Behind them, four columns had been rigged from golden velour.

He mounted the steps onto the higher platform, paused a moment to let a wave of feverish dizziness wash over him, then took his electric torch from his coat pocket and trying to look official, began examining the hollow interiors of the cloth columns with his mirror.

At the other end of this backdrop, a British Army officer, having just inspected the elaborate rostrum, was doing his own check of the columns. In passing, the Chekist gave him a polite nod, then crossed downstage to the uppermost of two podiums. It was at least two meters farther away from the first row than the lower, so he gave it but a once-over before descending the steps—two meters might reduce the efficacy of his bomb, perhaps sparing the eighth and ninth rows any fatalities at all. On paper, he'd computed the probable limits of the lethal blast overpressure, but now these figures tumbled past his inner eye without meaning. Enough meticulous reckoning. Many would die. Many would be deafened for life, a reminder that they had been deaf to the pleas of an enslaved mankind. And many would be left unimpaired to hear what he had to say.

He had no sooner started looking over the lower podium than a technician asked him to stand aside so he could adjust the battery of gray microphones.

"As you like," the Chekist said, noticing Govorov and his translator. They were staring up at him from the orchestra pit. He gave them an icy smile, and their gazes fell.

An unseen orchestra struck up a fanfare. It was apparently seated behind a thick drop curtain backstage of the velour columns. He hadn't counted on musicians being present. He had no wish to kill musicians. But a quick calculation reassured him that the upper tier of the rostrum would reflect the force of the blast out into the auditorium, although a few musicians might be deafened. Like Beethoven, then.

At last, the technician scurried off to his next task.

The Chekist crouched behind the podium. Within its wooden walls were three shelves—this was good. The more splinters the better. He locked both the case's latches with a tiny key that he then dropped into his jacket pocket, and slid the case so far back on the topmost shelf one practically had to be on his knees, as he was, to see it. He gave the string a tug, pulling the clothespin off the winding knob. The clock was now running.

Rising, he saw Molotov and his stodgy little retinue trooping down the aisle toward their seats. A bonus. Simply a garnish to the advent of a new world. He withdrew.

Thirty minutes.

From the wing his eyes paced off the distance back to the rostrum. He doubted the blast would injure him here, but even if it did he would find the strength to stagger through the smoke onto center stage and tell the world why he'd done this—his Nagan flashing from his fist as the FBI agents and MPs came barreling into the auditorium from the foyer.

That they would promptly kill him didn't depress him. On the contrary, he had never felt more alive. All the twisted roads of his life had now converged into a perfectly straight band of light that seemed to issue from his own feverish brow.

Movie cameras were whirring, plates snapping in still cameras, a Teletype rattling somewhere.

Twenty-nine minutes.

John Kost slammed his car door and began running through the rain. Martov had just refused to budge from the Dodge until Molotov and the rest of the Soviet contingent arrived. Nor would he let Pervukhin and Ruml help search the auditorium for Pugachev, as John Kost had asked.

He bolted up the slick steps of the Opera House—scattering a huddle of Indians in white turbans—and into the foyer, where an MP began to go for his holster until John Kost showed his badge. "A Navy officer is expecting—"

"John!" Jennaway himself hollered from across the echoing chamber. Through the auditorium doors came a light-opera tune, discordantly gay.

He drew Jennaway aside and struggled to keep his voice low and sensible sounding. "Dennis, Pugachev's going to do something here."

"What?"

"I'm not sure. Something big. A bomb, maybe."

Jennaway was watching him closely. "But what makes you think so?"

"His original mission was a bombing. But now there's more to it than that. No time to explain. Son—" He turned to a passing usher and once again brandished his gold star. "Run to the stage door and be ready to let us in. We'll be coming around the building. Hurry."

"What—?"

"Hurry!"

The youth dashed into the auditorium, and John Kost led Jennaway out the front into the rain. It was falling hard now, sheeting off the awnings. He could see that he was taxing the little trust he'd built up with the officer. "You've got to believe me—Pugachev's here. This is where he'd be today."

Jennaway let out a steamy breath. "Where's Cade?"

"On the way with Molotov's motorcade."

"The order to evacuate is going to have to come from you people or the FBI—"

"No!" John Kost snapped, throwing open the wrought-iron gate on the north side of the Opera House. News that the session had been evacuated due to a bomb would get to Beria even before it did Truman. The commissar might figure all deals were off—and hold Anna in Leningrad if she'd not already been put on a plane for Stockholm. Could he ever justify to Jennaway his willingness to risk hundreds of lives for that of a single child? If he stopped long enough to think about it, he knew he'd order the evacuation himself, but by not stopping to think he persuaded himself he could delay it a few minutes more. "There's no time to clear the house. We've got to find the bomb—or Pugachev—ourselves." Then he added, his voice jerky from his strides, "An evacuation will only complicate things. The panic."

Jennaway didn't look convinced, but kept silent for the moment.

"Help me, Dennis—where would he plant a bomb to kill as many as possible?"

"Depends." As John Kost began pounding on the stage door,

Jennaway counted off on his fingers: "What kind of explosive does he have? At this point I can almost swear it won't be military. Will it be tamped? Does he know how to use directional force? Does he want to kill with concussion or shrapnel—or does he want to bring down the building on everybody's heads?"

"Which would call for the least amount of explosive?"

"A directional fragmentation bomb."

"Then look at it that way, Dennis. Where? Where!" He went on smacking the yet closed door. "Open, dammit!"

"We can start by looking high. The catwalks above the stage, maybe."

The door yawned a few inches, and John Kost found himself confronted by one of Cade's men. The young usher was standing sheepishly behind the FBI agent, who then drawled, "What can I do for you, Inspector?"

He shoved past him and saw that the backstage area was jammed with musicians blithely going through "Lover Come Back to Me." Then he looked down at his arm: the agent had taken hold of it. "Let go," he said from deep within his throat.

The man hesitated, but then dropped his hand. "Sorry, I just—"

"This is what you're to do. Without alarming the delegates, search the offstage areas for anything suspicious. A package. I don't know. Anything."

"Am I looking for a bomb then?"

"Keep your voice down. Yes." Then he started up a narrow iron ladder whose uppermost rungs yielded to the darkness of the loft.

From the tormentor curtain across the stage the Chekist watched Vanka Kostoff talking with the FBI man posted at the door. With him was a martially groomed fellow in civilian clothes who was already grubbing around the counterweights as if hunting for something dangerous.

Kostoff had intuited his plan. But how?

Feeling light-headed, he grasped the curtain before he sagged all the way down to the stage flooring. His hands were yellow.

Jaundice. He had seen it all before: next his degenerating septicemia would give him delusions. If not already. Was that a grown man across the stage or a raven-haired child in a white *roobashka*?

He bit his tongue to keep from laughing or weeping or doing both until his giddiness slid him off the edge into blackness.

Had something within himself purposely betrayed his intentions to Vanka? Was he more taken with destroying himself than the governments of the world? Before he could come to any conclusion a gavel rang down on wood three times, and he laboriously brought the upper podium into focus. Stettinius, the patrician-looking American secretary of state, set down his gavel. "The first plenary session of the United Nations Conference is hereby convened. . . ."

Glancing back toward the door, he saw that the three men had separated, the FBI agent starting a search of the stage while Vanka Kostoff and his companion began climbing the ladder into the loft.

A nasal voice started blaring over loudspeakers. Truman, the new president, speaking by wire from Washington. He kept using the words *just* and *justice*, which infuriated the Chekist. This travesty had nothing to do with justice.

He stared upward at Kostoff's hands flying from rung to rung.

Gripping his revolver, John Kost inched down the bridge, a catwalk for lights just upstage from the house curtain. Jennaway followed him at a distance of ten feet, also with drawn weapon, but—at John Kost's urging—looking more for a bomb than Pugachev. John Kost himself would keep watch for the colonel, no easy trick with several battens branching off from the catwalk into the dim thicket of cables, lash lines, and lighting units that enveloped the men.

"Hold up," Jennaway whispered.

Stopping, still looking for the reflection of eyes in the dark clutter of the loft, John Kost waited for him. "What?"

"I don't know where the hell to begin."

"Why not?"

355

"It could be in any one of these light housings, John. And that'd be a dandy way to trip it too—wire the detonator to a bulb socket. Then somebody pulls a lever in the booth and off she goes. A shower of ball bearings. Nails. Whatever."

"Then let's start taking them apart." Applause told him that Harry Truman had finished his address. Secretary of State Stettinius began to speak, his words flowing up from the rostrum and ricocheting against the poured-concrete walls of the loft: "There can be no end to the tyranny of fear . . . of fear and want unless the proposed world organization commands . . . commands the allegiance of both the mind and the conscience of mankind . . . of mankind."

The look in Jennaway's face said his limits had been reached. "If you really think Pugachev's planted something, we should evacuate—now."

John Kost glanced through a narrow parting in the house curtain. He could make out Anthony Eden far below, lionine, handsome, weary looking. "Five more minutes—that's all."

Frowning, Jennaway began taking the inspection plate off a Fresnel. "This is worse than a needle in a haystack. I need to know *something* about the explosive to find it."

John Kost grasped at anything that might help. "We located his last hideout this morning. . . ."

"Come up with something?"

"No, it was clean. Except for a smell."

"Yeah?"

"Like ether. But not quite. It gave me a bit of a headache."

Jennaway stared at him, then lowered his forehead onto the backs of his hands.

"What does that tell you?" John Kost asked, alarmed.

"The son of a bitch cooked the nitro off some high explosive."

"Why would he do that?"

"So he could kill half the people in this place with something the size of a milk bottle."

"Where would you plant a bomb like that?"

"It can kill by concussion alone. The closer to the target the better. Like smack-dab in the middle of auditorium seating."

356

"I can't search there."

Jennaway began checking the other lights. "Start looking for dust disturbance on these."

"Where else would he plant it? Quickly, Dennis."

"The rostrum, under the stage, this unit in my hands if he decided to add shrapnel—Jesus, you name it."

"I'll see how the FBI is doing down there. Keep your gun handy."

"Sure."

In his haste to get down, John Kost missed a rung with his foot, slipped, and nearly pitched back into the plunging interplay of light and shadow. He hung on his arms for an instant, regaining his nerve, telling himself that the time to evacuate had come. If there was a bomb here—and he believed there was—they weren't going to find and disarm it before detonation.

Clambering down again, he landed heavily on the floor and looked for the FBI agent. But the man was nowhere to be seen.

He had no idea how to get under the stage and doubted it could be done without the help of the crew.

The rostrum then.

For some reason, perhaps to differentiate between his protocols as both presiding official and an opening-ceremonies speaker, Stettinius had gone down to the lower podium to make his remarks. John Kost could see nothing inside the upper one except a plait of radio and public address cables twisting up to the microphones. He braced his hands on his knees and stooped to have a better look. From this vantage the upper podium still looked unremarkable, but on the top shelf of the lower podium— whenever Stettinius rocked aside while gesturing—he thought he could see a briefcase.

A blind certainty took hold of him. This was it.

Yet, he waited for the secretary of state to end his speech. To storm on stage during the address would throw the MPs into an alert, triggering the evacuation he still wanted to avoid.

Then the pool of light covering downstage seemed to fade slightly.

Looking up, he caught the last wavering of the asbestos curtain before it went motionless. Someone had dropped it ten feet. Turning toward the pulley lines in the fly gallery behind him, he saw that it had been Jennaway, who had climbed down from the loft and now came to his side. "I gave up on those goddamn lights," he said breathlessly. "There must be two hundred of them. If it blows from up there, let's hope the fire curtain slows the shrapnel's velocity. If it's even a shrapnel bomb."

"It's not up there, Dennis."

"Where then?"

Crouching, motioning for Jennaway to do the same, he pointed at the briefcase inside the lower podium.

"Stettinius's?"

"We'll know any minute," John Kost said.

"You going to do the honors?"

Hunting for a bomb had been his idea. He had to do it. "Any pointers?"

"Yeah," Jennaway said. "Keep it level and don't sneeze. Shock, vibration, and heat don't mix well with nitro. Nice and easy until we get outside. Then walk—not run—away from it. I'll be two steps in front of you."

Both of them reacted to the applause as if it had been a shot. Stettinius walked away from the podium and up the steps to his gold-brocaded chair on the upper dais.

The briefcase stayed inside the podium.

"That's it," Jennaway said, his voice husky now.

John Kost quick-marched out into the heat of the lights, blinded by them to the murmurous audience. The MP at the edge of the forestage braced as he saw that someone not on the program was making for the rostrum. But then the soldier's attention was divided: Molotov was sauntering toward the lower podium from the opposite side of the auditorium, holding his pince-nez between his thumb and forefinger.

John Kost reached the podium first. He pivoted and said with a thin smile to the dignitaries on the upper dais, "A technician apologizes for forgetting something, gentlemen."

Stettinius smiled in return, which relaxed the MP into a parade rest again.

Drawing in a long breath, he reached inside the shelf and took hold of the briefcase, amazed that his hands were shaking no worse than they were. As Jennaway had told him, he brought it out on the level and kept it that way. Then, with a peculiar sensation that his arms were filled with helium, he backed away from the podium.

He looked askance at Molotov, who out of suspicion or confusion had halted well shy of the rostrum. "My apologies, Commissar," he said—in English—then started for offstage, making sure no cables lay in his path before fixing his gaze on Jennaway's strained face. The lieutenant commander nodded once, deeply, as if to say that if it hadn't gone off yet the removal was going better than expected.

"My b-brother delegates," Molotov had begun in his stammering Russian, "the point at issue is whether peace-loving nations are willing to create an effective international security organization. . . ." After each step Jennaway seemed no closer—John Kost told himself he'd feel nothing if the bomb went off in his hands; he would simply vanish in a burst of searing light, instantly atomized and digested by God. "You must definitely know that the Soviet Union can be relied upon in the matter of safeguarding the peace and security of nations. . . ."

He finally made it to Jennaway. "Where to?"

"Keep coming. Straight out the door."

John Kost crept past the usher, who was standing wide-eyed in the same spot he'd overheard the FBI agent mention a bomb.

Jennaway whispered, "I'm going to help you set it down when we get outside."

"Why?"

"It might have an antitampering device."

"What for?"

"To discourage handling."

"And *now* you tell me?"

"Would you've preferred knowing before?" Jennaway said, falling into some sort of professional jocularity John Kost couldn't quite share—not with his arms beginning to tremble and his stomach growing queasy.

"The door, Dennis."

"Got it."

John Kost stepped out into the rain. "Here all right?"

"Fine."

The door boomed shut and he jumped, his fingernails digging into the leather. "Lord God!"

"You're fine," Jennaway said. "Everything's fine. I'm going to take one side of it now." Together they lowered the briefcase to the pavement, then stood straight again. Raindrops drummed brightly against its lid.

"Done." Jennaway chafed his hands together. "I was serious about walking, not running away. If you trip, it's all over." He began ambling toward the iron gate on Van Ness Avenue, but hadn't gone far when he realized that he was alone—John Kost was still standing over the briefcase. "What're you doing!"

"We have to look inside."

"Later! We'll get a BD team to open it!"

John Kost shook his head, adamantly. "We have to know if this is it. Otherwise, the search goes on."

Jennaway stood his ground a moment longer, but then walked back. "This is absolute lunacy. . . ." Kneeling, he tested the latches, then tucked his hands under his arms and groaned, "It's locked! Let's get outta here, John!"

"I can't let it go off. Not even out here."

"Why? What's a few windows in the neighborhood? I'm rusty, John. I haven't done this in years. Hey, what're you doing there?"

John Kost had taken Ragnetti's picklock set from his jacket pocket and selected the narrowest pick and the tension tool. But trying to insert them in the keyhole in one of the latches, his hands began trembling so hard Jennaway said, "Give it up."

"I just have to rake the pins. There's nothing to it." And then the first latch opened with a click. "One more to go." He became conscious of the cold wetness spreading down his back from his collar. The second latch gave. He glanced to Jennaway. "What now?"

"We open it and go up in smoke. A mousetrap could be rigged inside to close a switch."

"I don't think there's a mousetrap, Dennis."

"I'll remember that." Jennaway slowly reached for the lid. As soon as he raised it the ticking could be heard.

Behind them the stage door flew open. Cade and the agent who'd helped them with the search were blinking against the rain. "Kost?"

"Get back—we've got a device here!"

"Explosive?"

"Yes!"

His agent ducked back inside, but Cade closed the door and puffing on his cigar, strolled over to the brick ring around a linden tree. He squatted behind it so that only his straw boater showed.

"Give me a hand here," Jennaway said, having pried out a felt-covered cardboard panel and exposed a false bottom. "Hang on to this first glass by the base. Tight but not too tight." Packed in a layer of cotton were two vials fifteen or so inches in length, filled with yellowish liquid. Taped to the one Jennaway had handed him were two blasting caps joined by wires to a partly disassembled alarm clock. He wound off the tape, then told John Kost, "Take both vials and set them inside the planter. Gently. Have Cade move away—just in case. You too."

John Kost had just laid it in the muddy earth at the base of the tree and was motioning for Cade to come away with him when a small bell started to ring. It was cut short by twin pops no louder than .22-caliber pistol shots.

He reeled toward Jennaway. A puff of smoke briefly hung around the officer's head before wafting skyward. He spun down into a fetal position against the pavement.

"Crap!" Cade shouted, lumbering up off his knees.

John Kost got to him first. Jennaway's eyelids were clenched and one side of his face was peppered with little black punctures that had not yet begun to bleed. Cade noticed the bloody left fist before John Kost did and unfolded it: Jennaway's thumb and forefinger had been stripped down to the bones.

His eyes yet shut, he arched his back and gave a growl full of self-reproach. "I should've gone after the clock first! Stupid son of a bitch!"

"Open your eyes," Cade said.

Jennaway did so. They seemed more white than blue and were laden with fear.

"Can you see?" John Kost asked.

The Chekist ranked it among the hardest things he'd ever done: to abandon his place in the wing of the Opera House stage, to forsake the instant of fire, of uproarious wind mingled with the screams of the dying. But the moment the FBI man started his way, he'd realized that if he were found on the premises, Vanka Kostoff would be all the more certain of a bomb and might order the auditorium emptied. He had to leave. His letter to Kostoff would have to be his final statement to the world.

Clutching his right forearm, its nerves barking for the morphine he was denying them, he gaped feverishly across Van Ness from the crowded corner with Grove Street. His head and shoulders were rain soaked. The half-staffed American flags in front of the Opera House and the Veterans Building were clinging wetly to their poles. Nickering with impatience, a police horse did a shuffle, its hooves clopping on the pavement and its dark haunches glistening as blackly as the policeman's oilskin suit.

One minute.

How loud would the blast be? he wondered. Curtains, human flesh, the stout granite-clad walls of the Opera House itself, distance, and even the rain would muffle it. But in less than sixty seconds, the survivors would begin streaming out the doors, clasping handkerchiefs to their mouths, sobbing, suddenly wheeling on the portico steps to remember those they'd left behind because of panic.

Thirty seconds.

He would wade into this melee and begin shooting those delegates with the short-lived good luck to have escaped the nitroglycerin.

Wiping his hot face in the crook of his jacket sleeve, he then watched the second hand of his pocket watch arc up to the twelve. "Now," he said.

But only a feeble report reverberated around the Opera House from its far side. It was so muted neither the mounted policeman nor the FBI agents sheltering in the portico gave any indication that they'd heard it.

But he knew at once what it had been. His bomb had just been disarmed, its blasting caps purposely detonated.

He shuffled over to a lamppost and wrapped his good arm around it. He stared off at the Opera House for a while, his eyes glazed, then suddenly wailed from all the pain pent up inside him, "Oh, Vanka, don't you see! There's an eloquence to final action, just as there is to final words—and damn you, you've just deprived me of it!"

He ignored the unsettled looks of the passersby and asked himself what then was left. He already knew, but asked himself again as if asking might rattle loose some all-encompassing solution. But no, vengeance was his last resort, lowly vengeance. Yet, it was also one of the great engines of history: a score is settled between two men, and in the process an empire falls and a new one arises, the old order is scattered and a fledgling one is jury-rigged from the debris. And this is how his own phoenix might rise from the ashes of the hour. His last hope was vengeance, for only by seeing Vanka Kostoff and those around him utterly destroyed might the world realize how this true revolution was not to be resisted. Killing Trotsky had meant nothing—his brand of revolution was as false as Stalin's. But this would be different. He was battling the Infant of Irkutsk, the raven-haired child with the face of an angel, for the fate of the world!

Letting go of the lamppost, tottering until he found his legs, he started down Grove Street. The tops of the buildings whirled above, leaning over as if they were made of rubber. He almost vomited.

A block later, he stopped beside a wire trash container and reached down into the sopping refuse for his trenching tool. Earlier he'd discarded it here, thinking he would never need it again. There'd also been the problem of getting it past the MPs at the Opera House, but this had had less influence on him than his conviction that he was forever finished with tawdry, small-scale violence.

But he'd been wrong.

30

JOHN KOST SWITCHED on the dome light in the idling Dodge to assure himself once again that the telegram was real, the flimsy yellow paper palpable to his fingers, that the afternoon hadn't pushed him over the edge into nervous exhaustion. It was from the American embassy in Stockholm and addressed to the State Department security man whose cubicle in the Federal Building he'd just left:

LITTLE PACKAGE SAFELY ARRIVED HERE STOP AWAITING WASHINGTON INSTRUCTIONS STOP

"Oh, the mercy of God!" Laughing, he jammed the stick shift into gear, and the usual grating noise betrayed his clumsy driving skills—no matter. Anna was in Sweden. The "awaiting Washington instructions" rankled him. Why did diplomats cringe at the threshold of each decision? But once again—no matter. Elena's child was free of Beria.

The rain had stopped and the clouds parted on a lustrous black sky. Although the Conference had let out a half hour before, the main north-south arteries were still jammed with cars trying to leave the Civic Center. Through his rearview mirror he saw that Leavenworth Street was in no better shape than the others, so he decided on Hyde, in any event the most direct route to Russian Hill—and Elena.

The downtown signals had been turned off in favor of human traffic control, and only with a blue-suiter's help was he able to nudge into the stream of cars inching north. He found himself behind a Silver Shadow filled with Arab royalty, the gold cord of their headdresses glittering in his headlights. When the chauffeur turned off onto Geary Street, John Kost noticed the Standard Oil logotype on the door. Looking forward again, he winced: brakelamps were shining redly in a long line; the jerky flow had come to a standstill again.

Ahead a block was a tavern with a public telephone.

He parked in the only space available, a fire hydrant zone, and trotted through air so pure and chilled he nearly choked upon rushing inside the stuffy bar. Then he could barely pick the nickel out of the loose change he'd gathered in his tremulous palm.

His father answered.

"Papa, put Elena Valentinovna on."

"She's just drawn a bath for herself. Later."

"Call her to the phone, Papa! I've got urgent news!" He flinched as his father tossed down the handset. The old man had been drinking more than his ration, and he reminded himself to make it clear to Elena that his father wasn't to be trusted with money. Martov had sent three hundred dollars along with her belongings, and the old man had obviously finagled her out of some of it. No more. But then this resolution slipped his mind as soon as her voice came over the line. "Yes, Vanechka?"

He started to speak, but his voice broke and he couldn't go on. He'd never imagined that exhilaration could be so wrenching; it was like sorrow in its intensity.

"Is it Annushka? Is something wrong!"

"No. Oh no. She's free. Your daughter's free."

A long, breathy pause. *"What?"*

"She's in Sweden. At the American embassy. I just got the confirmation."

Another pause. "How . . . how'd this happen?"

"I found a way—"

"Yes, yes—I knew you would," she interrupted, bursting into tears. "I knew it from the first time I saw you. From the start I saw how very clever you are." She snuffled, then cried happily, "I'm sorry, go on, tell me everything. Everything!"

"Beria met my demand."

"What demand?" Suddenly, despite her weeping, she sounded suspicious; but for the absence of sarcasm, he was reminded of Lydia's tone when she'd said that Beria would never forget this. "What'd you offer to do for him?"

"Listen, no time to explain now."

"You must."

"I'm only ten or so blocks away. But the traffic's wretched. That'll give you time to do something for me—"

"Yes?"

"Pack your things. I've got to move you—now."

"No, please, Vanechka. As I told you before—"

"Pugachev's still at large. He planted a bomb at the Conference this afternoon. It nearly went off. It would've but for a damned fine naval officer. He was injured."

"Oh, no—badly?"

"It could've been worse," he said with remorse. He'd been less than truthful with Jennaway, asking him to risk his life without knowing why. As soon as he could, he would tell the man everything. "Thank God he wasn't blinded. But the point is—Pugachev isn't finished. He's not trying to get out of the country. So I beg you—"

"I'll be ready when you get here."

He didn't know what to say for a moment. He had steeled himself for an argument. "Good. Thank you."

"Will I have to hide in this new place for long?"

"I don't think so. Pugachev's hurt. As of tonight, all the hospitals on the peninsula have his description. He's not going to last much longer without medical attention."

But then it seemed as if she'd heard none of this, his first admission to her that the colonel had been wounded: "Are you *sure* she's in Sweden?"

"Absolutely."

"Beria would lie to you. He'd say anything. Do anything. You mustn't believe his word."

Is this what was souring her joy? "I know," he said, annoyed by her inference that he was too naive to deal with the commissar. He'd just won the release of her daughter, hadn't he? "My confirmation comes from the American ambassador, not Beria."

"When can she come here? How can we arrange—" She stopped midsentence, and through the background static on the line he heard his father's front door boom hollowly against the entryway wall. He'd heard this sound countless times before when the old man had stumbled in drunk, spoiling for a quarrel.

"Lenochka!" he cried into the mouthpiece.

She hadn't screamed, which gave him hope that it had been his father staggering out for more vodka. But then this hope dissolved as soon as she said with a voice so flat it no longer resembled hers, "Too late, my darling. God keep you."

Then the line went dead.

She had hung up the phone because she didn't want Vanechka to hear her die. She knew she wouldn't die bravely; sobbing and screaming, she would beg for her life until the last breath.

The colonel stood framed by the opening of the door he'd just bashed in. His face was bilious yellow, and he was clutching a little spade in his left hand. He said nothing to her. Perhaps he saw no need. His presence was enough to steal her voice and take away her legs.

But then the floorboards creaked, and moving only her eyes, she saw that Mikhail Kostoff had come from the bedroom. A grave smile spread over his lips as he brought his saber up from his side. "I believe you're looking for me?"

"Don't flatter yourself, Mikhail Mikhailovich," the colonel said. "I stopped thinking of you as soon as you left Irkutsk."

368

Confusion seeped into the old man's eyes, dimming the courage she'd seen there the moment before.

The bulb in the handheld red spotlight had burned out, so when John Kost gave up tapping his horn from curbside and flipped on his siren, it only confused the drivers locked bumper to bumper on Hyde Street. A woman in a Nash was so unsettled by the shriek issuing from the grill of the unmarked Dodge she inadvertently shifted into reverse and accelerated into him, crumpling his fender and smashing a headlamp.

She got out to inspect the damage, but he hollered for her to get back inside her car and move it out of the way. Then he reached for his microphone and boosted the radio volume. The channel was jammed with nonstop chatter about the traffic mess, but still he tried to get through to the dispatcher: "Break for emergency traffic!" The drone went on about the need for more signal pots at Golden Gate and Van Ness, an officer asking for a backup to field sobriety test a drunk driver who spoke no English. "Break for emergency!" he shouted. "Break!" When no acknowledgment came from the Hall of Justice, he flung the mike against the dashboard.

Backing apart from the Nash, headlamp shards tinkling on the pavement, he muscled the steering wheel hard to the right and pressed down on the gas pedal. One by one, the tires crabbed over the curb ledge, and he started down the sidewalk, his siren clearing the strollers ahead of him.

The patrolman at the Bush Street intersection held up a frantic hand to keep him from crossing, but down off the sidewalk he plunged, the Dodge landing with a jounce that drove his head against the roof. The blow dazed him, but through his confusion he sensed something large closing fast on his side of the car.

A basso profundo blat deafened him in the split second before the collision. A bus horn, he realized as his head was rocked from shoulder to shoulder. Out his windshield the storefront lights stretched like taffy into ropy bands, and his tires began screaming above the din of the siren. After a dizzying revolution and a half, the Dodge came to rest pointed toward the gray Navy bus that had caved in its hindquarter.

Sailors began pouring out its folding doors, grinning with excitement—although one of them was dabbing at a bloody nose with his white hat.

"You there!" John Kost bailed out of the Dodge waving his gold badge. "Go to your call box!"

The Traffic cop cupped his hand behind his ear. "What!"

"Call box!"

"Turn off that goddamn siren, Inspector!"

"I want a cruiser sent to—" Then he gave up relying on the department. It was less than a mile to his father's flat. He started running, palming his revolver so it wouldn't jiggle out of his holster. He ran until his lungs felt scorched and a coppery taste coated the back of his throat, and then he kept on running.

Mikhail Kostoff smiled at her as if it were a plea for trust, a promise that he was in control of himself again.

Then he advanced.

The colonel waited for him, expressionless but for the haggard cast to his green eyes. "Where's your son tonight, Mikhail Mikhailovich?"

"How do you know me?" The old man kept adjusting his grip on the hilt as if already his saber was growing heavy in his bony arms. "Who are you?"

Taking a step backward, the colonel chuckled humorlessly. "I was your Vanka's Nagorny."

She didn't know what to make of this. Nagorny was the sailor who'd attended to the sickly Tsarevich Alexis and finally been shot for his loyalty to the imperial family. But what did this mean? Had the Kostoffs somehow run across the colonel before? Then recognition seemed to grow out of Mikhail Kostoff's befuddlement and he cried with anger, gyrating the tip of his blade in the colonel's face. "You!"

"Indeed, I."

"It was you who betrayed us!"

"It was your lack of vision that betrayed you." Then there was

370

a clash of steel as the colonel swung his spade down on Kostoff's saber, snapping it at the midpoint. With the backside of the same ringing blow he caught the old man alongside the head. Bleeding from the temple, he toppled against the kitchen table, either dead or unconscious—she didn't know which—and rolled heavily onto the floor.

The saber lay in two pieces on the linoleum.

The colonel was winded by this brief contest, and while he recovered his breath, she started for the broken blade, shrank from the enormity of using it, but finally lunged for the hilted half.

But before she could bring it up to fend him off, his shoe pinned it to the floor. "Don't even think of such a thing," he gasped, then sank to his knees, his chin glistening from a trickle of saliva. She backed off, and he let go of his grip on the spade to cradle his right forearm as if it were aching. A fluid too pale to be all blood was twining down off his hand onto the floor. She thought he might faint, but he didn't, and after a few moments he grinned, the whiteness of his teeth showing how severely jaundiced he was. "So the Little Boss decided it was time for me to go, what?"

She said nothing.

"Talk to me!" he shouted.

Her body jerked. "Yes."

"What were your orders?"

"To kill you when you came to me for your plane ticket."

"How?"

"Pistol."

"D'you have it now?"

She knew at once that her eyes had betrayed the truth: she was defenseless. But what did it matter if she had a gun or not? She had promised God at the outset of this trip that she would never save herself at the price of killing another. She would only kill for Anna, and now Annushka was no longer the issue.

As she began to creep toward the open bedroom door, he barked, "Stand where you are!"

She froze, but started moving again when she saw him bring

371

a revolver out of some sort of cloth attachment to his ankle. A large revolver. She was running for the bedroom—and the fire escape out its window—when the first shot came with a blast. Feeling the heat of a bullet whisper past her cheek, she dropped to the floor and crawled through the doorway, then rolled onto her back. The second shot kept her from closing the door with her hand, but then she extended her leg and kicked it shut.

On the verge of rising, she heard a roar simultaneous with the wood of the door splintering inward at about eye level. The icon above the bed behind her was swinging on its nail, its candle extinguished. "I'll get it from you with your guts!" he bellowed insanely.

"*What* do you want!"

"You! I want you!"

"But I'm nothing!"

"You're what he *believes* in!"

"I didn't go through with it! I never wanted to kill you!" All the while they shouted at each other through the door, she had been moving the hardback chair from the corner and propping it under the latch. Then she crouched behind the wall opposite where she thought the armoire was positioned on the far side—in time to hear two bullets crunch into the lathing.

She heard him jiggle the handle. "No! I beg you!"

He grunted in disgust and called her a whore.

No more bullets slammed into the bedroom. He had begun to chop away at the door with his spade. In her mind, the wood had become her own flesh, stiffened against the violation that was coming. She prayed, not for rescue but for the strength to keep her promise. To die innocent of blood.

John Kost turned the top of the stairs and immediately saw that several doors along the corridor were ajar. "Phone the police!" he whispered to one old pensioner who was peeking out. The door clapped shut against him, but then he heard a siren in the distance. Someone had already phoned. Instead of encouraging him, the approaching wail made his heart sink: people rang the

PD only after the fact. It was over. As Elena had said so eerily, he was too late.

He sprinted the rest of the way to his father's teetering door. Its top hinge had been ripped out of the jamb.

With no time for caution, he burst inside the flat, his eyes and revolver sweeping as one over the living room and kitchenette before fastening on the figure sprawled beside the wreckage of the table. His father. His head was bloodied.

Keeping his revolver trained on the open bedroom door, he moistened the fleshy webbing between his thumb and first finger and pressed it under his father's nose, praying to feel the faint coolness that would be breath, life itself, but his senses were so overwrought by his long run he could pick up nothing.

Then the old man's eyes twitched open and he asked in French what time it was.

"Stay down, Papa," he said in a winded hush. "Where's Elena?"

His wrinkled eyelids squeezed shut again.

John Kost rose quietly for the bedroom doorway.

He saw his father's saber in pieces on the floor (at least he'd tried!), and then where a crude hole had been chopped in the door above the knob. ID wouldn't have to do the impossible and make a toolmark comparison for him to know it was from the same vicious edge that had so disabled Aranov he eventually drowned.

This was his chance to pay back the man who'd murdered Nathan, he told himself.

But the bedroom was dark. He inwardly counted to three before reaching around the side jamb for the wall switch.

Steel thudded against bone, and he screamed so loudly he left his own ears ringing. As he collapsed to his knees, the flat blade dropped in front of his eyes again, connecting this time with his gun hand. The revolver flew deep into the shadows of the room, and he saw that both his left forearm and right hand were bleeding profusely, he could feel the flood soak warmly through his trousers. "Goddamn you!" Squaring his back against the wall, he thrust out his legs, catching the looming figure in the abdomen and driving him back over the bed.

Pugachev fell with a crash against the nightstand.

Silence.

He clamped his wrists under his arms to slow the bleeding. Partly from pain and partly in search of his revolver, he began squirming his shoes back and forth across the floor. He could see the outline of Pugachev's head showing against the rectangle of stars that was the open window. "Where's Elena?"

"Jumped, old fellow."

"What?"

"She leaped from the fire escape before you got here."

"You lying son of a bitch."

Yet, Pugachev's tone of voice was so blasé John Kost feared that he'd spoken the truth. The sirens—several of them now— were closer, perhaps three or four blocks away. But if she was gone, they were a mockery. But he went on grubbing for his Smith & Wesson with his shoes.

"Sit still, Vanka—I've got my Nagan aimed squarely at your face." Each breath Pugachev took was catching in his throat. "Hers was a hopeless situation. As soon as she strayed from orders, she had to realize her daughter was dead."

"Anna Lavrentievna's at the American embassy in Stockholm."

Pugachev paused, then asked, "Really now?"

"Really."

He chuckled, but it rumbled off into a phlegmy cough and then dry heaves. "Well, no matter," he said, recovering. "A plane must make many stops between Sweden and San Francisco. Did I take your left hand off at the wrist?"

"No."

"Good. I didn't want to, truly."

"But I'm bleeding a lot. I'd like to sit up to help stop it."

"Be my guest. You have good reflexes. Another fellow would've lost both hands."

John Kost drew in his legs, sliding his revolver back toward him. He had located it just as Pugachev told him to stop fidgeting. "Why?"

"Why what, Vanka?"

"This useless bloodletting when you have nothing left to do here." He reached down with both hands for his revolver, but they were either so numb with shock or nerve-damaged his fingers refused to close around the grips. "Is it just pride?"

"Oh, no. You must never think that. All the satisfactions of vainglory, love of rank and fame—they mean nothing to me. They've been overwhelmed by a single passion of liberty for all people."

"I still don't understand." His deadened hands simply could not manipulate his revolver, and he groaned under his breath.

"Then I've done a poor job of paraphrasing Bakunin."

"The anarchist?"

"Yes. You've read him?"

"This and that."

"What'd you think, Vanka?"

"I'm afraid my ignorance about mankind is less precise than his."

"Well," Pugachev said, sounding disappointed, "the police are coming and I have no time to argue. All that matters is this—I'm you in another world. That's all. The same selfhood on the other side of the globe. Don't deny it." His voice hardened: "And don't ever feel superior to me."

"What . . . ?" John Kost came close to passing out. Coming around again with a snap of his head, he thought he heard a car brake. Had the first cruiser arrived? "What do you mean? I'm nothing like you."

"Ivan," Pugachev said. "My Christian name is Ivan. I wanted you to know." Then he cocked his revolver.

By the time the colonel had hacked a splintery hole in the bedroom door and fumbled his arm through it to knock aside the chair propped against the latch, she was out on the fire escape, ready to start down the ladder. But then he said calmly from the open window, "Don't move—or I shoot." His tone grew gentle:

"You have nowhere to go, my dear. No place in this world will welcome you. You're as dead as I am."

She gripped the clammy railing with one hand. Her head sank between her shoulders. "Be quick."

But several seconds passed in silence, and finally she opened her eyes again. The bay lay darkly before her. She could see some lights on the island where Vanechka had been detained as a child. *Annushka is free!* she reminded herself. But she was holding a dagger down in the folds of her skirt, the old man's dagger she'd slipped from the nightstand drawer on her way out.

Suppressing a moan, she wheeled, the blade rearing back in her fist.

But the colonel was no longer standing at the window.

In shame she laid the dagger on the iron platform and stepped away from it. Relief shuddered through her. She had just been spared damnation, and she vowed not to fight for her life, not to flee either. Her faith would see her through this one way or another.

Suddenly, she heard Vanechka scream wordlessly, then howl in terrible pain, "Goddamn you!"

She glanced around the edge of the window as either the colonel or Vanechka toppled back over the bed.

It proved to be the colonel, for Vanechka then asked him from across the small room, "Where's Elena?" He said that she'd leaped from the fire escape. She wanted to cry out to let him know she was all right, but then it dawned on her that the colonel might take her hostage, shield himself with her so he might further hurt Vanechka.

Sirens seemed to be coming this way.

She sat on her heels, huddled in her arms, and told herself to wait for the police.

The men went on talking, but she found it hard to pay attention, so loud was the buzzing of her fear inside her head, so erratic and rushing her pulse—until a click made her jolt.

At once she knew what it was.

Scrambling across the platform on her hands and knees, she seized the dagger, then began to crawl over the sill. But the colonel must have heard her movement, for she found herself looking into the muzzle of his revolver. "You first then," he said without malice. Just a statement of fact.

A snick followed. Then another.

"It's empty! Climb down!" Vanechka shouted, rising unsteadily in silhouette. He was holding his forearms upright like a surgeon waiting for his gloves.

A siren echoed around from the front of the apartment building, then whined off.

The colonel reached down and came up with his spade. It was reflecting the waterfront lights. She cowered without thinking of the dagger still in her hand, losing her footing and falling against the railing, but his wild swing missed her and imbedded in the sill with a crunch. He ripped the spade free and wheeled on Vanechka, who stood motionless before him.

"No!" she screamed, yet couldn't make herself reach through the window with the dagger. Someone was hollering for John Kost from the entryway. A policeman. But something in his voice said he was reluctant to barge into the darkened bedroom. She gripped the dagger in both hands. Then the injustice of the moment, the hopelessness that would follow either choice, filled her with anger. The colonel could not keep on doing these things. It was right to stop him. It was right to save Vanechka. The conviction flowed into her like adrenaline. This would not be a sin.

"Good-bye, Vanka," the colonel said low, hefting his spade.

Then her thrust caught him in the upper back. But it didn't penetrate—she'd felt the tip of the dagger deflect off a bone.

He made no sound, but turned and looked her flush in the eye, his face obscenely quivering as he asked, "Still on orders then?" He was sweeping the spade toward her head when she raked the dagger across his throat; in the same instant Vanechka hurled himself against the backs of the colonel's knees, buckling him into the blade. His hand lost hold of the spade, and it flew out the window.

A moment later, it rang against the alley.

377

31

Vanechka had risen from bed at three o'clock and taken two painkillers, so she now trusted he wouldn't stir again until at least noon. His sutured wounds and broken left forearm were no doubt still agonizing him, but his exhaustion and the barbituates had combined to leave him sweet, quiet, remote, over these past ten days since the colonel had nearly killed him.

She wanted to kiss his sweaty brow, but dared not. His sleep might be less deep than it seemed.

Quickly, quietly, she dressed. She didn't linger over this or that in his apartment; the icons especially were avoided. Nor did she pause to wonder what might have been. This chance was a divine gift, a fleeting generosity not to be spurned because of personal longings, and all sorrows paled in comparison to separation from God. If she failed to believe this, she stopped being a believer, and on this morning Elena believed with a clarity that kept her from crawling back into bed and delaying the inevitable another few minutes. She was too weak for that.

So, she studied him a moment—his arm, L-shaped in its plaster-of-paris cast bent over his moist, black hair—and turned, depositing her hopelessly awkward letter of explanation on the dresser, and let herself out of his apartment.

The dawn was so foggy she could scarcely make out the Cadillac parked across the street.

Pyotr Martov sat alone in it with his side window rolled down. Hearing her heels clip over the wet pavement, he flicked away his cigarette and got out to help her. "Is he awake?" he whispered.

"No." She noticed how quietly he closed her door. He really was a timid man, but this morning she found it hard to resent him.

"How's he doing?" he asked, having hurried around the front of the Cadillac and gotten back behind the wheel.

"Fine."

"And his father?"

She couldn't help but to smile at how Mikhail Kostoff had wrangled an early release from the hospital in order to attend the Paschal service tonight. "Fine as well. I don't feel much like talking, Pyotr Aleksandrovich."

"I understand." And he sounded as if he truly did, enough so for her to reach over against her better judgment and squeeze his hand.

"You're braver than I, Lena . . .," he blathered on—only panic liquefied his crisp exterior in this way. On the night she'd begged him to avenge her against Beria, he had prattled like this. Perhaps he knew better than she what awaited her at the end of this drive. She took back her hand, and he switched on the windshield wipers. The headlamps were barely opening up the dark gray fog curling around the car. "That was always the problem, you know. I shrank. You confronted. But it's not in my nature, you see—"

"There's nothing wrong with your nature. It was just our mistake to marry. We should've stayed just friends. We were lovely friends."

"Weren't we though?" He laughed, but she could tell from his voice that he was close to weeping. Oddly enough, his was a sentimental nature when it wasn't consumed by the need to survive. Survival was the only glory he knew, and she pitied him for that. No one survived. "Would you like a cigarette?"

"Not now, thank you," she said.

"Are you sure you can't wait until tomorrow? Anna will arrive after midnight and—"

"No," she said sharply. Now, within only a few breaths of having praised her courage, he'd gone after it with knives. She couldn't see her daughter once again and then be strong enough to do what had to be done. She couldn't torture herself by seeing Annushka in the city where she'd grow to womanhood. Imagining later would have to suffice. But then she caught herself: perhaps Martov had really meant nothing untoward.

The silence between them began to solidify. He was driving very slowly.

They passed St. Basil's, its blue domes silvered by the fog, and her heart suddenly ached so she needed to say something. "You did well negotiating all this. . . ." The need for Martov's help had occurred to her during the ambulance ride with Vanechka to the hospital. Everything she'd overheard the colonel say to him in the bedroom was coming back to her: A *plane must make many stops between Sweden and San Francisco*. He had been right, of course. And at that instant, with the siren throbbing inside her head and Vanechka trying to reassure her with a sallow-faced wink that he was all right, she had realized what had to be done. Of necessity, it involved Martov.

In the following days the American government had proved reluctant to transfer Anna from Stockholm without Soviet approval, so Martov worked out a solution of sorts. As soon as Elena surrendered herself, Moscow promised to inform the U.S. embassy in Stockholm that it had no hold on the child. She knew that the Kremlin could break its promise and remain close-mouthed about Anna, as it had these past ten days, but to protect her against such a twist Martov had arranged for a State Department official to come aboard the communications ship moored off Pier 39 to ask her, "Are you being held against your will?" She would answer as she saw fit at that time. Also, Anna's plane would use the polar route, landing only at remote airbases in Alaska and Montana for refueling before flying on to Hamilton Field.

Of this Vanechka knew nothing.

She had put it all in her letter, along with documents drawn up by an American attorney giving him custody of her daughter. She hadn't asked him if he wanted such a burden: in desperation, she'd simply trusted that he would. She tried to convince herself that she was giving him back the child who'd been stillborn, but she couldn't fully embrace the notion if only because that baby girl had been another man's. With time would that have mattered to Vanechka? Yet, her choices were so few she refused to torture herself over them, and then something he'd said in the ambulance, as much as it had hurt her, made it easier for her to leave him Anna: "You don't have to be in love with me. I can live with that, Lenochka. But you musn't leave me. Ever." How could her paltry letter ever do justice to such a plea?

She realized that she'd started to say something to Martov and he was waiting for her to go on. "I want to thank you for your help. No one could've done as well."

"It was nothing," he said. "I just hope you've fully considered what you're doing."

"I have."

As Martov parked along the Embarcadero, the outlines of the communications ship bleared in and out of the fog, the very indistinctness of the vessel giving her a shiver. Then she blurted, "You musn't think I'm so awfully brave. . . ." She had started to cry and tried to hold her lower lip still with her fingers. "I can't start this voyage on a lie. No more lies."

"But you are. You're magnificently brave."

"I'm so afraid."

"I would be too."

"No. Not for me. For Annushka, for Vanechka—for the whole world. That's why I do this. I'm tired of being afraid."

He touched the side of her face. "What a curious thing to say on the last day of the war." His hand fell. "Let me walk you out to the wharf."

"No. Good-bye, Petrusha. I think we're still friends after all, don't you?" Before he could answer, she rushed for the pier. She ran until she glanced over her shoulder and saw Martov turning back for town. But only when she was aboard the dinghy, seated between two secret police sailors, gliding through the fog toward the hull looming up out of the slate-colored water, did this fearful sense of urgency leave her. She had not lost her courage at the last instant. And now her relief came close to besting her sorrow.

"Somebody *has* been out to the ship," Coffey answered, getting up from his desk to close his door because John Kost had been shouting from the moment he'd barged in.

"From our State Department?"

"Yeah. And he spent over an hour with her." Coffey poured him a drink, which John Kost felt like refusing, but then downed anyway. "She's aboard of her own free will."

"How can we be absolutely sure of that?"

"We can't. But we're reasonably sure. The State man made it clear to her we won't let the ship leave port if we think she's a prisoner."

"Let me go on board, Pat."

"Johnny, Johnny—"

"For the love of God, please."

"No can do."

"Who says?"

Coffey avoided his eyes.

"Come on, Pat—who? The chief? Hoover? Stettinius?"

"No."

"Who then?"

"She did, for Chrissake!" the captain barked. Then he shook his head and gently said, "She don't want to see you again, Johnny. She told the State guy that."

He sat in stunned silence for a few seconds, then held out his glass in his thickly bandaged right hand for a refill. The painkillers had worn off again. "I want you to listen to me, Pat. This isn't a threat. It's simply what I'm going to do."

"Now don't start shooting off your mouth—"

"War considerations can go to hell. I'm taking the whole story to the *Examiner*. Hearst has no affection for the Bolsheviks. I'll have him print what Pugachev did for Beria here. I'll hand over my case files. Let the chips fall—"

"You're doing nothing of the sort! By order of the chief of police, those cases are cleared by exceptional circumstances and sealed!"

"The Devil you say!"

"Shut up!" Then Coffey clasped his hand to his forehead as if he couldn't believe this was happening. "What're you threatening me for? This is Pat here, John. Recognize me?"

"I just said this isn't a threat. It's just what I'm going to do."

"Why'd you make me do this?" Coffey moaned.

"Do what?"

Coffey went to the door of his private lavatory and opened it. Sitting on the commode lid was Cade, champing on an unlit cigar. Revealed at last, he saw no further need in holding off the pleasure of lighting up. "You even walk out of this office in the general direction of the Examiner Building, John," he said, bringing the cigar to life, "and I take you into custody. The director's orders."

"Does Hoover have any idea what's been happening in this city for the past month?" John Kost demanded, suddenly dizzy from all his hollering.

"He knows everything." Then Cade added sarcastically, "Finally." He stretched his arms above his head, then strolled out of the lavatory and sat on a corner of Coffey's desk. "That means Truman knows too. So don't try an end run around the Bureau."

"Why won't anyone help this woman!"

"First of all, it's obvious to everybody but you she's got her own ideas," Cade said. "Okay? Whatever her reasons, she's on that ship because she wants to be. You may not like it—but that's the goddamn truth." He helped himself to a pull off Coffey's bottle of Irish. "Truman's got one thing on his mind right now—trying to get Stalin to live up to the Yalta Agreement so we don't invade Japan on our lonesome. You think I like this any better than you?"

John Kost bounded up from his chair. "Three cops are dead!"

"We know, Johnny," Coffey said quietly from the window. "And I know how much Aranov meant to you. But as an American—and not just an old gumshoe who loves this department and its boys as much as anything—I've got to stack up those three lives against the tens of thousands of GIs who'll be saved if Stalin gives us a hand with the Japs."

"Stalin won't lift a finger against Japan until there's not the slightest chance he'll get a bloody nose. Truman, all of you, are missing the lesson—the worst licking Russia ever took was from the Japanese. My father was *there*. And that defeat helped bring on a revolution. You're ignoring the past. You're—!" All at once he had to sit again.

"You okay?" Coffey asked.

He nodded even though he was close to vomiting. The nausea came as much from his injuries as the sense of futility that had just swept over him. It felt like being ushered into that white room to watch his wife die all over again. He rested his cast in his lap.

"John," Cade said, "I got to put two of my boys on you day and night until further notice."

"You already have. They followed my cab here from my apartment."

"That's right. Nothing personal. Go home. Get some more rest. I'll tell you right away if I hear anything—promise."

"Fog's lifting," Coffey said, still at the window.

From the Hall of Justice, John Kost took a taxi to the hospital. There he spent a few minutes with Ragnetti, who was so morphine-drunk he failed to notice his inspector's own injuries. Then he took his father down to the twilit street in a wheelchair, where they both climbed painfully into a cab and rode it in silence to a Russian cafe in Richmond District. The old man had a large gauze bandage taped to the side of his head, but as with his goiter, seemed oblivious to it.

The owner was playing an uninspired balalaika at the cash register, perhaps to mask the rumbling of stomachs on this, the strictest day of Lenten fasting—only tea was being served. In the midst of pouring a glass for John Kost, his father asked, "Where's Elena Valentinovna?"

John Kost started to reach for a sugar cube, refrained, then in a weary voice told him that she'd gone aboard a Soviet ship at dawn.

"Why?" the old man asked, slurping.

"I'm not sure. Maybe she thinks this will buy safety for her daughter and me. I only know that I love her, Papa, and I can't let this happen."

"Then what're you going to do?"

John Kost pointed out the front window at the two FBI agents lounging in a sedan parked across the street. "I'm being followed."

"That isn't what I asked," the old man said irritably.

"I don't know. At four this morning I pick up her daughter at Hamilton Field. . . ." His voice faded.

"And then?"

"I'm going to board that ship and take her off."

The old man was grinning through the wisps of steam off his tea. "That's rubbish. You'll do no such thing."

"I swear I will!" he said so forcefully the other patrons looked up from their tables.

His father continued to grin. "You're a Cossack after all, aren't you?"

He gave a noncommittal shrug. He wanted to say that he was an American and was utterly disgusted with Old World machinations. If these past two weeks had been a taste of the Russian way of life, he wanted no part of it. But he was in no mood for an argument.

"You're a Cossack if only because you truly believe at this moment you'll do this stupid thing," his father went on. "Right now, you'd rather die than not do it. But who can say what feelings tomorrow will bring? Come now, drink, hurry—I want plenty of time to shave and dress."

Let off by a patrol car, father and son arrived at St. Basil's fifteen minutes before midnight. The sky was deep, starry. The cars of the congregants filled all the curbside spaces within several square blocks of the church, forcing the FBI men to park halfway down to the waterfront and hoof it back up to assume their post on the corner. John Kost told them that, as the ceremony would be quite long, they were welcome to come inside the nave, or have some tea in the basement kitchen. They said no thanks, and he rejoined his father, who was huffing up the crowded steps, explaining about his bandage to all who would listen, "A Bolshevik did this to me!"

He looked forward to vanishing within the misty-looking incense, to letting these warm tendrils of human voice now spilling out the door wrap around him and carry him upward and away. But as soon as the ceremony began, even though he sang all the appropriate responses and crossed himself when called for, his attention ran away from the liturgy and fastened on Elena. Hitler was dead, *hateful hell has been despoiled*—as Father Aleksei had just sung, but he could only think of her. There could be no peace without her. Not for him.

He didn't feel betrayed. But he knew that would come later, when he'd ask himself again and again what had made her abandon hope at the very instant they'd won the freedom of her child. If that improbable release had been achieved against all the intrigue Beria could dream up, *anything* was possible. So what had blinded her to the infinitely efficacious grace of God? What then?

After countless readings—some of them a hasty, mad scanning, others as scrupulous as if her words were in hieroglyphics instead of Cyrillic—he still couldn't fathom the motive buried in her letter: *You must never doubt my love for you, my darling Vanechka. The worthiest love comes from need, not desire, although I satisfied both by knowing you and trusting in your kindness with all my heart. But need creates the greater love, yes? Isn't it so between man and God? And isn't it so between you and me, my beloved?*

A hand roused him by touching his arm above the cast. He was given a taper, and then a flame was passed from believer to believer, each keeping a child-glow of the holy fire, their faces ghostly looking for being underlit. Finally, out they trooped, the entire congregation led by Father Aleksei and his deacons, out into the night with the bells pealing and the FBI agents growing jittery on the corner as they were confronted by this strange civil disturbance, a blaze of candles, the choral singing echoing off the apartment facades and bringing on the lights behind the windows. Around and around the church the hundreds proceeded, seeking Christ risen from the sepulcher, Christ triumphant over venality and death. Sheltering his taper with his cast, John Kost prayed for Him to reveal Himself restored, prayed for him to alight *here* in the modernity of the automobile-jammed street—and to save the woman he loved. To let her drink from the cup of joy He had just set before her.

Then, as if suddenly convinced of the miracle of the Resurrection, the congregants hurried back inside the nave, where John Kost turned and exchanged three kisses with the man on his left. *"Khristos voskrese,"* the fellow said in the extraordinarily tender spirit of this night, his eyes filling. He had lost a son on Tarawa. *Christ is risen.*

"Vo istinu voskrese," John Kost replied. *Truly He is risen.* He turned to his father on his right and clutched him as best he could in his wounded arms. Astonishingly, the old man returned the embrace so tightly they couldn't find the space in which to share the traditional triple kiss.

"We were meant to be men alone, my Ivan Mikhailovich. Accept it. If you want peace in your heart, accept it. She knows what she's doing. Just as your mother knew what she was doing."

And there it was after all these years: his father had just freely bestowed his patronymic on him. Yet the old man's words had come with a promise of such great bitterness he found himself robbed of the pleasure he'd hungered for.

"Christ is risen," John Kost said.

"Truly He is risen," Mikhail Kostoff answered.

The sprawling, many-armed bay slowly took shape in the dawn light. John Kost followed Highway 101 down off the Marin Headlands and onto the northern approach of the Golden Gate

Bridge. His arms throbbed and itched from the effort of steering. Across the front seat from him, huddled against the door in a shoddy overcoat, Anna slept.

Sadly, she was a child used to being handled by and ordered about by strangers. Only by nearly going to blows with Cade had he kept the FBI and State Department from interrogating her at the airbase. "Come, Anya," he had simply said, and without a word she'd followed him out to his Dodge, a tiny girl with fine chestnut hair and transparently variegated eyes of blue and gray and green—probably her inheritance from Beria; still, he found them bright and innocent.

Both the FBI and State Department cars had promptly fallen in behind his. He could catch their headlamps whenever he checked his rearview mirror.

Midway across the bridge, he glanced eastward to take in the city's skyline—and suddenly let up on the accelerator.

A tug was pushing a ship away from the northern end of the Embarcadero. By the time he had reached the toll plaza and waved his badge at the attendant, the daylight was strong enough for him to see that the antennae-cluttered vessel was the Soviet communications ship.

"*Why now?*" he asked out loud.

Anna rose up drowsily, looked at him, then sank back against the door—although her eyes remained locked on him.

Speeding through the Presidio, he struggled to make sense of the departure. According to Martov, the ship wasn't scheduled to sail for Vladivostok until the end of May, by which time the most important business of the Conference was expected to be wrapped up. Had Beria decided that Elena's return to Soviet territory took priority over all else?

Yes, because what she knows is the most immediate threat to the bastard's survival!

He thought to drop off Anna at his father's apartment, but then realized there was no time. Trailing him down Lombard Street, the FBI driver was flashing his headlamps for him to slow down. Instead, John Kost gave the engine even more pedal before turning off for Pier 43. There he found the PD's motorboat being hosed down by a municipal worker after its graveyard-shift sweep of the waterfront. The crew had already returned to the Hall of Justice, and its relief had not yet shown up.

Cracking his door, he hollered at the worker, "I'm from Homicide! Fire up the engine!"

The man nodded and dropped the hose to snake back and forth across the wharf. Within seconds, the diesel was grumbling and leaking bluish smoke across the waters of the berth.

Hurrying around to Anna's side of the car, he lifted her under his right arm and carried her toward the boat, her legs flapping as he ran. "We're going on a ride, little one." He could see the rust-streaked Soviet ship inching past the end of the pier. Then, from the parking lot behind him, he heard the brakes of the FBI and State Department cars, but he didn't bother to turn as he asked the worker, "Can you operate this boat?"

"Sure, but I'm only supposed to motor it around the slip. You know, for gassing and maintenance."

"Then this is your lucky day—here, take the child." He cast off the mooring lines, then leaped aboard, groaning tight-lipped at the pain the jolt gave him. But he smiled as he accepted Anna from the man again. "Be fast about it, old fellow—I want you to catch that ship headed for the Golden Gate."

"Can I see your ID?"

John Kost showed him. "Please—quickly now."

"You sure this is okay?"

"Absolutely."

"Then who're those guys?" The worker had one hand on the throttle, but with the other was pointing at the agents who were flagging their arms and shouting for the boat to come back to the wharf.

"Ignore them. Full speed."

He later realized that he'd still held some hope, however slight, of stopping the ship until they actually closed on its stern a quarter mile out into the rollers beyond the Golden Gate Bridge. At that moment two sailors and a man in civilian dress appeared at the fantail railing. All three were armed with submachine guns.

"San Francisco Police!" John Kost cried over the bullhorn in Russian. "I am coming aboard!"

Their faces betrayed nothing except a vague contempt.

"What's going on here?" the worker asked, his voice jerky from fear and the chop of the ship's wake. "Am I gonna get shot!"

"No—relax."

Anna, at first delighted by the speed and spray, had now begun to cry. When he asked her what was wrong, she said that she was cold.

All at once the Soviets on the railing trained their guns on the pursuing boat. The civilian brusquely motioned for them to break off. John Kost reached inside his jacket, hesitated with his hand poised there, then glanced down at the child. His hand slowly dropped to his side.

"Ease off a hundred yards," he said at last to the workman. "Please circle it once before returning to port."

"I don't know—"

"Please, I beg you!" He then picked up Anna and perched her on his hip. She buried her face against his neck to be out of the chill spray. "Listen, Anya, I must tell you the truth. With us it's always going to be the truth, no matter how hard it is on us. Your mother is on that ship—"

"Mama!" She looked toward it with such joy he came close to breaking down. Yet he forced himself to smile as he cleared his throat and whispered, "We're going to make a circle around it. Only one. And we're going to pray that she sees us from one of those little round windows. We must show her that we're going to be happy together—even though we won't always be. Not completely. Not without her. This is the only gift we can give her now, so we've got to pretend very well. Do you understand?"

Her face told him that she was no stranger to difficult truths.

"Let's wave, Anya."

And when her small hand flew up against the spray, he kissed the crown of her damp head and starting weeping. "See? Even at four you're stronger than I."

EPILOGUE

San Francisco, 1968

He THOUGHT that he'd made it unrecognized through the moving ellipse of demonstrators until a shrill, familiar voice rang out, "Chief of Police Kost! How many kids have you gassed today!"

The middle-aged woman was wearing a calico dress with a tawny felt headband. Strands of red glass beads were clicking around her neck. Having stopped walking, she was in violation of the picketing ordinance, and one of his patrolmen posted outside the Opera House took his hands off his hips and started toward her. But smiling, John Kost motioned for the blue-suiter to let her be. She was allegedly still a professor of American history at San Francisco State College, although she was so ubiquitous at any public expression against the war he'd come to doubt whether she had seen the inside of a classroom in months. "Professor, I hope your carelessness with the word *gassed* is not intended. May I suggest a course in basic chemistry to assure you that tear gas is not Zyklon B?"

She had a rambunctious laugh, and he rather liked it. "And may I suggest, Chief, that you take a refresher course in Russian history?"

"For what purpose, my dear?"

"To remember how a quixotic and imperialistic war in Asia resulted in the Revolution of 1905!"

"If you think the circumstances in this country today are comparable to those of Nikolas Romanov's Russia—well, Professor, may I inquire as to what you've been smoking?" He continued up the steps, but then turned with a chuckle and said, "You know, even my dear mother would've been ashamed to dress like that. And she was a Gypsy."

The rookie patrolman in the foyer, stationed there to prevent protestors from gate-crashing this evening's Red Cross benefit performance of *The Sleeping Beauty*, recognized his chief despite the tuxedo and saluted.

"I appreciate the gesture, old fellow," he said, patting the young man's arm, "but we're not quite the Marines here." He hurried on toward the stairs, but once again turned. "You look quite smart tonight, I must say."

The boy saluted again. *Ah, well.*

He took his seat in the mayor's box and gave the Mrs. Mayor a glancing peck on the cheek just as the orchestra struck up the introduction. Almost at once his mind began to wander. His lack of concentration during performances more than any loss of vigor told him that he was pushing sixty. And it was incredible to think that, if he were still alive, his father would be nearly a hundred! Mikhail Mikhailovich had died two years after the war. But his lasting even that long had been a godsend; it had been a difficult time for the Homicide Bureau, rebuilding during an avalanche of cases brought on by the return of thousands of young men troubled by combat, and a difficult time for John Kost to try to rear a child. It would've been impossible without his father's help, which had been unstinting, joyful even.

Princess Aurora made her debut at her coming-of-age party, and the Mrs. Mayor whispered in his ear, "She really is lovely, John."

"Yes, she is," he said proudly, although he wasn't blind to the truth. She was not the beauty her mother had been. Then he

392

frowned. Already the conductor was having trouble with his baton. "Valse tempo," he said in a low growl, "valse tempo."

Pyotr Martov was recalled to the Soviet Union in 1947, a month after Mikhail Kostoff's death. If the old man's remains could be cremated, the vice-consul had offered to see that they were interred at the small Cossack cemetery in Novocherkassk where generation upon generation of Kostoffs lay in repose. But John Kost had regretfully declined: for bourgeois religious reasons, cremation was out of the question. He had no doubt that Martov would have gone through with this. Regardless of his personal failings, Pyotr Aleksandrovich was after all a Russian and knew what it would've meant to the old man to lie in Russian soil.

Death upon death, he mused inwardly, his eyes following only Aurora on the stage below, *memory at my age is just a litany of deaths*.

One afternoon in 1955, Ragnetti came back from a long lunch at Carlo's and laid his head on his desk. Thinking that he'd had too much to drink once again, the other plainclothesmen didn't disturb him. At quitting time, John Kost, recently promoted to captain of inspectors, strolled down to the bull pen to say good-night and found him dead. A stroke, according to the postmortem. Coffey, retired by then, went just as suddenly from a heart attack the following year.

Of Elena, Pyotr Martov passed on a few unconfirmed reports in the early years that she'd been spotted in this or that labor camp, but then he let it be known that his interest in his wife was putting him in jeopardy, and the reports stopped filtering their way into San Francisco. In 1953, when Lavrenty Beria was arrested by his fellow members of the Politburo and subsequently taken down into one of his own death cells and shot in the back of the head, John Kost was delirious with the hope she might be among those released as part of the amnesty following Beria's reign of terror. But nothing came of his inquiries as to her fate. However, each year on Holy Saturday, he did two things before going with Anna to the Paschal service: first, he wrote to the State Department, requesting that the embassy in Moscow determine what had become of Elena Martova, and then he had his police driver take him down to the consulate, where he formally demanded that the consul general once again inquire into the matter. He would do this until the day he died, for he wasn't so faithless as to deny the possibility of hope.

Mrs. Mayor leaned close to his ear, "Well, John, what do you think so far?"

"I'm afraid the Rose Adagio is more like a *funebre* adagio." In years past, he might have been tempted to have a word with the maestro during intermission. Tempo was no light matter. But such priggishness would only raise Anna Ivanova's ire, and in the heat of such scenes she lapsed into a contemporary vernacular he didn't think fit for charwoman, let alone a ballerina.

He sat back and tried not to be bothered.

There were times when he sensed, as Anna Ivanova flatly said she did, that her mother was dead. But on the brink of admitting darkness, his soul would suddenly writhe toward the light in a new direction, and he would find himself trusting that Elena was far removed from any kind of death, that she was at peace beyond human reckoning. For hadn't she come to God as so few ever do—through courage? *Most of us leave this world shrouded in our own cowardice,* he had once told Anna Ivanova, nearly shouting, vainly trying to make her see the truths of that spring in 1945, *but your dear mother went in triumph! She outbraved the Devil himself!*

Anna Ivanova insisted that she was an agnostic. A secular humanist.

"Ekh," John Kost muttered, crossing himself as the corps de ballet flowed around his daughter like angels.